O9-AHU-378

THE WORLD OF
DARKNESS

DARK DESTINY

PROPRIETORS OF FATE

Edited by Edward E. Kramer

WHITE WOLF
PUBLISHING

DARK DESTINY: PROPRIETORS OF FATE is
A product of White Wolf Publishing.

All rights reserved.
Copyright ©1995 by White Wolf Publishing.
All contents herein are copyrighted by White Wolf Publishing. This book may not be
reproduced, in whole or in part, without the written permission of the publisher, except for
the purpose of reviews.
For information write: White Wolf Publishing, 780 Park North Boulevard, Suite 100,
Clarkston, GA 30021.

The characters and events described in this book are fictional. Any resemblance between the
characters and any person, living or dead, is purely coincidental.

The mention of or reference to any companies or products in these pages is not a challenge to
the trademarks or copyrights concerned.

Because of the mature themes presented within, reader discretion is advised.

White Wolf is committed to reducing waste in publishing. For this reason, we do not permit
our covers to be "stripped" in exchange for credit. Instead we require that the book be
returned, allowing us to resell it.

Cover and Interior Illustration: Mike Mignola
Art Direction and Cover Design: Michelle Prahler

Table of Contents

This volume is dedicated to Karl Edward Wagner, writer, editor, and friend. May your adventures in life be surpassed only by those in eternity.

Foreward

History is written by the victors...
— Winston Churchill

Long before the advent of CNN, the written word documented our very existence. We assume that once an event is recorded for posterity, its historical significance and accuracy are well founded. In fact, much of our belief system depends on it.

While archaeologists, researchers, and the like continue to discover clues which they believe will vertify the existence of Sodom and Gomorrah, Noah's Ark and the Holy Grail, such proof has never been necessary for most of the adult population in the world to challenge the word of God (or some facsimile thereof). Even though the four Gospels of the New Testament display sharp inconsistencies with historical fact — no less the content of each other — we are told to accept each as truth, and the composite as ultimate truth.

Even scientific proof has been slow to alter the written word. In 1609, Galileo used a 20x telescope to prove what Copernicus published nearly a century earlier: the belief that the Earth was not the center of the universe. He was called to Rome for trial by the Inquisition and condemned to life imprisonment for "vehement suspicion of heresy." Galileo died while under house arrest.

In 1925, the state of Tennessee forbade the teaching of evolution. A schoolteacher, John T. Scopes, was tried that year for violating the law. Scopes was found guilty, but his conviction was overturned by the state supreme court, which nevertheless upheld the statute. Similar statutes were not ruled unconstitutional by the U.S. Supreme Court — until 1968.

History can also be created without a shred of proof. In 1800, Parson Weems, an itinerant evangelist and bookseller, wrote the *History of Life, Death, Virtues and Exploits of George Washington* based on his "biographical" sermons of the nation's first president. Although entirely ficticious, Weems' tale of George Washington and the cherry tree has clearly found its way into American mythology, as many elementary school references treat it as fact.

Under White House command, history can also be wiped from the face of existence. In 1944, General Eisenhower launched a top secret military operation off the coast of England in practice for the D-day invasion at Normandy two months later. A German U-boat on patrol surprised the operation, sinking one of the US ships and killing almost eleven hundred American soldiers and even more British and Allied troops. Families were simply told that their loved ones were missing in action. On the 50th anniversary in 1994, the American press first reported knowledge of "Operation Tiger," although many of its details remain classified to this day.

Which brings us to the volume you are about to read. Many of the events as described herein are clearly works of fiction — for today. The Masquerade is retained unveiled, and those creatures of the night remain just that. But these historical accounts give light to the insurmountable power of the Netherworld — where history is only in the making....

— *Edward E. Kramer*
June, 1995

Introduction

TO A MALIGN FIESTA

by Robert Anton Wilson

What is the function of the carbon-based units?
— *Star Trek: The Motion Picture*

Don't worry, I'm only kidding — not!
— *Truth or Dare*

When I think of the external or "historical" events of my childhood, everything seems like faded old newsreels of the Great Depression. Worried faces, run down buildings, violent strikes with cops smashing workers upside the head with billy clubs: all have that grainy look and that bad sound quality of NEWS ON THE MARCH — which always served us kids as a signal to run out and buy our candy so we wouldn't miss the cartoon coming next. Maybe poverty always looks that way, in memory. Maybe they invented the newsreel just to leave a suitably sub-standard film record of those malnourished days. Strange that some of these awful images come, in fact, not from newsreels but from things I actually saw.

But when I think of the *internal*, and therefore more vivid, memories of my childhood, everything comes into sharp focus and high contrast, full of artfully meaningful blends of light and shadow. The great horror movies of the '30s live on and on in the labyrinth of my consciousness, turning up in the most unexpected places: my reflections of Buddhism and physics, my thoughts about war and pacificism, names of minor characters in my novels. Those films carved a trace in the mind; the newsreels just represent the accidents of existence. I can still see Maria Ouspenskia, with all the art and craft of the great European theatres where she had worked, solemnly reciting to a tormented Lon Chaney, Jr.:

> Even a man who is pure of heart
> And says his prayers by night
> May become a wolf when the wolfsbane blooms
> And the moon is full and bright

I can't remember a single Roosevelt speech, or even a single Huey Long speech, as well as I remember those lines of cornball genius. And all the other dark memories flood over me at the very mention of — *wolfs*bane....

Ah, *Wolfs*bane: if you say it just right, with the proper rise and fall, you have mastered Step One in a good Bela Lugosi imitation.

Oh, Bela the Magnificent...I can never forget him as Igor, who although hanged by the neck ("Be*cause* I robbed *graves* — they *said*.") remained alive. And I especially remember him telling Basil Rathbone (Baron *Wolf* von Frankenstein — what a name!) that the — the — *thing* — on the slab was in a sense his, Frankenstein's, brother: "Your father make you, your father make *heem* ! But lightning was his mother!" God, did anybody ever combine total malignancy and demented overacting with such deep sincerity as Bela and cap it with such poetic flair? He always seemed to think he spoke high Shakespeare, and at his best he made you think you had just heard Shakespeare.

And the others, also great: Boris, the mute gaunt suffering monster, looking sadly at the little girl, wondering what to throw in the water after he ran out of flowers... Boris again, saying to the forgotten heroine of *The Mummy*, "No man has suffered for love as I have." (He'd survived 3900 years of undeath in a coffin, because he stole the magick scroll to make *her* immortal.) The Calypso singer, smiling insinuatingly as his song hints, and hints, and hints, but never says clearly what horror hangs over the Harlan family, in *I Walked with a Zombie*. Robert Armstrong standing by the dead body of the Big Fellow intoning the

Most Certainly Immortal Line In Film History — the line that may someday serve as the epitaph for Rush Limbaugh, if he has a stroke during one of his erotic-sadistic spasms about Hilary — "It was beauty that killed the Beast." The Wicked Witch of the West soaring through the sky and writing in letters of fire:

SURRENDER DOROTHY

Yes, yes: those moments, and hundreds like them, made up the true fabric of my childhood: their "trace in the mind" (a phrase I purloined from Ezra Pound) registers real lines of psychic force in the collective unconscious — or, if you prefer a more neurological metaphor, these moments aim directly at receptor sites in the brain where the stimuli that carry raw power imprint themselves in circuits of association and networks of poetic myth that boys and girls, and men and women, have experienced since we became human, or maybe even before that...

Somehow, out of 60 million years of primate psychology, humanity has emerged as the beast that knows its own dark side too well, and would prefer not to know. But we love to look at that dark side, safely projected into the proper realm of myth and fantasy.

Because that which we find within remains always and only a reflection of that which we also find outside.

To say it another way, that which we perceive outside contains only what we can perceive inside.

Hermes proclaimed that before I did, of course: "That which is above reflects that which is below." Phil Dick suggests that Hermes meant to say the universe has a hologrammic structure, i.e., the information of the whole appears in every part. You can hang on to that metaphor if you find it helpful.

Gort, klaatu barada nikto.
— *The Day the Earth Stood Still*

And take your cold companion with you!
— *Arsenic and Old Lace*

Yes: the creatures of those great old films, and of the book you hold in your hands, always co-exist with us, for, to paraphrase H.P. Lovecraft, they appeared in somebody's dream last night and they had names and images farther back than garden-girdled Babylon. And we spend eight hours out of every day in their company, even though most of the memories of those adventures fade before we have our first cup of coffee brewed.

Do they also influence history, as some of these stories suggest? Carl Jung thought so: he regarded Nazi Germany as a nation possessed by an archetype — a metaphor different in content but not in structure from the simple Christian notion of that nation as one possessed by demons. Archetypes, demons, stimuli that trigger weird brain circuits: use the language grid that best suits you. The only error would lie in denying that *they* — "night's black agents" — exist in some form, or refusing to realize that *they* track us every minute of every day.

That arrogant 19th Century error, fortunately, does not have many adherents any more. Not after Auschwitz and Hiroshima and Vietnam and Oklahoma City 4/19/95... We know better, now. We know that every bus, every car, every bicycle that enters our street may carry the demonseed, the spirit that wills annihilation, chaos and Mother Night. We know, even if we wish we did not know, that even the worst of the Camp Classics, even *Frankenstein Meets The Wolfman*, comes closer to the inner life of humanity, and its increasingly externalized frenzies, than any "sensitive" and "ironic" *New Yorker* story about adultery in the suburbs.

I perhaps push my thesis too far? I hyperbolize? Consider the figure on the bottom of this page.

Familiar looking, wouldn't you say? Well, if you belong to the shrinking minority that does not find him familiar, you have managed to avoid most of

the UFOlogical literature of the past twenty years and the hottest controversy in modern psychology — "repressed memory syndrome," the fashionable disease, or delusion, which increasing numbers of psychologists do not believe exists.

This creature looks exactly like one of the "Greys," a race of alleged extraterrestrial sex fiends, or bio-researchers — as you will — who abduct humans and perform sexual assaults or genetic experiments upon them. Literally thousands of people allege that they have suffered these Alien rapes or genetic alterations. The number of such alleged victims almost equals the number of those who claim their parents once forced them to participate in Satanic rituals involving human sacrifice, cannibalism and more scatological fantasy than a grade school lavatory wall.

Some (few) psychologists believe these "repressed memories." The majority very seriously doubt them. I say (once more) that we live with these creatures eight hours a day — in the realm where we also encounter mome raths, Dali's melting watches and things, in Joyce's words, "like gnawthing unearthed."

The important thing about this particular "Grey": the sketch does not derive from any modern UFO abduction story. Not at all. The occult drug guru Aleister Crowley drew it way back in the early 1920s. He said it represented an "Enochian entity" (a being from a "higher" astral plane than ourselves). Crowley even knew its name — LAM, which looks to me like *mal*, the Latin root for evil backwards, and also suggests the Holy Lamb of God in Blake's visionary poetry....

Let's not get drawn into a dispute about whether LAM really comes from an "astral" or an "extra-terrestrial" realm. We know where he comes from, if we trust our guts and don't get entangled in verbal cobwebs. The hypnotists who find him in "repressed memory" and Crowley, who found him in drug-drenched magick ritual, both opened the same gate, the gate to the antipodes of the human mind.

We're in moderately bad shape down here.
— *The Abyss*

Life's a bitch, and so am I.
— *Batman Returns*

As the Magus Linaweaver wrote (in a book so terrible I dare not mention its name), "Monotheism is the slippery slope to atheism."

A limited god does not really fit the idea of "god" at all; any "god" must transcend every limit and exceed all boundaries of every sort. Thus, only the advaitist (non-dual, pantheistic) concept of "god" remains free of contradiction and oxymoron. But nobody, least of all the pantheist, can distinguish the pantheist "god" from the "All" invoked (in "All is One") by all those New Age bliss-ninnies with their vacant eyes and empty smiles (what "archetype" or "entity" possesses them? I wonder...). And this "god" which equals "All" differs very little from the giant clockwork of atheism, except that it allegedly has feelings.

(But why shouldn't a mechanism have feelings? Didn't *Frankenstein* show us that any automaton that *acts* alive must *feel* alive?)

Emerson's Brahma, who says "I am the slayer and the slain," presumably enjoys the slaying even if He-She-It also suffers the pain of the victim. This view really implies a cosmos consisting only of a god playing with itself (Transcendental Masturbation) or playing hide-and-seek with itself (the view of Alan Watts and all Gnostic conspiracy buffs in the Phil Dick tradition). Take out the poetice metaphors and this view quickly collapses into atheism, as Linaweaver told us.

Thus, Nietzsche ultimately realized that "There are gods but there is no God — and this alone is divine." Beyond the advaitist/pantheist/atheist mythos, the real universe always shows what the Irish call an orderly chaos.

A phalanx of intelligences and powers, all differentiated, some cooperating and some competing — the view of the ordinary person about ordinary day-to-day reality — ultimately describes the cosmos better than any monotheistic or atheistic oversimplification. We can call these intelligences and powers "gods" or "goods" or "demons" or "evils," if we will, but those remain merely our own prejudices. Each entity has its own view of the situation — just as an old rat, in Burroughs memorable phrase, has decided opinions about wise guys who stuff steel wool into rat holes.

In other words, one and zero do not differ by very much — one god or no god, who really cares? — but infinity and zero differ very greatly. And we seem to live in a world of infinite complexity, infinitely many intelligences, infinitely competing and cooperating entities, very few of whom give a fried fart about human hopes and prayers.

In such a world — once described by Crowley as "a practical joke by the general at the expense of the particular" — super-Darwinism reigns. To put it simon simple: such a world contains AIDS and cancer. Any god who created it with purpose appears monstrous to clear judgment; any god who did it in "play" (as the Orient claims) appears idiotic; but a phalanx of often competing intelligences could easily have created just such a chaotic whirligig, with its accidental moments of sheer ecstasy thrown in along with its equally random terrors that walk by night and stochastic tragedies that stalk us by day.

If this seems arcane or (God forbid) "mystical," let me restate it more simply. None of the critters in this book, or in my favorite old movies mentioned earlier, scare me as much as several recent American presidents have; certainly, none of them has a record of mass murder equal to that of our most recent presidents. Just as we "elect" our presidents, we "select" our maps or models of the world. Whatever we elect or select, if it does not include murderous Evil, it does not fit the world that the majority of our fellow humans have collectively elected and selected.

Looking at the current Congress, for that matter, I would feel greatly comforted to think that some of them have as many flashes of almost human pathos as, say, King Kong had, or the Frankenstein monster had when (and only when) Karloff portrayed him. It would even feel good to think they had the wit and empathy of Hannibal Lecter, M.D.

But I see no sign of such redeeming qualities in politics. Perhaps, ultimately, the real pleasure provided by the great horror stories consists in giving us a world, unlike our own, in which even the most destructive creatures have a human side we can recognize and pity . . . .

— *Robert Anton Wilson*
4 May 1995

(anniversary of the Haymarket bomb, 1886;
Holmes' final confrontation with Moriarity
at the Reichenbach Falls, 1891; the Kent State
massacre of American boys and girls by American
troops, 1970)

The Sign Of the Asp

Nancy A. Collins

The Queen of Egypt, Cleopatra V Tryphaeana, entered the suite of rooms belonging to her third daughter and namesake, glancing about apprehensively. It was the first time she had set foot in her child's private chambers. The Queen and her husband-brother, Ptolemy XII Auletes, lived in a different wing of the royal palace, far removed from the quarters of the princes and princesses, separated from their children by, it seemed, far more than physical space.

The Queen was quite shocked to find her daughter's suite decorated with pottery, fabrics, and statuary of native design. To her dismay, there was what looked to be a shrine to the gods Re and Isis beside the one dedicated to Serapis, the household god.

A native servant girl appeared, blocking the Queen's entrance to her daughter's bed chamber. The servant, little more than a child herself, raised her hands to show that admittance was off limits. The Queen scowled, her eyes darkening.

"How dare you! Don't you know who I am?! There is no room in this palace forbidden to me!"

The servant girl, cowed by the Queen's indignation, said something in Egyptian, which provoked the Queen even further.

"Hades take you, wretch!" she spat, pushing the frightened child aside. "Speak Greek if you have something to say, not that barbaric tongue of yours!"

The decor of her daughter's sleeping chamber was similar to that of its sitting room, except that the room was dominated by a large gilded bed, swathed by finely woven linens and silks to keep biting insects from feeding on royal blood. It was there she found her daughter sprawled face down, her sobs muffled by a pillow.

Upon seeing her child in such a state, the Queen felt her anger fade, but she knew she could not let what had transpired at the dinner table go unpunished. It was important for her daughter to understand the duties her position demanded of her.

"Cleopatra?"

Cleopatra VII started, rolling over to stare at the Queen with swollen, tear-reddened eyes. "Mother?"

The Queen smiled gently as she settled herself onto the corner of the bed, resting one hand on her daughter's young shoulder. "You needn't look so surprised, my sweet. I just wanted to see if you were feeling well."

The ten-year-old princess' features took on a wariness the Queen found disconcertingly adult. "You know perfectly well how I feel, Mother! So does Father! I'm not sick, if that's what you're suggesting!"

"Are you sure, my pet? After all, what you said at dinner sounded more like the notions born of fever, not a well mind—"

"I'm *not* sick! I just don't want to marry Ptolemy! He's my *brother*!" Cleopatra punched the pillow for emphasis.

"As is your father to me."

"But you and father are different! He's you're demi-brother! Besides, he's the same age as you — even older!"

"True, we had separate mothers. Mine was the Queen, his a concubine — but I don't see how that has anything to do with you not wanting to marry Ptolemy."

4

"He's too young! He's four years old! When I'm eighteen, he'll only be twelve! Besides, I'm not the oldest daughter! Why aren't you making Berenice marry him?"

"Because Berenice *is* the oldest daughter, Cleopatra! She is ten years older than Ptolemy — such an imbalance cannot be righted. By the time your brother would be able to sire an heir, Berenice would be too old to safely bear one. However, she is useful to the House of Ptolemy in other ways. Your father's already making plans to marry her to one of King Mithradates of Pontus' sons—"

Cleopatra could not contain her disgust. "Mithradates? But father *hates* him! The Pontics are the ones who kidnapped him and Uncle Alexander and held them for ransom to the Romans!"

"I *know* how your father feels about the Pontics, young lady! But that still doesn't exempt you from your duties as princess!"

"But great-great-great-great-great-grandfather didn't marry his sister!"

"But all our grandfathers since him *did*," the Queen countered. "And as distasteful as you might feel it to be, it is the one concession the Ptolemys have made to the culture of this land. Since you are so fascinated by their barbaric language and religious practices, I thought that you, of all my children, would have the fewest qualms about following the rituals of the ancient pharaohs."

"It's just that Ptolemy's such a baby! And he's cross-eyed! Why does it have to be me?"

A flicker of sadness crossed the Queen's eyes. "Because your older sister, Cleopatra VI, died too young. Had she not tread upon the asp in the garden that day — then who knows what Fate would have bestowed on you? I was carrying you in my belly when it happened, just as I now carry my latest child," the Queen said, touching her gently swelling stomach. "Her nurse brought her limp little body into the palace, so that she might die in my arms. I then had the same nurse killed and entombed alongside her, so she would not go into the afterlife unattended. I prayed then to Hera that my unborn child would be a girl, to replace the one I had lost. I know it was wicked of me to pray for a daughter when my husband so desperately needed a heir, but I was weak. And when you were born, I knew the gods had heard my prayers and I named you in honor of the daughter lost to me."

"But why not marry Arsinoe to Ptolemy? She's the same age as he is."

"She and Ptolemy are twins. While marrying brother to sister is one thing, marrying twin to twin is still another! It would be like wedding self to self! Such unions breed monsters."

"But Geb and Nut were twin brother and sister, and their children were Osiris and Isis."

"And of what importance are barbarian gods to our family?" the Queen scowled. "And speaking of which, your father and I do not approve of your learning Egyptian! It's unbecoming for one of your station to speak such a crude tongue! Besides, I don't like it when you talk to the servants. I always feel you're conspiring with them!"

"Mother, they are not barbarians! They are our people!"

The Queen got to her feet, her features rigid with displeasure. "Hear me now, young lady! I will tolerate no more foolishness, even if you *are* the daughter of my blood! I may be the Queen of the Egyptians, but they are certainly *not* 'my people'! In the 300 years since our illustrious forefather, the great Ptolemy I Soter, came to this land, our family has yet to allow native blood into its lineage! We are Macedonians, not Egyptians! And with your marriage to your brother, the future king, so shall it remain!

"You should feel honored, daughter! You are to be the Queen of Egypt! Your father could have offered me no greater tribute than to make me his queen!"

"But father can't rule without you. *You're* the full-blooded heir to the throne, not him! He was born of a slave, not a member of the royal family! Without you, he would be deposed by his enemies!"

"Where have you heard such treason? All Egypt loves your father!" The Queen's eyes blazed with anger and Cleopatra inwardly cringed. Cleopatra V Tryphaeana was indeed formidable when enraged. But Cleopatra VII was very much her mother's child, and she was not about to back down. She might be trapped by her station, but that did not mean she had to surrender to destiny without a fight.

"They say he's a puppet to the Romans — that he will make Egypt a protectorate of their empire for fear of losing his hold on the throne! That's why he surrendered Cyprus to them! They say that's why he's going to Rome — to bribe Pompey, Caesar, and Crassus into backing him against his enemies in Alexandria!"

She was surprised when her mother slapped her. Her cheek stung and glowed red as an ember, but she refused to cry. She stared up at the Queen, who looked as if she wanted desperately to vomit. She had dared to speak the truth — something rarely uttered aloud amongst members of the royal family. After a long pause, the Queen finally spoke — her voice knotted tighter than a noose.

"You are to marry your brother, Ptolemy XIII Theos Philopator. There will be no further discussion concerning this matter, just as there is no discussing whether the sun will rise in the morning. And I expect those Egyptian idols to be disposed of immediately. Good night, Princess Cleopatra."

Cleopatra waited until her mother had left the suite before bursting into angry tears. She did not want to give the Queen the satisfaction of knowing how upset she truly was.

It just wasn't fair! Berenice was going to be married to a handsome prince while she was stuck with stupid, funny-looking cry-baby Ptolemy! She rolled off the bed and stomped into the sitting room, motioning curtly for her servants to leave her. It was not fitting that slaves see the tears of a princess.

Dusk had turned into early evening, although the moon had yet to make its climb across Alexandria's night sky, and the torches that lit the royal gardens outside her window cast a dim, flickering light, filling the room with febrile shadows. She stood before the small, ornately carved table that housed her shrine to the god Re and the goddess Isis.

Although she was by blood and tradition Macedonian, Cleopatra had been raised by her Egyptian nursemaid, not her biological mother. This was hardly unusual — it was common practice for royal children of all kingdoms to be farmed out to wet-nurses, to protect their mothers from child-bed sickness and to facilitate rapid replacement, should infant mortality strike. Still, the Queen had been far from attentive to the little princess. Even though she had named her in memory of her lost daughter, Cleopatra knew that her mother still grieved and, for some reason, seemed to hold her responsible for her elder sister's untimely death. As she knew from past experience, and as this evening's argument had so roughly proven, she could expect no help from the Queen in thwarting her father's plans for her future.

Her alienation from her mother's affections had forged a bond between the tiny princess and her Egyptian nurse, which resulted in her learning the Egyptian language and hieroglyphs, and her interest in their ancient pantheon of beast-headed gods. Her father snubbed his people's deities because they resembled animals, not humans, unlike the gods of his forefathers. Some, like Re, were simply disembodied body parts. Cleopatra knew he was a fool to

7

dismiss the ancient lords of Karnak and Thebes. There was power in their mummified hands — for those brave enough to use it.

Cleopatra took a cone of incense and placed it onto the back of a bronze burner made to resemble a scarab. After lighting the incense, she knelt before the shrine she had erected, raising her hands in supplication. The idol of Re showed the solar god as a squatting man with the head of a falcon, the golden disc of the sun balanced atop his head. In one hand he held the *Ma'at*, the solitary feather that symbolized Truth. Beside him stood a small statuette of Isis, carved from a single piece of ivory, the eyes outlined with kohl from the princess' own paint box. In the goddess' right hand she held a tiny ankh — the Egyptian symbol of life after death.

"Oh, great Re, you of the unblinking eye, I beg you: hear my prayers. Oh, mighty Isis, sister-wife of the eternal Osiris, mother to the glorious Horus, heed my words. Help me to find my true love, just as you sought for the body of your beloved along the banks of the Nile."

She repeated the prayer a dozen times, yet the idols showed no signs of springing to life or offering auguries. She repeated the prayer another dozen times, but still the graven images remained mute. Dispirited, the young princess returned to her bed chamber, where she quietly cried herself to sleep.

✠

Cleopatra—

She started awake with a gasp, uncertain whether the voice she'd heard calling her name was actual or one born of her dreams. She lay on her back, staring at the night-shadows through the canopy of insect netting that covered her bed. Sometime after she cried herself to sleep, her servants had come in and changed her out of her clothes and into a sleeping robe and tucked her in. She was so accustomed to being physically attended to she no longer woke when they administered to her. Still, she was certain that whoever — or whatever — had called her name was still in the room. And whoever it was, he or she was certainly not a slave.

"Who's there?" she whispered, trying not to sound frightened. "Answer me or I will call the guards and have them take your head!"

"There is no need for such threats, little princess — empty though they may be."

The intruder was suddenly there, emerging from the darkness at the foot of her bed as sudden and quiet as blood from a wound. Cleopatra gasped aloud at the sight of the strange figure, but more out of amazement than fear.

Whoever this pale, ruby-eyed stranger might be, it was clear from his elaborate dress that he was far from common-born, as he was outfitted in a manner unseen since the Middle Kingdom, over a thousand years past. He wore a transparent outer skirt of fine, unbleached linen over a loin cloth, the hem chased with golden thread. Nude from the waist up, his hairless, alabaster-white chest was decorated by a heavy pectoral made of solid gold in the image of a vulture clutching the sun in its claws. On his feet were sandals decorated with enamel and semi-precious stones. His long dark hair fell past his shoulders and he wore a Horus lock at his right temple, braided with a blood-red ribbon. Atop his head he wore a claft, the ceremonial headdress of the Great Sphinx, a golden asp resting on his brow.

"Who are you? And what are you doing in my bed chamber?"

"My, you *are* a brave one, aren't you?" the stranger smiled, his eyes gleaming like new wine in the moonlight. "The auguries were correct. You will serve us well — provided you survive your childhood, that is."

"I asked you your name!" Cleopatra struggled to keep the fear out of her voice as she sat up, clutching her bedclothes to her chest. "I am to be queen — and I expect an answer!"

The stranger's smile widened, although not enough to show his teeth. "I am called Sek. And I am here in response to your prayers."

Cleopatra blinked. "My prayers?"

Sek nodded, motioning with a pale finger in the direction of the vanished sun. "The gods in Heliopolis heard your prayers and sent me to help counsel you."

"Are you a god?"

"Not as you understand the word. Once I was a living man — a prince of ancient Thebes. Now I am a messenger in the service of Re."

"Oh." Cleopatra looked somewhat disappointed. "I was hoping you were a god. Why didn't Re come himself?"

Sek shook his head, scowling at her blasphemy. "If Re was to appear to a mortal — even a princess as noble as yourself — the power of his glory would reduce you to cinders within a heartbeat, as Zeus inadvertently destroyed Semele, mother of Dionysus."

Cleopatra eyed the pale stranger. "You know of Zeus and Dionysus?"

Sek shrugged indifferently. "When one is dead, one knows all things — even the gods of the conquerors."

"Then you know my future?"

"The eye of Re sees more than one path. It sees the end of all journeys, even those unmade."

Cleopatra frowned. "You're not making any sense!"

"Forgive me, princess. I do not mean to be oblique. What I meant to say is that there are numerous futures, as there are spokes on a wheel. The trick is to pick the correct path and avoid the ones that lead to emptiness or despair."

"Will I end up married to Ptolemy, then?"

"Yes. But it will be a marriage in name only — true love will come to you under the sign of the wolf."

The princess made a face as if smelling something bad. "A *Roman*? My true love will be a Roman?!"

"Not just *any* Roman, sweet princess — but the greatest son born of the Republic. Together, you will unite East with West and rule an empire undreamed of since Alexander! From your union shall emerge a new race of pharaohs, who will build monuments to your glory that will put the Great Sphinx to shame! At least, that is what the future holds in store for you, provided you are willing to make sacrifices."

"Sacrifices? What sort of sacrifices?"

"Blood, of course."

"B-blood?" Cleopatra echoed, her demeanor suddenly that of a ten-year-old girl, not a haughty princess.

"No other sacrifice is worthy of the gods," Sek explained. "If you wish to enjoy the protection and council of Re the All-Seeing, it is necessary that a human sacrifice be made to him at the dark of the moon."

"But Re is a sun god — why must the sacrifices take place in the dead of night?"

"While Re spends the day traveling the skies, observing all that transpires in the mortal world, it is only during the night that the wisdom gained during his ride across the heavens can be learned. Re speaks to those he favors in their dreams, but to receive these dreams requires the spilling of human blood. All you need do is have a slave sleep at the foot of your bed and I will escort them to where Re's priests shall attend to them and send them to their god in the proper manner." He held up a necklace from which dangled a tiny bronze asp. "Have them wear this, so that I might recognize them as sacrifices." With that, he dropped the bauble onto the foot of the bed. As he turned to go, the dead prince lifted a hand in blessing.

"You have been given the chance to steer your destiny by the foresight of Egypt's gods, Cleopatra. Choose wisely." And then he was gone as quickly as he had appeared, swallowed by the shadows that filled the corners of the room.

When Cleopatra woke that next morning, she remembered the strange dream of the pale stranger and the prophecy he had made of her finding true love in the arms of a Roman. It was almost preposterous enough to make her laugh — except for the necklace she found curled on the foot of her bed. It was a black silken cord, from which dangled a bronze asp.

She didn't know whether to be frightened or excited, so she hid the thing in an unguent jar and placed it under a loose flagstone in the corner of her room.

✛

"Why aren't you crying?" Arsinoe asked in between her own sniffles. "Mother's dead and you're not even *trying* to be sad!"

Cleopatra glanced over at her four-year-old sister, who sat on a wooden stool painted gold and fashioned to resemble the royal throne of the Ptolemys. The play-throne was one of several elaborate toys littering the royal nursery Arsinoe inhabited with her twin, Ptolemy XIII.

"That's Ptolemy's throne," Cleopatra said accusingly.

"So? Ptolemy lets me sit on it. I'm to be his queen."

"No, you're not."

"Am too!"

"Are not. Father said so before he left."

"Things are different now! Father's in Rome, not here. Berenice is the queen now, not mother! Berenice says father is betraying Egypt to the Romans! She won't let him be king anymore."

"I wouldn't put much store in what Berenice says, if I were you."

"Berenice is the queen! She said Ptolemy would be my husband!" Arsinoe made a face and stuck her tongue out at her older sister. "You may be ten, but Berenice is fourteen! She knows more than you!"

"Berenice doesn't know everything."

"And you do?"

Cleopatra looked away from her younger sister. Arsinoe was the same age as Ptolemy XIII but far more intelligent — and aggressive — than her twin brother. And now that their mother was gone — dead of childbed fever from delivering her sixth and final child, Ptolemy XIV — Arsinoe was beginning to test her kitten's claws, challenging Cleopatra for power.

"I just wouldn't get used to Berenice being queen, that's all."

⚜

Princess Cleopatra hurried down the corridor toward the throne room. The halls echoed with the sounds of Roman legionnaires cursing, the clatter of shield on sword, and the screams of the dying. Four years had passed and now father was home.

A tall, burly figure lurched out of the shadows, grabbing the princess roughly by her upper arm. It was a Roman, smelling of rank sweat and worn leather, his eyes blazing with battle fever. In one hand he held a naked short sword, its blade wet with blood. Cleopatra was so terrified she could not find her voice to scream.

"Here she is, sir!" the Roman boomed, dragging the frightened girl behind him in the direction of an officer.

"Unhand her, you fool!" snapped the commander. "It's the queen we want! She's just a princess!"

Chagrined, the legionnaire let go of Cleopatra as if she'd suddenly metamorphosed into a scorpion. "I'm sorry, Commander Antony! I didn't realize…!"

"Of that I have no doubt, Silanus!" Commander Marc Antony replied tartly. He turned and smiled as soothingly as he could to the trembling girl before him. His Macedonian was flawless. "A thousand pardons, princess! Silanus is a good soldier — if somewhat overzealous in some matters! I'll have one of my men see that you're safely escorted to your father's side." Cleopatra stared up at the handsome soldier towering over her, too surprised to do more than nod her understanding. Within seconds he had disappeared into the swirling smoke and chaos of the palace coup, leaving her with one of his retainers. As she was taken to her father, she realized it had been four years

12

since she had been told her future love lay in the arms of a Roman. Cleopatra wondered if it might not be with one as dashing and handsome as the young officer who had so gallantly come to her aid.

Ptolemy XII Auletes was seated on the throne he had vacated four years before, the horsehair flail and scepter of his office once more in his hands. Before him lay prostrate the entire royal court, including the eight-year-old Ptolemy XIII and Arsinoe, and the four-year-old son he'd never seen, Ptolemy XIV. Cleopatra could not see Berenice anywhere.

When Auletes saw Cleopatra, he smiled and held out his hand to her. "Come, my daughter. Come sit by your father's side. I have missed you, my child."

Cleopatra knelt before her father, and although she knew she had nothing to fear, she could not help but tremble. After four years of civil war with his eldest daughter, Auletes had succeeded in bribing Aulus Gabinius, lieutenant of the Great Pompey, into supporting his return to Egypt. And now the time had come for those who had opposed his rule to pay.

"Father — where is Berenice?" she asked quietly.

"She will be with us soon, my child. Ah! Here she comes now!" Auletes gestured with his flail.

The Roman soldier who had so roughly grabbed Cleopatra was striding toward the throne, picking his way through the field of prostrate courtiers. In one hand he held his bloody sword — and in the other Berenice's head, still dripping gore from its neck.

Cleopatra quickly looked away, but found herself meeting Arsinoe's eyes. The eight-year-old stared at her older sister with an intensity that transcended mere sibling rivalry. Cleopatra could not help but smile as she thought to herself, *See? I told you not to become used to Berenice being queen. I told you.*

✠

"You are to marry your brother Ptolemy in a fortnight, my child," Auletes announced to his daughter over a meal of crocodile eggs and hippopotamus steak.

"As you wish, Father."

Auletes lifted an eyebrow and regarded his daughter intently. "I am surprised, my dear. I suspected to hear you railing against the match."

"You have been away a long time, father," Cleopatra replied evenly. "Your memory of me is that of a ten-year-old child throwing a temper tantrum because she could not have her way. I am almost fifteen years old now — I am a woman. And I have come to realize you and Mother were right — I must accept my responsibility as queen."

Auletes' eyes saddened at the mention of his dead wife. "It grieves me that I was not here with your mother when she died. You must believe that, Cleopatra. I loved her dearly. She was my sister, wife, and queen. Perhaps that she died delivering a half-wit is my punishment for surrendering Cyprus to Rome." He glanced up from his plate at his daughter, his demeanor brightening somewhat. "Child, you know as well as I that Ptolemy is not strong enough to plot Egypt's fate. Were that you were born a man, then I could die secure knowing I had a son worthy of carrying on the family name! All I ask of you, child, is that you keep Rome from swallowing us whole. The wolf of the Tiber is a hungry beast, intent on devouring the world, if it can. While it is true that I promised great riches to both Caesar and Pompey so that they would reinstate me on the throne, that does not mean that Rome has the right to interfere in the affairs of Egypt! We are still a powerful, independent kingdom — and I want you to swear to me that you will never allow Rome to annex Egypt, as it has done with so many of its adversaries over the years."

Cleopatra took her father's aged hand in hers, squeezing it gently. "Have no fear, Father. No such fate shall ever befall Egypt as long as I and my children draw breath."

"It does my old heart good to hear you speak such words, my dear," Auletes sighed. "But what is this I hear of your handmaiden disappearing?"

Cleopatra's smile flickered for a moment, then reappeared. "Not disappeared, Father. Dismissed. Her mother died of the fever, leaving several young sisters and brothers behind. I gave Asma her freedom so she might raise them."

"Cleopatra, you are far too soft-hearted when it comes to your slave-girls," Auletes sighed, shaking his head in admonishment. "You treat them far more kindly than they deserve."

✛

Cleopatra watched impassively as the golden sarcophagus containing the remains of her father, King Ptolemy XII Theos Philopater Philadelphus Neos Dionysos Auletes, was sealed away in its marble tomb. Although the Ptolemys prided themselves on remaining aloof from the people they had ruled since the days of Alexander the Great, they had wholeheartedly embraced the old pharaohs' burial rituals. Although barely eighteen, Cleopatra had already approved the plans for her own tomb. And although she had been married for over three years, the fact that her tomb had no place for a husband's bones spoke much about the state of her marriage.

☩

She was but fifteen, Ptolemy XIII only nine, when they were wed. Although Cleopatra's desires were those of a normal, healthy young woman, as far as Ptolemy was concerned bed was a place to play with his toys. Frustrated, Cleopatra had been forced into a celibate life, waiting for the day her husband-brother would be old enough to discover his manhood. However, now that the boy was finally entering puberty, he seemed far more interested in spending his seed with his twin, Arsinoe, and not his legal wife. Auletes had scolded his son repeatedly about neglecting Cleopatra, but the youth had fallen under the influence of Pothinus, a particularly loathsome eunuch, and ignored his father's request that he sire a legal heir as soon as possible.

Since his return from Rome, Cleopatra had served as Auletes' queen, as the ancient traditions of their adopted people demanded that a man and woman should rule side-by-side, in honor of the gods Osiris and Isis. Now Ptolemy XIII Theos Philopater was the king, and as she pretended to listen as the priests of Serapis recited the prayers for the dead, she watched Pothinus stroking the boy-king's hair and whispering in his ear. She did not need to hear the eunuch's words to know he plotted against her. But as to the nature of his plans — well, that could also be divined.

Cleopatra's gaze fell on the young slave beside her, tending the jug of water should the royal thirst require slaking. What was his name again? Naeem? Nahir? Little matter. Come the evening she would present the lad with a small token of appreciation for his loyal service — a necklace in the shape of an asp — and give him the honor of sleeping at the foot of her bed. What greater honor could a slave ask?

☩

Cleopatra rose from the bed, careful not to disturb Caesar. Her bare feet glided across the rug that, hours before, had hidden her from her brother's soldiers. As she looked out at the night-garden, she reflected on all that had happened in the three years since her father's death.

Shortly after Auletes' death, the surviving members of the Roman Triumvirate, Caesar and Pompey, had a falling out. Ptolemy XIII, counseled by his pet eunuch, had chosen to help Pompey by providing him with ships and troops. Cleopatra, who, even without her gift from Re, was a far more astute politician than any of the men in the court, had quarreled mightily with her co-ruler over his decision. The up-shot was that Ptolemy ordered her expelled from Egypt.

Lucky to escape with her life, the exiled queen promptly set about raising an Arab army in the northeast frontier. It was then that Pompey the Great — fleeing his defeat at Pharsalus — arrived, seeking refuge and expecting to be welcomed with open arms as an ally of the king. Ptolemy marched down to the coast, ostensibly to welcome the Roman general, but he and his counselors had chosen not to risk offending the victorious Caesar. Pompey was executed within moments of setting foot on Egyptian soil.

Shortly thereafter Julius Caesar arrived, seeking his enemy. But the great general had not been overjoyed when Pompey's head was placed before his feet. And it was in so sorely misunderstanding Caesar that Ptolemy and his clique had made their fatal mistake — as Cleopatra had known all along they would. Caesar was a far cry from the fifteen-year-old king. Although he had hunted Pompey as one would a wild boar, he had not desired to disgrace his former son-in-law in death. It was the Roman way to offer men of noble mien the honorable solution of suicide. Ptolemy, however, had assumed Caesar would want Pompey's head to ride upon a pike when he returned to Rome to celebrate his triumph.

But it seemed Caesar was far from eager to return to his homeland. He had marshaled a mighty army to come to Egypt and put his enemy to rest once and for all. But since Pompey was dead, he had to do *something* with his legions. So he elected to stay and put an end to the civil war between brother and sister so that he could be paid what their late father owed him, thereby paying off troops that would otherwise return to Rome empty-handed and more than a little angry. Having arrived in Alexandria and seized the palace quarter, making the Princess Arsinoe and Prince Ptolemy XIV his captives, Caesar ordered the warring factions to submit to his arbitration. Grudgingly,

Ptolemy had left his army and traveled to Alexandria in the company of Pothinus. However, he left strict orders with his troops that should his sister try to make her way to Alexandria, she was to be seized and killed.

But as Sek had warned her of her brother's treachery, Cleopatra decided to smuggle herself into the palace by hiding within a Persian carpet that was intended as a present for Caesar. And so the twenty-one-year-old queen of Egypt presented herself to the fifty-one-year-old Roman dictator, rising at his feet clad in a diaphanous gown and the finest of her jewelry.

Needless to say, Caesar had been impressed. He had been even more impressed when the Queen of Egypt proved herself to be a virgin. She glanced back over her shoulder at the bloody stain on the bedclothes that marked her deflowering, then smiled to herself as she imagined the look on her brother-husband's face come the morning when he found her already in Caesar's presence.

She studied the aging warrior's sleeping face and remembered the promise that Re's messenger had made to her over a decade ago — that she would find her true love with the Republic's greatest son, and that her Roman lover would make her the queen of queens. Surely who else could he have meant but Caesar, the undisputed ruler of the Roman Republic, soon to be named its emperor? Still, Cleopatra felt a dissatisfaction tugging at her heart. True, Caesar was indeed dynamic — he was even attractive, in that way that power makes even the homeliest men desirable. And it was evident by his lovemaking that Caesar certainly knew what pleased the ladies. But there was something about him that failed to make her heart race and her breath grow shallow, as she had always imagined it would when she finally met her true love.

Perhaps she should call one of the slave girls and have her sleep at the foot of the bed? She shook her head. Not with Caesar here. That would be too much of a risk to take. Plus, she had discovered over the years that often Re's prophecies were as obscure as they were useful. Many times they were so vague that she had only a general idea about which of destiny's paths was the safest to tread. And, sometimes, as with the death of her mother and Berenice's execution, the future she glimpsed was too painful and personal. Sometimes it was best to trust her own instincts, which, as her father had said, were far sharper than most men's. Besides, she did not need the help of the gods to tell her that Julius Caesar would be more than willing to settle the differences between herself and her brother-king to her satisfaction.

✢

"Hurry, child! Hurry!" Cleopatra gasped as she dragged her child to the awaiting boat.

"But, mother," Caesarion protested. "Why are we leaving in the middle of the night? Where is father?"

"You — your father is unable to come with us," Cleopatra explained, trying her best to control the tears welling in her eyes. It would not do for the boy to see her cry just yet. Better he not know his father's fate until it had come about.

"But why must we return to Alexandria? I like it here in Rome!"

"Hush, Caesarion! Be quiet! You don't hear your uncle complaining, do you?"

Three-year-old Caesarion glanced at fifteen-year-old Ptolemy XIV. Although Ptolemy was married to his mother, and was therefore his step-father, Caesarion thought of him as his uncle and nothing more. His real father was Julius Caesar.

Ptolemy smiled vacantly at his nephew and pointed at the harbor. "Boat," the King of Egypt said, then clapped his hands, pleased with himself.

Caesarion had no real memory of Egypt, as he had come to Rome when he was little more than an infant. Caesar had commemorated the arrival of his mistress by dedicating a golden statue of her and his newborn son in the temple of Venus Genetrix — a far grander greeting than the one Arsinoe had received, dragged behind Caesar's chariot in chains after he had destroyed Ptolemy XIII's troops.

His father had placed all three of them, Caesarion, Cleopatra, and Ptolemy, in one of his villas on the Tiber, outside the walls of Rome, and he often came there to get away from what he called the "noise and schemes of the Senate." The last time he spent the night, he promised Caesarion that he would bring him a wolf cub for a pet — "as befits a Roman prince." When Caesarion heard his mother talking to someone in the villa garden, he automatically assumed it was Caesar returning with the wolf he'd promised. But when he looked out the window he saw his mother talking to a strange man dressed in even stranger clothes, his skin whiter than milk. Caesarion could not hear what the pale stranger had said to his mother, but whatever it was, it was enough to upset her and make her decide to flee Rome in the middle of the night.

"Mother—"

"Caesarion, you must be quiet, child! No one is to know we're leaving!" Cleopatra whispered.

"But, Mother — who was that man?"

Cleopatra glared down at her child. "What man?"

"The one in the garden. The one you were talking with. He was dressed very strangely, mother. Was he one of father's slaves?"

Cleopatra's face grew rigid, as if it had become a mask. She bent down and grabbed her son by his shoulders, her fingers digging deep enough to leave marks. The boy cringed and tried to pull away, but he was held fast.

"You saw *nothing*, is that understood? It was all a bad dream, do you hear me? It was a nightmare, nothing more."

"Y-yes, Mother," he squeaked.

✠

Ptolemy XIV Theos Philopator II sat on his bed and played with his toys, oblivious to his sister-wife as she mulled over the latest dispatches from her spies in Rome. She had fled the city in the nick of time, as it turned out. Before the blood was dry on their daggers, several of the assassins had arrived at the villa she had shared with Caesar, only to find the place deserted. No doubt that wretch Cassius would have delighted in tearing free Caesarion's heart from his breast, all in the name of the precious Republic. Murdering bastards! At least the heirs to Caesar's powers were taking care of the assassins. However, the true danger to herself, her kingdom, and her child lay in these self-same avengers.

The Second Triumvirate that arose from Caesar's death was composed of Marc Antony, Octavian, and Lepidus. Cleopatra already sensed that Lepidus was of little concern to her. But the other two — that was a different matter. Marc Antony was Caesar's friend and military protégé, having served under him in Gaul. When Caesar first introduced them, Cleopatra immediately recognized him as the young staff officer who had come to her rescue years before. At thirty-nine, he was still quite dashing and virile in appearance. Octavian, Caesar's great-nephew and legal heir, however, was little more than a youth. At nineteen he was spindly, gangly, and plagued with uncertain health. He also seemed unduly dependent on a low-born lout called Agrippa. Cleopatra

19

remembered, with a shudder, the one time Octavian, in a fit of drunken passion, attempted to seduce her while his uncle was away from Rome. He reminded her all too much of Ptolemy XIII for her liking. She also suspected Octavian of destroying Caesar's original will, which favored Caesarion over him.

Still, which one should she side with? Which one would prove the strongest, and thereby take Caesar's place? Her heart told her Antony, but then she had thought the future secure with Caesar, too. No, she needed more than her native wiles to decide which was the right one to seduce.

She turned from the dispatches to her cosmetic table, with its impressive collection of unguent jars, mixing bowls, paint boxes, and wigs. Her hand dropped onto a tiny lacquered box, the lid of which was marked with the sign of the asp, then glanced back at her brother-husband, still busy playing with a toy crocodile.

She had taken Ptolemy XIV as her husband and co-ruler upon the death of his elder brother, as the laws of Egypt demanded. At least he'd proven far more tractable and easy to control than her first husband. Cleopatra held no true ill-will toward the boy, although her father had held him responsible for the death of his beloved queen. Ptolemy XIV was harmless, forever locked within the mind of a young child. Still, if she was to someday present Caesarion as the legal heir to the Roman Empire, he would need the experience that can only come from holding the scepter and learning the ways of court intrigue, and the sooner the better. And the only way that could happen was if she named him her co-ruler, as Auletes had done with her, years ago.

"Ptolemy, dear?"

The King of Egypt looked up from his play, smiling quizzically at his queen.

"Come here, Ptolemy. I have something I'd like to give you," she said, gesturing so that he might come closer.

Ptolemy hopped off the bed and hurried over to his elder sister's side. Cleopatra was always nice to him — nicer, anyway, than Arsinoe and Ptolemy XIII had ever been. As it was, Ptolemy XIV's memories of the twins were becoming fuzzier with each passing day. Arsinoe was no longer living in Egypt, having dedicated herself as a virgin priestess to Artemis somewhere in Asia Minor, while Ptolemy XIII was dead. In any case, they were no longer around to pinch his ears and dump salt in his porridge.

"See what I have for you, my sweet? Isn't it pretty?" Cleopatra said, holding up a necklace whose pendant was shaped in the form of an asp. "It is a gift, my husband," Cleopatra said as she placed it about his neck. "Something to wear to keep the nightmares away from you as you sleep."

Ptolemy plucked at the necklace; he was a little disappointed. He'd hoped it would be a toy or a sweet of some kind. But still, it *was* pretty and shiny.

⊹

Cleopatra sat within her mausoleum, contemplating the lifeless body of her lover, his head cradled on her lap, as she awaited the arrival of a pale messenger.

"Milady," Sek said, stepping from the lengthening shadows as if he'd been there all along. Cleopatra did not look up. She knew that the messenger appeared just the same as he had the first night she first saw him, twenty-nine years ago.

"Octavian approaches. Antony is dead. Egypt is lost. You lied, herald."

"Not always. But in this instance — and those leading to it — yes."

"Why? Why would Re treat me so cruelly — have I not always honored our contract?"

Sek shook his head and smiled crookedly, revealing a flash of ivory fang. "Re is merely a god created by men to explain the passing of the day, the changing of the seasons. I serve forces far older — and darker — than those of a mere sun-king, my dear. While my name is indeed Sek, I never was a prince. I was a Theban wizard who surrendered my art for power and eternal life offered me by a member of Clan Ventrue. In the centuries since I drank of his tainted blood, I have served the Kindred well, operating as a shadow within the hearts of mortal men — and women."

"But if you were not Re's herald, how is it you could have known such things as my mother's death? Caesar's assassination?"

Sek waved a languid hand in dismissal. "Scrying the near future is nothing for one versed in the darker crafts, little queen. And it was necessary to make you believe in my abilities."

Cleopatra reached out and smoothed Antony's hair, still damp with sweat. "You prophesied that Antony and I would defeat Octavian and Agrippa, that the empires of Rome and Egypt would unite, and that I would be made Queen of Queens and become immortal, my beauty undying."

Sek shrugged. "Such a future could have been yours — but not in this world. My scheme was to cripple and destroy the Roman Republic, not elevate you to empress. My masters find the concept of the Republic quite — distasteful. It worries them. A government without kings and princes? Civic power granted to elected officials? Such ideas are dangerous. Humans are troublesome enough to deal with without rational thought and logic becoming common characteristics! No, the Kindred has decided that the Republic is far too evolved a concept for human society, and I was elected to help defuse the situation — just as I was picked to demolish that wretched Hellenic fad called Democracy by encouraging the rise of your kinsman, Alexander the Great.

"It did not matter to me if I destroyed the Republic by creating a world where you won or Octavian did, as long as the demolition was assured. As I once told you, Destiny walks more than one path."

"But how can the Republic be destroyed if Octavian has won?"

"Believe me, once the little wretch returns to Rome, he'll prove tenacious when it comes to releasing the reigns of power, no matter how much he claims to be a Republican. It will take decades, but the Republic will wither on the vine as Caesar takes his toll on Rome." Sek moved forward, his wine-red eyes glittering in the dim shadows like those of a serpent. "But grieve not, sweet queen. I may have lied as to the future of your mortal plans — but the immortality I spoke of was not an idle promise!"

Cleopatra looked up then, only to cringe when she saw how close Sek was. Without thinking, she tightened her grip on Antony's corpse. "What do you mean?"

"I am prepared to make you an offer, Cleopatra. One that I have made only once or twice in the long centuries since I became as you now see me. I would give you the gift of the Embrace. All I ask is that you give freely to me your life's blood, which I will replace with a drop of my own, from which you will arise immortal. Your beauty will never fade, and Time will be forever at a standstill. I do not offer this rashly, my child — only those mortals who impress me with their strength of mind and character, who display unusual aggression, ambition and courage; only these do I consider worthy of the gift that is mine to give. Over the years I have watched you grow from a tender princess to an iron-willed queen. You would make a worthy addition to Clan Ventrue, daughter of Auletes."

"But what of Antony?" Cleopatra whispered. "Can your sorcery return him to me?"

Sek shook his head. "He is beyond my reach — even if I was disposed to help him. No, Mark Antony is as cold and lifeless as the Republic he once fought so fiercely to defend."

Cleopatra raised her head, meeting Sek's cold stare with eyes as dark and hard as onyx. "Before I make my decision, grant me one last boon. Tell me what Fate holds in store for me and mine, should I refuse."

"As you wish, my beauty." Sek's ruby eyes rolled back into his head, revealing blood-tinged whites. "Within moments of reaching Alexandria, Octavian shall put your son, Caesarion, to the sword, and he will also order your sons by Antony, Helios Alexander and Ptolemy Antonius, slain as well. He will then return to Rome and drag both you and your daughter, the Princess Selene, in chains behind his chariot. He will put you to service in the temple of Venus Genetrix as a temple harlot. Egypt will become Rome's granary, and the Ptolemies shall disappear from the face of the Earth as if they had never been."

Cleopatra shook her head wearily. "Such a choice!" She laughed without humor. "Either to be dragged as a slave through the city through which I was once borne as a queen, or to spend eternity the consort of a monster! Life and unlife. Neither holds much interest for me. I shall turn my back on both, if it's all the same to you."

Sek crossed his hands over his chest, mimicking the attitude of the god Osiris, Lord of the Dead, and bowed stiffly at the waist. "As you wish, great queen."

Cleopatra wiped at the tears in her eyes and, when she opened them again, Sek was gone. In his place was a small, plain wicker basket, inside which something rustled and hissed quietly to itself. As she placed her hand inside, Cleopatra reflected on the immortality she had so easily rejected. To live forever, beautiful and unchanging, like the goddess Isis before her — but Isis at least had her husband, Osiris, to accompany her throughout Time Never-Ending. But to face eternity without Antony—? Better it end like this, even if meant being swallowed by the sands of the great desert.

What use is immortality without love?

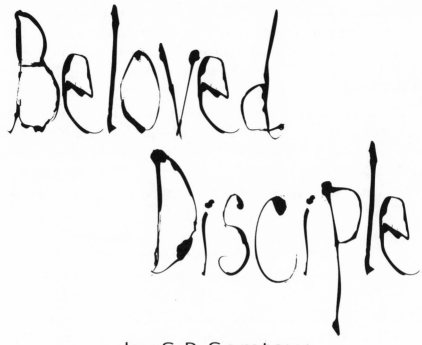

by S.P. Somtow

F irst off, I never fucked him.

I know, I know, Your Holiness, Your Eminence, Monsignor, distinguished fathers of the Roman and other churches; some of you are going to be disappointed. I've heard that there's even a church named in my honor, the Church of the Beloved Disciple, with the implication that I'm the patron saint of homosexuals, which is all very flattering, especially knowing how many of you Reverend Fathers suffer from certain... proclivities which you hypocritically practice even though they are forbidden by your religion.

Not that it never occurred to me. For in any other country in the Empire or beyond, it would have been perfectly natural. But this was Judaea, and Joshua ben Joseph, Jesus to his Greek friends, was very, very Jewish: no pork, no graven images, and no buggery.

He was so pure that I don't think he even masturbated. But he had a passionate hankering for all those things that make a man immortal: philosophies, ideas, poetry. And a hankering for me, too, since I was what, at the time, he was not: I was, so to speak, the real thing.

I am immortal. I am a vampire.

He was a dreamy boy — no more than a boy when I first met him, though old enough to turn a few heads in Cornwall — for the Celts, when it comes to boys, were more Greek than the Greeks, as you would know if you read Caesar's *Gallic War* unexpurgated.

Cornwall, you protest! Jesus was never in Cornwall. Oh, but you surely know William Blake's poem:

> *And did those feet in ancient time*
> *Walk upon England's mountains green?*

As late as the nineteenth century there still lingered some memory of the truth: that Joseph of Arimathea, one of the most influential men in Judaea, owned shares in a Cornish tin-mine, and had become rich from the manufacture of bronze; that he once had occasion to bring young Joshua to distant Britannia, the most barbaric outpost of the Empire.

Joshua's father was another Joseph, a rabbi of the Essene sect, so learned and so diligent that they nicknamed him The Carpenter. His mother, Miriam, doted on his little brother James, and ignored him. They were, in modern parlance, dysfunctional.

I learned all these things when I was in Cornwall for the winter solstice.

The solstice was a marvelous thing. You cannot imagine what you have lost by turning your backs on the paganism you so shamelessly plundered for the trappings of your own religion. You still burn the yule log. But the Celts burned living things: virgins, children of particular purity and beauty, lambs, chickens, cattle, all imprisoned within monstrous wicker statues, so tall they dwarfed the trees, the houses, even the menhirs or votive monoliths that the Celts loved to erect in honor of Bridget, their great goddess.

This was, you understand, before the rampant Romanization of the area. I visited it less than a century later and found a health spa, a marble shopping mall and a slave market, next to a temple to the God Vespasian. The Old

Religion had become unfashionable. I see you're smiling, Your Holiness; the same thing seems to have happened to your own Old Religion.

But not to digress, the solstice was a wonderful time for hunting humans, and on the night of the great sacrifices I was mingling with them, sniffing the night air, redolent with the fragrance of excited blood. Bloodlust was blowing in the wind. Druids strode among the populace, and so did I, in the same white robes, a wolf in wolf's clothing.

The feet of the wicker men were already aflame. They held the lowlier life forms; the humans, lashed together inside the statue's chest and head, would have ample time to reflect on their mortality. Most seemed resigned, though a few screamed and tried to free themselves, much to the merriment of all. I moved through the throng. There was snow on the ground, but the heat from the wicker men was turning it to mush. Boars were roasting on spits, and tourists were being fleeced by cunning vendors into buying any number of sacred stones, elixirs, mistletoe love charms, and the like. Among those tourists was a small group of Judaeans; and one, apart from the others, was gazing intently at the holocaust, almost as though he were feeling the victims' suffering with them. This was the boy called Joshua ben Joseph.

I could single out the peculiar scent of his blood, even in this chaos. It was a sweet blood. In today's all-too-scientific parlance, you might say that I detected a complete absence of adrenaline; his was a terrifying kind of inner calm, almost as though he were already one of us. It was this calm I found most beautiful about him. I wanted to make him kindred to me. I did not want to feed on him and then abandon him to the worms and fishes.

I do not breathe, and so it was I was able to stand behind him, quite close to him, without his noticing. I wanted to hold off the moment of attack, to savor the fragrance of his blood, as a mortal lover longs to delay his climax until he can sustain himself no longer.

At last I could no longer rein myself in. The sacrificial victims were on fire. Smoke billowed through the crowd. Blood, I thought to myself; blood, blood. I coiled, prepared to pounce.

"Don't," the boy said.

It suddenly occurred to me that he had known I was there all along; perhaps he had even been toying with me.

"I have a sense about these things," he said, and turned to me. Looked me over with his soulful, serious eyes. "Joshua," he said. "And you... I suppose you have many names. I'll call you John."

"All right."

"You're not a druid at all, are you?"

"What am I?"

"I'm not sure, really. I think you're sort of an angel."

"Hardly. I'm what you might call a fisher of men. You often talk to angels?"

"My whole family does. They're always at the house. An angel told my mother she was going to get pregnant with me, you know. Other people laughed when she said it was an angel; they said it was a Roman centurion named Pantera. Another angel told my father he should marry my mother anyway, but he still doesn't like me."

"You're here without them."

"Yes, I made a scene at my own bar mitzvah, got into a big argument with some learned men, so they sent me away with Uncle Joseph to cool off. Wasn't a scene, really. All I said was that the whole of the Torah could be boiled down to a single sentence: 'Do unto others what you would have them do unto you.' Rabbi Hillel says that all the time. I was just quoting him. They don't call *him* a dangerous radical."

"I'm assuming this Rabbi Hillel is a learned, venerable scholar rather than an insolent pip-squeak like yourself."

"I keep trying to go about my father's business, but I never seem to get it right."

"So they don't think you should be a rabbi."

"That's right. They want me to get into bronze, like Uncle Joseph." The Roman occupation had made Joseph of Arimathea a very rich man.

We did not talk for awhile. The wicker men were fast being consumed, and the Celts were rolling around drunk and indulging in the usual debaucheries. The druids were droning an interminable paean to the sexual forces of nature, and I needed to slake my thirst. A suitable prospect ambled by at just that moment. I entranced her with a look, sipped a little from the nape of her neck even as she stared into empty space, seduced by my eyes, which seem to mortals like a yawning void. Joshua watched me, alarmed and fascinated. "You're a strange kind of angel," he said at last, as I let the woman go and she stumbled into the crowd. "You're beautiful, and that in itself is dangerous. The way your skin sucks in the moonlight. It's probably really cold, as cold as the moon."

"Yes." If only he knew how cold. I have stood in the country of the midnight sun. But what I am is a thing more desolate still. "Tell me about that sense of yours," I said. "Most people are completely clueless about what's lurking in their very midst."

"Well," Joshua said, "I just make myself go very still, and then it's like I'm outside myself."

"Samadhi," I said.

He started. "What language is that?" Almost as if he had heard it before.

"A language of India. It's something ascetics know how to do... leaving their own bodies, turning themselves into creatures of pure spirit, floating above the world. Only they have to meditate for years first."

"Oh!" he said. "You've been to India!"

"Occasionally," I said. I did not tell him how long ago.

"So have I," said the boy. And he told me all about it. I'm not sure how much there was to it. It was all so mythic: the massacre of the innocents, a flight by camel across a great desert, then forests, palaces, sages, teeming cities; and him so young through all of it, he could not possibly have remembered so much. I think he was told some of it, surmised some, imagined most of it. He had the gift that all great leaders have: He could take the wildest fancies and make them palpable.

Before long, I was telling him some of my own adventures in India. Encounters with hermits in the jungle. How I once sipped the blood of a maharani as she rode to a tryst with a secret lover on the back of an elephant. How I had sat at the feet of the Buddha and heard him tell me that the world is only a dream. He came alive as we talked. I was almost convinced he *had* been there.

"You see," he said, "we do have something in common."

"More than something." For he had seen the void, and he had not been afraid.

From that moment on, I wanted to make him my beloved disciple, to teach him the ways of love and death, to be his guide through the labyrinth of night. But he had other ideas. "'One day,'" he said, "'they'll hold this festival in my name. But I think I'll get rid of the human sacrificing.' Even then, Your Holiness, he was suffering from what has come to be known as a messiah complex."

A bearded man, richly attired in the Hellenistic fashion, his head covering the only indication of his Judaean origins, called out to Joshua: "Let's go back now, Joshua. This place reeks of pork."

Joshua surprised me by putting his arms around me, and his lips to my lips, also in the Hellenistic fashion; I held him a little longer than was seemly, but only because I wanted to savor the pure, still fragrance of his blood; perhaps, he mistook my meaning, for he then said, "I'd love to, but you see, I'm Jewish; we're not allowed to."

He stepped away from me, a slender, shadowy figure that soon blended into the crowd. A hint of that strange fragrance hung in the air, for the fires had died down and the celebrants mostly passed out from too much partying. I wandered among them for awhile, feeding here and there. But their lust-drenched blood was too rich, too ripe.

He's only a minnow, I told myself. I've tossed him back in the river. But I couldn't shake the suspicion that it was I who had been let go. Who was fishing for whom? It depressed me so much I went to a cave in the Himalayas and slept for thirteen years.

✝

When next I saw him, he was in his thirties. I, of course, had not aged.

"John," he said. I hate the name John. You will note that I have contrived to omit it from *that* gospel. But Joshua had changed. Getting dunked in the Jordan by his cousin the mad guru had caused him to undergo what you might call a "religious experience." The messiah complex was in full swing, and he'd caught a bit of the infallibility bug, too, Your Holiness. Yet he was no fool. He knew me at once. Even though night was falling and thousands of people had gathered to hear him preach.

I had braved the twilight to come and see him, cowled and caped like Mr. Death to protect myself from the dying sun. He had been preaching all day, mostly, it seems, a rehashed rendition of Rabbi Hillel's doctrines; but there was a healthy dose of Buddhism in it too, the whole non-violent "blessed are the meek" angle, half-remembered from the stories I had told him about India.

Like a guru in Benares, he was surrounded by disciples fetching him wine, bread and fish, sitting at his feet so that not a pearl could escape.

They stared at me, with my pallid mien, my unblinking gaze, the fact that I do not breathe except occasionally, for a touch of verisimilitude. One of them,

30

tall and bearded and reeking of fish, was about to shoo me away, but Joshua ben Joseph silenced him with a barely perceptible flick of the wrist. I smelled the strange tranquillity of his blood. I knew at once that this was the memory that had drawn me back from the sleep of the dead.

"Now *I'm* old," he said, laughing, "and you're the callow boy. You'll have to be *my* beloved disciple this time round." We both laughed, but the companions didn't. I made them uncomfortable. "Peter," he said to the tall one, "don't you know an angel when you see one?"

Warily, the disciples looked me over. One of them — I could tell from the family resemblance that this must be James, the favored younger brother — said, "Is he Jewish?" They were eating, you see. It wasn't as rude as you might think; dining with goyim violates one of their innumerable mitzvot.

"Don't be such a brat, James," Joshua said. "Haven't you been listening? I've changed the rules."

"You're such a fucking egotist," said James. "No one minds you being the messiah — everyone and his mother's the kwisatz haderach these days. But you start saying '*I've* changed the rules' and people are going to think you're crazy." He wouldn't eat another bite, but the others were less fastidious.

"I'm not crazy," he said slowly. "There's got to be five thousand people camped out here tonight. They need something. I'm giving it to them. There are miracles. The blind *can* see. Today" — he looked straight into my eyes — "you've seen the dead walk." Peter poured me a krater of wine. "He never drinks wine," Joshua said, and made me laugh again, and baffled the others even further; grumbling, they turned away from us and began debating some arcane aspect of the Torah.

"We've got to talk," Joshua said to me. He got up suddenly from the rug they'd laid out for him. He gripped my hand. The coldness of my flesh didn't make him flinch. I didn't feel his blood quicken. Only the preternatural calm. He led me a little further uphill. It was sheep country here, crags protruding out of sparse vegetation; the moon was rising now, and you could see all the followers, bundled up, dotting the slopes and on down into the valley; the sheep analogy felt particularly poignant. "I've been... well... waiting for you to come back," he said.

"What for?" I said.

"You're still the same. The childlike eyes. You don't need to breathe the air. You *are* an angel. I know I wasn't wrong when I was a boy, in Cornwall, at that awful sacrifice."

"Maybe a dark angel."

"You have to help me, John. I'm the captain of the ship, but I don't know which way to go, and I don't recognize any of the stars."

"Rabbinical teachings are hardly my thing. You haven't tried asking your father?"

"Which one?"

"Touché," I said. Inside the head of this brilliant, radical rabbi there was still the angry little boy, uncertain of his parentage, whose mother saw angels where others saw centurions.

"I've been suckered into this whole messiah scheme," he said, "but I'm all wrong for the role. I don't understand politics. I've never led an army. I don't even believe in an independent Jewish state. Have you heard of this guy, Herod Agrippa? Now he'd make a fine messiah. He's had military training... and he went to school with everyone who's anyone in Rome, so he knows the enemy... speaks Greek like a native... plus he's got royal blood. The messiah's supposed to have royal blood."

"Genealogies can always be faked."

"Yes, but—"

"So why don't you just endorse him?"

"Yes, but... well, I know it's hopeless. The Romans are the greatest nation on earth... well, the *only* nation on earth. No messiah has ever succeeded before... it's essentially a losing proposition. Unless..."

He had no intention of asking my advice at all. He was bouncing ideas off me. We cast no reflection, you see. That's because we are your reflection. We hold up the mirror to your dark souls. Chew on that one, Your Holiness! I stood beside him, on the hilltop, overlooking the sea of sheep, showing him his true self in my vacant eyes.

"Unless," he went on, "the redemption of Israel is really a metaphor for something much bigger, something cosmic. Unless the kingdom is not even of this world. Do you follow me? Like the world you come from, the world of shadows. That's it, you see. If I build my church on reality, then I'm building it in the sand, and Rome is the infinite sea."

"What are you saying?"

"Nothing, really. Except..."

"Except?"

"Can't you stay, this time? I know I can't turn back the clock to that time in Cornwall, and of course I'm just as Jewish as I was then, so I don't commit abominations, but... you're the only one who understands. There's more to life than... you know, life."

Had I been human, my heart would have raced, my hormones would have started to hum, because Joshua was on the verge of admitting that he loved me, even though he couldn't quite bring himself to suck my dick. He still didn't quite get it, Reverend Fathers. I was going to have to use the direct approach. You never have much time, with humans. You blink and they're dead.

"I'll stay, but you're going to have to give me something," I said.

He sighed.

"No, no, you fool," I said. "I only want a little blood."

"Wouldn't be kosher," he said. "But I guess you wouldn't care about that. Well... why not? The whole world's going to be drinking my blood soon enough."

He pulled back his right sleeve and offered me his wrist. I knelt down, worried a little scab with a fingernail, then sipped it, one drop at a time. It was something to savor. That otherworldly calm seeped into me. A memory of my mortality surfaced for a moment. My mother's milk. I had not thought of mortality in a thousand years. For a moment I almost thought my heart was beating. As I drank, he stared out over the sleeping congregation. His eyes shone in the moonlight. Some humans become aroused when I feed on them, and cry out as in orgasm; he only made himself go far away.

Finally, faintly, I heard him say, half to himself, "They crucify you through the wrist; did you know that? A lot of people think it's through the palms, but that would just rip right through."

And that, Your Holiness, Your Eminences, Reverend Fathers of the Church, was the extent of the Beloved Disciples's carnal knowledge of the Son of Man.

✠

It took some time for Joshua's followers to get used to the idea that I was there to stay. Judaea was a pretty tense place, a messiah under every rock, political activists railing in every street corner, and the Romans sitting around

33

crucifying people almost at random. I wasn't a spy, and I wasn't one of the peasants, and I was surely no theologian. But it was necessary, for various numerological and historical reasons, to have twelve apostles, and Joshua always got his way.

I was there for it all: the miracles, such as they were, though you people have become a lot slicker at these things; the triumphal entry into Jerusalem, carefully stage-managed so as to function as an elegant midrash on selected passages of the Tanakh; I was there for the passover shabbat, wherein Joshua made no mention of his body and blood, such pagan concepts being quite distasteful to him; and I was there for the awful climax and its bathetic denouement.

After they dragged him away, the apostles called an emergency meeting at Joseph of Arimathea's house. Joshua's parents were conspicuously absent, as usual; but there was another Miriam, an ex-prostitute, who was Joshua's first and most devoted groupie and could not be kept away. Joseph — a liberal — didn't mind having harlots in the house, though he did draw the line at publicans.

"It can't end this way," James said. It was as if, having been the family's darling all his life, he couldn't stand the thought of being permanently one-upped by Joshua's martyrdom.

"So what do *you* suggest?" said Peter. "We can't very well storm the dungeons; we'll *all* get strung up." He stared shiftily about; on his way to the meeting he had denied knowing Joshua three times. The fetor of his fear permeated the chamber. They were all stinking drunk, except for me.

I sat in the shadows, thinking of other things. Between mortals and immortals, love always ends in an unending longing. I wished we could have gone to India together. Or even to the world on the other side of the ocean, which I had heard about from a sage whose skin was the color of wine. I relived our first meeting again and again. Their lives rush by so fast, I thought. Larva to chrysalis to butterfly to putrefaction.

It was Joseph of Arimathea who said, "But it's so simple. Let John bring him back from the dead."

They all looked at me, looked away, drank deeply. I said, "It's a gift that can't be taken back. And he has never asked me to make him immortal."

"We need him," Peter said. "You can see that. We're like a chicken with its head cut off. If he comes back, everyone will see that the God of Abraham, Isaac and Jacob is more powerful than idols of stone and brass."

"When's the execution?" I said.

"Friday," said Joseph of Arimathea, who, being a man of influence, had a tendency to know these things. "The Romans will give him a fair trial, but there's really no way they can let off someone who's openly being called the King of the Jews."

"But his kingdom's not of this world!" said Thomas, who never believed anything he was told.

"The Romans," I said, "are completely literal-minded. That's why they own everything."

"It's politics as usual," said Joseph, "and Pilate has to protect his ass back home. Can't blame him, really." But he was on the verge of tears. I've often wondered whether it was not he, rather than the legendary Pantera, who stuck it to the rabbi's fiancée, for he loved Joshua far more than the other Joseph ever did.

It was Joseph who convinced me, not the squabbling, self-righteous rabble who called themselves his apostles. No, I take that back, Your Holiness. It was I who convinced myself. Perhaps it was selfishness. But you, Reverend Fathers, have never faced eternity. You just wouldn't understand.

Oh, but you preach eternity from your pulpits. Eternal bliss, eternal damnation. Fleecy clouds and fiery brimstone. You don't know what the fuck you're talking about. After the first few hundred years, every color becomes gray. Every song is a single note. Every mortal is another scurrying piece of vermin, and all that is left is the ache that can never be slaked, and the loss that festers forever. You are fools to say *forever* so lightly. A long long time, my friends, is not forever.

"I'll do it," I said softly. "But somehow we have to get him to drink my blood."

"Is that kosher?" said James. No one so much as looked at him for the rest of the evening.

✝

Humans can never get used to crucifixions, but for me an almost clinical detachment is possible. In their own way, the Romans bent over backward to accommodate the practices of their wayward subjects. Usually it takes days for the victim to die, but the Judaeans had a religious taboo against leaving corpses hanging after sunset (or was it only on Saturdays?), so they had compromised by using novel techniques for speeding up death: the flogging and the nails were, grotesquely enough, designed to shorten the agony. That was Roman know-how for you.

The "display" crosses you see in religious paintings were not a common feature of these operations. Actually, criminals were strung up only slightly above eye level; you could look right into their faces, even spit in their eye; and people often did. Public executions bring out the worst in mortals. You all know that Joshua ben Joseph was crucified between two thieves, but actually the whole hillside was crammed with crosses. Under Roman law, virtually everything was a capital offense.

It was afternoon, and so I almost didn't make it there. But about three or four o'clock it became preternaturally dark; a nightingale began to sing outside the room at Joseph of Arimathea's mansion where I was lying. I came to suddenly, bewildered because my sleep seemed so short. There was no one in the house. I made my way to the crucifixion hill.

In the tribal north, there had been at least a sense of elation and celebration about the wicker men. Here there was nothing of the kind. Here only beggars and lepers lurked about, and a few idle curious; the Roman soldiers, jaded, went about their business, nailing them down and stringing them up. Unrecycled crossbeams lay on the dirt; the smell of stale blood clung to them, mingled with the scent of fresh-gushing blood which permeated the hot, dry air.

I made my way through the forest of the dying, and at length spied Miriam — the whore, not the mother — standing almost at the summit of the hill, where three recent crosses formed a sort of triptych of suffering. The smell of Joshua's blood was faint, but it still held that eerie calm. I went up to Miriam, told her we had to go through with the plan.

She said, "Wait. His mother's here."

Then it was I saw another woman, one who had remained conspicuously absent throughout Joshua's ministry. She looked up at her son now, and I do not think she wept.

And I also looked but did not weep, though for another reason: I cannot.

It was going to have to be done soon. And still I was unsure, because, Reverend Sirs, it takes more than an invitation for a man to enter my eternal kingdom — not a sprinkle of water over a baby — not a few murmured phrases. To borrow a cliché of your modern pop psychology, Joshua had to want to

36

change. I was almost sure I had seen that longing in him, at our very first meeting... but might it have been something else?

I watched for a sign. His agony begged description, but then all agony does, in the end, doesn't it? They had crowned him with thorns. Blood caked his forehead. There were flies. Vultures, too. The causa poenae, tacked to the cross, read "*Rex Iudaeorum.*" He gazed back at me, his eyes already beginning to dull. In his mother's eyes I saw... disappointment, perhaps. She looked at Miriam the prostitute and for a moment I thought she was going to claw her eyes out. Then she saw me.

I do not look Jewish. I am clean-shaven as I was in life, which the Judaeans considered a sign of Hellenistic effeminacy. I have a certain clarity of complexion, a glow; all vampires do. That is why the ugliest of mortals becomes beautiful once he has heeded the call of night. I could tell that she did not admire my otherworldly looks; rather, she instantly assumed the worst — that I must be the masculine counterpart of Miriam the whore. She looked at me and to her dying son, and I could just imagine her thinking maybe I was the reason her Joshua could never settle down and have kids.

Then Joshua gasped, "Mother, he's your son now. John, kiss your new mother."

She gaped at the outrageous insinuation. I wanted to tell her it wasn't what she thought it was, but I daresay it would have made even less sense to her. Just like human beings, to stoop to a bit of domestic bickering at a moment like this.

I was surprised that he could still speak. The process of crucifixion is actually one of asphyxiation, of the body slowly sagging and collapsing the lungs. The power of speech soon goes.

"I'm thirsty," he said.

A small detail was marching uphill, pausing in front of each cross to smash the criminal's legs. Without the anchor of nailed-down bone, the body caves in on itself and squeezes the life right out of itself. Another practical Roman solution to the Jewish taboo about corpses being strung up past nightfall. No time to lose. I found a sentry, nodding off against a boulder. I shook him. "Let me give him something to drink," I said. I dropped a silver denarius in his helmet. He grunted, let me borrow his javelin for a moment; I pierced my left wrist with a fingernail and squeezed out enough blood to wet a sponge, held it up to his lips; blood trickled onto his tongue, which was already beginning to protrude.

When he tasted blood, something about him changed. Was it the touch of the first breath of eternity? Softly, he said, "It's done." But what was done? Surely not his crazed master plan for establishing the perfect Jewish society, God's Kingdom on

Earth? Or was it an acceptance of his vampiric destiny? Only the night would tell.

He closed his eyes. The darkness gathered. But I left swiftly, for these unnatural darknesses have a way of lifting, and I did not want to be stranded in sunlight even on the short distance from the execution site to the tomb that Joseph of Arimathea had prepared — a luxurious tomb, for he had intended it for himself.

✠

Once inside the tomb, I waited awhile; in time, my circadian rhythms, interrupted by the unnatural darkness of the afternoon, forced me back into slumber. I slept more than twenty-four hours; when I go out by day, even in darkness, my body needs a little longer to repair itself.

When I awoke, he was hunched on the lid of the stone sarcophagus, tearing the bloody linen off himself. "I'll get that," I said. I ripped away more pieces of his shroud. His wrists were regenerating nicely, but there was a deep puncture in each one, wide enough to stick a finger through.

"What did you do to me?" he said. "What have you made me?"

I said, "They begged me, your apostles. And I've seen it in your face. You want this. You've looked eternity in the eye before, Joshua, and it didn't scare you."

He didn't answer. He was staring at his hands. They were white as the limestone sepulcher itself. Yes, I knew he was no longer mortal. There was no source of light in the tomb, and yet he saw with the eyes of night. And for those who see as we see, he was light, cold, phosphorescent, pale.

"This isn't what I had in mind, John," he said.

"Don't call me John anymore," I said, and instead cried out my own true name in the language of night, which only the dead can speak. In that instant he also knew his true name, which cannot be spoken here.

I sensed his confusion, sensed also the incipient pangs of the great hunger; and slitting my wrist once more with my fingernail I gave him sustenance, becoming mother to him as well as midwife. He did not complain that the blood violated his dietary taboos; he knew already that to cross into our world is also to abandon the very concept of godhead. "I was hoping to be resurrected," he said. "But at the last minute I despaired; I tried to pray but all I could hear were the words of the psalmist about having been forsaken by god; that's true, isn't it? Instead of god, you came."

"And once you called me an angel."

"You still are. *Angelos*: messenger. But who sent you? That's what I can't figure out. Is this how we're going to defeat the Romans... by turning Judaea into a kingdom of the undead?"

"Just the sort of harebrained grand scheme you'd come up with. Get the long view, Joshua. You already *have* defeated the Romans. Do you know how old I am? I was old when the citadel of the Hittites was plundered and razed. Where are the Hittites now? A few scratches of cuneiform in other people's history books. Where are the Trojans now? The Minoans, the people of Thera, the Carthaginians? I've already defeated them, because I'm still here, remembering the taste of their blood, and they are dust. If you ask me a question, and I pause till the fall of Rome before I answer you, it is only a blink. The mortals cannot see the grand spectacle of their own lives; they cannot be as passionate as we, nor as pitiless. Don't you feel the thrill of it?"

"If you say so," he said.

But perhaps he didn't. I recalled the odor of his blood. The tranquillity that had so intoxicated me... it had survived the transformation. Why had I been lecturing him about the sweep of history? He had felt all of that without even having experienced it, even as a mere mortal. It occurred to me that perhaps it was not my blood that had brought him back from the dead. Maybe he was some kind of natural vampire, self-creating, self-sufficient. I had never encountered anything like that, but if you think about it, there's got to have been at least *one* vampire to start the whole cycle off....

This was a disturbing line of thought. So I said, "Well, Joshua, if not for the sweep of history, then at least for knowledge. We've spoken of India, but there are other lands too... Cathay... there are some of us who have found a whole new continent to the west... there are more worlds to conquer than your Roman Empire."

"And we shall conquer them, my friend," he said. He had freed himself from his winding-sheet now. He embraced me, and said, "We'll find new worlds and fresh philosophies."

"You mean it?" I said.

"You know that I can't lie," he said. Such is the loneliness of eternity that I welcomed what he said without considering its ambiguity.

✛

Your Holiness and others... I see that you are becoming heartily troubled by my narration. But it gets worse.

You all know the story of the empty tomb. We met up with the rest of the apostles at Joseph's, and a couple of other times. They all thanked me — somewhat perfunctorily, to be sure — for bringing Joshua back from the dead. Miriam and Joseph (the rabbi, not the tin tradesman) and the rest of that mixed-up brood went through a transformation of their own. Having shit on their wayward eldest all his life, they resolved to put him on a pedestal; the fat, spoiled little brother led the campaign to make Joshua's proto-Marxist precepts into the biggest new sect of Judaism.

A book of those down-home little parables and precepts was circulated underground — much like Chairman Mao's little red book — it's the "lost" book that Biblical scholars — which many of you, Reverend Fathers, are not — call "Q". I know, it was a cheap trick, using Xeroxed pages of my personal copy of "Q" to cause this, ah, ecumenical support group to be convened, and, yes, I *will* present you all with the entire manuscript after I've had my say — but how else was I going to get your reverend asses all in one room *and* to believe in the authenticity of my tale?

In any case, you'll find that the scholars were quite correct: virtually all of "Q" is quoted at length in the four canonical gospels. You won't find anything new in it. The scoop, Reverend Fathers (oh, I do apologize, Sister, I didn't notice you among all the male chauvinists) is in what I'm telling you. I know you're all spazzing already, but please hold your sphincters for just five more minutes.

Something really, really weird happened next: *Christianity.*

Joshua and I were gone for, oh, twenty years or so. It was wild and glorious... the vampiric equivalent of a honeymoon. Yes, we went to India. We fed on pilgrims as they stripped to bathe in the Ganges. I did most of the hunting. Joshua saw the necessity of it but was still queasy; he was still adjusting. We rode through jungles, were received by maharajahs, drank the blood of virgins, were venerated as gods in some cities, reviled as demons in others. Yes, we did set sail to what you now call America, so you Mormon elders may consider Mr. Joseph Smith's febrile imaginings, at least in part, vindicated. Joshua did not preach. Instead, he listened. He was like an empty vessel into which men poured what was best and worst in themselves. And I admired him for that, because in transcending mortality he had not lost compassion, which is usually the first thing to go. He grew in compassion, in fact. I had not known that this was possible.

In time, we came back to the Levant, and it was in Ephesos, a town most famed for its huge gold statue of the Great Mother, that we first encountered Jesus Christ.

It was, in fact, in front of the famous statue (in Ephesos they call the mother-goddess Diana) that we first heard the name being bandied about. It was night and they were sacrificing — strange how that motif crops up again — and we were hunting. The place was a spectacle, all towering columns and clouds of incense and everything gold and ivory and the statue itself as tall as a ten-story building. No babies being sacrificed here, though; we were well inside the civilizing boundaries of Rome. In the shadow of a fluted column, voices were whispering about Nazareth.

Joshua pricked up his ears. "They haven't forgotten me," he said, and smiled.

Good news. Baptism. The Kingdom of Heaven... The Redemption of Mankind... The Resurrection... it all sounded hauntingly familiar. There was a meeting later that night, we overheard. In a back room of a local synagogue.

The crowd was an odd one. I had never seen so many goyim in a synagogue, and they didn't cover their heads. There were women, too, sitting right alongside the men. A lot of riffraff — slaves, the homeless, prostitutes — Joshua liked that. He had always gone down well with the proles, with that stuff about the first shall be last and blessed are the poor and camels going through needles' eyes and all that. One or two rich people, too. We blended right in; no one so much as stared at us.

The thing was as brilliantly stage-managed as a contemporary revival meeting. There were warm-up speakers who gave testimonials about the efficacy of using the ineffable name of Jesus as a kind of mantra; Joshua chuckled a little at this, but as the meeting went on he became more and more solemn.

The keynote speaker was a man named Paul. Bit of a flamer, a Liberace type... a real live Roman citizen, as he never tired of pointing out. The tale he told was an amazing one, a sort of throw-it-in-the-blender mélange of every popular cult in the Roman Empire. Jesus was the son of God (like Hercules) and that bitter yenta of a mother was transformed into an eternal virgin, much like the Great Mother herself who was worshipped at the Temple of Diana down the street. Like Adonis, Jesus had died at the beginning of the spring fertility rites and been resurrected on the third day. Like Odin, he had been strung up on a great tree. Adam's dismissal from Eden was no longer what everyone had always thought it was — a profound, poetic metaphor for the human condition — but a temporary inconvenience to which Jesus would soon put an end, especially since he was coming back any moment now to snatch up the faithful and punish the sinful. The whole of the Tanakh was just Part One. All this was gospel truth because Paul, formerly Saul, had once persecuted Christians... and Jesus had come to him in a vision and set him straight.

Mixed in with all this phantasmagorical mythology were many of the homely parables and radical sociological viewpoints that Joshua had actually preached. It was very inspirational, very feverish, very much like a rock concert. Women were weeping and fainting and having orgasms; men were having attacks of glossolalia; cripples were tottering around and blind men claiming they could see while banging their heads on pillars.

Paul's rhetoric climaxed with an appeal not to resist persecution — to welcome martyrdom, as it would mean instant acceptance into the bosom of Jesus. Crucifixion, flaying, burning, being devoured by lions, all were but painful preludes to paradise.

It got better. Next came a magic ritual — a pagan parody of that sad last passover meal we had all had together, the night they came to take him away. They broke bread, and after a few incantations pronounced that it was Joshua's body; a flagon of wine became his blood. Such irony! It made me relive once more the moment I had first savored that blood, so innocent of inner turmoil. Eating the sacred body of the god-king was a custom as old as the Stone Age, but Paul had managed to trivialize even *that* most ancient and potent of metaphors. Fucking Roman citizen, indeed! He certainly had their literal-mindedness.

"I can't take much more of this," I said, and we fought our way through the throng as someone bore down on us with a collection plate.

But suddenly Joshua stopped me. "We have to talk to him," he said. "This is insanity. We have to stop it."

"They're only humans," I said. "This will all blow over."

"But it's my name they're using," he said. "It's my name they're dying for."

"Your *human* name," I said scornfully.

"Yes," he said.

You know, we don't change all that much when we cross over to the darkness. Alive, Joshua had attracted me because he grasped eternity so completely; now that he was dead, I saw that his comprehension of mortality far surpassed my own. He had not been comfortable in their world, and now he still had not found his home.

I had to humor him. It was not in my power to douse this spark of difference in him; it was what I loved most about him.

Easy enough for us to blend into the shadows, to drift along the dusty columns until we found a back room, where a young man stood flexing in front of a polished shield. We stood behind this youth (too absorbed in his narcissistic endeavors to look over his shoulder — we cast no reflection in the shield, of course) and waited.

Presently we could hear a hymn being sung, fervently and discordantly, by the crowd outside, and Paul came storming into the room. We stepped back into gloom. Paul and the young man kissed passionately. "A strong showing tonight, Timothy," Paul said. "I think we've collected enough to hit the big time."

"You think we'll actually get to play Rome?" said the boy. The adoring gaze he had for the old man turned sour when Paul looked away, and I recognized the sullen mien of the street hustler. Definitely rough trade.

"Rome? Honey, we're going to *own* Rome!" said Paul.

Many theologians and sociologists have argued that St. Paul was a closet homosexual who imposed his misogyny on the misguided Christian masses; but let me tell you, Your Holiness — in spite of your recent encyclical — that civilized people in the first century were far too sophisticated to be hung up on such minutiae as sexual preference. Later, of course, when St. Augustine decided that sex was dirty...

We interrupted before the scene could become X-rated, materializing out of the shadows. "Paul!" Joshua said. "Do you know who I am?"

"No," he said, mystified. Timothy shrugged and went back to flexing.

Joshua held up his pierced wrists. You could see the smoky flicker of the wall torch through the holes.

"You're not…" said Paul.

"I am," said Joshua ben Joseph.

I stayed out of it. It was Joshua's fight. I lurked in the background. Outside, the hymn singing crescendoed to a cacophonous climax.

"Why are you doing this to me?" Joshua said softly.

"James and the others… they said you'd risen from the dead, said they'd seen it with their own eyes… thought it was the greatest new gimmick… but it's true, then. Dear me, who would have thought it?"

Joshua said, "I'm not Dionysus. God didn't come down from heaven to screw my mother. I'm not Osiris, come back from the dead to guide mortals beyond the grave. I'm not the Corn God, ripped in pieces to fertilize the earth and then reborn as king. I'm just a rabbi who hung out with hookers. I wanted my friends to become better Jews, to understand what the Torah's really trying to say instead of hiding behind their petty regulations."

"What good are the Jews? They crucified you."

"No, they didn't. The Romans did."

"They made them do it."

"You don't make the Romans do things. I broke a Roman law. I would not render unto Caesar something which belonged to Caesar — sovereignty. I wasn't talking about political sovereignty, but you know how literal-minded the Romans are. Why would the Jews have had me killed? For claiming to be the messiah? There's a new messiah every week, and they don't get crucified."

I had to speak up. "He has to blame it on the Jews," I said. "He's preaching to the Romans. Roman complicity in your death would be a real no-no. What do the goyim know about the workings of the Sanhedrin? As far as they're concerned, a bunch of swarthy, middle-eastern religious fanatics is capable of *any* depravity… even deicide. Have to bend the truth a bit here and there, don't you, Paul?"

"The truth! And what, as Pontius Pilate said to you, Jesus, on the morning of your crucifixion, *is* truth?"

"He didn't say that," said Joshua. "He didn't even talk to me. He had a dozen other death warrants to sign that morning, and he didn't want to miss lunch."

Paul was fuming. "You're just like your brother James," he said. "I've built this majestic structure of powerful, rich images that trigger the imagination, that make men's spirits soar. I'm giving hope to the downtrodden and picking up a few denarii along the way. So what if it's a house of cards? So what if it didn't really happen that way? I've found the core of mythic truth in your tawdry little bio, and I'm going to make you the biggest thing since the invention of the wheel, you ungrateful insect. This new religion is going to take over the world. It's got everything. Tragedy and pathos, terror of judgment, the catharsis of forgiveness. It's the grandest religion yet invented."

"But I don't want a new religion," said Joshua ben Joseph. "I'm Jewish."

☩

After awhile, Paul seemed to calm down a little. "I'll need to regroup," he said. "Maybe I can still salvage some of this."

While he guzzled wine, we told him some of our own adventures. We got drunk together... he and Timothy on a couple of kegs of Samian wine, Joshua and I from a pint of Timothy's blood which he obligingly let me draw... after I told him I could do it painlessly.

Paul became so drunk he even stopped speaking Greek. In tearful Aramaic, he told us searing childhood tales about his father whipping him for sucking off the stablehands. No wonder he preferred being Roman to being Jewish! No wonder he wanted to bring the gospel to the goyim!

That was what it all boiled down to, after all. He wanted to be accepted, to be loved for what he was, this poor little sissy boy who had the misfortune to be born into the one culture where they stoned sissies. One could almost sympathize. After awhile, indeed, one did. "Forgive me," Paul was weeping into his goblet.

"I forgive you," said Joshua.

"Thank you... thank you, abba," said Paul. I realized then that he wanted his real father to forgive him... that the source of the angst that drove him was his fear of having disappointed his earthly father... he had created in his mind a surrogate father, all-merciful, all-forgiving, to succor his own self-loathing. And Joshua understood all this... truly understood it... and felt compassion for this lonely little man... a compassion as deep as any love he felt for me.

45

I envied the world, because not even death had sundered Joshua from his love for it.

Paul invited us back to his home. "I want to hear more stories," he said. "I want to learn everything you can teach me. After all, you are my Redeemer. You ought to have a hand in the religion, especially since it's all about you."

Very softly, Joshua said to me, "He just doesn't hear me."

But we went home with him anyway, and as dawn approached we bedded down for the day in a cozy wine-cellar.

Night fell and I rose from my dreamless sleep. I found my beloved disciple lying on the dirt floor, unmoving, in a pool of still, cold blood, with a stake through his heart.

Paul and Timothy had gone on to Rome.

And I too fled, for the inchoate feelings that raged through me were too much like my memories of pain.

✛

He must have known. He had a sense about such things. He must have realized that Paul could not long abide the shattering of his great glass cathedral with the hammer of blunt reality.

He loved the world. He loved beautiful things, cities, trees, animals, and even more so, people. It must have pained him more than I can imagine, to choose to leave the world behind. Why, then? Was it that he could not face the prospect of his name being taken in vain by thousands, thousands who would become millions, billions? Did he sense that his homespun stories about shepherds and widow's mites and mustard seeds would become the official religion of the Roman empire, that that religion would plunge the western world into a Dark Age for a thousand years, that it would spawn senseless massacres, enslavements of entire peoples, wanton destructions of countless noble, ancient, beautiful cultures?

I don't know.

Your Holiness, Reverend Fathers, Your Eminence, and... yes, Reverend Sister... this is what I know.

He was good. I have never known anyone before or since who has truly deserved that adjective. He was brilliant. He loved, deeply and with complete

46

commitment. He possessed an absolute empathy even for the dispossessed. These qualities were in his very blood.

The blood of mortals is spiced with the hormones of desire and fear, but his was not. It was to other blood as a sparkling mountain stream is to the murky effluvium of a city faucet. It was the Platonic absolute of blood. It was pure. It was the holy grail of bloods, the true taste of which all other tastes are but an echo.

We are much alike, you who have hocus-pocused a million gallons of cheap wine and call it redemption, and I who have savored your savior's actual blood. We cannot believe he is gone forever. Love such as ours, we desperately think, cannot stay unrequited forever. The Absolute is by its very nature Eternal.

We live — you for a few heartbeats, I for all time — in the hope (the fear, too) that he will come again. He *must* come again.

The river of time is long. I know. Trust me. One day he will. Suddenly. Without warning.

Like a vampire in the night.

The Westfarer

by James S. Dorr

K now this: The world   is wide and bowl-like,

Its extremities up-curved   at every corner,

To north, ice-locked Thule,   night-bound Nifelheim,

Home of Hel, goddess,   of death's hungered gnawing;

To south, fiery Muspel,   hall of bright Surtr,

Birthplace of sun and stars,   flame's heat and searing;

To east, dawn, beginnings,   destiny's first day,

The morning of men's lives,   of mead and brave sailings;

To west, only endings.

THE WESTFARER

I sing now of west-faring,

I, Signy, Helmsdottir,   bondsmaid and seeress,

Dark haired, dark fortuned,   sailmaid and dire traveler,

Sing I of wanderings,   of three men, and one more.

The first I sing, Bjarni,   the son of glum Herjolf,

Made sail south to Ireland,   then Iceland and Greenland,

Was caught first by north wind,   then calmed in a white fog

His ships drifting westward,   saw at last woodlands

And hills unfamiliar;   north then he set helm,

Disdaining to beach there,   until, dim in cloudbanks,

His tired eye saw ice fields,   and, so turning east again,

Entered at last the fjord   of Eirik Redbeard.

This, then, was Greenland,   Bjarni's last landfall,

From whence sailed the second,   Leif, Eirik's eldest son,

Blown, too, by winds west,   backward on Bjarni's course

To a land of black stone,   high and ice-summited,

Which named he Helluland   hailing cliffs' flatness;

Next founded he Markland,   fairer and forested,

Willow-wrapped and with spruce   meet for ships' siding;

Yet went he on south and west,   seeking new wonders,

Till he found a grass valley,   frostless in winter,

Its streams filled with salmon,   its dew sweet as honey,

Its hills vine-encumbered   and heavy with wine fruit.

Here Eiriksson wintered,   then, weighty with new lore,

Returned he to Brattahlid,   byre of his father,

From whence, third, came Thorvald,   thane and Leif's brother,

To west to the new land,   and north for exploring

Found inlets and rivers,   ice-laden Kjalarness,

Named for his keel's scraping   on hard sand bottom,

And found he there *Skraelings*   or, as we say, "Screamers,"

The men of this new place who,   making no welcome,

Set on him with arrows   until, slain, his crew made sail

Heavy with grief, home.

             Thus weave the Nornir

The fates of men, earthbound,   unvisioning futures,

Save that I, Helmsdottir,   am cursed with seeing!

             ☩

Listen as I sing: The fourth man *I* sailed with,

Thorfinn Karlsefni,   from Iceland to Eiriksfjord,

Greenland's south settlement;   I, Signy, first of three

Women I tell you now,   and, later, one again.

Second was fair Gudrid,   gaunt Thorvald's widow

Who, at Eiriksfjord, betrothed   Thorfinn our captain.

Filled she that winter   his ears with wonder,

With tales of the travelings   of the first three I sang

Until, with spring's budding,   three ships he fitted,

Broad *knarrs* meet for blue water,   deep and strong-bottomed

And high, with their oaken strakes   near overflowing

As goods he had brought aboard,   cattle and brood-sows,

Corn-seed and women —   yes, wives we took with us too —

Seeking to settle   these new strands of plenty.

Oars straining, we pushed to sea,   then, with the wind

Raised sails of dyed wool-cloth   as red as sun's setting,

Our masts tall as ice clouds   kept pole star to rightward,

As, wave-thunder tossing,   we followed the whales' track

Until the black, flat stone   of Helluland sighting.

Thence bore we to larboard,   as had Leif before us turned,

Sails tacked to carry us   south with the current,

Until we passed Markland   and came to a place of streams,

Fast racing waters,   and there, winter near us —

So long had we journeyed! —   spent we our first snow time.

Huddled we now in huts   cursing the harsh wind

That blew ice and coldness,   beyond expectation,

As some called aloud to Thor,   others to Odin,

Others the White-Iesus   worshiped of Christers,

While I, alone, friendless,   away from the hearth fire,

Banished with bond-slaves   to sleep in far corners,

Dreamed, shivering, of shadows.

                    This was the first sharing:

This, my first Norn-vision,   gifted by Verdandi,

She of the Always-Now —   later would I, weeping,

Come to Skuld's blessing,   the skald-sense of Will-Be —

This showed me ice creeping   from west and north crevices,

Steadily southward,   until, the world shifting

Once more back to sunlight,   again at last came spring.

And so again did come spring,   so sailed we further,

Surprised by the land's cold   that not Leif nor Thorvald

Had claimed to encounter;   yet climbed we the wave crests,

Our ships' timbers groaning,   as groped we again to south,

Finding both fruit-vines   and honeyed meadows,

Until came we to a bay,   arm-like, encircling,

Protected from currents   and storms' harsh keenings,

And here we entered,   made fast our anchors,

Built byres and longhouses,   pens for our meat-beasts,

Sowed rye and barley   thus for our abiding.

And dreamed I this place at night   not yet of coldness,

But shadows, of shapes melting,   shifting in moonlight.

☩

Autumn brought Screamers,   our first meet with Skraelings,

Ugly-haired, squat men,   with broad cheeks and huge eyes

Who crept, their feet soundless,   in sandals of furred skin,

Until, nearly at our gates   whooped they their greeting

In shrill ululation,   in shrieks and mad soundings.

Their tongue we knew not,   yet gestures made Thorfinn

To show we desired trade,   their furs for our dyed cloth,

Red as the sun's rays,   and also sweet milk we gave

Fresh from our grazed beasts,   frothing and well-fatted,

But one thing we would not   offer despite their wish,

That being weapons,   our steel swords and spear points.

Alas, it turned not well,   our metal they lusted for;

One took to stealing   and quickly we slew him,

Then others screamed foully   and fled to the forest,

Leaving us for that night,   but the next morning

Returned they in numbers   near overwhelming.

Screeching, they shot at us,   sharp arrows coursing,

Then with clubs fell on us   forcing us backward,

Driving us to rock cliffs   where clung we in despair

To our lives' last hour.

                My tale would be over

Save, as I sang before,   just as three men there were,

Three who began it all,   braving, first, western seas,

So, too, were three women: I, Signy, song-teller;

Gudrid the second,   fair bride of Karlsefni;

And third now bold Freydis   Eiriksdottir,

Who, in heat of battle,   tore loose her byrnie

And, baring her breasts to all,   took in hand sword's blade,

Stung it against her teats   terrifying,

Through magic of womenkind,   milk and blood mixing,

Birth and death drawing   in dire steel together,

Our enemy Skraelings   who, screaming the louder,

Fled once again forestward,   leaving to us the field.

So passed the second year   of Thorfinn's settling

Of grape bedecked Vine-Land.

                           The winter grew on us,

But milder now, easy   for us to endure the cold,

Save it seemed fiercer   the closer to spring it came.

Then the next growth season   came back the Screamers,

But cautious now, canny,   content with harassment,

Unwilling to brave the walls   we built in winter,

Protecting our village —   but came back, too, visions:

✤

This time I attended   a band of armed hunters,

A servant to skin the deer,   scrape from meat, entrails,

To clean and to carry,   as my masters cared me to.

Thus marched I through the wood,   marveled at autumn,

Its early arrival,   trees orange with brightness,

And how left the Skraelings   with passage of summer.

At night cooked I meat for men,   shared in their mead, too,

Until in a stone place   surrounded by boulders

Our fur skins we wrapped us in,   fitfully slept then,

And dreamed I of shadows.

                           In shade form my vision

Took me to a stone land,   much like that I slept in,

But north, by a great lake,   choked full with ice mountains,

And there saw I men as wolves —   men clothed in wolf-skins,

But shifting, arising,   grown huge now, slavering —

Men who as wolves themselves,   howled forth in anger.

Listened I to their words,   heard I their hatred

Of ship-borne men such as I   lately had sailed with,

Of eastern men, artisans,   builders and hunters,

Despoilers of virgin earth,   bane of their Vinland.

Showed me the future then,   of farms and homesteads,

Of axe-leveled forests,   fields cut from wood they felt

Earth-Mother owed them,   they, Her erst protectors,

And, thus to prevent such wyrd,   this their revenge was:

The cold, they commanded;   men's crops would they wither

Through ever-harsh ice seasons,   increasing winter-blight,

Hamper thus sea-lanes,   snow sending southward

Not just in these western lands,   but the world over.

Then saw they me in my dream,   huddled in sleep-dress,

But feared they the magic   of Freydis — *all* women —

Just as did the Screamers   that first meeting's season

And so left me, waking,   warm, curled in fur blankets,

Once more with my own kind.

                    But woke I now, shrieking,

Beholding the slaughter   of men slain around me,

Of dark entrails steaming   in sunlight of morning,

Of throats ripped and tooth-chewed,   limbs torn from bodies,

All heaped in a fell hill —   thus arose I, alone!

Snatched I up sword and shield   lest I find Skraelings,

Or wolf-manlings — Fenrir's folk —   lurking in forest;

I knew not, my breasts I bared,   prayed their protection,

As trod I not bravely,   but trembling through wood-trails,

Until at last, fainting,   came I from the forest

To homestead and Freydis,   to Gudrid and Thorfinn.

Told I then of slaughter,   of gore stained on stone ground,

And warriors took oath   to rush into woodland,

To search out the Skraelings,   to lay at rest slain men,

But when at last night fell,   returned, finding nothing.

✠

Thus came our third winter: Behind walls we waited,

Feared frost, the snow's howling,   the wolf cubs of Fenrir,

And when spring's days lengthened   took ship and departed.

We sailed north to Greenland,   anchored at Eiriksfjord,

Glad of the ice-glint   of that far land's glaciers;

Told we our tale there,   then, fearful to tarry,

Sailed eastward to Iceland,   from there to the sun's rise.

And yet I had visions —   no more would they leave me! —

Of winters grown worse,   of ice-sheets increasing,

Of blight ever following,   haunting our footsteps,

Of Skraelings across the sea,   sailing in skin boats,

In Greenland itself fared south,   *Inuit* seal-catchers,

Following cold to come   soon to the farmsteads:

There saw I too,   as I say, a fourth woman,

A fourth after we, the three,   left for the east-lands,

A Skraeling, Navaranak,   whispering to Norsemen,

And then, again, to her own,   sowing forth enmity.

Then saw I *umiaks*,   skin boats of Skraelings,

Disguised well as ice floes,   sneaking through fjord-mouths,

Approaching the homesteads   as men, inside, sleeping,

See not flame and arrows   until they lie, dying;

And thus, too, passed Greenland,   last of west thane-holds,

And nearly as well, Iceland,   as cold increases,

As winters grow bitter,   the blight of the wolf-men,

That ever spreads south.

☩

But sing I one more tale,

One last before ending,   of earth and its future:

Of one final seeing   that comforts my night-sleep.

Know you that the world   is vast in its bowl shape,

Its northern side rising,   but south, too, up-curving;

That where Hel and Nifelheim,   home of Wolf-Fenrir,

Hold sway in their highness,   so too, south, opposing,

The mountains of Muspel   grow men wise as foxes.

In dream-vision saw I this,   one man among them

Prostrating before a queen,   begging this bounty,

That from her pawned jewel-hoard   be hired ships and seamen,

A sailing to west be planned,   with ships' holds groaning

With byrnied and armed men,   with barrels that shoot fire,

And — see I this also,   ye wolf-folk and wolflings,

This wyrd I foretell *you* —

                    These foxes spread northward.

The Comedy of St. Jehanne d'Arc

by Caitlín R. Kiernan

Canto I

Malta, May 1486

The girl comes down the winding trail that leads from the old Roman house to the colonnade by the sea, her bare feet sure on the slick and uneven path, flagstones smoothed by centuries of sandals and wind. She is careful to make enough noise so that the vampire will know it's her coming, will recognize the purposeful clumsiness of her approach. And she finds him, pale skin like Carrara marble beneath the setting moon, skin like pearls and marble and the eggsac silk of spiders, standing more alone than usual on the wide portico, staring north across the sea, toward Sicily and, beyond that, holy Rome.

He says nothing, offers no sign or acknowledgment of her, and she stands a few feet behind. Listens a moment to the black heartbeat of the Mediterranean bashing itself patiently against the high cliffs, and, to the east,

61

the lights of Valetta twinkle like grounded stars or fallen angels. The wind smells like almost nothing, now, but the sea, salt and water, blood or semen.

"Another hour and Radu would have been at your throat," the living girl says, speaks boldly as if she were not mortal or had no other need to fear.

The vampire clears his throat and attempts a rasping laugh, dry as the parching wind.

"Monsieur Radu is a fat fool and an ass," he says, and she sees the bucktoothed Magyar again, leaning across the great cedar table, pounding both meaty fists into the wood like some petulant, demon-child demanding its mother's immediate and undivided attention. "Radu would have us all cringing like rats in the catacombs, whispering between the dusty Christian corpses for fear of one Jesuit spy."

"He has the Austrians and Wallachs on his side now," the girl says. "He has the Turks afraid of their own blessed shadows."

The vampire doesn't reply, says nothing else for a long and brittle moment; tilts back his pretty head and flares his nostrils wide as if looking for something on the air. She breathes deeply, searching with senses sharpened by the blood he gives her, past the rocky walls of the estate and the omnipresent sea, past olive groves and sleeping goats and the rolling countryside. Catches the musk of ash and cinder, like an accent, and then it's gone and there's nothing but the windy Maltese night.

"*Everyone* is afraid, Marie," he says, finally. "Those who escaped the stake but cannot escape their memories are afraid because they have never truly believed it was over. Those who only have the stories that their sires whisper like curses are afraid because it doesn't seem that such a thing could even have happened."

The vampire pauses and looks back, past the girl, toward the house, the moonlight on the roof and every window dark.

"We are all afraid."

The girl says nothing, has heard this all before and more and waits quietly in the night's worth of shadow that has accumulated in the colonnade.

☦

Canto II

Rome, June 1426

The old chamber deep beneath the cobbles of Via Leone is too close and much too warm, and it seems to Mengette that they've been down here for ages. Nights and unnoticed days lost to this rat's maze of tunnels and vaults hollowed into the city's belly, winding into the bowels of the Vatican itself, the work of slaves and heretics dead a thousand years. Perfect, constant darkness that hides them and holds their secrets.

The stale air smells like clotting blood and the acrid, gray smoke of the technomancers' opium; the thicker, darker smoke from the lamps and tallow candles rises up to the high ceiling and hangs there like an oily ghost. Mengette de Poitou stands behind her sire with the other loyalists, those who would have the Dauphin Charles on the throne of France and send the British scurrying back across the channel, and holds her cold tongue while the Burgundian finishes his rant. She does not meet his red glare, blooddrunk eyes like hateful rubies, minds her station and stares instead at a crumbling section of the wall over his left shoulder.

"This has gone past insult," he says again, voice like glass and wagon wheels. "Does Monsignor believe that we will sit still while this council takes sides and thinly disguises its contrivances as action for the greater cause?"

The Master Prelate rises from his chair then, gathering like a storm of white flesh and damson silk.

"You've stated your opposition, Bedford," he says, a diplomat's velvet tone and no hint of the ragged impatience shining from his eyes. "Your objections have been entered into the record. But the ballots have been cast, and I must support the council's decision. I sympathize with your dislike for this so-called Dauphin of Viennois. He is weak and surely unworthy of any throne, but for the moment our common interests are best served by a sovereign France and he is convenient."

Bedford de Troyes sneers, flashes his ivory-yellowed canines, curdog snarl and spits dramatically, spatters the tabletop and the robes of the mages seated across from him.

"Then damn this council and damn everyone sitting here who is so blinded by their fear of the Pope's butchers that they will be puppets for the Armagnacs."

"Better we should be puppets for England," Mengette says, almost a whisper but loud enough, deceiving calm and her eyes never waver from the spot of wall behind the Burgundian. But she can feel his eyes shift her way, hating gaze like an inquisitor's white-hot brand. Her sire takes her arm, firm warning squeeze and his long nails sink easily through the woolen sleeve of her blouse. Familiar pain, and she grits her teeth against it.

"You know that's your right, Bedford," the Prelate says, and Mengette can hear the tattered weariness creeping into his voice now. "We have all entered into this alliance willingly, of our own volition, but I urge you to forget these mortal allegiances, and consider now what's best for the Kindred and the cabals represented here."

The Burgundian laughs roughly, an uglier sound than his voice, wipes a bloody string of spittle from his chin, and his eyes release her to sweep the length of the table.

"I agreed to fight against the Inquisition, against the Mendicants and the Church, not to make an Armagnac savior of some Canaille bitch and then send her off on a holy war against my own people," and he steps back and away from the table, spreading his long arms wide as if he would embrace them all.

"You are all insane and my part in this madness is finished."

The four vampires waiting nervously behind him step quickly aside to make room for their lord's exit, but he pauses and levels one thin, barbed index finger at Mengette's sire.

"As for you, Etienne, don't be too surprised if your maiden meets with the wolves long before she meets your Dauphin."

Her sire, still holding tight to her arm, only nods his head slightly for a reply and the faintest smile creases the corners of his mouth.

"I warn you, Bedford" the Prelate says, "A threat against the girl's life would constitute a threat against this council."

"Then take it any way you please, Monsignor," and he turns and steps out of the murky pool of light, vanishes into the hungry shadows crouched in the doorway.

"Shouldn't we stop him?" asks the hawk-nosed sorcerer sitting on the Prelate's left; the Prelate does not answer, instead looks questioningly toward Etienne.

"I had expected as much from de Troyes, Monsignor. We already have agents waiting in Domrémy. The girl Jehannette is well guarded."

"Then I'll remind you and your brood, Etienne Marcel, that our decision here tonight, inasmuch as it *seems* to benefit your own plans for France, is motivated only by our conviction that this course will further obstruct the efforts of the Mendicants and bring us one step closer to ending the inquisitions. We will pursue it only as long as it continues to serve this purpose."

"Of course, Monsignor," but the satisfied half-smile still lingers on Etienne's lips; finally his claws retract and Mengette can move her arm again, feels the slow trickle of stolen blood from five neat punctures just above her elbow. She doesn't pretend to understand it all, to grasp every coil and convolution of the council's serpent mind. The anger and frustration in the eyes of the Burgundian dog is enough for now, and the warm promise of English blood.

Canto III

Domrémy de Grus, August 1426

Jehannette does not often leave the sanctuary of her father's house, now that she has reached the age of discretion, now that the *écorcheurs*, the skinners, roam the roads and countryside, bandits and unemployed mercenaries more like ravening beasts than men. She has not eaten in four days, not since the bowl of broth she took on Friday; she may eat something tomorrow, perhaps a bit of bread and cheese, so that her mother doesn't worry, so that her brothers won't talk of forcing her again. When she fasts, the voices come more easily.

St. Michael, who came to her first, over a year now since she heard his voice like soft rain and the silence after thunder, before lightning, looked up to find the archangel, the captain-general of Heaven's armies, watching over her prayers. He did not carry a scale for the weighing of souls, but a gleaming sword and shield more brilliant even than his white wings. Argent feathers and his light so pure that the summer sky above the garden had seemed to fade to deepest twilight and the sun had glowed no brighter, by comparison, than a dying ember.

And St. Catharine of Alexandria next, and then, later, St. Margaret of Antioch, and neither of them the dour women she knows so well from the crumbling statues in the village church. Beings made of light and impossible music, things there were no words for, their martyr's crowns woven of nothing so simple as gold and gems. The old women of Domrémy cross themselves when she passes, and the wives whisper that she is mad.

But tonight she waits for the newest voice. Kneels bare-kneed on the hard floor below her window and finishes her prayers, all the prayers that her mother has taught her, the *Ave maria* and *Credo*, and waits for the voice that has come to her every night for almost a week. It has not named itself, but speaks like a woman, if women spoke with the crystal tongues of angels. This voice that speaks to her not of the glories of Heaven but the troubles of the world, of the Dauphin and the plight of besieged Orléans, the darkness that will befall all France if the English archers are allowed to finish what they began at Agincourt.

Jehannette has not seen the face of this new messenger, has been commanded to keep her eyes cast down and listen. The voice always seems to come from just the other side of the wall, although it is as clear as if the speaker stood beside her, or somewhere in the room behind her. Unlike the others, it comes only at night, long after the household is asleep, and never lingers after sunrise, and sometimes that makes her afraid that it might not come from God, that it might be something of darkness and not light. But it always speaks to her from the right and not the left.

Saints and angels have their reasons, she knows, and knows too that they are not hers to understand or question.

"Jehannette," the voice says at last, and she answers quickly, "Yes?" but keeps her eyes on the floor, supplicant, meek.

"This is the last time I can come to you," it says, and she almost cries out then, fights not to stand and throw open the casement window, teeters helplessly on the knife edge of temptation.

"There is no more time for words, Jehannette," and the name she has always hated is beautiful and there are tears tracing warm rivulets down her cheeks.

"Please do not leave me here," she sobs, the same way she has begged the archangel, St. Margaret and St. Catharine. "Please carry me back to Heaven with you."

The voice does not respond immediately, and she prays desperately that this hesitation might mean that it is considering her request, that she will not have to spend another day learning the toil and drudgery of housewives. That she will not have to marry the boy to whom her mother and father have promised her and spend her life serving only his needs. That her virginity will not be defiled.

"No, Jehannette. You should know that I can't do that. You have very important things to do here, while you are alive."

"I don't understand," she whispers, hating the weakness she hears in her own voice, loathing the tears that she can't hold back.

"I have told you everything I can about how and why your country has fallen into the sacrilegious hands of the English, these godless men who would grind even the memory of the kingdom of France beneath their heel. And as this nation has been lost by the treacherous actions of one wicked woman, Isabella of Bavaria, it must be redeemed by the bravery of another woman, a girl who is good and pure, a maiden from the marches of Lorraine."

Her heart seems ready to burst from her chest, dragged still beating from her breast by the fear and passion that swells in her like God's own fire.

"Go to the Dauphin's court, Jehannette, to the rescue of the rightful king of France. Go as soon as you are able. Tell him that he will be consecrated and crowned at Rheims, and become the lieutenant of the King of Heaven. Tell him that you will lead his army against the Angloys-Francoys, and that he cannot fail, for even St. Louis and Charlemagne are on their knees, praying for him."

There are no words, nothing she can say that will not sound foolish and proud, so she says only, "Yes."

"And, do not forget, you will repeat the things that I have told you to no one but the Dauphin himself. Do you understand that? If the Burgundians should learn of your purpose, they would surely try to prevent you from reaching Vaucouleurs.

"In the morning, look atop the wall beside your garden gate and you'll find a token of God's faith in you. Wear it always, Jehanne, and He will never be very far away."

And then she is alone in the night again, and the only sound is her heart and the barking of a dog somewhere in the village.

Mengette de Poitou stands in the deeper night gathered in the shade of the garden wall. She takes the small pouch from underneath her tunic, old leather stained by time and fingers and the blood of her kills, and removes the ring that she has carried from her sire's court in Auvergne. A plain gold band, a mannish thing, engraved with the device of the Franciscans' Jhésus-

Maria. She sets it carefully on the top edge of the garden wall and the gold and her white hand, curved nails like glass, flash back the moonlight dully.

She slips noiselessly through the open gate and along the empty streets of Domrémy, past sleeping houses and then the fields and their nervous cattle, to the company of horsemen waiting on the road to Vaucouleurs.

Canto IV

Orléans, 7 May 1429

Dead night, almost Sunday morning now, surely, and the Daughter of God lies half dreaming beneath skies smeared charcoal black and fiery from the funeral pyre that her soldiers have made of the English bastille, Les Tourelles. Orléans is delivered and her wounded shoulder burns in sympathetic agony for the broken battlements and dead men and the stars hidden behind the billowing smoke.

Her page, faithful blur of chestnut hair and perfect, girlish lips, sits somewhere nearby, and when she whispers his name, he wipes the beading sweat away from her forehead. His fingers move like velvet insects and the damp cloth is cool against her skin and smells faintly of rosemary and the nostalgic stench of wet sheep.

She cannot remember if she has prayed, but cannot remember the words, either, the precise and calming Latin, and drifts helpless beneath the flames that crackle and spit like hungry, living things. Demons loosed by her hand and her words and the incontestable commands of her voices.

Jehanne closes her eyes and watches the coward Glasdale turn and flee back toward Les Tourelles, across the narrow drawbridge, dragging his army out behind like shattered legs. She rides along the riverbank, high on the back of her borrowed charger, impossible horse of bone and wheat and blood-stained glass, screams after him, fashions curses of her anger and vengeance. And the bridge collapses beneath their weight, sticks and straw, and the swirling Loire sucks them all down to endless night and its muddy bosom.

Whore, he called her, and she sees silver-bellied fish nesting in the empty sockets of his skull.

The world rolls fevery in choking smoke and she's down in the ditch again, climbing the tall ladder they've raised for her. Her standard clutched in one hand and its flapping, white banner, fleur-de-lis of silk and the Virgin's blue, snagged in the stumbling wind. The crossbow's bolt makes an urgent sound, bees and the downstroke of a scythe, and for a moment she doesn't fall, stands at the crumbling lip of the trench, the battle's rage all around her, and waits for the angels to catch her. Instead, there are the fearful, panicked hands of her men, frightened voices, who carry her back down into the earth and the bolt, jutting from her shoulder like a feathered accusation pointing to indifferent Heaven.

And the black-eyed soldier pushing his way through the rest, carrion crow bending low over her and offering his charms, healing spells to end the pain and close the wound, and she pushes him away, swears that she would rather die than sin. The soldier spreads his ebony wings, rises cawing from the ditch, and she pulls the shaft free herself. The blood flows across her breastplate before they remove her armor, wrestle away the steel and the crimson-soaked leather and mail beneath. Wipe away the life seeping from her and rub in ointments of olive oil and fat. Jean d'Aulon stands at her feet, has not allowed her standard to touch the dirt; his tears sparkle like diamonds in the midday sun.

"Jehanne," the angel says and she opens her eyes and Jean has left her alone. The room is dark, only the dull glow of the sky through the window.

"Are you in pain?" the angel asks, its wet, red lips close to her face, alabaster skin and well-water eyes that seem to go on forever. She thinks that she smells blood on its cold breath and knows she's only bleeding again. She tries to answer, but her mouth is very dry.

"Don't speak," the angel says. "Save your strength." It touches her cheek, fingertips so chilling cold that they seem to scorch her flesh and Jehanne gasps,

slips, pulled back into the roiling smoke that stings her eyes and silts her face and hair with ash and glowing cinders. She floats somewhere between Heaven and the smoldering world below, and the angel is still at her side. They pass over the needle spires of a cathedral and Orléannais voices cheer her and offer their joyfully solemn *Te Deum* to the fire-stained sky.

"Talbot has ordered a full retreat," the angel says. "In the morning, the English goddons will leave Orléans forever."

And they are rising, buoyed higher and higher by the wild night breeze and the heat from the inferno that had been Les Tourelles, through the smoke to an indigo blanket speckled with the pin-pricks of Heaven's cleaner fire.

"You've done well, Jehanne."

"You are taking me back with you, then?" she asks hopefully and the angel shakes its head, smiles and its glinting teeth are more terrible than the swords of all her fallen enemies.

"No, not yet. Your wound is not nearly so bad as it looks. Orléans was only the beginning," and below them the countryside is spread like a banquet of fields and sleeping villages; the angel raises one white arm and points east.

"Tell Alençon that the time has come to take Jargeau, and then Meung and Beaugency. You'll stand against Talbot again, at Patay, and then, Jehanne, *then* you will ride to the liberation of Rheims."

"Am I that strong?" she asks, shivering at her own blasphemous self-doubt and the wind that rushes past her ears, shivering at the bloody work that lies ahead, waiting somewhere beyond the dark horizon.

"And even a thousand times stronger," the angel says and pulls her close, wraps her in arms that feel like stone, as they plunge back toward the earth and the merciful oblivion of sleep so deep there are no dreams.

Canto V

Limoges, August 1429

All the others have gone, have been dismissed, sent off to their respective intrigues, and Mengette de Poitou waits alone in the great hall of her sire's castle on the Vienne. The unsteady light from the sconces and torches along the walls washes over her like memories of Orléans and Rheims, Jehanne's victories and the battle-orange skies Mengette has risen to again and again during the spring and this long summer.

And the things that she has heard tonight still don't seem real, impossible contradictions, denial of everything that has been accomplished. She has never before felt betrayed by Etienne Marcel's words or deeds, has never questioned herself as an extension of his blood and will. But to be told at this late date that the council in Rome has seen fit to alter its plans, that they wish to pursue a new tack that will encourage diplomatic solutions between the new king and the English, that they do not wish for Charles' army to march on Paris after all...

Her gut rumbles, impatient sound like chained dogs, reminding her that she has not fed tonight and sunrise is only a few hours away. But the hunger seems too distant to matter very much, suddenly as detached as her loyalty, and there is no joy or release in the thought of its warm, red conclusion. She wants only to escape these binding walls and the firelight and hide her

70

confusion and outrage in the night waiting for her beyond the ramparts. She will not sleep here this day, will bury herself beneath the soothing, worm-riddled mud along the river's banks.

Etienne finishes with the fat sheaf of documents that has come from the prelates and lays them carefully to one side. Then he raises his head and regards Mengette with those bottomless, jade-flecked eyes that she has trusted for the twenty-five years since her death, has loved even as she loves France.

"I am sorry," he says. "This is not the course I'd have taken, but then I think you know that."

She cannot look at him with these thoughts boiling like scalding oil inside her and turns her face to stare instead at a tapestry hung nearby, brocade and jewels and the perfect white stab of the unicorn's horn.

"You're asking me to undermine everything that has been accomplished in the last three years, to turn my back on Jehanne and the army when they're so close."

He sighs loudly, hisses out between clenched teeth the particular weariness that only immortals can suffer, and she hears the rough *scrunk* of his chair against the stone floor as he pushes himself back from the table and stands.

"*No*, Mengette. I am *ordering* you to abide by the decisions of the Council. There are other considerations now. I wish it were not so..."

"*What* considerations, Etienne?" she says, interrupting, struggling against the instinct and training that would keep her quiet, spits the words like a mouthful of plague-tainted blood. "Tell me, please, if you will, *what* considerations? The lies that the Duke of Bedford would use to delay our advance on Paris while he strengthens his defenses? Jehanne's army could take Paris tomorrow if the king would only allow her to..."

"Mind yourself, childe," he says, all ice and steel and a sound like far away thunder in the back of his voice, and Mengette takes a cautious step backward.

"Of all my offspring and all my court, you are my most beloved, Mengette de Poitou, but I won't humor impertinence, not even from you. Do you think I haven't already agonized over this enough, without having to hear *you* question me?"

Her eyes burn, and the scene on the tapestry blurs behind the film of her red tears.

"I am sorry," she whispers, despising the strain and fray, despising the words themselves. "I'm trying to understand..."

"*No!*" he growls. "There's nothing here for you to understand. You follow my orders, *because* they are my orders. Once before the vote went in our favor, and because of that France has a king again. This time it has not and it's our turn to show that our first allegiance is to Kindred. The council exists to obstruct the Mendicants, not to choose sides in every petty human dispute.

"Is that clear, Mengette?"

"Yes," she says, and feels the warm trickle of blood she can't spare from the corner of each eye.

"That's good, because there's something else I have to tell you, and I suspect you'll like it far less than anything else you've heard tonight."

She wipes viciously at her eyes, smears dark streaks across both cheeks.

"There is concern about the Maid's followers. They're fanatics, and they're preaching that her victories against the English are miracles, God's will made manifest through this strange girl who dresses like a man and sends battle-hardened soldiers running in fear of their lives."

"France is filled with the *pastoureaux*, Etienne. You can find a score of children, girls *and* boys, preaching their gospels on any road in Auvergne or Lorraine."

"Jehanne is no *pastoureaux*, Mengette. She calls herself the Daughter of God and these people believe her. By encouraging her delusions, we have also encouraged their belief in miracles and sorcery, and the council fears that if something isn't done to bring her down, her acts might even increase the power of the inquisitions.

"If she can move people to believe that God walks among them, it's all that much easier for them to accept that evil might also have a face and a body, no?"

Mengette turns back to him then, no longer caring what he sees on her face.

"She has become too dangerous, Mengette."

"Are you telling me to kill her?"

"No," he says, and she catches a dull glint like guilt or moonlight off lead in his eyes. "For the moment, she's still more useful to us alive. The prelates think she might even be turned against the inquisitors directly, as a means of discrediting the *officium inquisitionis* once and for all."

"Jehanne was cleared of witchcraft in Poitiers before Orléans," Mengette says. "She was under examination for three weeks and the Archbishop's report..."

But Etienne only smiles and waves a hand dismissively.

"Archbishop Regnauld himself is in hiding from the English. Believe me, it would be easy enough to arrange a new trial for the girl, especially if she were to fall into the hands of the Burgundians or the goddons. The Duke of Bedford has already made enough accusations."

"But Jehanne is everything but a saint in the eyes of half of France..."

"Precisely. It is simple enough, Mengette. There is a good chance that if the papal inquisitors denounce Jehanne, or better yet, send her to the stake for heresy and sorcery, there will be a popular uprising against the Mendicants and Rome will have to relax its interrogations or risk revolt."

And her head is spinning, sucking blackness at the far corners of her vision, and she knows that he's right, and there's nothing she can say. Even if she dared to argue with him again, there's nothing she knows to deny such clear and obvious logic.

"At any rate, it will be no concern of yours," Etienne says and sits down again, folds his white hands like sleeping doves across his lap. "Preparations are being made. I have at least spared you any active role in this."

"Thank you," she says and waits to be dismissed.

"I know that I can trust you, Mengette," he says, and she hears the warning and guarded suspicion, and the fragile hope that he has not misplaced his faith in her, has not misplaced his love.

"Yes," she says, almost *Yes, Sire*, but is certain that would have been too much. Her deception is thin, April ice scabbing over dark, swift waters, but she has been taught the alchemies of masquerade and artifice well enough, and Mengette de Poitou looks deep into his eyes and her face is nothing but relief and gratitude and unquestioned acceptance of the part her dark gods have written out for her.

Canto VI
Beaurevoir, 25 October 1430

After Gien and King Charles has sent his army away like bothersome children; tied her hands and he deals with the Burgundians and the goddon pigs who hold their straining leashes, truces and guile. After she has played his privy council and he kept her around as a breathing token, living legend, witness and holy proof of his success.

It is long past midnight, and Jehanne lies in the muddy ditch that surrounds the castle of Beaurevoir. The rope, hurriedly fashioned from what she could find in her chamber, blankets and bedsheets, shawls and wall hangings, sways in the chilling autumn breeze, dangles like a knotted tongue from the black mouth of the tower's second story window, latest prison and she wonders how long she has lain here, how many minutes or hours since the loud *shrrip* of fabric tearing and no angels to break her fall. There is the sky overhead, infinite audience to her failure, and the dank smell of the moat and the pain that wraps her in velvet needles.

When she closes her eyes, she still sees the white thing at the window, tangible perversion of her visions; the thing that spoke with the crystal voice she followed all the way to Rheims, the voice she had not heard (nor St. Michael nor any of the others) since the King dispersed his mercenaries. She remembers its eyes like a nightbird's or a stalking cat as it pulled itself over the sill and dropped soundlessly on all fours to the chamber's cold floor.

The sky is better, not so cruel, and the pain and she does not know why she isn't dead. She tries to pull herself up the steep and slippery bank, digs her fingers deep into the mire but there is so little strength, so many shattered bones and muscles that refuse her bidding.

"Jehanne," the thing said, mouthed her name, as it stood slowly upright, flesh like living stone in the dim moonlight, image of a young woman carved for the altar. It turned away for a moment, then, looked back the way it had come and her heart slammed itself against the cage of her chest, another prisoner. She crossed herself, reached for the sword that had not hung at her side since her capture on the bloodied fields outside Compiègne eight months earlier. Since she'd given her parole to Jean de Luxembourg, and been locked away, first at his castle of Beaulieu and finally Beaurevoir.

"What manner of spirit are you?" she said, the old bravery masking the bright fear in her voice, but she knew the answer well enough, something evil sent up from the pit to torment her in her miseries, something to shame and mock her sacred revelations; further proof that she had been forsaken.

And the white face turned, the pantomime of great sadness or pity etched in its predator's eyes, and Jehanne remembered the full, dark lips and the wolfish smile from the fevered dreams after Les Tourelles.

74

"I am Mengette de Poitou," it said, "Ancilla and blood daughter of the clan Ventrue," and there was no mistaking the voice, sweet nightvoice that had come to her first at Domrémy, after martyred Catherine and Margaret. Ringbearer and battlefield messenger and murmuring soother the times she'd lain wounded and doubting.

"I've come to take you out of here, Jehanne."

Jehanne reaches the top edge of the ditch, her fingers raw and nails splintered but finding grass instead of mud and bare stone, and she hauls herself forward until she lies flat on her belly, gasping against the ache and exertion, the nausea and crushing dizziness. It's hard to see through the dried blood crusted in her eyes, but there's no sign that anyone has noticed; if she can only crawl a little further, as far as the tower of La Follemprise, a few hundred yards, no more, if she can find a horse in the stables and pull herself into the reins...

"And to put an end to the lies you've been fed," the white spirit said, anger rising in that voice, and took a cautious step away from the window, a step toward her bed.

Jehanne wanted to squeeze herself insect thin into the secret, dusty spaces between the granite blocks at her back.

"Keep away from me, spirit," she said.

"I'm not a spirit," the white thing said, faintest exasperation or impatience like a fresh bruise she could hear. "I am a Cainite, a blood-drinker, but I assure you, Jehanne, I am as much flesh and blood and bone as you. I let you deceive yourself into thinking I was an angel or a saint, Jehanne, because I knew that they would follow you, that you could lead and France would follow.

"It was I that left the Franciscan's ring on your father's garden wall."

And she looked down at the gold band on her right hand, the precious metal scratched and pitted from the war and her careless disregard, and "No," she said firmly, shaking her head and pressing harder against the stone wall. "No, it is a lie. You would have me abandon my faith and give myself up to despair."

"*Listen to me, Jehanne,*" the creature hissed, and it was standing over her, although she'd absolutely no sense that it had moved, had taken steps and crossed the small room.

"*There isn't time for this shit.* Even now, Jean de Luxembourg is crumbling under pressure from the Parisian clergy to give you up to the English. And *when* he finally delivers you into their hands, Jehanne, you will not be sent to rot in some London prison. You will be tried as a heretic and you will be found guilty and then *you will be burnt.*"

The last four words punched themselves into the soft belly of the night, scarring the shadows and she *considered* the possibility, that this creature was telling her the truth, not simple temptation but the darkest revelation, that everything had been a lie. Worse than a lie, blasphemy; that she dangled at the end of marionette strings and had proclaimed herself the Maid of God on the authority of monsters.

Jehanne lies at the gravely edge of the road that would take her on to La Follemprise, if she could drag herself another foot, and if she could stand once she reached the stables... She can hear an owl in the rustling oaks nearby, lonely, hungry cry and she flinches, mouse flinch, rabbit flinch, waits for the wings and the merciful razor hook of its claws. Coughs, and there's fire in her ribs and blood in her mouth.

And the only mercy in this night is the gathering blackness, the numbness that oozes from the pain and seeps inside her; she lays her face against the grass, dew cool, no longer cares if she reaches the gates, wishes only that she could stop hearing the white thing sowing its glassy seeds of doubt and sacrilege inside her.

Sapphire voice, silver words, tongue too red and wicked for anything so petty as lies.

"We have both been used," the white thing said, and she tried to push it away, push *her* away, this beautiful young woman with her wolf's smile and the smell of fresh earth like a honeyed and buzzing cloud of flies about a corpse.

"No," she said again. "No, my voices *said* if I were tempted to abandon my quest, that I must not listen," hardly even a whisper *she* could hear and the white thing shook her, pulled her close, face to face. And those eyes.

"*I* told you those things, Jehanne! I can repeat every command, every fucking reassurance and pious half-truth I ever muttered to you in the night!"

"*No,*" Jehanne said, firm refusal, hollow triumph, and it yowled its terrible frustration, trapped animal sounds, sorrow past tears or the memory of solace. Dropped her violently to the narrow bed; the slats cracked and the frame split like winter-dry tinder.

"Leave me, spirit," she said, "I will not listen."

76

"I have crossed my lord and all my kind to come to you," it said, "I have risked an eternity to set this right, to..."

And then there was noise beyond her door, the hurried feet of her guards and nervous voices.

"I will remember you in my prayers," she said.

"Jehanne, I will not leave you here..."

But the iron rattle of keys and the old tumblers rolling like rusty dice, the door shoved open wide and they stared stupidly at the crazy Armagnac bitch sitting on her broken bed and nothing else and no one in the room. She said not one word to them, ignored their angry questions, kept her eyes on the window and finally they left. Laughing and cursing her and themselves.

Jehanne waited another hour before she moved.

And now the blackness, numbing, acid chill, taking away the hurt and the truth and even the unholy recollection of those eyes. When the light comes, she thinks at first it must surely be the sun, brilliant morning, before the archangel speaks and his words rain down on her like healing flame.

Canto VII
Rouen, 30 May 1431

The trial is over.

Still enough hours until dawn that she does not think about the sun, crouches cat-sleek on the roof, slate tiles cool beneath her palms and splayed fingers, and from here Mengette de Poitou can watch the men working by torchlight in the Old Market.

Mengette. Outlaw, outcast. Traitor to her clan and the Roman Cabal and all Kindred. She has aged more in the past five months than in the quarter century since her Becoming, the five long months past and buried since good King Henry paid his ten thousand pounds to the Burgundians and Bishop Cauchon himself rode to Arras to see that the Maid reached Rouen without incident.

And Cauchon's judges, his grim clot of Abbots and Archdeacons, have listened to Jehanne's heresies and fantasies, have scribbled their statements and examined and cross-examined and marveled at her wicked arrogance. Have at last read out their *libellus* of formal charges: schismatic, apostate, liar and

77

soothsayer, blasphemer; finally wringing her surrender, half-hearted recantation, amid the pomp and ceremony of a public excommunication in the cemetery of St. Ouen.

There is no evidence of life from the body she straddles, limp sleeper, no moan or hint of movement, and she licks the cooling blood from her hands, keeps her eyes on the men in the square below.

Raising the scaffolds, roughhewn phallus of dry boards smeared with pitch and almost twice as high as usual; no ordinary pyre for so notorious a witch. The stonemasons have almost finished the low barricade that encircles the stake like a bracelet, heft the last few slabs and she can hear clearly the gritty scrape of their trowels, iron against stone, as they slop their mortar, as clearly as she can hear their labored breathing and the drumbeat of their hearts.

Clever, she thinks. *Clever bastards*, and it's easy enough to see what they intend, how the wall will brace the burning structure so that the wood does not fall in upon the condemned. So that she will die more slowly in the heat and the flames.

Mengette stretches for a better view and the wound above her left breast aches, jabs icy disapproval, two days old and barely even begun to close. The bolt only missed her heart by inches, its silver-tipped head burying itself deep in her solid, dead flesh; the latest archer sent by Etienne or the Cabal, she'd never know which and it'd never matter, either. She left him lying in a ditch on the north road out of the city, his crossbow driven through his obedient assassin's heart, food for the hungry sun.

Instinctive moan and her hands move to cover the wound, the careful lump of bandage underneath her tunic, colder spot beneath the dressing where her body had refused the borrowed warmth of the blood. And the girl sprawled on the tiles sighs, softest gasp of sympathy or pain; she isn't dead, not yet, but emptied almost to the point of death, so close to the edge of the pit that there's no turning back for her.

Mengette bends close, lifts the pretty head that lolls freely, as if maybe the neck has been broken, brown eyes wide and glazed, hair still boy-short, but grown longer now than the familiar *en ronde* cut. Jehanne is wearing her male clothes again, relapsed since Trinity Sunday, four days ago. And that was all that Cauchon and his forty judges of God and law required, clear proof of the insincerity of her surrender and the folly of her rehabilitation. The vote on her sentence was unanimous.

"Hold on," Mengette whispers and Jehanne's eyelids flutter. Her skin is as pale as Mengette's dim memories of winter skies. "Don't let go yet, Jehanne."

Months she has waited, hiding herself away in Rouen and the Norman countryside since January; sleeping days in the earth or empty crypts, abandoned cellars, she kept her night vigil as near Jehanne's cell as she dared. Living like some filthy outlander or Caitiff rat, dodging the assassins and the city's own undead. And finally the death sentence, Cauchon not even bothering to hand her over for a secular trial. And there had been no more time for waiting or indecision.

Mengette learned of the passageways from a thief she killed the last week of April, secrets handed over with his life, useless barter: the underground maze leading from Devant Les Champs, winding beneath the castle and up into Jehanne's tower cell. And in the morning, when the watchful Dominicans, Martin Ladvenu and Isembart de la Pierre, come for the Maiden, they will find instead the peasant sorceress waiting in her place, another innocent condemned to the fire. They will not alert Cauchon of Jehanne's escape, would never risk the Bishop's wrath, and besides, she knows that Jehanne's delusions are as infectious as plague and how those two have listened to her, how close they've come to believing in the truth of her voices. They will think, perhaps, that this is a miracle, that the saints have spirited her away and left behind this young witch, proper fuel for the papal spit. And the shaming garments of the execution will conveniently hide their lie: long, black dress, the mitre and veil on her shaven head, her clothes and body smeared with pitch and sulfur up to the neck.

Giddy on triumph and unseeing, Cauchon will parade the impostor through the streets, to the waiting scaffold and the assembled crowd and the torch.

"Forgive me," and Mengette cradles the dying girl's head in her lap, lifts her own wrist to her lips, pulsing, swollen interlace of blue-green veins and arteries, and quickly rakes her canines across the skin. Beneath the cold and silent dome of Heaven, Mengette de Poitou begins the embrace, blackest dance and Death can never quite keep up. As she closes her eyes and Jehanne's tongue stirs suddenly awake, she imagines that she can hear thunder, or angels crying in the sky.

✢

Canto VIII
Malta, May 1486

The girl, whose name is Marie Garlande, watches the eastern horizon, blanched now with the soft purple stain of false dawn. The moon has slipped into the sea and the stars are going out, one after the next. The vampire has not moved for more than an hour, seconds and minutes she counts like coins in her head, time-keeper Marie, and when she speaks he shows no sign of having heard.

"Sometimes I almost forget her face," he says, and Marie keeps her eyes on the east, her mind on the deadly swift fade of night to dusk. "Sometimes there's nothing left but her name and I almost can't see her face, or remember her voice."

Marie has only the vaguest impression of the woman, the Anarch traitor, Mengette de Poitou, dead and dust forty years before her birth. But she knows the story like she knows the constellations and the thousand shades of blue between midnight and sunrise.

Mengette, bloodmother of her lord and sire-to-be, who delivered Jean from the stake when he was still the Maiden Jehanne; Mengette, who was herself burned by order of her own sire a year before his death at the hands of Bedford de Troyes.

"There will be no Camarilla," he says, and the strain in his voice is like the game that he plays with the rising sun. "Radu and the Malkavians will have their way and this time the Mendicants won't be so blind."

"They'll listen," she says, trying to find the confidence to be convincing, to get him past this and moving.

"Why do you believe that?" he asks, and turns, half-turn, and his sexless face outlined against the sky. Marie wants only to be back in the house, safe behind thick, cool stone and falling asleep in his arms, her head against the breasts bound in silk and leather, the still heart.

"Because they'll have no choice," she says.

"You fool yourself, Marie. Half of them are so sick of the Hunger that they secretly welcome this new inquisition. They *want* someone to end it for them, because they're too afraid or have been caught so long between life and death that they can't imagine taking a side."

"We should go back to the house, Jean," and she no longer tries to conceal her impatience, her fear. "They'll be wanting to close the gates for the day," she says.

For another minute, the vampire does not move, waits until the first crimson thread burns above the restless waters, and only then does he shield his face with one slender hand, looks away before his eyes can flash to steam. Marie catches the faint glimmer from the gold band and, without a word, he is moving away through the shadows.

And Marie follows him, back up the cliff to the dark and sleeping house.

At the Edge of the World

by Lisa Lepovetsky

ungry, we're hungry. We need more food.

I know, my dears, I know — I'm doing the best I can. We're watched too closely here; we need to find new feeding grounds. Just a little longer... these things take time to arrange....

✛

The old wooden ship sliced through the thick black waves like a dull blade. Marcus didn't know which moans were louder, those of the ailing sailors or those of the ship's boards straining against their wooden pegs and one another as the bow heaved through the crest of one wave into the trough of another. But then, he really didn't care. He was going to find the New World.

He had waited nearly a year for this voyage, and nothing was going to ruin it for him — not the gnawing fear of what lay ahead, not the constant groaning of his mates, not even their terrified stories of monsters that lurked beneath the oily surface of the ocean. He didn't really believe those stories, anyway. He knew who the real monsters were, and they didn't live in the depths of the sea. They wore human faces and walked upright side-by-side with men.

Through aching, bloodshot eyes, Marcus peered at the faces of the men around him flickering in the light from the lantern. Pale, gaunt faces, twisted into fearful grimaces from sickness and the terrible nightmares that tortured their sleep. For the last three nights, the lantern had remained lit by silent consent, though supplies were dangerously low and the first mate, Mr. Hurgens — Marcus' father — said he feared they had drifted off course. The men were afraid, though only Marcus knew what it was they had to fear. Only he held the dark secret.

Which one? he asked himself for the hundredth time. Or could it be possible that there was more than one monster aboard?

He closed his eyes and repeated the prayers his grandmother had taught him. His cracked, swollen lips moved silently around the familiar syllables, though the meaning behind the ancient language had long been forgotten. As a boy, in their small city on the coast of Spain, Marcus had thought it was a game, chanting the strange words with the old woman, drawing the signs in the air. It had been their secret game, and they only played it when Marcus' father and mother were absent, behind the stone walls of the big house.

Captain Hurgens had never liked his mother-in-law, and after she'd made the treacherous journey from her little village deep in the Balkans to live with them, he'd insisted she remain in her own rooms, except for meals. Several times a week, Marcus would sneak away from the others after his studies and head back to her apartment. The walls were hung with gaudy tapestries depicting bloody battles and strange mythical creatures. Incense burned continuously. It filled the air with a sweet acrid haze that scorched his lungs and made him dizzy.

Grandmother always seemed surprised and delighted to see him, though he was sure she'd been expecting him. There was always a cup of fresh, sweet fruit nectar and a biscuit waiting for him on the heavy, scarred table, no matter when he appeared. Her eyes half-closed, she listened to his breathless stories about what he'd done since he'd last been there, nodding her old head and smiling. Sometimes he'd been afraid she'd fallen asleep, but if he stopped talking, her eyes would fly open and her bony scarecrow claw of a hand would motion him to continue.

Finally, when Marcus had run out of steam or could not finish his story, Grandmother would smile around the four brown teeth still remaining in her mouth and point to the shelf over her bed. Marcus never had to ask what she wanted. He'd hurry over to the shelf and take down the huge moldering book leaning in the corner. The leather cover felt warm in his hands, and a bit too soft, as though it were skin still covering the bones of a living creature. Marcus was at once attracted and repelled by it.

While he was small enough, Grandmother had patted her knee for him to climb onto; later, he'd drawn a stool next to her chair and leaned over her arm as she turned the dry, yellowed pages. The pages were filled with strange, twisted letters in fading reddish ink. Grandmother didn't read to him from the book — it was written in a language from a place and time now long dead. Instead, she told him the old stories and showed him the terrifying sketches. And she told him what must be done.

"You must not suffer the wampyr to live," she'd whispered, her voice shaking with emotion and age. "Their hunger is insatiable, and they cannot exist peacefully with normal man. But their power is great. Some say they cannot bear the sunlight, but the old ones, the Cainites, have learned how to survive even this."

And so the words flowed from her like a river, and Marcus wrapped himself in their wisdom. After telling the legends, Grandmother would chant the words of prayer and protection, older than the city Marcus lived in, old already before there were cities or countries. And Marcus spoke them with her.

Marcus had trembled as she slowly turned the page. He knew what he would see, dreaded and needed it both. Tiny flakes snowed from the edges of the ancient vellum as the arthritic fingers drew the page across, and then it was there: the full-page drawing of the wampyr, feasting on its female human victim. The woman lay prostrate on a large cushion, head back and eyes fixed despairingly on the face of her attacker as he drank from her wrist, his thick lips fastened leech-like to her pale flesh. The face of the wampyr was mainly in shadow, but his gaze glowed white-hot, boring from the drawing straight into Marcus' eyes, sensually hypnotic and yet totally terrifying.

By the time Marcus was sixteen and had begun to explore the sea with his father's men, new sounds were heard beneath the usual patter of news and gossip — rumbling undercurrents of wonder and suggestion. Marcus gradually became aware that his grandmother wasn't the only one who thought creatures lived among the people. Not the wampyrs, perhaps, but there were whispers of old ones with darkness in their hearts who wore the faces of humans but hungered for them in the night.

At the same time, visitors from neighboring lands hinted of those who thought there might be new lands to explore to the west, far across the oceans. Marcus' father traveled for weeks at a time, returning from each voyage with new word about the intrepid explorer, Cristobal Colombo from Portugal. Colombo had convinced Queen Isabella and King Ferdinand to finance his journey west to find a new route to the East Indies. Those traveling the eastern routes were suddenly falling prey to vicious attacks, or simply disappearing. Some thought Colombo mad, but Captain Hurgens spoke of him with the fever of anticipation in his eyes.

The captain came home to dinner one night after a trip to the palace, his eyes unnaturally bright and his cheeks flushed with excitement beneath his dark whiskers. He held his news until the evening meal, when he fairly exploded with the announcement that he was taking a ship westward with Cristobal Colombo, to help him discover what might lie that way.

"I believe in this New World they talk about," he said around a mouthful of stew, "and I intend to do all I can to make sure Colombo does not fail. I have been selected to travel as his first mate."

His wife's eyes filled with tears, and she drew a deep shuddering breath before speaking. Her voice was quiet and still. "I fear," she said simply, "that you'll never return."

"I'm an experienced sailor," he said. "My men are clever and brave, the best in the country."

"But the kraken," she warned, "and the leviathan. They could swallow you alive. Assuming you don't first fall off the edge of the world."

"Perhaps the mapmakers are wrong and Colombo is right," Captain Hurgens countered. "Perhaps there are more lands across the ocean before the edge of the world. Nobody has ever attempted to go farther. If the old theories are right, then I shall be the first to see the edge of the world."

"And what shall I do while you're gone?" she asked quietly.

He looked confused by her question. "Wait, of course."

Suddenly, Grandmother had spoken. She rarely spoke during meals, and

Marcus had always assumed it was because she feared the captain. But she sat as straight as her bowed spine would allow and stared him down.

"This is the work of the wampyr," she said. "They need to find new feeding grounds, and want you to open the way for them."

Captain Hurgens stared at her, startled for a moment, then laughed. "You old fool," he scoffed. "Your mind still lives in the Carpathian mountains. This is science expanding its borders, finding new worlds to explore, not some supernatural nonsense. Go back to your potions and frogs, old witch."

Grandmother said nothing, but left the table. Marcus' mother flushed a bright angry crimson and glared at her husband.

"She's my mother."

"Do I not know that? It's the only reason I suffer her to live here with us. You should be grateful."

The captain cleared his throat, moving back to his original topic. "Colombo will leave Spain within the year. Marcus is old enough now; I've decided he should accompany us on this voyage."

Marcus felt pride warm his breast, though a ripple of fear tickled the back of his neck. His heart ached when he heard his mother's horrified gasp.

"Both of you?" she asked. But it was settled, and they all three knew it.

A week later, Grandmother was found dead in her room — "night death," the physician called it. Her heart had simply given out. But Marcus sneaked a glance at her wrist before the maid came in to bathe and wrap her body for burial. He breathed a quiet prayer of thanks when he saw no mark there.

In less than a year, Marcus waved good-bye to his mother from the stern of the ship they nicknamed the *Santa Maria*. He was sure he would never see her again.

And now they had been at sea for a month. The men were falling ill one by one, growing pale and listless, their eyes fearful, their fingers twitching spasmodically. Some wept or cried out in their sleep. Only he and his father and Captain Colombo seemed to be immune to the strange malady. And only Marcus knew why: there must be a wampyr on board, and the wampyr had left them for last, making sure of reaching land — if land there was — before killing them.

Telling his father would do no good — Marcus would either be beaten for a liar or fear-monger, or worse yet, be ridiculed by everyone on board as a coward.

Someone snored in the far corner, and Marcus sighed. Other than the occasional cat nap, he hadn't slept in — what? five days? a week? more? He couldn't remember; his mind seemed riddled with holes. He'd stopped sleeping when they'd dropped the first white-shrouded corpse off the starboard railing while the rest of the crew watched, their faces pale as fungus, their eyes red-rimmed and dead. "Night-death," the ship's doctor had called it, but young strong sailors did not die of night death. Only old grandmothers from the far mountains, who had already lived their full measure.

Ashes to ashes, his father had said. *Dust to dust*. But there was no dust in the ocean, Marcus thought, and no ashes. Only miles and miles of water and the creatures who lived there, waiting to devour what providence tossed their way.

As the body sank slowly into the dark waters, one arm came loose from its muslin wrap and floated out to the side. In that moment, Marcus was suddenly reminded of the drawing in his grandmother's book. He knew then how the man had died, and how they were all going to die unless he did something to save them.

But what? he wondered as he struggled to stay awake in his hammock. The prayers weren't enough. He had to destroy the wampyr before he and it were the only ones left alive on the ship. In the last three days, as many men had been dropped into the churning black waters. Their numbers were dwindling quickly. The men were frightened, and their fear made them angry. Just two days ago, there had been rumblings of mutiny. Several of the men had even smuggled weapons from the armory, heading as one toward Captain Colombo's quarters.

But Mr. Hurgens had interceded. He'd barred the captain's door, insisting that Colombo must succeed if any of them were to survive this journey. Marcus knew his father had suppressed the incipient rebellion, but he couldn't recall the details. Only that the results were quiet and bloodless. *Bloodless*. The word echoed in his brain like thunder. And today another man, the leader of that still-born rebellion, had been offered to the sea. Marcus tried to remember what Grandmother had told him, the legends, the old ways from her village. But he was so tired, so tired.

Marcus felt himself nodding off and forced his head up and his eyes open, though they felt gritty and swollen. His gut ached painfully, and the restlessness he'd been feeling lately gripped him again fiercely. He swung his legs to the floor, and padded across the cold boards in his bare feet. Perhaps the night air would help him to think.

He climbed the wooden rails and emerged into the crisp salty air. A three-quarters moon hung like a deflated sheep's bladder in the eastern sky, illuminating the deck. Marcus stretched and moved to the port stern, where he found the mess left by the ship's carpenter before he died yesterday. Nobody had yet cleared away the tools and pegs and long shafts of wood. Marcus knelt and touched the rough edges thoughtfully, some memory tugging at his consciousness.

Marcus heard soft footsteps behind him. He whirled. His father stood outlined in the moonlight, wisps of hair drifting around the edges of his hat in the wind like small serpents.

"Father," he said with relief, "you frightened me."

"You have nothing to fear from me, Marcus," the first mate said. "I am here to watch over you and protect you."

"It's not I who need protection, Father," Marcus sighed, sitting back on his heels.

"Who then?"

"The men. They're in grave danger, Father; danger not only to their bodies but possibly to their mortal souls. I must speak with Captain Colombo tonight."

"What's this about?" His father moved a step closer.

"I know this will sound mad," Marcus said miserably, his eyes cast down to the deck. "But I'm sure there is a wampyr aboard the *Santa Maria*. That's why the men have been dying — not the night death or some strange plague. The wampyr is draining them of their life."

His father was silent a moment. "What makes you think this? Everyone works here; we have no slackers on board. Does the wampyr not sleep in the day and feast at night?"

Marcus was surprised by his father's reasonable reaction. He'd expected scorn, ridicule, even disappointment. But not this. He raised his eyes, about to respond with Grandmother's familiar explanation of the Cainites. But he looked into his father's eyes and saw a glow there, two red-black vortices that shimmered and swirled like windows into Hell. And he knew.

"It's you," he whispered, "you're the wampyr."

The first mate said nothing. Marcus rose, a long pointed shaft of wood trembling in his hands. He pointed the sharp end into the center of his father's chest. *You must not suffer the wampyr to live,* Grandmother had said. But she had not known that would mean Marcus killing his own father. Or had she? His hands were clammy around the wood.

"I remember now how Grandmother told me the old ones killed the wampyr," he said, his voice hoarse with emotion. "But first, tell me — why?"

"The hunger. The clan must feed to survive, and there are too many of us back home. The humans are becoming suspicious, even when we hide the evidence of our feeding. We must find other vessels to satisfy our needs."

"But you don't even know if there is land to the west," Marcus protested. "We may yet fall off the edge of the world."

"We may," the first mate agreed solemnly. "Which is why I'm the only one of the clan to explore this route. I was chosen to ensure that the captain succeeds, if success is possible. If I don't return, the others will seek other sources."

Marcus felt sweat trickle down his spine. "How many are there?"

"Too many for the food available. We have been feeding on the travelers along the eastern routes, but those are increasingly rare. Fortunately, our pillage encouraged explorations west."

Marcus' heart froze as a terrible thought occurred to him. "And Mother — is she…?"

"No, she knows nothing of my darker side. I married her for political reasons, and to propagate. Her mother was a thorn, however, when she became suspicious."

"You bastard!"

Marcus raised the wooden shaft to strike, but the first mate raised one hand. "Before you try to slay your father, you should know something."

"I know all I need to know," Marcus spat.

"I am not the only one who is feeding from the men. I have endowed one other with The Life."

Marcus stopped cold. He had not considered the possibility of two wampyrs on board. He straightened his shoulders.

"Then I must kill you both."

"It's not that simple, I'm afraid," the captain said. "You are not only my son — you are also the other wampyr."

Marcus thought of his faulty memory of recent nights, of his swollen and sore lips and the blood caked on them, of his increasing restlessness. He knew his father spoke the truth.

"Then the wampyr must die," Marcus croaked. And before his father could stop him, he drove the sharp end of the wooden shaft into his own breast.

As his father wept over him in the gathering darkness, placing his lips to the blood, Marcus realized his mother had been right. It was indeed possible to sail beyond the edge of the world.

Blood Month

by Brian Herbert & Marie Landis

On the Anglo-Saxon calendar it was called "Blood Month," November. It was the time of slaughter, when animals were butchered, smoked and salted for the winter months. The first day of the month began with the feast of All Hallows, an ancient celebration expelling evil spirits from the dead. The Church called the day All Saints.

At the edge of town the predator watched the festivities and sniffed the odor of fresh blood and human sweat. The townspeople were simple folk who slaughtered and drank and fornicated and slept. Easy to catch, but not the game the predator sought. It turned its attention toward the great stone castle that towered a short distance from the town.

In the dark woods by the castle, the predator leaped to the branch of a tree and selected its intended prey. It waited for an opportunity to pounce, but the plump female animal was surrounded and protected by its herd. Perhaps the female would lag behind and could be trapped. Fangs glistening, saliva dripping, the predator saw that the female was neither ill nor wounded. It was best to retreat to the shadowed darkness. There were easier catches to be made.

✝

From the window of the palace, bare-footed and still wearing the long white chemise she'd slept in during the night, the Queen watched her husband sail down the River Thames in his ship of state. She gripped a jeweled crucifix, sporadically squeezing it with a trembling hand. The gold chain attached to the crucifix slithered between her fingers like a metallic snake and made soft hissing sounds.

Bitter tears filled the Queen's dark eyes. After only thirteen months of marriage her beloved husband was leaving. Would he ever return?

Philip's reasons had sounded lofty enough, a professed need to be with his father, the King of Spain, who was considering abdication and wished Philip to take his place. She suspected her husband's true reason. He'd left because she couldn't bear him a son.

"Why can't I have a child?" she cried. "I've lived a life without sin, I've devoted myself to my husband and my God. What have I done to displease them?"

A half-dozen ladies-in-waiting and two handmaidens fluttered about her like a flock of small birds twittering their sympathy.

The Queen brushed them aside and paced back and forth.

It was August, 1555, and she, Mary, Queen of England, was nearly forty years old. It seemed to her that she'd married too late, past her time of childbearing. Even the lowliest peasant woman could bear children, in twos and threes like litters of puppies. Even a whore could give birth.

Once, she'd believed herself pregnant. Her stomach had swollen, her breasts had become distended. Shops in the town closed and prayers were said for a happy delivery. There were celebrations and parades. Then Mary's doctor told her she was not pregnant. She had dropsy, an accumulation of fluids in her body cavities.

Her desire to give Philip a son was all-consuming. He'd shown her the first affection she'd ever received from a man. Her father, King Henry VIII, had abandoned her, and now her husband was forsaking her too.

She spoke aloud of her loneliness, of her mistreatment by those she loved, of the lack of loyalty that her subjects displayed.

"My people betray me with their lack of faith when they reject my religious beliefs. Bishop Gardiner, my adviser, has told me that mercy to the country requires the execution of traitors."

Her ladies-in-waiting listened and nodded their heads in agreement. They'd often heard the Queen weep and wail her frustrations.

"What is our Queen saying?" asked the youngest handmaiden, a girl of thirteen years.

The older handmaiden, Leanora, pulled the girl to one corner of the room and whispered an answer. "When the Queen was a child, the Papacy refused to support King Henry's divorce from her mother, Catharine. The King snatched control from the Papacy, ended his marriage and banished Mary and her mother. He claimed Mary was a bastard, since he was no longer married to her mother. Since her ascension to the throne, our Queen has reinstated the old religion."

The young handmaiden frowned. "Could King Henry do all those things to a church?"

"He was King. He could do anything he wished. He wanted a lively bitch for his wife, not a grim, pious woman like Catharine of Aragon. This Queen is somewhat like her mother. Not much fun in bed, I suspect. The only quality she inherited from her father is his cruelty."

"The Queen's husband will return," said the girl. "They are man and wife."

"You are an innocent. If the Queen had married someone her own age, instead of a foreigner almost young enough to be her son, she might have held a husband."

On the opposite side of the room, Mary continued to pace like a caged animal.

"I can't breathe in here, there's no air in this room. I must go outside. Bring something for us to dine on."

The handmaidens scurried to clothe their royal personage properly. They dressed her in a long-sleeved tunic of crimson silk, a fur-lined surcoat and a mantle fastened at her neck with a brooch of emeralds and pearls. They wrapped her waist with chains of gold and silver and slipped boots of soft leather onto her feet.

Then, in an obedient line, the ladies-in-waiting followed their Queen onto the grass that grew to the castle's outer stone walls. The two handmaidens fetched almonds in honey and slices of cold peacock breast and a bucket of ale.

They seated themselves in a circle and listened to their Queen complain as they ate with their fingers. As was proper, the handmaidens sat away from the others.

"I hope she says her complaints quickly," said Leanora from her safe distance. "Someday she'll complain herself into eternity."

✝

From the top of an outer wall that surrounded the castle, the predator, concealed by its own unique camouflage, viewed its prey once more. The female had changed since the predator's visit a year earlier. Despite the thick layer of clothing she wore, an odor of illness emanated from her, physical changes in her body. Nevertheless, he wanted her and meant to take her at his pleasure. Sometime when the herd was not surrounding her.

For a brief moment the predator made himself visible to her.

Mary screamed. "I see the devil! On the wall. He's looking directly at me with eyes of fire!"

She could not be consoled or cheered.

"My Queen, there is no one on the wall," Leanora said. "Only shadows cast by trees."

The Queen continued to scream. "Make him go away. He is trying to steal my soul!"

The youngest handmaiden knelt before her Queen. "My uncle has given me a new Bible." She laid the book at the Queen's feet. "He says it will save a soul."

"Abomination!" answered the Queen. She rose from the grass and nudged the handmaiden's gift to one side with her foot. "Wretched girl, remove yourself from my presence. You have given me the New Testament, the words of heretics!"

Leanora grasped the young handmaiden by the arm and tugged her back to the castle kitchen. "That was a foolish gift. What madness came over you?"

"I only wished to comfort her."

"Our Queen is right, you are a wretched girl. And a stupid one, too. If you want to keep your life, leave your Protestant opinions to yourself. Do you know how many people our Queen has approved for execution, since she attained the throne two years ago?"

The girl hung her head.

"Over a hundred," said Leanora. "Queen Mary and her advisers see enemies everywhere, particularly Protestant enemies. She began the terror before your arrival. And she's not finished yet, I fear!"

"My uncle says the Bishop is responsible."

"With the Queen's approval. She started by executing four clergymen. You may know of them, since your Bible is the same one they use. John Hooper, Bishop of Gloucester and John Rogers, Vicar of St. Sepulchre's in London. And there were two others whose names I do not recall."

Leanora took the young girl's hands in her own. "I dislike telling you this, but I say it for your own good. John Rogers was the first to die. They tied him to a metal stake and placed a bag of gunpowder between his legs so his death would be swift."

Leanora paused and took a deep breath. "Gunpowder, a gesture of kindness? His death was neither swift nor kind. John Rogers was burned until he was nothing but ashes. He left behind a wife and eleven children, the smallest still a suckling at its mother's breast."

The young handmaiden released her hands from Leanora's and placed them over her eyes.

"Don't hide from the truth, girl. Think what it must feel like to be a living torch! Next came John Hooper. The gunpowder didn't ignite, and he suffered in agony for almost an hour. Do you want that kind of punishment? If you don't, keep your tongue still."

The girl shuddered.

Leanora, not certain she'd made a big enough impression, added, "Most of the Queen's victims have been working people, like you and me. Their only crime is that they learned to read the Bible. The wrong Bible. Do you understand? Like the one you gave the Queen."

The girl whimpered. "I can't read."

"Religion!" spat Leanora. When she saw the despair on the young girl's face, she softened her voice and put an arm around her. "Believe what you will, if it makes you happy."

In the Queen's chambers, her ladies awaited dismissal. After they'd accompanied her back to the castle, the Queen had remained silent. Her face was expressionless, as blank as a doll's, but her lips moved in prayer: "Keep me from the devil, I pray you keep me from the devil and all his legions."

When the Queen did not dismiss them, the ladies-in-waiting lifted the edges of their tunics and curtsied to indicate departure. Quietly, they closed the door behind them and scurried down the corridors toward their own quarters.

"Is she ill?" asked one.

"I think she's gone mad," answered another.

"I wonder what he... the devil looks like," said another.

Alone, the Queen continued to stare at the walls of her room. The demon was there, she was sure, inside the thick layers of stone and wood and mud, hiding in the darkness. She could almost see the outline of his body in the oak that paneled the walls, etched there in the grain of the wood.

There was a sudden thump and the sound of voices outside. As though she'd just wakened from a long sleep, the Queen leaped to her feet and rushed to the window.

"Who's there?" she called. "What are you doing out there? I command you to go away!"

Something large and dark flew through her window and splattered on the wooden floor. Queen Mary stared down at the obscenity that lay at her feet, the body of a large dog, its head shaved like a monk's scalp, and a thick rope tightly wrapped around its neck. Its swollen tongue lolled from its mouth. The animal had been hung or strangled some time ago, and its stench was overpowering. It was a symbol, a crude, rotting effigy of a monk. Her enemies wanted her to know what they thought of her beliefs.

She put her head out the window and looked about. But no one was there.

"Monsters!" screamed the Queen. "Heretic monsters!"

✠

It watched three men scurry away from the castle after they'd hurled the dead beast. The predator had its own agenda for Mary, a game that could last for a long time, depending on the nature of the prey. But it was best to remember the timing of a kill. If the game went on too long and wore the prey down, the prey might weaken and die before it was meant to. And that was not the purpose of the game.

✠

On the last November of her life, the Queen woke from another nightmare and lay shivering in bed. For a long time she'd suffered a variety of ailments that left her drenched with sweat and filled with foreboding. She had dismissed all of her handmaidens and only a soldier stood guard outside her bedroom. Since the day in the courtyard when she'd first seen him, the devil or one of his demons continued to haunt her. What good were guards against an evil spirit?

Sometimes she saw the devil's image in the depths of her closets or along a dark corridor, a small glimpse of something tall and muscular and evil. Sometimes it appeared at her chamber window, long-toothed and ravenous, grinning at her as if it knew all her secrets.

And no matter what potions she took, she still saw its face in her dreams. Her religion was her only solace, her only lover.

The Queen was caught by a fit of coughing and spit black bile into her handkerchief. She slipped from her bed and walked on bare feet down the castle hallways, ghostlike in her night dress. And after a while she sat on the cold floor and rocked back and forth like a small child afraid of the dark.

Her handmaiden, Leanora, brought her back to her chambers and covered her with soft blankets and pulled the curtains that hung from her four poster bed.

"Sleep well, my Queen," said Leanora.

"The devil has brought this sickness upon me," answered Mary.

"No, no," comforted Leanora. "It is the ague fever."

"They call me *Bloody Queen Mary* behind my back," said the distraught woman. "Did you know that?"

"You are the Queen," said Leanora. "You must rise above name-calling."

After Leanora left the chambers, Mary pulled the covers over her face and prayed. Alone. She clutched the jeweled crucifix tightly against her breast, her eyes closed against an evil world.

"Have you deserted me, God, because I have not yet destroyed all the heretics?" she asked. "I'm not a difficult woman. I have compassion for the poor. On Maundy Thursday I washed and kissed the feet of forty-one elderly women and gave them alms. But who has ever done anything for me? I am abandoned. Please send a sign that you forgive me, O God."

"I forgive you," said a voice as soft as velvet.

She opened her eyes. In the darkness of her room a great light blazed, and within it stood a figure so beautiful and radiant that she almost closed her eyes against its glory. The figure wore a white robe and its skin was the color of milk. Its golden hair hung in ringlets across broad, winged shoulders and its brilliant blue eyes revealed purity of heart. Her prayers were answered.

An angel!

"Let me hold you," said the angel, and without further words he put his arms around her. She fell asleep immediately, like a babe against its mother's breast.

In the morning he was gone, and she was pleasantly lethargic. It was a dream, she thought sadly, just a lovely dream.

A few nights later the angel reappeared, and this time she was awake enough to realize she had not imagined him.

"Will you hold me again?" she asked. "May I make my confession to you?"

"I will hold you and listen," the angel answered.

"A demon haunts me," she told him. "It haunts me because I've been too merciful and forgiven people I ought to have condemned. It grieves me that so many of my subjects are opposed to the one and true religion that Philip and I have attempted to reintroduce to the nation."

She took a breath. "There are dozens of sects rising like poisonous toadstools, publishing their literature, spouting their creeds. Religious revolt means political revolt. Those who oppose me suggest my actions are motivated by revenge against my father, who changed his religious beliefs and England's as well. I have attempted to undo the harm he did. But I do not hate him or his memory."

"And you believe your motives are pure?"

"I know in my heart that I carry the banner of my beliefs for the proper reasons. I am performing God's work. Even if some Catholics object to my methods or feel shamed because of them, I will continue to do what is right."

"Killing those who oppose you?"

"Only those who do not believe in the true religion. If they are heretics, their blood must be spilled in the name of God."

A beatific smile came to the angel's face, a smile that surrounded and warmed her, as she had not been warmed in years.

"I need absolution," she said. "My illness takes a bit of me each day. Will you give me absolution before I die?"

The angel stared at her with brilliant blue eyes. "Not here, not in this castle. But if you come to me tomorrow at dusk, to the south edge of the town, I'll give you what you need."

The following evening, the Queen dressed in silks and fine woolens. Her surcoat was lined with ermine and her mantle with soft beaver. She asked Leanora to arrange for a carriage. When the time came to leave, Leanora dressed Mary and combed her dark hair. Despite her age, the Queen's Spanish mother and English father had bequeathed her exotic good looks that shone through her illness.

"Will I accompany you?" asked Leanora.

"Not tonight," answered the Queen. "I am meeting with an important person. I need only the driver to take me there."

The carriage rolled forward with the Queen inside. On top of the coach, the driver was bundled in a long, black coat.

Clouds scudded across the evening sky, and a veil of darkness fell over the earth. Wind blew and rain cascaded down upon the horses and carriage, large drops that turned to nuggets of ice. The horses galloped faster as they were pelted with hail. Mary peered from her carriage into the storm.

Something ahead on the road? An animal, a person?

She put her trembling hands in the fold of her surcoat and held them still. The town was only a short distance away. They'd be there soon. Everything would be fine.

Suddenly there was a shout followed by a groan, a long, painful sound that grew fainter and fainter. The wagon careened sharply to the left and then to the right, and Mary realized with sudden fear that the driver was no longer in control. Possibly no longer in his seat atop the carriage.

Where was he? Had he fallen from his perch on the carriage?

She wrapped her arms about herself and began to mouth the prayers that would protect her. Someone would come, sooner or later, to save her from the cold storm and the night.

"I am here," said a velvet, angelic voice. "As I promised. To give you what you need."

And the angel leaned over her and placed his mouth against her cheek and ran sharp teeth across it.

She pushed him away and stared into his beautiful, terrible face that was filled, not with light, but with a funnel of darkness.

"You are the devil!" she cried.

"I am your savior," answered the creature.

The Queen began to pray again, asking her God for protection.

"Useless words," said the creature. "Hell is your destination, not Heaven." He pushed his face against her neck and bit deeply. Blood filled his mouth and he drained her slowly, with great pleasure. She struggled for a short time then grew passive.

"I am giving you something better than Hell," he said. "I will give you centuries of existence. And that is more than you did for my Sire."

Her question was no more than a whisper. "Your Sire?"

"He was among those you sent to the fire. But he was not a Bible reader, only a hungry visitor caught by accident with the ones you condemned. He was leader of our clan, and because of your behavior he's dead and our numbers have been reduced."

She moaned, but did not pull away.

"This is Blood Month," said the predator. "A fine festival for slaughter and blood letting. I am a vampire, and so shall ye become... to replace the one we have lost."

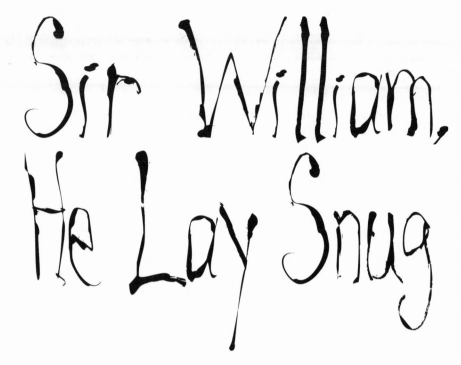

Sir William, He Lay Snug

by Roland J. Green and Frieda A. Murray

Being Extracts from the
Diaries of Elizabeth
Loring, late of Boston,
with Some Narrative
Emendations

I
1775

eat. The sun burned from a clear, cloudless sky, without wind enough to stir so much as a leaf, even near the water.

Noise. Ragged musket fire, punctuated with screams, turned to an indistinguishable roar that hardly ceased all day, save for perhaps the space of a breath.

Smoke. Beginning at noon, when the firing commenced, smoke obscured Breed's Hill, breeding rumor, breeding anxiety; foul air breeding the worst of humors.

I was able to find a place from which I could watch what has come to be called the Battle of Bunker Hill, safe from both the contending armies and the sun. It was the widow's walk of the Pettisgill House on Foster's Lane; some ingenious person had contrived a canopy of canvas over the greater part of it.

The view, therefore, was superior, though little could actually be seen, even through a telescope. Twice I was able to obtain the use of one, as the house was well-furnished with them (Pettisgill had sailed often to the Mediterranean before coming ashore).

As to the rest, although it was near the solstice, and New England lacks the clouds and mists that make old England a favorable clime for our kin, I am hardly one who cannot endure the sun. I dressed myself as I am accustomed to do when walking out, complete with sun masque, and, with the aid of the canopy, I suffered no injury.

Though I had been as close, or closer to, the battle than many residents of Boston, I cannot describe it without the benefit of knowledge that came to me later; most, though not all, from human informants. Bunker Hill casts a luster on the courage of the soldiers of both armies, though not on judgment of their leaders.

The Rebels assumed a position on two Charlestown hills, behind rudimentary fortifications, and awaited British attack. They appeared to have given little thought to the possibility of the British landing behind them, or barring their retreat by a bombardment from the ships in the Charles.

The British gave still less thought to such stratagems. It appears that they either expected the Rebels to incontinently flee at the first appearance of British regulars in battle array, or wished to demonstrate that such regulars could drive the Rebels from any position on the face of the earth.

The Rebels did not flee, but held their position against several vigorous assaults before exhausting their ammunition. They suffered fewer than half the thousand or more dead and wounded of the British, and most of these fell in the disorder of the retreat — which the British should never have allowed them to accomplish.

A great loss for the British, and quite possibly for the Rebels also, was Major John Pitcairn. He was one of the officers who hoped to settle this entire situation peacefully, and he did his best to maintain civil relations with those outraged by the Quartering Act, even to imposing a most rigorous discipline on his own men.

On the other hand, a noteworthy casualty among the Rebels was Dr. Joseph Warren. It is generally accepted that he has both knowledge of our existence and the skill (thanks to his medical training) to be a serious danger to us. Add to this his friendship with Paul Revere, who has access to abundant silver, and one can see how much mischief Dr. Warren might have wrought.

Fortunately, he is no longer among the living. A loss to the Rebel cause, but a gain for our folk. This is not the first time since the Tea Party that I find myself of a divided mind about the outcome of an event or the fate of a person.

"It won't be the last, Bets," was Joshua's only reply. "So you'd best be used to it before the next battle."

The art of being consoling or even courteous to a partner is not in him, I fear. But that is also nothing new. I do wish, however, that he would not call me "Bets."

I hate the name. I loathe it, I despise it, I turn from it as from holy water. Joshua knows this. But as long as I must work in conjunction with Joshua, I must endure it, as a dying mule in Spain must endure the presence of vultures.

"How long will that be?" I asked, in the hope of receiving a civil reply.

This time I was not disappointed. "A good while, I suspect. The British can hardly break out of Boston with the forces they have now, and the Rebels won't break in without artillery."

"A drawn bout, as it were?"

"Yes, which is a victory for the Rebels." Anyone hearing the way he pronounced the last word would have been certain that he regarded them as diseased Kine.

"Every day the Rebel army remains in existence, the more folk of the Colonies are likely to rally to its cause. If they do not join the ranks before

Boston, they will certainly cause mischief for Tories or suspected Tories or anyone they dislike in their home towns."

We looked at each other. "Anyone they dislike" could mean grave trouble for our sort in disputed areas, particularly those kin who, from long years of peaceful existence, had grown careless about disguising themselves. But trapped as we were in a city under siege, and with much work to be done here even had we not be so situated, there was little we could do to help those beyond our reach.

Still, few of our folk were likely to be Loyalists. Patriot sentiment had grown ever since the Quebec Acts.

The intent of most of us in undertaking the perilous and painful journey across such a large body of water as the North Atlantic was to settle in a land where mortals, while numerous enough to provide sustenance, lacked the numbers and time (and in many cases, the disposition) to spy on their neighbors. Also, a land where knowledge of our kind was scant, the yoke of government and the church light, and witch-hunts of any sort discouraged. The Quebec Acts and the Crown's subsequent efforts to levy taxes and quarter troops made it evident that only with political changes could we expect to gain that which we had risked so much to find.

I had not expected that the changes might come only at the price of a war which, much more so than yesterday, seems doomed to be long and bloody. One, too, which will result in stricter Royal governance, perhaps outright military occupation (I can see no other outcome).

Acts of Parliament were the root of these hostilities. Cannot this war be fought in Westminster, amending or repealing the Quebec, Navigation and other Acts which the Rebels now term "Intolerable"? Blood is not spilled on the floor of the House of Commons, as it has been (most wastefully) on the streets of Boston.

Joshua chides me for this, saying that I am, as always, too kind in my thoughts toward mortals. My reply is that war can turn any land into a howling wilderness, where neither our folk nor mortals are well-situated. (As he should know, having survived the Thirty Years' War, but it seems to have hardened him excessively even for one of our kind. I must remember, though, that he has been a Cainite some five hundred years, and can have but little humanity left.)

However, I cannot disagree with him that there is much to be done, especially if matters may still be accommodated short of a prolonged war. We shall begin by calling upon all of those British officers with whom we were previously acquainted, and offering them hospitality and sympathy.

Diary

June 28 — Paid our respects to Sir William Howe. He is rather fine-drawn from the weight of responsibility and the wound he received while most gallantly leading the light infantry at Bunker Hill. He remains, however, a well-made man of excellent sense, agreeable conversation, and enough wisdom for half a dozen of his rank.

He even invited me to sit upon the foot of his bed, saying that the doctor had forbidden him wine and spirits, but that my presence there would take away more pain than all the madeira in Boston. As my outer aspect is that of a fair-haired, blue-eyed woman, past first youth but not yet showing signs of age, the invitation (and Sir William's prior appraisal) did not take me by surprise. I obliged him by accepting the seat, for as long as decorum allowed.

Afterward, Joshua said he was certain that Sir William had a *tendre* for me.

"And how apt a judge of such matters are you?" I could not resist replying. Joshua seldom has problems with unwanted human desire, being Sir William's opposite in nearly every respect.

"Listening to you boast of the attentions paid you is an education in itself," he replied tartly. "And if Howe remains interested, that interest may open doors to us."

I noted that he had not been so encouraging about Generals Gage, Burgoyne, or Clinton.

"Gage will be bound for England within weeks," Joshua replied. "Burgoyne will allow no woman to influence him, but neither is he one to cooperate with other commanders. Clinton is a diligent mediocrity and junior to Howe.

"If there is a British general here with the capacity to beat the Rebels in the open field, it is Howe. But he is a Whig," — this referred to British, not Cainite politics — "and they do not support military action against 'their fellow Englishmen.'"

I would not doubt Sir William's ability, but if he is disinclined toward armed coercion of the Colonies, there may yet be a role for diplomacy and persuasion.

July 16 — Dined with Sir William and a numerous company of the more middling sort of Loyalist. I suspect the greater number there had not fully made up their minds, but, being in the city, were turning a courteous face to the general.

Sir William drew me aside for a few minutes private converse. I thanked the Third Mortal that colonial dressmakers do not cut their bodices as low as European ones, or he might have noticed the peculiarities of my breathing.

Howe spoke thusly: "So fair an English rose deserves an English — bed," he said.

"Nay, the briar twined round me preserves me from plucking," I replied.

He toasted me and escorted me back to the company, with a just barely perceptible squeeze to my elbow and pressure of his forearm on my farthingale.

⁜

December 21 — Supper party with dancing, hosted by Sir William. An abundance of fish but no beef, the only mutton from sheep who had perished in dire straits, and the other courses diminished in proportion. Twenty couples only.

Rum, brandy, and wine still in ample supply, and one could not help numbering those who drank more than usual. Even those of sober mien seemed downcast and lowering in spirits.

Tales from London suggest few who wholly oppose coercion of the Colonies, still fewer who realize the effort that may be required. Rumors in Boston run strongly to the effect that the Rebels are bringing artillery from inland to reinforce their siege lines.

Sir William most attentive, but strictly within the bounds of propriety. He claimed my hand for several dances and insisted on taking me in to supper. He keeps his rather saturnine complexion even in the depths of winter, and his wit under the burden of commanding a besieged garrison. Indeed, it had improved. A mortal would be flattered by an expression of such interest from a man who clearly has ample choice among the ladies, even in a besieged city.

1776

February 28 — Secret message from one of our own with Washington's army confirms imminent arrival of Rebel siege artillery.

March 5 — Rebel artillery in position to bombard city. Much fear, for both the city and the garrison are gravely weakened by hunger (theirs and ours) and smallpox. British troop discipline holds, however. Suspect Howe's influence, and, to do him justice, Burgoyne's.

Howe has two choices. Assault siege lines, probably leading to another Bunker Hill, or evacuate Boston. Too sympathetic to plight of citizens to risk bombardment and assault, even if he had the troops to sustain such a battle.

March 11 — Joshua informs me that decision to evacuate certain. Has packed essential Cainite and human appurtenances, also about six hundred pounds in gold.

I wonder what he sold to raise this sum and question the need.

Joshua (more reasonable in manner than usual under such circumstances) reminds me that maintaining human semblance in Halifax (crowded with exiles and troops, with everything thrice dearer than usual) will be expensive. Arcane or dark methods of obtaining resources would endanger our larger mission, which is to create refuges for our folk in British North America.

I reply that I have no intention of endangering that effort. Apologized afterward for tart reply to greater than usual courtesy. Joshua as indifferent to apology as to courtesy.

March 17 — Boarded brig *Sarah Logan* of Barbadoes, with forty-two other Loyalists. Sailed for Halifax on the evening tide.

March 27 — Have been at sea for ten days. The ship is dangerously overcrowded; a hundred souls in a vessel meant for half that number. I am keeping to my cabin — not much larger than a coffin! — under pretext of illness. This occasions no remark; more than half those aboard the *Sarah Logan* are genuinely ill or convalescent.

Actually, the illness was pretext only when I first came on board. Ten days of dealing with the Atlantic Ocean, even inside, away from the sun and its reflection on the water, has drained our vitality. Even Joshua is subdued.

Ah, well, unlike a mortal, I don't actually have to *eat* ship's rations!

April 1 — Landed in Halifax toward noon. The Captain bade us farewell, saying how well I looked for a woman sick for so much of the voyage. Joshua said the man was only being gallant, not indicating suspicion.

Halifax is smaller than I had thought, built on a superb and easily-fortified natural harbor. Five thousand mortal souls, if that many, regularly reside here, plus several times more soldiers and sailors with more arriving each day from both rebellious Colonies and Britain. Nor are we the first Loyalist exiles from New England.

Beyond the town limits are extensive forests, modest farms, and fishing and timber-cutting villages. A far cry from Boston, as it lacks a university, bookshops, and taverns where respectable folk may gather (although not the sort where soldiers and sailors may drink themselves sodden).

April 9 — Armies with banners may be terrible to foes, but they are the same to those trying to share a town the size of Halifax with them. We eventually contrived two rooms in a house owned by an elderly couple, both with failing sight.

Joshua arranged for a small rent augmented with work about the house. Our story is the same as many a mortal's; having fled from Boston with little, we must carefully husband what we have brought. Most of the mortal exiles, looking at the army gathering here, talk of returning to what they left within the year. More than ever I find myself of a divided mind, for Sir William appears to have decided that only an unmistakable defeat, or defeats, will stop this rebellion.

✠

Old Charner called from the bottom of the stairs.

"Message for Mrs. Loring."

"Tell the man to leave it. I am indisposed."

In truth, I was sorting the herbs our folk use when they inadvertently take sustenance from diseased Kine. They could be obtained in Halifax, but at prices that made it painful to contemplate a long sojourn in the town.

"Says it's to be given into your hands, ma'am."

I rose and secured the door by both the natural mechanism and other means. Then I went downstairs.

The message was a letter from Sir William Howe, addressed in an unfamiliar hand, no doubt that of an aide or secretary, but the interior in his own bold hand.

Madam:

Please accept this first payment of my debt to you, restoring what you left in Boston. Consider this letter a promissory note for the rest, redeemable when the Rebellion is crush'd.

Yr most obedient servant,

William Howe

Or at least part of the message was this letter. The rest was three well-strapped boxes. I could not pretend to be indisposed and still open them, even apart from revealing my strength.

"Please allow them to remain here until my husband returns. It appears that some person among the Crown's officers has heard of our intention to assist in the hospitals."

"You won't be bringin' sick folks over here, will you?"

"Not unless there are too many afflicted for the ordinary hospitals. Even then, we shall be sure to ask you first."

That satisfied Mr. Charner. Joshua did say when we were alone that he did not altogether care for the way Charner looked at him while he was bringing up the boxes. (Joshua has the aspect of a man who was powerful in a youth now some years behind him.)

With none to see, we could open the boxes with ease. Their contents left me surprised, bemused, and excited all at once.

There were a profusion of caps, fichus, and laces, and bolts of the finest muslin and linen, hair powder, feathers and fans. There were shoe buckles in another box, and an elegant parasol. There were finished garments also. I tried on a sacque, and found that it would need very little alteration. Sir William had gauged my measurements quite accurately.

"If this is all from Sir William…" Joshua began. His hesitation showed that he was less easy in his mind than he usually is or pretends to be.

"I recognize his hand," I said briskly.

Joshua looked straight at me. "I think you have caught his eye more than we realized. Did you expect this?"

"Not a fraction of it."

"So." He appeared to consider. "We must return south when Sir William does."

"Into the midst of the war?"

"The midst of the war is where Sir William will be found, and we now have a chance to influence him. I know what your skills are," he continued. "This is the sort of chance the Council expected you to seize."

He has the right of that, for seldom do I need vitae, or blood. My preferred sustenance is mortal lust, or energy, or vitality. Moreover, I can give as well as take this sustenance, just as any of us can bleed for each other, or, under some circumstances, for mortals.

"Well, Halifax would not be my choice for a long stay," I conceded.

"Nor mine," he said seriously. "And the rest of Canada is worse, Bets. Vast it is, but much of it is wilderness. Most of its folk are Indians, quite ready to kill anyone not of their tribe, or French peasants, of the ignorant breed who will burn the handiest old woman in their village if a child of theirs falls to a fever. You have never lived among such, and I can assure you that you would not enjoy the experience."

He looked at Howe's bounty. "Pack all that up again — securely. We don't want the Charners to ask questions. And don't forget that sacque you're wearing."

"Sir William showed excellent judgment in selection," I said. "He doubtless spent some time imagining how I shall look in it, and how I shall look when it is removed."

Joshua's laugh was not a pleasant thing to hear.

Diary

May 29 — We have discreetly turned much of Sir William's bounty into more portable forms, although we retained the more recognizable pieces. Since we had so indicated to the Chandlers, we spent some time at the sailors' hospital. It is a wretched place, and only duty to my own kind would take me there again.

As it happened, Joshua found one of us there, a sickberth attendant. He is a blood-drinker so new to the life that he had never learned how dangerous it is to take the blood of scurvy victims. He was not well when Joshua found him, but herb simples and our united wills largely healed him.

In gratitude, he told us of a Hessian officer who is one of us, a Rhinelander.

111

That is Joshua's native territory; we will hope for the officer's full cooperation in a number of matters.

Much activity in the harbor and at the quays. Five ships came in today, and lighters are moving both men and stores in great quantities.

June 19 — Sir William's expedition sailed, as generally believed, for New York. Rather, it began to sail. More than a hundred ships need time to wend their way to the open sea. Even those that sailed today were a splendid spectacle, however, like a city afloat.

July 30 — Word received that the "Continental Congress" of the Rebels, meeting in Philadelphia, has proclaimed the independence of the colonies from Britain. One can understand their reasons without approving of a measure that is certain to make the conflict more prolonged and bloody, and a reconciliation afterward more difficult.

☩

October 28 — Most of New York is reported firmly in British possession, the British having routed the colonial forces, although with serious losses on both sides.

Nonetheless, Howe cannot or will not press the Rebels vigorously. Several times they have escaped annihilation, as they did at Bunker Hill. They maintain an army, although much reduced by desertion among the militia, and are driving Loyalists from the country into New York, even as they did at Boston. They even have garrisons on the New York side of the Hudson River.

Whatever Sir William's original sentiments, his duty requires him to crush this rebellion. The fate of the colonies could, in the end, resemble that of Scotland after the Battle of Culloden. It is high time to go south and stir the pot directly. Joshua is seeking a ship, while I order and pack our remaining goods.

November 6 — Bought the sickberth attendant out of the Navy, as we will need a manservant in New York. He will use the name of Peter Jones. He is expected to find or, if needs be, create a suitable maidservant as soon as possible after we reach New York.

November 10 — Sailed this day from Halifax for New York, aboard the *Loyal Scot* of Bristol. A former West Indiaman, she is one of the few ships left in Halifax since Howe set sail. She is older and hardly in better condition than the *Sarah Logan*. One hopes she will complete the voyage safely.

Our quarters are more spacious this voyage, and far from overcrowded. The ship is well-laden with army stores, but the only other passengers are a party of soldiers hitherto unfit for duty through sickness or injuries, under the charge of two entirely disagreeable sergeants. I fear I shall have to feign illness again, to avoid being asked to dine at the Captain's table.

Joshua says I am fit to tempt any being capable of being tempted by female flesh. I hope this look survives the voyage, for the human Englishwomen of New York are said to be very fine, and the Dutch not ill-favored.

II
Diary

November 24 — Landed in New York. A faster passage than we expected, although the soldiers at the pumps for much of it. No fog, but mostly cloudy skies eliminating danger from sun. We are well enough, but it is good to be on land again.

December 1 — As of today, we are established in a modest house on Bleeker Street. Peter Jones' search for a maid has yet to bear fruit, so we are a trifle understaffed for a respectable appearance.

Otherwise, all that is needed for the household can be purchased at a good price, as many Rebels departed from the city with only what they had on their backs or carried in their pockets. The Crown's officers have not stinted themselves on buying comforts, but here we are ahead of many of the Loyalists fleeing from the Rebel terror in New Jersey and Connecticut.

Also, Peter Jones appears to have gained wisdom as well as experience since Halifax. He says that he is seeking a maid among those young women who will not be missed if the conversion goes awry and a body must be slipped by night into the Hudson.

He adds that this may lead him to search among the free blacks or even the slaves. However, this may prove troublesome. Those of us who rely on colored slaves for blood or vitality have mostly taken the Crown's side, lest the slaves be declared emancipated if their owners join the Rebels. But writs of emancipation are frequently ignored, and many a free black has been enslaved on a white man's bare word. A sordid squabble over slave ownership is the last sort of notice we wish to attract.

Except for the maid, all we require is some sign of continued interest from Sir William — or some sign that his interests have turned elsewhere. In that case, Joshua and I must seek some other means to exert influence on the British conduct of the war.

December 12 — Prodigious good news! Joshua was called to Sir William's headquarters and offered a position as chief contractor for supplying the prison hulks in Wallabout Bay. Upward of a thousand Rebel prisoners are already confined there, under brutally oppressive conditions.

Joshua is delighted; indeed, I have not seen him so since the Boston Tea Party. This is an excellent opportunity to increase our portable wealth. Also, he will have a suitably secret means of communicating with any of our folk who may find themselves in the hulks. Finally, he believes this confirms Sir William's interest in me.

"Quite the gentleman, Howe," Joshua said, with what was more smirk than smile. "But I'll reserve judgment until I see the *quid*."

December 14 — Joshua was correct about Sir William, and is crowing about it in a manner befitting a cock on a dunghill. I have been invited to one of the several residences or quarters Sir William maintains. I do not know whether their purpose is to house his staff, make him a more difficult target for would-be assassins, or offer privacy for assignations.

✠

Sir William reached for the brooch with which I had pinned my fichu. They were both his gifts from Halifax; the brooch had a Cupid intaglio.

"What of the briar, Rose?" he asked, his finger on the fastening.

"La, I fear the knight has won his way through," I said.

He laughed, unfastened the brooch, and slid the fichu off my shoulders. The royal blue of the sacque beneath made an alluring contrast with my skin. His gaze traveled to my chest. I gasped, as if I had been holding my breath, and began to breathe in a fashion calculated to hold his attention.

And more. I had taken no more than a dozen breaths — probably less — when his hands passed the boundary of the sacque and were on my skin. I raised my head and captured his dark gaze with my own.

Sir William's lust was not the crude, hasty sort. A rake he was, but not one whose passions drove him to haste, ill manners, or brutality. He was one who savored the leisurely gratification of his appetites, and was anticipating a night of delightful exploration.

As was I.

✟

The clocks were striking two in the morning of December 17. Sir William lay on the bed, clad only in his shirt, deeply asleep but not unconscious. I had not drained him to that extent.

I was (for the moment) sated, having taken much and given little. In spite of a season of rough if intermittent campaigning, the general had vitality to spare, if presented with a suitable objective.

It would be well if that objective were not the Continental army beyond the Delaware River.

I drew him into my arms, then put my lips to his skin and took just enough blood for my next measure. A mortal's blood is a trail, however tortured and twisted, to the depths of his mind. Deep in Howe's mind I left thoughts of comfort, of ease, of holiday celebrations, of letting his army rest for the winter.

I whispered the tag about retiring to winter quarters, from Caesar's *Gallic Wars* as I withdrew. Then I relaxed, certain that Sir William would not wake until sunrise.

December 24 — Joshua is delighted with first month's profits from prison-hulk contracts — sixty-two pounds eight shillings ninepence. At this rate, not only shall we prosper but we shall be able to pay for other Rebel enterprises, beginning with the escape of those of our folk who fall into British hands.

I am less delighted with my own situation. Sir William is undoubtedly a man of much experience with women. When we meet I must at one and the same time use my vitality to persuade him that he is having a splendid tumble, use more of it to plant suggestions in his mind, and finally draw enough of *his* vitality to replace my own without drawing so much that he will collapse or even become moderately sick. Blood can be substituted for vitality to a certain extent, but I am unaccustomed to a blood-heavy diet. Moreover, exsanguination can be recognized, even by those persons called Army doctors (to whom no self-respecting farmer would entrust the care of his swine), much more quickly than devitalization.

All of this is as demanding as it would be for a mortal woman to actually do what I feign. When I sleep through the day now, it is *not* because I cannot face sunlight!

1777

January 5 — At my latest rendezvous with Sir William, he confirmed (without being asked) the tales of Rebel victories at Trenton and Princeton; they have severely shaken the British hold on New Jersey. General Washington appears to have learned a good deal about the art of war since his defeat on Long Island.

I used power of suggestion, afterward, to persuade Sir William to remain in New York even now. If the Rebels retreat across Delaware, as is likely, they will be impossible to catch. If they remain in New Jersey, they can be cut off from the river by quick marches. No British soldier need sleep for weeks in the snow, either way.

January 24 — Joshua says that Howe's refusal to leave New York is provoking ill-feeling among Hessians, both officers and men. They feel they were sacrificed to no purpose at Trenton.

I suggested that we use some of the profits from contracts (altogether, more than a hundred pounds now) to encourage desertions among the Hessians. Start by purchase of civilian clothes — the red coat makes one a target for every sharpshooter, especially in a snow-covered countryside.

✠

April 15 — At my latest meeting with Sir William (no bedsport; he had a quinsy), I learned that Hessians have deserted in alarming numbers. I prepared a herb tisane, which much improved his throat and spirits with no further effort on my part. This improvement was surprisingly agreeable to me; Sir William is normally a man of such joviality that seeing him cast down left me a trifle *distraite*.

He did confirm that, without substantial reinforcements, he will not be able to divide his forces in the field and still adequately garrison New York. Would that he could capture the Rebel army, but General Washington will hardly repeat the errors of Long Island for the convenience of the British. Nor has Howe the force for a long season's chase through rough country. The combined forces of Howe and Burgoyne (the latter presently in Canada) might suffice, however. And New York itself could be left in a very perfect (or at least sufficient) state of defense.

Why not go south, I suggest, to Philadelphia? A threat to the Rebel capital might bring Washington's army to battle. The Rebels now have *two* armies in the field. If Sir William can destroy one, or at least take it out of play, Sir Henry Clinton may be able to deal with the other without having to depend on the cooperation of Burgoyne.

Howe is sympathetic to this last proposition, as Burgoyne is proving himself an able field commander, but a little *too* independent of mind. Sir William asks if, in lieu of Burgoyne, I will accompany him into the field.

May 1 — After an occasion in which he believed he enjoyed an exceptionally fine frolic, Sir William is in a mood to believe black is white if I told him so — although not for long. His will is of a robustness almost equal to his appetites.

I set myself a more modest goal: to persuade him to advance on Philadelphia by sea rather than by land. New Jersey is full of good places for Washington to fight delaying actions and ambush supply trains. Going around by the Cape of Delaware avoids both problems.

This will also cost at least two months' prime campaigning season, which Washington can use to train recruits and bring in militia. This strategy is double-edged, for a Rebel army able to defeat the British in a pitched battle, rather than wear them down by ambuscade, might encourage the Ministerial party in Parliament to support repression of the colonies, regardless of the cost.

✝

September 24 — Advancing on Philadelphia. The country is quite attractive, as is the weather, although the occasional fogs provide welcome relief to me.

I have traveled independently until now, as not even a general can commandeer quarters for his mistress aboard a ship of the line. Now I move with the army's baggage train, and Sir William has provided every care for my comfort, including a traveling carriage with its own guard of British and Germans (from someplace other than Hesse, I believe). Although considering the state of these American tracks — they can hardly be called roads — I would prefer to ride.

With a few words about the richness of the countryside, I have persuaded two of the German guards to consider desertion. They may actually do so if Washington advances again after the recent drawn battle at Brandywine Creek.

October 5 — I can now draw appropriate conclusions about the Battles of Brandywine and, more recently, Germantown. The Rebels still cannot defeat British regulars in the open field, but they can sustain action against them all day and withdraw in good order.

The American army is more than a manure-booted militia, and as a result, *the Americans can no longer be crushed without vast resources and a terrible effusion of blood!*

October 18 — Encamped outside Philadelphia. Reports from north suggest that Gates is making good use of the terrain — hills and forests — against Burgoyne. And Sir Henry Clinton, leading the British forces remaining in New York, has made only modest advances up the Hudson. He seems even more cautious than Howe, and apparently without any assistance from our folk!

Sir William has obtained quarters in an abandoned tavern, quite sufficiently comfortable for our purposes, especially after two months at sea and on the march.

✝

Sir William's neckcloth was crumpled and loose, and his waistcoat hung askew. A kettle, not a bowl, of rum punch was being kept warm over the embers in the fireplace. Though his head was turned in my direction, he seemed not to see me, or perhaps to see beyond my facade, to what I really am.

"I've tried," he said, and the slurring of his words told me how much this usually hard-headed man had had to drink. "I don't want to see '46 again. One Butcher was enough, b'gad."

I made quite whole-hearted, if soft-spoken, assent. The Duke of Cumberland's bloody-handed campaign in the wake of Culloden had driven mortals and Cainites alike from Scotland and all but ruined the land. Many,

118

in fact, had come to the colonies. What would happen if the Crown sent another general of the same stamp as Cumberland, with orders to waste the Colonies like the Highlands and an army sufficient for that purpose!

Sir William made his way to the kettle — that he walked rather without stumbling was a marvel! — and dipped his tankard. Punch is meant to be drunk in glasses, and I could tell by the odor when the lid was lifted that this was exceedingly potent.

I watched him and worried. Had I drained enough to drive him to drink?

"Perhaps you should have some supper, sir," I suggested. I put as much enticement in my voice as I could contrive. "Pray send for some; it's only a quarter after nine."

He gave no sign of having heard. "The way they fight, like the savages! What would happen if we left them to their own devices? In a few years they would be living in lodges and scalping each other, just like the savages." Now his eyes seemed to look even beyond me, into a future that held such appalling spectacles.

I said nothing, not wishing to encourage this line of thought. His augury seemed no idle fancy. Yet no one had thought that the Americans could keep together for two campaigning seasons. They might have other surprises in store for us.

"Englishmen have no business fighting each other. Civil war..." His voice trailed off, and I was relieved to note that the tankard stayed on the table.

He was quite right about civil war, which injures Cainites as well as mortals. I and many others had to go to ground in Cromwell's day. We had likewise been as pleased as any mortal with the peaceful solution of 1688.

I placed my hand on Howe's shoulder. Drunk he was, but I could not sense that it had brought him any relief. Neither had it drained his vitality to any great extent.

The depth of my concern surprised me. I truly did not want to see that magnificent vitality drained by defeat, let alone sordidly destroyed by drink.

He raised his head and looked at me, and it hardly took a vampire's vision to see the rum was beginning to exact its price. I stepped to the chamber door and spoke to the orderly.

"Tea and hot soup for the general, and quickly!"

✠

October 20 — Reports from the north are very encouraging. Gates is doing even better than expected against Burgoyne. British losses are heavy and this year's campaign has gone completely awry.

Sir William is plainly discontented and seems torn several ways. I cannot think of any way to use this uncertainty, so I have made no attempts of late to influence him.

Letter from Joshua — profit from contracts now running to eighty pounds or more each month. But he also wrote that deaths among the Rebels in the prison hulks are over one hundred a month.

October 28 — A sad day for the Loyalists. Burgoyne is ready to surrender to Gates, at Saratoga.

My own spirits are low also, from saying farewell to Sir William Howe. He and his brother the admiral are resigning their commands in America, and returning to England. They may be able to help the situation in Parliament, where they both sit.

Howe says he will bear fond memories of me, and he hopes that Americans and British, despite all the bloodshed, will remember that they were once brothers and may be so again. He does not expect this in his lifetime, however.

We exchanged real embraces, without my seeking to enter his mind. I felt almost like a mortal woman. My tears afterward were also real.

1778

April 11 — The French have recognized the colonies as an independent nation and signed a treaty of alliance with them!

This treaty also makes war between Britain and France almost inevitable. The French want revenge for the Seven Years' War and will hardly have a better chance for it. With the French fleet in the Atlantic, the British supply carriers can be attacked, and King Louis may even send troops, as well as supplies, to America.

✛

Joshua agreed with my conclusions about the probable course of the war over the next few years.

"In fact, I think the Americans now have a serious prospect of victory," he concluded. "Wherefore, I fear we may have to think about returning to England."

"Have you received orders, or is this your own idea?"

"Think on it, Bets. We are known and notorious Loyalists as far as the British, other Loyalists, and the Rebels are concerned. That will help us in England, where there are more than a few men there who will need watching or even influencing for years to come, if they are not to make mischief even after the peace."

I had to admit the truth of that. But even a mortal could have sensed that Joshua had not told the whole truth. "That is not the only reason, is it?"

He shrugged. "My association with the prison hulks has not given me a good name among the Rebels. We would be harried, if not hunted, on this side of the Atlantic. At the best, we would have to move to the frontier or far to the south."

"To someplace that would make Halifax seem like Boston?"

"Exactly so."

I considered. No one connected with those hulks could have avoided odium altogether. But knowing Joshua, I doubt that he even tried.

"Another time," I said, "you might remember that a good reputation among mortals can be useful to us."

"Was my position, reputation or not, so useless? All of our folk in the hulks survived, and most have escaped."

I glared at him. "If they were all as unscrupulous as you, I hardly imagine that they needed your help to survive."

Now he returned glare for glare. "Mortals are of small account in our plans. Or were you so fond of Sir William that he weakened your judgment?"

"Joshua, you talk as if we were really married!"

"If I were a mortal and really married, I hope it would not be to a fool like you!"

I would have flown at him for those words, and he would have had to use his full strength to save himself, but for the charge we had been given. We could not dissolve the partnership by mutual slaughter, or even uncontrolled tempers, until its work was done.

Still, I shall have to find one or two discreet friends among our folk, and more among the mortals. Joshua may stop short of an open breach, but a *secret* betrayal is not known among our folk, even those with more scruples than

Joshua. At the very least, it must be plain to Joshua that anything that happens to me will happen to him soon thereafter.

To avoid more such heated exchanges, I went for a brisk walk. Or as brisk as the streets of New York on such a day of chill rain and gray skies permitted. Even my strength could not give me a full stride after the mud and other matters plastered themselves on my boots and skirts.

By the time I returned to the house, I had found time to contemplate the future with a cooler head. I must look to finding friends in England as well as here, and Sir William's name should not be useless in that endeavor. I do not anticipate reestablishing our connection, but doubtless he has friends who feel they owe him favors.

Also, I know England better than Joshua does. He may feel safe in a country where the Church of England prevails. He does not, I think, know as well as I do that the Scots Presbyterians are of the same cloth as the New England Puritans.

Nor is England devoid of those who have traded, lived, or served in the West Indies and in India itself. More of them than he thinks have learned enough native lore to be able to detect our folk — and by means that dear Joshua may not be able to recognize!

England will be safe enough. Indeed, for a while it will probably be safer than America, as Joshua says. I can always return in a generation or two, if I so wish.

Indeed, I probably shall. England, after all, has changed out of all recognition since the reign of the great Elizabeth, when I was mortal. If the Americans win their independence, and do not fall to pieces fighting each other, they may well be worth a visit in much less than a single century.

The Great Man

by Doug Murray

The Great Man groaned as he pushed himself upright on the bed. *There they are again!* He looked around. *One over there, another... there!*

The Emperor allowed himself to settle back against his pillows. He had seen ghosts before. Many of them. He had seen them every time he thought of the thousands who had died for him. The Old Guard. The Grand Armee that he had raised and wasted in his dreams of conquest. *Those spirits I would expect,* he thought, *not these strangers!*

He stared at the largest of the vaporous forms. It had a wide face, flat features... *except for the nose.* A tiny smile formed on the Great Man's face. *People made such fun of my nose.* Familiarity touched him. *I've seen those faces before!* The Great Man closed his eyes for a second, searching his memories, trying to remember....

"He sees us!" My companion seemed surprised.

"Of course he does!" I moved to the Emperor's side, unconcerned. After all, he couldn't touch me. "He's very near death. The wall between us is weakening."

My companion's face hardened. "Good. My people have been waiting a long time for him."

The Great Man's eyes suddenly opened, staring directly into my face. There was power behind those eyes. Even now, on his deathbed, the Emperor was not ready to surrender.

I watched as he marshaled his meager strength. I saw him moisten his dry lips. *He's going to say something!* I smiled at the effort. *Probably ask who we are. Tell us he's not afraid!* That was good. Fear should come later, as he slowly began to understand what eternity held for him. I saw his lungs fill and nodded to him, waiting for the usual speech.

It did not come. He reacted to my movement, realized that I could see him. It gave him pause, and I could see his brain work as he tried to fit me and my companion into his world view.

I smiled. Yes, he was special. He would be a challenge.

The Great Man came to a conclusion and reached for the bell pull.

"He's calling for help!"

I shrugged. "Let him. His servant will not see us."

My companion reached out for the bell, stopping it from ringing. "I prefer that he be cut off from the world for the moment." His face closed in remembered sorrow. "As he cut us off from the larger world."

I shrugged again. It really made no difference one way or the other.

The Great Man pulled the cord again and again...

Nothing happened.

I saw the beginnings of concern in the old eyes. He knew he was alone. He knew that he could depend on no one for help.

"What will he do now?" My companion had returned to my side.

"I'm not sure." I thought back to other times, other victims. "He's different from my other subjects." I reflected on their actions. "Perhaps he'll pray."

My companion snorted. "As if that could do any good."

"True." I nodded, thinking of my own experience. "But he has no way to know... wait a second." I bent down. The old man was sinking into his bed, fighting to keep glazing eyes open. "I think he's going to pass out."

"Will he die?"

I looked at the body before me. "Not yet."

My companion nodded, an ugly grin on his face. "Good. He hasn't suffered enough yet!"

✠

The Emperor fought the lassitude that fell over his body. *Not yet! I'm not ready to sleep yet!* He shook his head, forced his eyes to stay open. *I know those faces! I saw them in...*

Egypt! It was in Egypt! The Emperor's eyes closed. The world drifted away....

✠

I was full of dreams then... The Emperor sunk into the past, away from the ghosts and fears of the present. *I saw myself founding a religion, marching into Asia, riding an elephant, a turban on my head, and in my hands the new Koran that I would have composed to suit my needs.* He shifted in his sleep. *I would have combined the experiences of the two worlds, exploiting for my own profit the theater of all history, attacking the power of England.* His heart beat faster. *And, by means of that conquest, renewing contact between the East and all of Europe.*

✠

"What's he dreaming about?"

I looked down at the face: His fast-moving eyes told me he was in the midst of a dream. I touched his mind, just brushing the fringes. He was still too strong for anything else. I caught a glimpse of the Sphinx. "I think he's dreaming about you and your people."

My companion nodded. "Good."

✜

Egypt was waiting for me. His mind filled with heat and dust. *A dead place. Filled with tombs...*

The Emperor's men had landed at Alexandria, moving quickly inland. *There was no resistance until we reached* Shubrabbit....

The Mamelukes had started as an order of military slaves. They were contemptuous of the Europeans, having defeated and captured Louis IX some years before.

They thought we were like the damn nobles...

They charged. Picturesque charging tribal warriors armed with sword and lance. *Against modern muskets!*

It was a slaughter.

Later, at the Battle of the Pyramids, the Mamelukes lost over 2000 men. *And we lost less than thirty.*

Cairo, the heart of old Egypt, fell. *The tombs were magnificent.* The pyramids, which had stood guardian over the Great Man's victory, seemed to proclaim the Emperor to the skies. *There were bits of history everywhere!* The Armee moved to refit and rest. The Great Man began his conquest — present and past. *I brought my scientists. They worked to bring order out of chaos, just as I did....*

The Emperor moved to take possession of the wealth of Egypt. It would pay for the troops and supplies he would need to conquer the hated British. And then it happened.

The damned Navy betrayed me again!

✜

"Look at how fast his eyes are moving!"

"That must be quite a dream."

My companion glared at the sleeping man. "I hope it's a nightmare!"

✜

It was a nightmare. The fleet, under the command of Admiral de Brueys, was busy preparing a feast — *celebrating!* — when the British fleet appeared. *The idiots didn't even sail out to meet them!* The fleet was caught at anchor, almost wiped out.

That defeat ruined all my hopes, all my plans. No reinforcements were possible, and the British victory brought new heart to the Austrians and Russians.

Worse, it turned the Egyptians into enemies.

I should have handled that better....

Idle artillery men, bored with heat and insects and dust, fired their guns at the Sphinx, damaging a relic older than all European civilization.

The Sphinx! That is the face I saw.

The scientists hurried through their work as well. Despoiling ancient graves, cutting open mummies, trampling old religions as they did so.

It all finally ended with a humbling evacuation under British eyes and guns.

Damn the British!

✠

The Great Man's eyes flew open, peering wildly into the shadows, coming to rest on the face of my companion. They stuck there, staring intently.

"I know you..." The words were weak, but intelligible. "Egypt..."

My companion leaned down, face contorted in hatred. "Yes! I am Egypt! Egypt, where you destroyed the tombs of my people! Shattered our plans for the afterlife!"

"He can't hear you."

My companion turned to me, face still angry. "When will he be in my hands?"

I looked down at the wasted body. "Soon. I have been keeping the doses small, drawing his death out slowly..."

My companion nodded. "It will do. I can wait."

The Emperor watched the two shades talking, although he could hear nothing. *Am I deaf?* He had seen the hatred in the glaring eyes of the flat-faced one. *That one has the face of the Sphinx!* The Emperor stared. *How can that be?*

127

He sank back into his bed. *Does it matter? I have no strength to fight.* He fought his eyes open. *And yet I cannot allow myself to die like this!* He watched the faces above him. *Not with them waiting and watching!* He let his eyes close. *I must live! Live to be Emperor once more!*

He let his eyelids drop. Sleep came again. Blessed sleep. *Emperor of all the world!* He faded away, going to a land of green hills and blue-clad me. *If I could only find Ney....*

I smiled as I caught the thought. Ney was going to be the Great Man's fetter. Ney and the hated Navy...

✟

Fetters. I had thought nothing of them in life, save as instruments of my work. They had no other meaning. How could they? We are taught, almost from birth, that we can take no emotional or physical baggage from one world to the next. The Bible makes it quite clear in its constant appeals for faith and charity.

It's a lie.

We do bring things with us. All kinds of things, be they word, deed, crime — even attachments to people or places that we love or hate. All of these hold us in the Shadowlands, forestalling us from ascending to our final destiny.

I'd been surprised at *my* fetters. After all, when you serve God as I had, you expect to be taken directly to Heaven.

Expectations mean nothing here. Look at my masters, the ancient Egyptians. For millennia they planned very carefully for the afterlife: preserving their bodies, building huge tombs of stone filled with food, wine, clothing, furniture — anything and everything they might need or want.

Fetters.

They were a trap, holding the Egyptians in the Shadowlands, unable to pass into the afterlife they'd planned so carefully for. Still, it wasn't as bad as it could have been. At least they were well supplied and relatively comfortable in their great Necropolis.

Then the Great Man had come with his scientists. They'd gone to work with a vengeance, breaking into tombs, stealing... excuse me, *borrowing* artifacts and bodies. They cut into mummies, opening their flesh to the light of new days, defiling them, cutting their fetters.

Thousands were released — into the roiling heart of the Tempest, never to return.

Those Ancients who remained were enraged. How dare this man destroy everything they had worked so hard to build?! They *had* to find a way to gain revenge.

Eventually, they did....

✠

"He's not dying, is he?" My companion glared down at the sleeping form. "I don't have my people in place."

I shook my head. "Just asleep. Retreating into dreams." I allowed a tiny smile to play across my face. "That's how his life will end. Retreating." My smile hardened.

My companion turned to me. "Retreating." His hand touched my shoulder. "Yes, I like that."

We both looked down at the still figure below. "I wonder what he's dreaming about."

I touched his mind. "The last battle." His eyes moved rapidly behind their lids. "Many of his dreams concern the last battle."

My companion smiled. "We'll give him other things to dream about."

"You won't feast on his soul?" Professional interest on my part.

"That would be too quick."

I looked at him, saw the hungry way his eyes looked at the Great Man. "I see."

I did, too. I had learned about punishment during my time among the living. It had been my specialty. *I* had been the master then, Grand Inquisitor of all Spain. A force to be reckoned with. God's Sword on Earth, they'd called me, and I had done my job well, with diligence and energy. I uncovered more than 100,000 heretics in Spain alone. Think of that! More than 100,000 souls purged of sin and returned to God's bosom!

Of course, it was a little hard on the bodies those souls were attached to, but that wasn't my fault. I didn't create the problem, I just solved it.

And what was my reward? Was I carried to heaven to sit at the right hand of the Father, as the Church had promised?

No, I ended up here, in this forsaken limbo between heaven and hell.

With 100,000 fetters holding me in place.

I looked down at the Great Man, lying still and silent in his sheets. Would this one add to my fetters?

I didn't care.

✛

Ney, where are you Ney... The Great Man saw the battlefield spread before him. Thousands of troops were marshaled in tight fighting squares, rifles pointing in all directions, like some deadly porcupine. The Great Man smiled. His men were the best. He knew that, had known it for years. The others fought for money. His men fought for the Emperor! It was these men who would bring him victory this day.

If he could get word to Ney for one last cavalry charge.

"Runner!" A Hussar hurried forward, hat raised in salute. "Take this to Marshall Ney!"

The Hussar took the message, tucking it into his pouch. "Yes, My Emperor!" He turned to leave, then stopped.

"Excuse me," he said. An Imperial Aide turned to him. "Where do I *find* Field Marshal Ney?"

The Aide pulled the Hussar to the side, out of earshot of the Emperor, who was already planning his next move. "No one knows."

"Then how...?"

The Aide shrugged a gallic shrug. "Do what you can." He glanced back at the short figure of his leader. "If you find him, we still have hope."

"And if I don't?"

The man shrugged again.

The Hussar hurried off, determined to succeed.

✛

He failed, of course. My masters made sure of that. There were places where the wall between the Skinlands and the Shadowlands was thin. At those places, it was possible, if one had the power, to reach through, affect the world of the living.

My masters had the power — and had been ready to use it. When the Emperor marched near one of those weak spots, my masters were ready to make their move.

Marshal Ney had never been defeated in battle. His cavalry had ridden to honor and victory each time they had been called upon.

Until now.

My masters found a new enemy for Ney to fight. An enemy that didn't fight back in the normal ways — and could not be defeated with gun or sword.

That enemy was rain.

Rain that fell day after day, night after night, turning the fields of Belgium into a giant morass.

Ney found himself in mud so deep his horses sank to their withers. So thick that his cannon limbers bogged down completely, forcing him to abandon his batteries.

Still, he pressed on, determined to reach his Emperor's side. Yard after yard, mile after mile, he forced his men. Driving always toward the sound of the guns.

Sounds also created by my masters.

⊹

"Ney. *Why didn't you come...*" The Great Man was muttering in his sleep, the words a constant litany. A servant appeared with a tray. A light meal for the Emperor the servant loved and would die to protect.

I smiled. Such devotion was wonderful — and useless. I reached out, touched the man's small mind, exerted the tiniest bit of control, *Just take the bottle, little man.* He picked up a bottle from the counter — a bottle carefully marked with the symbols of ant poison. *It's just sugar. Your Emperor likes sugar.* The man poured a touch of the powder into the coffee. *That's right. Just a touch...*

I watched, smiling, as the servant turned to his master, tenderly helping the Great Man drink his coffee. I wondered if future historians would discover that the Emperor had died of poisoning rather than from natural causes. I shrugged. With *my* fetters, I would likely be around long enough to find out.

The Great Man took days to die. Days in which my companion and I did everything we could to terrorize him. As he grew weaker, I was able to touch his mind with more power, force dreams upon him, show him the truth of the Shadowlands.

Show him the pain of his future.

He began to show signs of fear. Not much, but a little.

My master smiled. "You're beginning to reach him."

"Indeed. It just takes time." I smiled. "And patience."

My master looked down at the wasted body, the feverish eyes. "He can't last much longer."

"A few hours. No more."

The Egyptian nodded. "I will gather my people." He looked down at the still form. "We will reap his soul, bond his shade."

I nodded.

✠

The Emperor finally succumbed the next morning. I must confess, try as I might, I was never able to instill real fear in him. Even at the moment of his death.

The little room was crowded then. As my master had promised, the Egyptians had gathered in force, ready to reap the Great Man's soul before it could pass beyond the Shadowlands.

"There he is!" My master was the first to spy the new wraith. "Grab him!" Egyptians scurried about. "Shackle him!"

Mere seconds later, the Emperor of the French was dragged in front of the Pharaoh of the Egyptians. The Great Man, Napoleon, was a different creature now. Not the wasted half-man we had watched die. This was Bonaparte the Conqueror, General of Generals.

Even shackled hand and foot, kneeling before an unknown foe, he exuded confidence and power.

My master, Ramses the Great, Pharaoh of Pharaohs, sneered down at his captive. "So, Emperor, we meet at last!"

Bonaparte struggled to look up. The plasmic caul still clung to his face, impairing his vision. Still, the eyes under the caul were clear. There was no fear in the Great Man.

None.

"Who speaks to me?"

Ramses snarled, then reached down and tore the caul off. "I do." He stepped back, trying to intimidate the Frenchman with his height. "I, Ramses, Pharaoh of all Egypt!"

It didn't work. Napoleon blinked away the aftereffects of the caul and looked around, shrewd eyes taking in the Shadowlands, nimble mind weighing possibilities. "Is this Hell?"

Ramses nodded his head. "To you, it is indeed Hell!"

Napoleon shrugged with gallic simplicity. "Well, I always expected to come here."

The Egyptian gestured to his followers. "And here you shall stay!" They put a collar on the Emperor's neck, one with a leash that led to Ramses hand. "Now come, my little Frenchman. My friend and I have many things to show you."

"Not yet."

The Egyptians were stunned, whirling to see where the strange voice had come from. Only Napoleon was unsurprised, smiling with satisfaction.

"At last!"

Men in the uniform of the Grand Armee of France appeared, as if from nowhere, rifles and bayonets ready, faces aflame with hope.

The battle was short and bloody.

"So, my friend." Napoleon was unchained now, standing next to his field Marshall. "At last you appear."

Marshal Ney nodded, face flushed with embarrassment and remembered pain. "I could not fail you a second time, my General."

Napoleon grinned down at Ramses and his men, shackled together at the Frenchman's feet. "You have not." The Emperor peered around and nodded. "This world is not too different from the one we knew."

"Not at all, my General."

Bonaparte nodded. "So, we have a new Empire to build." He winked at me, not a touch of fear in his eyes. "A new world to conquer."

Emperor of the Shadowlands. I nodded, my mind taking it all in. The Great Man was forging his own fetters — the strongest, most eternal of all.

The fetters of forever.

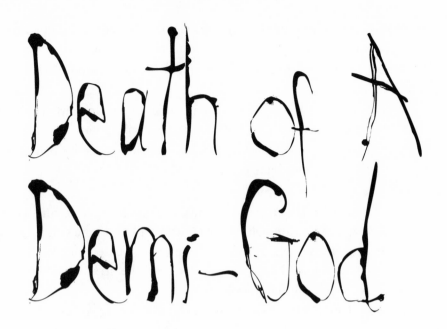

Death of A Demi-God

by Basil Copper

WHERE THE HELL is the axe?" Grady said.

His face was white and he spoke through clenched teeth, but his voice was steady. Ryan didn't answer. His eyes were blurred as he stared round at the blood-spattered walls.

"One must have been used," Grady said, more to himself than anyone else.

"Undoubtedly," Ellis said.

He was the police surgeon and his white smock was smeared with dark blood as he knelt in the shambles of the poorly furnished room, lit only by the wavering light cast by two oil lamps.

"My problem relates to the head," he said evenly, the glow of his cigar momentarily lighting the gray stubble on his cheeks. He had seen too many

135

violent deaths to show his true feelings to his younger colleagues, but even his iron nerve was shaken by the violence of this savage crime.

"It must be somewhere around," he continued. "Unless the murderer took it with him."

The fragrant blue smoke of his cigar went straight up to the dirty ceiling, momentarily blanketing the stench of death in the squalid room.

"Hardly, doc", Ryan said, speaking for the first time since he had been called to the scene. "He must have been covered in blood in any case".

"You may be right," Grady said.

He was a big man and his tightly buttoned blue uniform made him seem bigger still. He was a reassuring sight to Ryan, whose nerves were still jangled by what he had gone through. For the first time he focused clearly on his companion's face, taking in the steady grey eyes and the grizzled mat of hair that made his face vaguely Roman-looking.

"Find the husband," Grady went on, as though talking to himself. "It's usually the husband in these domestic matters. Jealousy or drink."

"You're sure she had a husband?" Ellis grunted, rooting around the floor, his hands encased in rubber gloves.

"That's what it said on the card on the door."

It was Grady speaking again.

"George and Virginia Munson."

"Ah, well," Ellis said in a resigned voice. "Your job. You represent the law, after all. Been dead about four or five hours, I'd say. A girl — or woman rather — about thirty-five years of age. That's all I can tell until we get her to the morgue. Though I can't be certain, the murderer probably decapitated her with the first blow. Then, for some reason I can't figure, he just kept on raining blows until his strength gave out."

"How do you make that out doc?" Grady asked.

Ellis shrugged, still bent over, his face suddenly wan in the lamplight.

"Instinct and experience. He started on the head and torso. The cuts get less deep until we get to the extremities of the legs. The final blows barely broke the skin, as though he suddenly dropped the axe. It had to be a man. No woman would have had the strength to do this."

"Guess you're right," Grady said. "The floorboards are all splintered up near where the head should have been."

136

"It hadn't escaped my attention," Ellis said dryly. "It will all be in my report in the morning."

He looked up at the cheap clock on the mantel. Even its face had not escaped the red rain from the thing on the floor. He made out with some difficulty that it was long past one a.m.

"Better make it the afternoon, boys. Even I have to sleep sometimes."

There was a great edge of weariness in his voice that was not lost on Ryan. Ellis then gave a sharp exclamation that made him jump.

"Ah! There it is! Rolled under the dresser."

He dived into the far corner of the room, came up with a golden object all dappled with scarlet. Ryan had to look away.

"Pretty little thing, wasn't she?" Ellis went on, using his professional voice. "I haven't lost my touch. Mid-thirties was about right."

He looked at the still figures of the two men in their blue uniforms, his cigar smoke going up in an unwavering line in the oppressive silence of the lonely room. From far below, on the lower floors of the tenement, came furtive sounds; the murmurings of many hushed voices. The remaining tenants being interrogated by the two men's colleagues; prevented from venturing any higher.

"Shouldn't you boys be taking notes or something?"

The ironic tones in his voice were not lost on the two officers. Ryan pulled himself together with a palpable effort.

"Sure, doc," he mumbled, making a show of going through the drawers of a shoddily-built bureau on the far side of the room which had mercifully escaped the scarlet mist carefully avoiding the thing on the floor. From the corner of his eye he could see that Grady had resumed his official persona. He noted that there was an empty tin box on the table that looked as though it might have contained money.

"Time the wagon was here," Ellis grunted. "Little more I can do."

As he spoke there came the heavy tread of booted feet on the stairs and two men in uniform appeared at the door with a stretcher covered with a canvas tarpaulin. The younger clapped a handkerchief to his face on entering and turned away, retching. Ellis made a disparaging clicking noise with his tongue.

"I said experienced men only," he admonished the older attendant.

Ryan stepped in quickly, before anyone could speak.

"I'll take the other end," he said.

He fought back the realization that on no account could he have stayed in that room alone at that late hour. Grady shrugged. His face was impassive and phlegmatic in the dim light of the lamps. Ryan knew that he understood his own feelings, but he was a professional and would not condemn him for that.

But all Ryan said was, "I'll send another officer up."

He was glad to escape the claustrophobic atmosphere and once on the ground floor relinquished his burden with relief and saw it slid into the van.

The images of the night stayed with him all the way home.

- 2 -

Ellie was still up.

"How did it go?"

Ryan did not trust himself to reply. He took off his jacket and slumped down into a chair, reaching gratefully for the coffee Ellie carefully poured for him. She always kept a brew going on the kitchen stove. He let the steam bathe his tired eyelids before taking the first invigorating gulp.

"Bad?"

He nodded.

"I'd rather not talk about it, if you don't mind."

Their eyes met in mutual understanding, and she moved quickly to a position beside him, stooping to cradle his head in her arms. Then, just as quickly she had disengaged herself.

"Have you had anything to eat?"

He shook his head, his thoughts jumbled, so that he found it difficult to speak.

"Just make me a sandwich, if it's not too much trouble."

He still had difficulty keeping his voice steady. She was smiling now, went rapidly into the kitchen, her heels making sharp rapping noises on the floorboards. He watched her out of sight, then turned again gratefully to the coffee. Later, in bed, they reached for each other in the scented darkness and eventually drifted into sleep. But Ryan had troubled dreams and found himself awake in the early hours. He could see by the pale light filtering through the shutters that it was about five a.m. At first he could not remember anything except that he had had a night with his rest so disturbed that he could not recall anything similar unless he went as far back as his childhood.

It had to do with yesterday's horrific murder, of course; he could not put it down to anything else, which was another cause of worry. It would not do for a police officer of his long experience to become too affected by the incidents connected with his investigations. It was unprofessional and quite outside his normal reactions. He turned toward Ellie but she was sleeping the sleep of a young person in perfect health, her measured breathing strangely comforting. She was twenty years younger than her husband and a very beautiful girl; he still could not believe his good fortune in obtaining such a prize. He was not good-looking but he had a strong and rugged personality which he supposed had something to do with his attraction for her.

He turned back again and closed his eyes, but sleep would not come, despite the fact that he had had only four hours' sleep in the last twenty-four. His mind went on endlessly turning over the incidents of the previous night before once again reverting to the fragmentary images of the dream. But still they eluded him and eventually he drifted off into an uneven sleep. Not unnaturally, he awoke feeling out of sorts. After a hasty breakfast with Ellie, during which neither of them spoke very much, he rode downtown to the Bureau.

Grady was not yet in, or else was out on some mission of his own but the Chief sent for him. He was closeted alone with him for more than an hour; he was more serious than Ryan had ever seen him, his big, square face with the cropped, Germanic haircut, clouded and angry. Not with himself and Grady, Ryan had to admit; the newspapers already had hold of the story and had splashed the lurid details.

Nor was there any trace of George Munson, as might have been expected. A trail of blood had led to a nearby woodshed when a search was made at dawn; obviously the husband had cleaned himself up there with a bundle of rags but there was no trace of him or the axe used in the crime, if indeed an axe had been used. But Ryan had long experience of Dr. Ellis' expertise and he had no doubt in his own mind that they were looking for an axe, as well as the perpetrator, and he told the Chief so.

All in all, it was an unsatisfactory interview, from both points of view and Ryan came out no further forward in his mind, while he was certain that his superior was no wiser than when his subordinate came in. But he sat down at his mahogany desk in a somber corner of the office, far from the windows, and concentrated on his report. He had made a good many notes on the previous night and it took him a while to compose on the official form, after a number of false starts, though he had been fortified by more than one cup of coffee.

Grady came in eventually, and sat down at his own desk opposite, with a curt nod of recognition, as was his way. Presently he too was summoned to the presence of his superior and was absent for a long time, allowing Ryan an adequate period in which to complete the documentation. He would, of course, compare it with Grady's own, but he had no doubt that his fellow officer's findings would closely parallel his. The Chief came over to his desk while he was still working on his notes.

"We're getting posters out," he said, in answer to Ryan's unspoken question. "You'd better check the text and let me know. Here's a copy of the details."

He put the handwritten sheet on the desk in front of his subordinate and went out without any further conversation. He never wasted words but Ryan had to admit he was an outstanding officer; punctilious, thorough, fair, and slow to blame. Ryan knew as well as the Chief that it was only a matter of time before Munson was captured but the routines had to be observed, not to mention protecting the public and warning them of the dangers from a man who was apparently a homicidal maniac. For questioning by both Ryan and Grady the previous night had elicited no possible motive from other residents of the tenement.

Munson had apparently been a model tenant; his wife a demure and respectable woman. The husband had worked as a printer for a major publisher in the city and his wife was a seamstress who did a good deal of her work at home. It was true that Munson had exhibited streaks of unwarranted jealousy from time to time, but nothing to explain the horrific murder which had shocked the entire city. The Chief did not seem to be giving the slaying a very high priority, despite the immense publicity the case was arousing, but then Ryan supposed that it would be only a matter of time before the man gave himself up or was captured. The public was being warned; that was the main thing. One major difficulty was that a thorough search of the murdered woman's apartment had revealed no correspondence from relatives or friends, with whom he might have found shelter.

"It's a dead end, then," Grady grunted.

He had come in quietly and was looking over his colleague's shoulder as he compiled his report in his neat, sloping handwriting.

"Apparently so. But it shouldn't be long before he's caught."

Grady sat down opposite, straddling one of the office's polished mahogany chairs. In the background the work of the Bureau went on, amid occasional hushed comments, as though the other officers were in church. Weak sunshine came in through the dusty windows, stenciling irregular patterns on the floor. Grady lit one of his fragrant cigars, the match making a harsh rasping noise in the relative silence of this corner of the office. For some reason it irritated Ryan's nerves and he moved uneasily in his own chair. Grady caught the movement and for a fraction his eyes expressed amusement.

"I wouldn't be so sure. This is a big city. And there's nothing to stop him taking a train to Canada or a ship to Europe for that matter."

"Except that all train stations and ports are under surveillance," Ryan reminded him.

Grady shrugged.

"That situation won't last long. Can't spare the men. Too many other things to look after."

He turned to his own desk, which was at an angle to Ryan's and riffled irritably through a bulky docket of official documents.

"We need a ten-day week to get through all this stuff," he said, waving his cigar butt, the blue clouds of smoke enveloping his face.

"So we put this case aside?" said Ryan bitterly.

Grady shook his head.

"I didn't say that. The Chief knows we've got too much on our plates. He's putting more men on. Sanders and Costello."

Ryan brightened. He knew them both and they were first-class.

"So what do we concentrate on?"

Grady fumbled in his inner jacket pocket.

"This for the time being."

He came up with a faded photograph. It depicted a sallow-looking man of emaciated physique. He wore a straggling beard and he had piercing, deep-set eyes that seemed to bore right through the onlooker. Ryan made a thin whistling noise through his teeth.

"A nasty-looking customer. Where did this come from?"

"Found it in a corner of Munson's bureau last night, after you left. The Chief knows about it and the likeness is going out, together with the description. Odds are he's shaved off the beard by now."

Ryan shivered slightly as he again looked at the photograph.

"Those eyes would give him away anywhere."

Grady made a disgusted clicking noise with his tongue as he removed the cigar from his mouth.

"Model tenant indeed," he said dryly. "An obvious candidate for the lunatic asylum once he's caught."

He got up abruptly knocking the ash of his cigar into an earthenware bowl on his desk.

"I thought we might ask around the neighborhood before starting on these."

He indicated the fat dossier on his blotter.

Ryan smiled thinly.

"Good idea. I could do with some fresh air."

The two men went out quickly, looking neither to right or left, as though they thought the Chief might put his head round his office door to tell them he had changed his mind.

- 3 -

It was turning cold already, though not quite autumn. Winter would be hard and early this year, Ryan thought, as he trudged the wide boulevards, his thick leather jacket buttoned tightly across his chest. It had been a long and fatiguing day; he and Grady had combed the neighborhood, showing the photograph but had obtained no further news of the elusive Munson. All the staff of the local stores and saloons knew him well but no one had been able to place him later than the day before the murder.

Neither had anyone noticed any apparent change in his demeanour; a decent type of person had been the general description; self-effacing and "a man who kept himself to himself," as more than one witness had testified. Both officers had pages of scribbled notes but nothing that would lead them to the apprehension of the criminal. Repeated questioning of the inhabitants of the tenement, had thrown up no further information, and the two men had even separately interviewed more than fifty employees at the printing works where he had been in charge of a machine but there again no one had noticed anything unusual about the man before his sudden and unexpected disappearance. He had been there for seven years and was regarded as a punctual timekeeper; a man neat in his appearance; in fact a model employee, according to the works manager.

Now Ryan was beginning to regret the wasted hours when he and Grady could have employed their time profitably on more productive and equally urgent cases. One consolation, if consolation it could be so described, was that their two colleagues new to the assignment, Costello and Sanders, had fared no better. Now, as he made his way homeward, dodging through the drifting crowds that thronged the sidewalks and the lighted shops, he began to think Grady may have been right in his suppositions. Perhaps the man had gone to Canada; or even sailed for Europe. There may have been a good deal of money in the empty tin box; the man's life savings, perhaps.

Best to concentrate on other things, and let more urgent matters take the foreground. With these and other thoughts still wearily churning around in his mind he went up the path to his house, noted the windows were dark, and reached for the key secreted on a high beam on the stoop. Ellie kept it there for emergency, and it was easier to use than delving through thick layers of clothing and his leather jacket to reach his pants pocket. He remembered then that Ellie had said she might be visiting friends that evening and would not be home until about ten.

Sure enough, after he had unlocked and replaced the key in its usual place, he found a note in the kitchen, cold food laid out under cloths and a big pan of soup on the stove that needed only to be heated. As he ate his lonely meal he scoured the daily newspaper to see if there had been any sighting of Munson, but saw nothing; nothing, that is, except a tart editorial that asked what the police were doing when everyone might be murdered in their beds. Ryan smiled grimly and threw the newspaper on to his leather armchair.

He felt tired and out of sorts tonight. More than usually so. He might turn in early and leave the lights burning for his wife. He sometimes did this because his routine was exacting and he kept very irregular hours, occasionally going whole nights without sleep. Ellie well knew this and understood. It was only nine o'clock when he crept upstairs, washed quickly and got into bed. It was half-past ten when he awoke at the faint slam of the front door. It was a habit long ingrained in him; he slept like a cat and was aroused at the slightest untoward noise. More than once his quick reflexes or intuition had saved his own life and that of less cautious colleagues.

Ellie came in and sat on the edge of the bed while they exchanged the

DEATH OF A DEMI-GOD

news of the day. She had had an excellent evening; and their old friends sent their best wishes. Then she withdrew to prepare her own supper and lock up for the night. By midnight she was in bed too and the pair slept on in the comforting darkness of the big room; but there was a change from the usual routine that evening. Ryan dreamt a hideous dream. He rarely dreamt and normally could not remember any details. But this one was so vivid and real that it stayed with him long after he awoke with the pale light of dawn filtering through the window blinds.

It had begun with soft voices calling and then the darkness had lifted to reveal a shimmering mist that danced and eddied. The voices went on with their enigmatic chanting, and for some reason that he could not pinpoint, Ryan felt a deadly fear gripping him. This was entirely foreign to a man of his iron nerve and even within the dream he felt ashamed and baffled that such a feeling would invade his being.

There was a whiteness within the mist; then, as it cleared slightly, it resolved into the form of a nude woman who advanced toward Ryan with a lascivious expression on her face. She was very beautiful indeed and for some reason she reminded the dreamer of his wife. Blond hair cascaded round her face and as she advanced to grasp him in warm arms he was aware of two needle-points of fire that transfixed his very soul.

There was something behind the naked woman that Ryan felt so menacing as to threaten his very existence. The needle points resolved themselves into two eyes of fire, so vile and insidious that they paralyzed his will and all his faculties. He must have lost consciousness within the dream for the next thing he remembered was that the images had disappeared, as is the way with dreams, but the two coals of fire were framed in a face of horrific darkness and mystery set beneath the brim of a wide felt hat such as Spanish grandees of old wore. For the rest, the figure was draped in a long dark cloak.

But these sparse details were worse than anything more explicit might have been and Ryan felt such stark fear that when he awoke his body was beaded with sweat and his night clothes were absolutely drenched with the perspiration of terror. It was already light and when he looked at the clock it showed a quarter of six. He found his teeth were chattering and his limbs deathly cold and he fought to regain control of himself as the light gradually strengthened. This was something so outside his normal experience that his brain seemed paralyzed, hardly able to comprehend what was happening.

Ellie was still asleep and as Ryan tried to calm his shattered nerves an insidious lethargy seemed to be stealing over him. He seemed weak and debilitated. He slept a little and when he finally awoke he could hear Ellie rattling coffee cups in the kitchen below. He put his hand to his face and was horrified to find it came away bloody. He staggered up and went to the bedroom mirror. He then saw that the right-hand side of his throat was slightly swollen and bleeding. He sponged himself with a towel at the wash-basin and was puzzled to see there were only two small insect bites just below his jaw-line.

He resolved to say nothing to Ellie; there was no need to worry her. He had noticed that, despite the advanced season, there were a great number of gnats, mosquitoes and other insects invading the city. No doubt something had stung him in the night. He put the matter from him and dressed and shaved quickly, fortified by Ellie's smiling face as she brought him his first cup of coffee. By the time he was at breakfast, most of his fears of the night had faded, though he could not shake off the darkest depths of the dream. But he rode downtown on the streetcar and when he arrived at the Bureau he was himself again. There was no sign of Grady but despite what he had said the night before there was a copy of Dr. Ellis' post-mortem report on the murdered Munson woman on the desk before him.

He read it slowly, as thought about to hear something fantastic. Instead, the report confirmed his own unofficial and inexpert thoughts on the matter. Death had been instantaneous, as he had already surmised, at the instant of decapitation. He read through the document with increasing inattention, but was brought up with a start by a penciled notation at the end of the two sheets of paper. The cogent content was as follows; "Incredible that such a puny man should have such tremendous strength to wield what appears to be a huge woodsman's axe as to decapitate this unfortunate woman with one clean blow. Bizarre — attention should be directed to this."

Grady came in at this moment and Ryan sat watching him as he sat digesting the report at his desk opposite. He sat back with a sigh as he read the penciled note at the end and set fire to his cigar as though he had come to some important decision.

"I've been giving some thought to this," he said eventually. "My sentiments exactly."

He was silent for a few moments, his brow corrugated as he again studied the report, puffing at this cigar, so that little stipples of red fire pitted his cheeks.

Ryan cleared his throat with a thin rasping noise.

"So we're still on the case?"

Grady creased up his face in what might have passed for a smile.

"Let's say we still have an interest. This is just a copy for information. Sanders and Costello would already have had the matter in hand since last night. But it reinforces my own thoughts. The murder was utterly pointless and without motive, if we can believe the people we've interviewed. Munson, a weedy and rather weak sort of man seem possessed of superhuman strength. Fantastic as it may seem, it would appear that he was either drunk, under the influence of drugs — though we found no evidence of that in the apartment…"

He broke off, his gaze fixed vacantly on the frosted glass panels of the Chief's inner sanctum.

"So what are you saying?"

Grady looked suddenly weary and out of sorts. He put up a hand to his forehead and wiped away minute beads of sweat.

"I don't really know. I hesitate to venture…But he appears to have been acting under the influence of some outside force…"

"I was already thinking on those lines," Ryan said. "Better not tell the Chief."

Grady smiled naturally then, revealing crooked yellow teeth.

"You're right. Feet firmly on the ground."

"Not to say in the cellar," Ryan replied.

The two men were still laughing quietly when the far door opened and the close-cropped iron-gray hair of the man they were discussing, appeared. The two officers were grave and composed as they advanced across the littered floor. Grady carried the thick dossier of unsolved cases that awaited their attention.

- 4 -

Ryan was again dreaming. The circumstances were similar to those that had obtained before, except that on this occasion he was in some dank cellar. There was the mist; the chanting voices; and the nude woman with blond hair, but whose features he could not make out. She briefly faded to make way for the vision of the creature in the wide-brimmed hat and dark cloak. The features were shrouded in blackness and only the red needle-points of the eyes, like

DARK DESTINY: PROPRIETORS OF FATE

those of some wild beast, stood out in the hypnotic display that kept the dream Ryan rooted to the loathsome floor of the place. There was a putrid stench in his nostrils and he actually screamed as the foul thing approached and sank the wolf-like teeth into his neck.

He was wide awake now and the alarmed features of Ellie appeared above the lamp, bringing back sanity to the scene. But there was no doubting the blood which dappled his neck and added to his terror when he staggered to the mirror. But his wife swiftly took charge and sponged away the emissions with her handkerchief. As always she laughed at his fears. She pointed out that he had cut himself shaving the previous day and that, in the grip of the dream, he must have clawed at his throat and re-opened the small wounds.

Ryan was calmer now and eagerly gulped at the brandy which she produced. He sat down by the dressing table, his trembling over, and had to admit that there was some sense in what she said. Now that the blood had been wiped away he realized that the areas of broken skin were tiny and that she might well have been correct in her assumptions. There were other scratches on his throat, he noticed, which could have been made by his cutthroat razor. He noticed too that there were tiny flecks of blood on Ellie's nightdress; as soon as he pointed that out she sponged them with a handkerchief soaked in cold water. As before, the dawn light was creeping through the blinds as he apologized profusely to his wife.

She was, after all, years younger than her husband, and vibrant with youth and beauty; inclined to throw off all these darknesses which were almost insensibly beginning to surround him. He decided not to return to bed and slowly dressed and sat by the fire in the sitting room while she prepared coffee and sandwiches. But he felt better after a short rest; indeed sleep claimed while he sat in a high-backed chair awaiting breakfast. He felt drained and enervated and his wife had to arouse him several times after she had set the tray down before him.

It was raining when he set out for the Bureau and he felt chilled to the marrow and greatly depressed, but decided to keep his thoughts to himself. He had not even told Ellie of his inmost fears and had pretended to agree with the bright face she put on things. He caught a streetcar and arrived at the Bureau an hour before his usual time and had to ring for a member of the night staff to let him in, as he had left his office key at home in the present disordered state of his mind. He sat on at his desk restlessly shuffling paper until the sound of distant footsteps and bells ringing told him that the normal work of the day was taking its accustomed path.

However, he became more animated with several cups of coffee and Grady's arrival. He had exciting news. One of the night officers coming off duty had dropped in at his house on the way home to tell him that there had been a report during the night that Munson had apparently been sighted on the outskirts of the city, taking refreshment at an all-night coffee stand. He had shaved off his beard but his wild, staring eyes had given him away and he had fled. The area had been cordoned off by officers but there had been no further news.

Ryan was excited too, though he tried not to show it.

"Have Sanders and Costello taken over, then?"

Grady shrugged.

"Your guess is as good as mine. It's up to the chief. I'm supposed to see him as soon as he gets in."

He looked up at the big mahogany case clock on the wall.

"If I know him he's still directing operations. In the meantime we shuffle the paper until further notice."

But the day passed with no sign of the Chief and the two men carried out routine assignments, while inwardly impatient and burning with curiosity. The big man came in at about three p.m., gray and haggard; as Grady had surmised he had been up all night taking charge of the search but if it was Munson and the patrons at the coffee stand had been correct, he had slipped through the net. The Chief was obviously not in the best of tempers, having had only two hours' sleep, and in detailing the reports on the routine operations, the matter of the two officers' assignments had passed over.

He stayed until five o'clock and then left for home, leaving strict instructions that he was to be alerted by the night duty officers, if there were any further developments regarding the axe murder. Costello and Sanders came in shortly after he had left; like the Chief they had been out all night and were not in the best of tempers themselves. Costello was a burly man with a thick mustache, and his Italian descent was evident in his explosive conversation and his pointed comments on the veracity or otherwise of the frequenters of late-night coffee stands. Things were quiet that afternoon and as if by tacit consent, after comparing notes on the case, the four men left the

Bureau a little after six. But instead of going home, Ryan, by a sudden whim, walked four blocks south.

To his relief the lights in Dr. Mandel's surgery were still on. The two men were old friends and Ryan did not wish to involve Ellis in his problems as it might get to the ears of the Chief and other personnel in the Bureau. Mandel was an elderly, stooped man with thinning white hair and gold pince-nez, but his outward appearance was deceptive. He was amazingly agile for his age and would work round the clock if he had to. His partner was busy in the next consulting room but Mandel had a gap between patients, and produced a half bottle of whisky from a drawer of his desk. The two men drank in silence for a couple of minutes, in a shared tranquillity that obtains only when people are completely at ease with one another.

"Some official business?" the doctor asked eventually, his kindly grey eyes regarding Ryan keenly from behind the gold pince-nez.

Ryan shook his head.

"Just a little medical problem, Donald."

The other listened sympathetically as Ryan outlined the details. The latter thought it best to say nothing about the two strange dreams. Mandel became brisk, reaching for his stethoscope.

"Let's just run the rule over you. Take off your vest and open your shirt."

He made notes on a pad as the examination continued. He gave a grunt at length and sat back in his old swivel chair.

"Heart and lungs sound enough. No problem there. From what you tell me it sounds like anaemia. Too much work and probably scrambled meals."

He got up and moved the lamp closer so it illuminated Ryan's face and the upper part of his body.

"Let's have a closer look at those sores."

He picked up a huge magnifying glass from his desk and grunted again as he gazed for long moments. He sat down once more and scratched something on his pad.

"You can put your shirt and vest on again. Nothing abnormal there. What's your age now? It's been so long since we last met socially that I've forgotten."

Ryan told him. The doctor ran a thin finger over his long nose.

"We get a lot of that among men of your age. Sometimes caused by the rubbing of unsuitable collars. Tiny lesions, you understand. Or slight impurities of the blood. Usually, they come and go. But keep me informed."

Ryan stood up, stammering his thanks. He reached for his pocket book but Mandel waved him away with a smile.

"No fee among old friends. Buy me a drink next time we meet."

Ryan thanked him again and put on his overcoat as there came a faint tapping at the consulting room door. He had his hand on the knob when the doctor said, "Give my love to Ellie. She well?"

Ryan grinned.

"Never better."

"That's good."

Ryan opened the door to admit the nurse and an emaciated-looking man who seemed as though he might expire before he got the doctor's desk. The police officer was closing the door when he heard Mandel's optimistic voice.

"You're showing a marked improvement, Mr. Crabtree!"

Ryan's smile lasted him all the way down to the street. He walked northward for another two blocks and had his prescription filled at a late night chemist's. He took one of the large pink pills with a glass of water at the counter without much conviction that the medicine would do him any good. But at least I know what I have not got, he told himself mockingly. The walk home must have tired him more than usual, but Ellie had a hot meal waiting and he ate with renewed vigor. The two passed a pleasant evening together and that night, to his great relief, he slept a dreamless sleep.

- 5 -

"I did the best I could," Dr. Ellis said. "Took some reconstructing, I can tell you. But all the findings confirm my preliminary diagnosis."

He slid back the drawer and pulled the sheet off the dead face with a dramatic flourish worthy of a music hall comedian performing some coup de theatre, Ryan felt bitterly. He did not know why Grady had dragged him down to the morgue, but as he stared at the waxen, smashed wreck of what had once been a beautiful woman, he marveled at the patience and surgeon's skills Ellis had brought to the task.

He was conscious of Grady's grim face at the doctor's elbow but was hardly aware of what Ellis was saying, as he droned on, " . . . severed the carotid artery and the spinal cord at one blow. The wound was delivered with such ferocity that it split the table clean in half and the head rolled into the far corner as you saw the other night."

He turned a beaming, professional visage to Ryan.

"Of course, this must all be normal routine to you gentlemen, but to me it represents a unique opportunity to exercise my forensic skills . . ."

"Hardly normal, doc," Grady interrupted him. "And I'm not disputing your genius with the knife and needle, but where exactly does this get us?"

Ellie held his hands wide, a pained expression on his face.

"All the technical details have to be delineated in the report. The rest — that is the reconstruction — is just icing on the cake."

"Oh, is that what it is," Grady said ironically, lighting his perpetual cigar.

Ellis replaced the cloth and slid the drawer to with a decisive crash.

"Well, you saw the note I attached to my preliminary," he said. "The man was either drunk or under the influence of drugs when he did this. Or he could be mad, of course."

"Maybe," Ryan said slowly. "Or perhaps he wanted us to think that he was mad."

Grady's eyes opened wide with surprise and even Ellis seemed a little taken aback.

"But to what purpose?" he asked, leading the way back to his cluttered office, behind the frosted glass screen, where the stink of chemicals was less pungent. He opened a sealed bottle that stood on his desk.

"You'll not say no to a large prussic acid, I take it?"

The two men assented and Ryan hastily averted his eyes from a bloody-aproned assistant who was dissecting a corpse on a marble slab, glimpsed through the half-open office door.

"There you have me," he said, answering the doctor's last question, that seemed to be still hovering in the chemically impregnated air.

"But it's a possibility, isn't it?"

Grady half-closed his eyes as he rested his cigar in the brass shell case that stood on a corner of the desk. He smacked his lips appreciatively at the first taste of the bourbon. Ellis held out his arms expansively again.

"But to what purpose?" he asked the ceiling. "After all, these were obscure people. Now, if it had been a society lady…"

"We shouldn't be here," said Ryan with a taut grin. "It would be handled higher up. It was just a thought."

They drank on in silence for a few minutes more and then Grady got up abruptly.

"No doubt you have far more important things to do, doc. Thanks for the drink." Ellis grunted and saw them to the door. The stench of chemicals again seemed to permeate their very clothing.

"Final reports tomorrow morning," the doctor said succinctly.

And he added, as they were hurrying away.

"Don't forget to tell the Chief."

"About what?" Ryan asked, with a puzzled look.

"About my technical virtuosity," Ellis said with a twisted grin and the light of an artist in his eyes. "The reconstruction of a corpse."

His mocking laughter followed them out.

That night Ryan awoke with a choking cry in the small hours, as though he were suffocating. He had had a similar dream to the others, but this time the naked woman and the cloaked figure were more distinct and vivid. The blond girl kept her face averted but the man with the red pin-points where his eyes should have been was more menacing than before if that were possible. The mist swirled about them and the unseen choir kept up its unearthly chant. Even within the dream Ryan was aware that such recurrent images were a comparative rarity. People did not dream the same dream night after night; it was true that they might do so on as many as two or even three occasions when some problem in particular was worrying them but apart from the current cases that he and Grady were investigating, there was nothing in his private life to worry him.

This time things were more serious. Ellie had been awakened by his strangled utterances and when the room was bright with light he was shocked to find he was weltering in his own blood. What was worse, Ellie's own night clothing was stained from his emissions. There was horror in her eyes and as she drew her arm across her face it too came away scarlet where he must have brushed against her in the frenzy of his dream. He felt feeble and his head was splitting as though the mist in the dream had some acrid reality. He gagged once or twice as Ellie held the rim of the brandy bottle to his lips and then he was himself again.

"My God! My God!," he repeated over and over again. "What the hell is happening to me?"

Ellie had her dressing gown on now and cradled his head in her arms, sponging away the blood from his mouth and neck with a damp cloth. He had opened his eyes again and was arrested by the startled look in her own.

"You seem to have cut yourself somehow in your sleep."

She pulled back the stained sheets.

"How on earth did that get there?"

Fear again clouded Ryan's mind as he found his open cutthroat razor lying beneath him in the tumbled mass of bedding. Its blade was all stained with his own blood. Tremblingly, he felt his neck. He could not fathom how the razor had got there unless he had absent-mindedly cast it into the bed when he had tumbled in the previous night. It was true he had been dog-tired but normally he would never have been so forgetful. Was he losing his sanity? Or were these terrible dreams eroding his nerves and causing him to do strange things? He could in fact, have rolled over on to it in his sleep, if the blade had been uppermost. Ellie was crying now and he hastened to take her in his arms and soothe her, taking care that the bleeding had stopped.

When she was calmer she asked, "Should you not see a doctor?"

He shook his head, trying hard to keep his voice steady.

"I went yesterday. Dr. Mandel found nothing wrong with me. Just a slight anaemia and overwork is what he said."

Ellie shook her head.

"All the same there is something badly wrong. You really need a good rest."

Ryan felt calmer now.

"It will be better once we find this Munson creature. Then the pressures will ease a little."

Ellie pouted. She looked ravishing kneeling on the bed at his side, her face flushed with emotion. He was conscious too of the great concern in her eyes.

"Sometimes I wish you had found some other line of work…" she began.

He put his hand gently across her mouth.

"We've been all through that, darling."

She signed deeply.

"That's true. Just wait until I change the bedding and we must get back to sleep. We'll discuss this further tomorrow."

But when things had been set to rights Ryan lay awake for the rest of the night, his thoughts painfully twisting and turning. He did not know what was happening to him. Perhaps the horrors of the Munson case were really beginning to get to him. Normally his nerves were like Grady's; unshakable and he had seen some other things almost as horrific which had left him comparatively unmoved. He and Ellie ate their breakfast that morning in a unique and foreboding silence.

- 6 -

"Are you awake?"

Ryan came to with a start. There were a dozen surprised and disapproving faces round the big table. The Chief's face beneath the frosted hair was stern and condemnatory as he stared down from the end of the room.

"This is a most important meeting and everyone here must know exactly what he has to do."

"I am sorry, Chief," Ryan said, concentrating with an effort. "The truth is, I haven't been sleeping at all well lately."

"You are not alone there," the big man replied, the acid still in his voice. "Now I want everyone's utmost attention and I require you to study and absorb every detail of the diagram on the blackboard before you leave the office. It gives the disposition of every man and all the other forces at our disposal."

Ryan again felt himself sinking into lethargy, fought against it with every fiber of his being. He was conscious that Grady was staring at him curiously, though everyone else was concentrating on the Chief's exposition.

"This is the first occasion on which a French Prime Minister has honored our city with his presence, and we must be fully alert and extremely conscious of our responsibilities. Particularly in view of some recent developments. Violence is not exactly rare in our profession, unfortunately, but there are signs that it is intensifying following the national crisis we have recently passed through."

As he went on Ryan was increasingly aware that he was rapidly losing attention. He again wondered what was happening to him. There was an insidious lethargy invading his limbs and his brain and he dug the fingernails of his right hand into his left wrist below the level of the table, so that he drew blood. But his action overcame the condition temporarily and he followed with increasing interest the diagrams on the board and the sheets of notations that were passed round the table. Ryan had his own notebook out now and was jotting down salient points as the discussion continued. The Prime Minister's visit was not for another two days but Ryan resolved to liaise with Grady and walk some of the routes involved.

All the men in the room that morning would be armed when the day arrived and Ryan's own viewpoint was on the top of a large warehouse that overlooked the route that the important visitor and the city dignitaries would take. Ryan had a powerful pair of field glasses in a locked bureau at his home and he resolved to take those also. When the conference was over and some of those present had dispersed to their various duties, Ryan sought out the Chief to apologize for his earlier inattention. The sternness of the big man's face relaxed somewhat as he listened to his subordinates explanation and at the end he gave the other man a gentle smile.

"I understand," he said. "We are all under strain."

He sat down at his desk glancing across at Grady, who had been joined by Sanders and Costello and the three were now standing in a semi-circle listening to the conversation.

"The truth is, gentlemen, we could do with another fifty officers in this division, as you probably know. But the City budget will not stand it and we must do the best we can with the tools at our disposal. I take it you have all seen the notice-board in the foyer of the Bureau. If anyone wishes to report sick now is the time to do it."

He glanced round interrogatively at each man in turn. No one spoke.

"Very well then, gentlemen. That is all for the moment."

He turned back to the littered surface of his desk as the four men filed out.

"I was watching you," Grady said sotto voce as they made their way back to their own desks. "You don't look well to me. Why don't you report sick if that is the case? There's no disgrace involved."

Ryan shook his head.

"It's nothing," he lied. "Just a temporary upset."

Grady sat down and paused while he lit the stump of a cigar.

"No trouble between you and Ellie, I hope?"

Ryan shook his head, a smile lighting up his haggard features.

"Not at all, I'm glad to say. I'm out of sorts, that's all. I've seen my own doctor and he's prescribed me some pills."

Grady swiveled back in his chair.

"That's all right, then. We'd better do our own check on this State visit. As you heard I'm to be two floors below you in the warehouse. We'd better work out some signal in case of trouble."

"Sure."

Ryan pulled his own chair over to Grady's desk and the two men sat taking notes and making route sketches. They arranged that Ryan would let down a slate on a line to Grady's window position with a chalked message if it became necessary. It was a crude and primitive method but an immensely practical one, as Ryan would have a more commanding viewpoint, while Grady would have a clearer picture of the details of the procession and crowd movements. Both would carry sticks of chalk and it would take only a few seconds for Ryan to receive an answering message by hauling the slate back up.

These matters settled the two men took lunch at a nearby café and later separated on various inquiries the Department had in hand. Toward dusk Ryan had finished up and returned home. Again, Ellie was visiting friends and relatives, and he had the house to himself. But the shadows were long tonight and the rooms seemed dark and oppressive. A nameless fear hovered at the back of his mind, as though something momentous was about to happen, so he poked up the fire and ate the meal Ellie had left for him. Afterward, he spent some time in cleaning and oiling his revolver and put two boxes of cartridges in his overcoat pockets to take to the Bureau the following morning.

The sonorous beat of the massive grandfather clock on the upstairs landing seemed somehow menacing this evening. He sat by the fire and checked his watch for the third or fourth time. It was eleven o'clock. Ellie was late coming back again. Finally, he could stand the monotonous sound of the clock no longer and mounted swiftly to the upper floor and stopped the pendulum. The silence flooded in, as significant as the sound had been, and with it again came the fear that had no visible source.

Then there came a metallic click as thought something had broken within the clock case and he realized he was not alone. Something white and glimmering in the shadows of the landing. His heart rose to suffocate him and its beating was so dull and heavy it seemed as thought it must burst within his chest. A sweet voice calling; a distant choir; and thin mist; the shimmering whiteness advanced toward him and he saw, as though in the grip of paralysis, the nude woman of his recurring dream. She made lascivious gestures as she glided toward him, but still he could not see her face. Then she had passed

156

him, his limbs were loosened and he followed her submissively as she beckoned him onward.

Incapable of resistance, his passage was as insubstantial and trance-like as when he was in deep sleep. At last, by what means he could not fathom, they reached the confines of a dark wood. Here the alabaster form of the woman paused, and then darted aside. Apart from the shock of hair, Ryan could still see no details of the face, except once, when a smile glittered in the darkness as she backed slowly toward what looked like a long, low manger or trough, hewn of rough stone. Then Ryan truly felt fear as an odious, cloaked figure appeared from the crackling branches that fringed the dank clearing. Ryan kept his eyes fixed upon the ground but inexorably he felt his will being eroded by the power of the foul thing that confronted him.

The two eyes, like red-hot pokers, that were all that was visible beneath the broad-brimmed hat, transfixed him like a lightning bolt. Words of foulness came from the shrouded figure, instructions so vile that Ryan summoned all his powers of resistance. The naked woman moved closer to the cloaked figure and whispered something to him that Ryan could not catch. As the creature stooped to listen to her, his cloak fell aside and he too was naked; the two indulged in a grotesque, carnal embrace and then, just as the figure moved as though to glide toward him, a distant church clock struck and the vision faded, the power that held the police officer in thrall waning.

There came the sudden clicking noise and Ryan, to his incredulous relief, found himself back on the landing of his own house, drenched in perspiration, his limbs heavy, his heart weary beyond belief. He must have re-started the clock because its sonorous ticking was still resounding in his ears. Fingers of the strengthening day crept palely through a far window and he saw with incredulity that it was past five a.m., though only a few seconds appeared to have passed since he first saw the vision. The woman was not there now, to his immense relief.

But as he moved back to the bedroom he found that he was in his night clothing and it was drenched in moisture. He put his hand up to his throat and his fingers came away scarlet. As his sanity reeled he glanced down in the strengthening light and saw that his feet were bare, all streaked with blood and mud. Barely conscious he dragged himself down to the kitchen, stripped naked and washed himself in soap and cold water, hardly knowing what he was doing. Somehow, he found a towel and dried himself.

Fortunately, the blood was no longer flowing. He put on an old shirt and

157

trousers from the laundry basket and carefully washed every trace of blood and mud from his night clothing. Then he put it at the bottom of the heap in the basket where, hopefully it would eventually dry, divesting himself of shirt and trousers and crept quietly upstairs. Ellie was sleeping deeply on her side of the bed. He quickly dressed and crept downstairs again, sleeping fitfully for an hour or so in his big armchair, waking in starts, his teeth chattering with abject fear. Only the cool butt of his revolver beneath his trembling hand brought him some semblance of reassurance. His nerves were somewhat calmer and he was again outwardly normal, making breakfast in an atmosphere of bird song and sunlight when Ellie eventually came downstairs to join him. Only his clenched teeth and monosyllabic conversation betrayed his inner tension.

- 7 -

"You all know what you have to do!"

The Chief's voice was harsh and staccato above the distant rumble of traffic.

"Unfortunately, we have five hours before the procession arrives so don't let your minds wander or your vigilance relax. It may be that someone in the crowds already gathering has an evil intent. If you see anything suspicious arrest that person, male or female, black or white, and use the threat of armed force if necessary."

The Chief looked round, his jaw squared, his eyes blazing. Ryan had never seen him in such a formidable mood.

"I don't care if we have a lawsuit on our hands. I'd rather have that than anything go wrong today."

There was a murmur of assent from the assembled officers and then a great rush for the stairs. The Chief had been right. The broad boulevards were already thronged with hordes of people that would swell to thousands by the time the procession arrived. Grady was quiet as they shouldered their way through. They gave up trying to find a public conveyance in the end and decided to walk downtown to take up position. As the Chief had said, there was plenty of time.

It was a fine, dry sunny morning in early November, with an icy edge beneath it; conditions which normally would have filled Ryan with pleasure. But the events of the past fortnight had shaken him to the very foundation of his being and he was aware that Grady was only too conscious of it.

"Did you bring the slate?" he asked in as light a tone as possible, more for conversation's sake than anything else.

Grady patted the capacious canvas satchel he carried at his side. It contained a flask of coffee, sandwiches, his revolver and shells, and other material, which included the item his companion had just mentioned. He also had a lethal-looking hunting knife in a sheath at his belt and another revolver in an inside pocket. Grady was a man who did not believe in leaving anything to chance.

Tactfully, he made no mention of Ryan's haggard appearance; he knew there was something troubling his partner but he also knew that he could rely on him to the death if necessary. Now he grunted disgustedly, shouldering his way through the press with quick, decisive steps.

"I'd better come topside with you before we settle down. And you can survey things from my window lower down. That way we'll know both viewpoints."

On arrival at their post at the warehouse, to which they had been given keys, the two men plodded up a rusty internal iron staircase, which gave creakingly under their weight, and with every passing moment Ryan's depression grew. Eventually, they forced open a metal door, which gave with a shriek that set Ryan's teeth on edge. They were on a flat roof which jutted out from the main building and which had a fine view of the broad avenue beyond, with the narrow street beneath, which the procession must traverse. There was still three hours to go but already the sidewalks were thick with people, lining the route four deep. The sun, momentarily behind a cloud, then re-emerged, brushing the distant scene with gold and striking sparks of fire from the wavelets in the broad, sluggishly flowing river that bisected the horizon.

"Well, you got the better part of the deal," Grady said in a disgusted tone.

The two had already inspected his dusty cubbyhole two floors below, but as the Chief pointed out Grady would be able to discern far more detail on the sidewalks than Ryan in his more elevated position. The officers dragged out a couple of small empty beer barrels from the debris in the warehouse corridor and settled down to moodily munch the first of their sandwiches.

"Yes, but it will take far longer to get down to the ground floor," Ryan said at length, taking up the conversation where they had left off earlier.

Grady shrugged, reaching for an unsmoked cigar which lay on the parapet at this elbow, along with his flask and the packet of sandwiches.

"The Army boys will take care of things," he said. "They'll be lining the route, though why the procession wants to come this way beats me. This thoroughfare is far too narrow."

"But it would be easier to pick off any possible assassin down there," Ryan replied, shading his eyes with his hand as he gazed down over the parapet.

"Unless he throws a bomb," said Grady gloomily.

The two men exchanged bleak smiles. Presently, Grady went below to take up his post, "in case the Chief comes by," and Ryan let down the slate on a long cord; when they practiced for half an hour or so they found that they could transmit messages by this system in just over thirty seconds. Ryan then tied the end of the cord round an iron stanchion that jutted from the parapet, which meant that the slate more or less finished up on the window sill of the room occupied by Grady. He laid his revolver on top of the barrel vacated by his colleague and gave himself up to some serious thinking.

As he did so a tremendous melancholy swept over him. Dark shadows seemed to be enveloping his marriage; his career in the police; and even in his personal relationships with various people. So intense were these feelings that he could almost imagine that the horrific vision of the man in the broad-brimmed hat would appear to him at the dizzying height he now occupied and he looked up startled, as a shadow swept across his face. But it was only the flight of a bird and when the sun again passed behind a cloud a few moments later, it merely re-emphasized the darkness in which he felt himself to be surrounded.

For though his earlier experiences were easy to pass off as dreams, the grim reality of the blood from his neck and his lacerated feet could not be explained away by any normal criteria. He was still sitting there, as though in a trance, when a sudden urgent jerk on the cord from below returned him to reality. Swiftly, he hauled up the slate. The message read; PROCESSION APPROACHING FROM THE WEST. He quickly rubbed it out and chalked his own response before lowering the slate back to his colleague. He had his field-glasses out now and soon located the slowly crawling column, it looked like black ants at that distance but presently resolved itself into a marching band, soldiers and horses and then the leading carriages containing the dignitaries.

160

Now his main purpose, as that of Grady below, was to sweep the crowds immediately below him for any suspicious circumstances. The martial tunes rose up in waves and so insidious and nostalgic was the music that Ryan was hard put to preserve in his mind the main reason he was there. But he did his best to ignore the stirring tempo of the band and raked the crowds below with his glasses. But he soon found that his lenses were so powerful that the close-up views were so near and out of focus that the exercise defeated its own purpose and he soon returned the instrument to the leather case round his neck, finishing off his sandwiches as he surveyed the ground, now near, now far, with the naked eye.

Even so, the swirling patterns of humanity that shifted and swayed so far below him made close scrutiny difficult and he guessed that Grady down below was having the same problems. The procession was now only some hundred yards off and Ryan noticed a particular pattern in the crowd to his left. The music rose in great waves and he sensed rather than saw, by the position of his colleague's head at the open window below, that he too had been arrested by the rippling motion among the great broken mass of humanity.

The band, the military outriders and the militia were now directly beneath him and an open carriage was sliding into view when there were screams and loud shouting from the crowds, which broke up in disorder immediately below him, penetrating the thin screen of sentries and spilling across into the ranks of the military band. The officer next heard three or four shots ring out and the screaming redoubled. He could already hear Grady's feet pounding on the iron rungs of the staircase below and he lost no time in following. With sobbing breath and strained lungs he at last reached ground level and had no difficulty in breasting the thinning crowd, which had broken ranks and was streaming away into the side streets.

The stern face of Grady, his badge and the drawn revolver had already cleaved a path through to the area of the procession's head and like a small vessel in the wake of a much larger one, Ryan was able to keep a yard or two behind Grady's burly form which, arms tucked into sides, was going at a great rate to where a crowd of military and civilians had concentrated in thick knots up ahead. Ryan spared a moment to look back to find that the procession had now diverted from its original route and had passed up a parallel street headed by what appeared to be another band keeping up the same martial air.

But he had no time to see anything more for a few seconds later he came up against a dense ring of soldiers holding rifles at the ready, bayonets fixed and shining in the weak sunlight. Grady's credentials had already secured his entry and Ryan swiftly followed to find a strange scene unfolding itself. The leading carriage had stopped and civilians in formal clothing mingled with excited bandsmen, Army officers and detectives. Ryan was startled to see the Chief there, the light of triumph in his eyes. There was blood on the ground, Ryan now saw and a patrol wagon was going away swiftly in the opposite direction to that taken by the main part of the procession.

"What's going on?" Ryan asked Grady.

The latter shook his head.

"Some scheme of the Chief's. Successful apparently, judging by the look on his face."

An excited officer came up then, waving a sheaf of documents. He crossed to the Chief and the two men conferred. The big man spotted Ryan and Grady at that point and beckoned them over.

"I expect you're wondering what all this is about. We got Munson, that's what! Costello wounded him in the leg. He had a big knife and was obviously going for the French Prime Minister!"

"He wasn't hurt?" Grady asked.

The Chief laughed.

"He wasn't here! I had a duplicate carriage full of our men disguised as the official party, to head the procession. I thought something like this might happen and my supposition paid off. We were ready for him this time, and I've temporarily muzzled the press. The Prime Minister won't know anything about this, because I had the procession diverted half a mile back. He probably thought those shots were fireworks!"

Ryan could not suppress his admiration.

"Then the case is solved."

The Chief nodded.

"Principally because I told no one about this. Then our officers in the leading carriage thought it a routine precaution. I even had a duplicate band to head up this section. One cannot be too careful. We live in dangerous times."

He glanced round at the tangled group of soldiers and officials surrounding him.

"Ryan, Grady, Costello and Sanders come with me. The rest of you rejoin the main procession and carry out your detailed orders."

The mad eyes stared vacantly from hollow sockets and a thin trail of spittle ran down the stubbled chin. The man Munson sat slumped in a padded chair in the Chief's office, his bandaged right leg resting on a stool before him, seemingly oblivious of the barrage of questions that had been hurled at him during the last hour. The Chief's face was grim as he towered over the group of officers who sat or stood in a semi-circle round the captive, whose hands were manacled in front of him.

"Undoubtedly mad," the Chief said through clenched teeth, for the third or fourth time since the cross-examination had begun. "I don't really know why we're wasting our time."

"There is a point, Chief," put in Sanders, a thin, sallow man, who seldom spoke.

Encouraged by the look at his superior's eyes, he went on doggedly, "He may well be insane. Probably is. But how did he know of the importance of this State visit? He's been on the run since his wife's murder and living rough by the look of him."

"Just exactly what are you getting at?"

The Chief's face was barely visible through the thick haze of tobacco smoke in the room but there was no doubt of his interest.

"There may be a purpose in all this which we haven't yet discovered," Sanders went on. The Chief shrugged.

"You might have something. But I've had enough for today. I'm off for some supper. You four take over. You know where to find me if he cracks."

The room slowly emptied as Grady went on with the questioning, Sanders, Costello and Ryan taking over vacated chairs and gathering in a close circle round the wounded man, who glared in front of him like a wild beast. The cigarette smoke slowly cleared and Ryan started on his second cup of coffee. They had offered some to the prisoner but he had dashed the mug to the floor with such fury that the attempt had not been repeated. The belief that the man's insanity was not simulated had been gaining strength in Ryan's mind ever since the interrogation had begun.

No one but a madman would have carried the murder weapon around with him for days, for the blood-stained axe had been discovered thrown on a vacant lot at the rear of the warehouse, when a massive police search had been carried out following Munson's aborted attack on the supposed visiting

Prime Minister. He had been carrying a huge woodsman's knife and two other murderous weapons had been discovered in a leather pouch on his person. These were workman's gimlets, their deadly points sunk into corks, which could have been purchased at any hardware store. Innocent enough when carried by a workman but such tools would have pierced a victim to the heart in two seconds when death would have been instantaneous.

No doubt Munson had felt, in his twisted brain, that these would have been ineffective among such a dense crowd that surrounded the processional carriages. But Sanders' remarks earlier had taken root in Ryan's own mind and had strengthened his feelings about the murder of Munson's wife and the weird circumstances surrounding the man and his mental state. The darkness that had clouded Ryan's life of recent weeks had lifted and he was now professionally absorbed in a case that would have made no sense at all to a layman. Not that the professional investigators were doing much better at the moment, Ryan thought wryly. He stared intently at the man slumped in the chair before them, steadfastly ignoring Grady's relentless questioning. Not a flicker of emotion passed across his white features and he seemed oblivious to the intense pain the bullet wound in his leg must have been causing him.

Ryan took in the sunken eyes; the emaciated form; the stooped shoulders and the almost degenerate features and marveled that the man had been able to wield the enormous axe with such force as to sever his wife's head from her body. Or why such an attractive woman had married such a man, come to that. He wished too that Dr. Ellis had been there to give his valued advice but he understood that the doctor was currently out of town on some family business. Now he switched abruptly back to the present as Munson commenced to sing some obscure ballad in a high-pitched voice. Or rather to utter gibberish to a well-defined tune for the officers in the room could not make out any words or phrases that made sense.

Then Ryan's mind began to cloud over and horror seeped into his brain for the sounds the madman was making were similar to the devilish chanting he had several times heard in the dreams that had so troubled him. Grady, of course, was unaware of these implications and made a noise indicating disgust as he proceeded to light on of his inevitable cigars. He cleared his throat and turned to Ryan.

"Better if Costello had shot him through the head. It would have saved the State a lot of time, money and trouble. I doubt if he'll ever come to trial. Unless he's the best actor in the world."

He looked at Ryan sharply.

"Are you all right? You look very pale."

His colleague shook his head impatiently.

"It's nothing. I haven't been sleeping very well lately, that's all. And to be honest, this creature disgusts me."

Grady had an ironic smile on his face now, as he puffed contentedly at his cigar.

"That's not a professional attitude. You've seen worse criminals than this one."

Ryan mumbled some banality. Grady was right, of course. He had seen far worse. But coming on top of the axe murder; the terrible dreams he had been having; and then the capture of this homicidal maniac, who had obviously intended to murder the French Prime Minister, it was all too much. His legs suddenly turned to water and he buried his face in his hands. Grady was at his side in an instant, held a flask of whisky to Ryan's lips.

"Drink this, old chap. It will bring you round."

The homely words had an instant effect. Ryan took two deep gulps and was himself again.

"Sorry about that. It's just that this case is beginning to affect me."

"Time you took some leave," Grady said sympathetically, putting the stopper back in the flask and screwing it home.

"Later," Ryan said.

He stared across at Munson, who was moaning something brokenly in a language neither man could understand. Despite his leg wound, he started writhing about. Just at that moment footsteps sounded in the corridor outside. The officers turned as the door commenced to open but were transfixed by the behavior of their prisoner. With an amazing burst of energy he rose to his feet, ignoring the pain of his wound and, as though he heard an inner voice, hissed, "I hear, Master! I obey! I come!"

Then he screamed something in a guttural voice the men in the room could not make out and before anyone could move had dived across the office. He went crashing through the plate-glass window and fell like a stone to the sidewalk eight stories below.

The Chief cursed and blundered into his subordinates as they all rushed to the window to stare bitterly at the turmoil below. Beneath the pallid glare of the street lights Munson lay, his skull smashed like a rotten apple as passers by gathered round like flies on a wound. Black blood ran from his shattered corpse as ink is absorbed by blotting paper. Ryan turned away, sick at heart. All four men muttered their apologies. The Chief patted each man's shoulders in a rare and strange gesture of tenderness.

"It could not be helped," he said. "I saw what happened. There is something extraordinary here. Something beyond normal comprehension."

He stared down grimly at the milling mass of people below.

"It has saved the hangman a rope, at any rate. Or forty years in a lunatic asylum."

He turned back from the shattered window, oblivious of the staring faces of the police officers at the door.

"You'd better all get on home," he said. "We'll work out the reports tomorrow. There is nothing more to be done here tonight."

Later, in a smoke-filled restaurant two blocks away, as they finished their meal, Ryan and Grady broke the doom-laden silence between them.

"Did you hear what he said just before he went over?" Ryan asked.

Grady nodded.

"It's beyond my experience."

Ryan leaned forward across the table.

"It was as though he had just received some orders from a supernatural source," he said in a trembling voice.

Grady stared at him, disbelief in his eyes.

"I'll pretend I didn't hear that. We're police officers. We have to go by the facts."

Ryan shook his head.

"It won't go in the reports. This is between ourselves."

Grady lit another of his cigars.

"I'm listening."

"He intended to kill the Prime Minister. Right? So maybe he was acting under orders. The murder of his wife was absolutely pointless. It goes against the grain of the man's entire history. But suppose the death of this unfortunate woman was to establish a pattern, as it were? A smaller crime, however horrific, to conceal a greater, the murder of the Prime Minister. Something utterly evil and entirely outside our experience is behind this business. The man was a tool of outside force and nothing more."

166

The two men stared at one another without speaking for what seemed like ages.

- 9 -

Winter set in early that year, with flurries of snow and heavy rainfall. Ryan trudged the broad boulevards with a heart as heavy as the lowering skies, though the cases he and Grady had to deal with engaged his professional attention most of the time and prevented too much introspection. He and his colleague had often discussed the Munson case together with Sanders and Costello; Ryan had kept his innermost thoughts to himself, of course, but the other police officers who had knowledge of the affair, were equally in the dark as to the motives that had impelled the terrible crime; the attempt on the life of the French Prime Minister and the subsequent suicide.

Only Grady and Ryan had heard the murder's last words and they had not spoken of them to anyone, not even their own wives. To Ryan's immense relief there had been no repetition of the terrible dreams from which he had suffered so badly, and as the week went by with no sign of any recurrence he began to breathe more easily. But he could not get over the fact that the physical aspects of his experiences could not be explained away except by sleep-walking, and that had never happened to him in his whole life.

He could not reconcile his waking visions of the nude woman and the foul creature in the cloak and wide-brimmed hat; nor his lacerated and mud-stained feet, especially as there had been no other physical sign of his having been outdoors. For, surely, in that condition he would have left traces of mud and blood in the hall and living room to say nothing of the stairs. But there had been no signs whatever though when Ryan had cleaned himself the towel he had used was soaked with blood and grime. As to the marks on his throat they had never properly healed and on occasion, for no apparent reason, they had begun to suppurate. It put him in mind of religious articles he had read concerning the appearance of stigmata on victims' hands and feet, if the parallel were not too blasphemous.

But even the most sensational or horrific incidents tend to fade from the human mind with the passing of time and so it was with Ryan. He had taken a few days' leave at Christmas and he and Ellie had been to stay for a much delayed visit to Ryan's aged parents, whom he had not seen for almost a year. The visit had been a great success and he and Ellie had behaved as though they were in the first days of their marriage. This had pleased the old people greatly, to see their son and daughter-in-law so carefree, and when the visit came to an end the parents had promised to visit them in the city the following May.

Back in the Bureau Ryan found things much the same, except that the number of crimes waiting to be dealt with seemed to have increased two-fold. Grady and his other colleagues had soon apprised him of the incidents involved and the right and wrongs of the department's policies. As the first weeks of January came and receded Ryan again found himself beset by gloomy thoughts. It began with small things as usually happens; trivial incidents that are often the harbingers of darker and more sinister events to come. So it was with Ryan and the fears lurking at the back of his mind were now slowly advancing from the shadows to engulf him. Or so it seemed and he wondered more than once whether his mental state might not be to blame. After all, so many years of witnessing the more horrific side of human nature could not fail to have a cumulative effect, and the repetition of hideous crimes and the terrible scenes that often greeted him and Grady when they were called out on cases, usually involving homicide, had begun to erode his once calm and steady nerves.

The dreams that had originally beset him started to return, but fortunately for his sanity, not in such a horrific form. These were but pale shadows of the former horrors but they served to disturb his sleep; torture his waking hours; and were a constant reminder that his mental state had not yet returned to normal. It began with mist and shadow during the dark days of winter; the former in reality, though the lowering weather had already begun to colour and distort his thoughts. Then the darkness and somberness returned inside his head. Ellie was worried; Ryan could see that, but she said little, though occasionally he intercepted a worried glance over the supper table and when he uttered some banality to distract her, she would bite her lip and turn away.

Then the dreams took an even more distorted tone and the twisted landscape in which Ryan found himself when in the vale of sleep, began to be interspersed with whispers. It were as though, hidden behind a gnarled tree trunk, he overheard a sinister conversation between a man and a woman. And gradually, through night after night of such morbid visions, he started to discern coherent passages. Presently they resolved themselves into a vivid phrase which, through gradual repetition, drummed itself into the sleeper's waking consciousness. And the words were these: "Remember, he must be fit and well for the great day." Just that and no more he was able to make out from the insistent mumblings which invaded his subconscious and persisted during his waking hours.

Ryan felt like a walking shell and one evening, after a particularly stressful day investigating criminal activity, he felt he must again consult his doctor. But he had one more call to make before his duties ended and this involved Dr. Ellis. He was on duty at the Morgue, as he often was, and Ryan made his way there, through echoing side-streets, whose shadowy corners still bore traces of the recent snow. The doctor was in his office though two of his assistants were working among the shrouded corpses up at the far end of the big room. Ryan had brought one of his official reports with him for Ellis' files and the doctor wrinkled up his eyes as he scrutinized it.

"Ties up exactly with what our examination revealed. This woman was stripped and raped but somewhere she had secreted a six-inch steel hat pin. Though her hands were bound, during the night she managed to get hold of it and stabbed the bastard through the heart."

"Served him right," Ryan grunted. "No doubt she'll draw a light sentence."

"No doubt."

"But look here. I have something to interest you."

He led the way among the slabs with their sheeted tenants to the far corner where a yellow lamp cast its pulsating light down on the silent occupant of the table. Ellis adopted his lecturing mode, putting his right hand up to the lapel of his stained white jacket as though addressing a class of students.

"Now hear this. Here's a man of my own profession. He is due to leave for his vacation. He lives alone and he is not due back for his professional duties for three weeks. So no one misses him. He is not married and has no close relatives. His nurse and other professional colleagues do not raise any alarm until a month has passed. Now you're the detective. What do you deduce from that?"

Ryan adopted his own professional manner.

"Fairly simple, doctor. Like most medical men he is careless about his own physical condition and his health in general. He is preparing for his holiday; maybe suffers a heart attack or a stroke and dies at home. Letters pile up on the mat but everyone expects him to be away."

Ellis grinned.

"Well done. Correct up to a point. But now look at this."

"He whipped the sheet back with one of his theatrical flourishes. Ryan

169

was shaken to the core. Despite the physical deterioration and the work of decomposition that had taken place, he had never seen such an emaciated and grotesque parody of a man that lay there, with its waxen, shrunken features and caved-in chest through which the ribs showed like so many barrel staves. The face seemed vaguely familiar but persons were so changed by death that sometimes even their nearest relatives did not recognize them as Ryan had noted on more than one occasion.

"I fail to see..." he began, when the doctor held up his hand to stop him.

"I haven't finished yet. A case unique in my opinion. Death within two to three weeks before discovery. But mark this, my friend. The body absolutely drained of blood. Hardly a spoonful left. Punctures on the neck as though made by fangs. What human agency would be responsible for that, eh?"

He chuckled as he gazed down at the corpse.

"If we weren't living in the modern age I'd say this was a classic case of vampirism."

"Vampirism?"

Ryan was bewildered.

"What's that?"

Ellis made a clicking noise with his teeth.

"You really should read up on these esoteric subjects. They might come in useful in your profession. Especially in the present circumstances as I'm having to report this to your Chief as undoubtedly a case of murder. Vampirism, my boy. Mythical creatures that went on living for hundreds of years by feeding on the blood of the living!"

He chuckled again.

"Known since Roman times and often mentioned as the stuff of legend. Creatures supposedly unable to walk the earth in daylight. Traditionally they could only be killed by having a wooden stake driven through their hearts. All rubbish, of course."

The doctor's eyes narrowed.

"But nevertheless here we have a classic case of a victim of one such creature, though the thing is medically impossible. I may say that there was no trace of blood anywhere in the house. The corpse was slumped in a chair, his veins completely emptied by some blood-sucking apparition."

He raised his hand in mock horror.

"Bless my soul, Ryan, you aren't a victim too, I hope? I see by that bandage on your throat…"

The laugh died at the anguish on Ryan's face. The officer took one step forward, put a trembling hand to his eyes.

"But it can't be! I was on my to see him after I leave you!"

He had just recognised in the hideous caricature of a human being before him, the wasted visage of Dr. Donald Mandel.

"For God's sake…" Ellis began when Ryan's legs buckled and he fell in a dead faint on the mortuary floor.

- 10 -

Ryan was away from his duties for a week. When he came to himself again he saw Ellie's concerned features hovering over him. She nursed him tenderly through the fever. From what she let drop Ryan guessed that Ellis had been tactful. He had mentioned nothing to her about Mandel and when Grady came in to see him the following week, he was more himself again, though the horror of Mandel's death and the circumstances surrounding it lingered. Grady had told him that Ellis said the chemicals used in the dissecting room had overcome him and this, combined with the recent strains he had undergone in investigating various cases, had reached on his nervous system. As though by tacit consent neither the doctor nor Grady went into any further details, though Ellie's concern was evident.

But she kept her own counsel and Ryan resumed his duties at the Bureau in the second week in February, with the cloud partly lifted. He had no more dreams, he thanked God, but he could not erase from his mind the insidious whispers and their import, "Remember, he must be fit and well for the great day." Surely it could not have referred to Dr. Mandel's dissolution; in any case it did not make sense. Some form of premonition, perhaps? He hoped not. He would not be able to carry out any of his duties at the Bureau if things went on as they were.

Dr. Ellis' jocular remarks about vampirism had set him thinking; the doctor himself had laughed at such primitive superstition but how could such a healthy and vital man as Dr. Mandel have been drained of all blood when there was no evidence of any struggle or bleeding within the house? Ellis was still investigating possibilities but in his own heart Ryan did not think that he would ever get to the bottom of the matter. The autopsy had revealed that

Mandel had been a perfectly healthy and active man before the mysterious leaching of more than seven and a half pints of blood from his system.

If it had not been for Ellie's tender consideration of his health and sanity Ryan felt he could not have survived the winter this far. His blood had thinned to the point where he felt the bitter cold more keenly than ever , and he remembered poor Mandel's remarks about his anemia and finally rediscovered the box of pills he had prescribed, in his desk at the Bureau. He commenced the old routine of taking four a day but he had to confess that they did not seem to make much difference. But as the year advanced he recovered something of his old momentum and he could tell by Grady's more cheerful demeanor that his partner had noticed his slightly improved condition.

There had been one point in his illness where Ellie was about to send for his parents but Ryan had stopped her in time. He did not want them worried unnecessarily and there was little they could actually do to help. Ellie had stayed at home most of the time when he had been ill in bed and he could not have had a more conscientious nurse. Not that he would have expected anything less from her; she was a model wife and a wonderful companion and though his duties necessitated their spending a great deal of time apart, she fully understood what he had taken on when he joined the force and had loyally supported him throughout the ordeals through which he had passed.

The Chief, with his great understanding, had given him largely administrative duties the first week he had been back in the office, which had greatly eased the strain on his nerves and he had concentrated on paperwork and codifying the criminal records which had simplified the rather complicated procedures which had hitherto obtained and had speeded up the processing of reports, particularly for the identification of individual criminals. The Chief had asked him to let him know when he again felt confident enough to take up his normal duties and it was with this in view that Ryan had sought him out one bleak evening when the wind blustered round the building and rattled window frames and shutters.

A few days after he had resumed his normal routine, he was trudging home after all-night duty, when he suddenly saw the dome of the Capitol rising from the pallid mist, the first rays of the sun turning it to a pale rose as though it were some version of an Eastern temple and his heart was temporarily uplifted by the sight. The euphoria lasted him all the way home and after he had consumed the hot breakfast Ellie had prepared for him, he went upstairs and fell immediately into a dreamless sleep.

He was so far improved for several days that he began to believe that the dreadful shadow which had haunted him for so long had lifted forever. Yet he could not erase all the other terrible circumstances from his mind, and another fearful thought kept edging into his troubled brain; had he not been going to consult Mandel about his problems when the doctor had been conveniently found dead before Ryan could obtain the help he so desperately needed? He used the term ironically, for a dim perceived pattern was beginning to emerge, though he could not find the key. Whirling about in his inmost thoughts were the axe murder; the whole Munson affair; the French Prime Minister and the aborted attack; the mysterious command that only he and Grady had heard; the equally horrific suicide of the murderer; and the recurring repetition of the phrase that someone should be fit and well when the great day came. Could not that someone be himself?

For his brain was now working in an official capacity, and he realized only too well that the inexorable thrall in which he had been held was relaxing its grip. But for what purpose? And all that was to leave aside the insidious night attacks on his person; an unseen presence draining both his will and his vitality; apart from the terrible nightmares; and the physical manifestation which included the wounds on his throat; his nocturnal wanderings with the nude woman and the evil figure in the cloak; and the all too obvious lacerations to his legs which proved that he had physically ventured out at night over rough and muddy ground.

Paradoxically his health was now so robust that he was able to sift and evaluate all these jumbled thoughts without losing either his sanity or his courage. Every night he now slept with his loaded revolver under his pillow, more for effect than anything else; for he had little hope that the bullets would have any impression on the seeming supernatural phenomena that had so long held him in their grip. Obviously, he did not voice any of these thoughts to Ellie, but he started keeping a diary in a thick, leather-bound volume he found in a corner of his desk at the Bureau. In case anything happened to him it would give Grady and his colleagues some idea of what he had been up against. He imagined that the book had been left there by some predecessor who had never had occasion to use it.

This he resolved to utilize in order to keep a meticulous record of his thoughts and actions concerning the weird incidents in which he had become involved; there would be nothing regarding official police actions unless they had some bearing on the events he was describing. He kept to his decision and wrote up his notes during his all-night watches and soon had a dossier running to some fifty or sixty pages. Then one morning in mid-March, he opened the drawer and felt around in it. His fingers came out covered in light gray ash. There was no sign of the book and it was obvious that some hitherto unknown agency had been concerned for the volume had been completely consumed by fire without harming the rest of the drawer or its contents.

Then Ryan knew stark and utter fear; he realized that he was being watched in some unimaginable manner and that he had been picked out for some evil purpose of which he had no knowledge. Still he did not tell anyone of his thoughts and inmost fears, for he sensed that if he did so not only would he be in mortal danger but the person in whom he had confided also. In some obscure way, just as his energy had been drained from his body, so were his thoughts and movements being observed and analyzed by some elemental force.

He was extremely worried too, about Ellie, and contrived to send her away for a week or two with a cousin in the country. This meant that he was alone in the house when not on night-duty, which was the worst time; paradoxically, the presence of his loaded revolver beneath his pillow gave him strength and confidence, though he knew that it would have little or no effect against those dimly perceived powers gathering around him. But still his health improved and his dreams remained untroubled for a while. Ellie, on her return, noticed the change and responded to his more cheerful mood.

The dreariness of winter was now giving way to early signs of spring and the pace of life in the city began to quicken. There was more traffic on the streets and people were able to move about freely now that the snow had gone. But chill blasts from the river persisted and the fact that it was still too early to discard heavy clothing was brought home one afternoon when the wind carried with it small flurries of snow which lay about the streets until rain at nightfall washed it away.

It was toward the end of March when the Chief called Ryan into his office for a private conversation. His strong face beneath the thatch of iron-gray hair was more benevolent than his subordinate had noticed in recent weeks, and he held a dossier in his hands which Ryan saw bore his own name on the inked label. It was his record in the force, in fact, and Ryan waited with a heightened heartbeat as the Chief riffled through it. He put it down on his blotter eventually and made an inked notation on the last page. The he clasped his hands together in front of him and regarded Ryan steadily for what seemed like minutes.

"I've been keeping an eye on you during the last weeks," he said in a pleasant voice. "It seems to me you've shaken off whatever was troubling you. God knows, the Department gets enough lousy assignments that would send an ordinary member of the public off his head within a few days."

Ryan's faint smile echoed the Chief's own.

"I feel fine now, sir," he said, hoping his superior would not notice the faint trembling of his hands in his lap. Ryan observed that his superior looked white and ill himself. The strain of office, he supposed.

The Chief gave a bleak smile.

"I understand that Dr. Mandel had been a particular friend of yours for some years. I can imagine the shock of finding out the way he died must have pushed you over the edge for a bit."

Ryan nodded assent, hardly trusting himself to speak.

"Good," the Chief said crisply, as though finally disposing of the point. "I have a very important assignment for you and Grady. I am putting my complete trust in you both. Sanders and Costello will be your back-up on this occasion."

He took a large-scale folding map of the city from a drawer of his desk and spread it out while Ryan moved his chair round so that they could both study it in detail.

"You've read the papers recently, I take it? Good. Then you know what we're talking about?"

"Certainly sir. I have a few ideas about security I'd like to discuss with you."

The Chief shifted in his big swivel chair.

"Of course. That's what we're all here for. The assignment won't be going up on the board in the usual manner."

"Why is that, sir?"

A shadow passed across the big man's face.

"It all stems from that Munson business and the French Prime Minister. Nothing must go wrong on this occasion and I want to retain the utmost secrecy. There are too many people in and out of this building every day. The conferences will be held in this office behind locked doors and I want every man involved sworn to secrecy. That means wives, family and other relatives are to be told nothing. Understood?"

"Understood, sir."

"Good. Now let's get down to details."

Ryan spent another hour in the Chief's office and when he came out his step was lighter and his jaw set firmly. Many ideas were beginning to course through his mind. The night staff had come on duty but Grady was still at his desk, obviously awaiting his colleague's return. He raised his eyebrows interrogatively.

"The big assignment?"

Ryan sat down at his own desk and started putting papers away and locking the drawers.

"Yes. We're going up in the world, according to the Chief. What do you think?" Grady bit his lower lip.

"It's a big responsibility. But then we're used to that."

He stood up abruptly.

"We can't talk here. Let's drop in for a cup of coffee on the way home and chew over some ideas."

- 11 -

It was still reasonably early when Ryan arrived back at the house and Ellie was just about to prepare supper. She was delighted to see him home so soon and they exchanged their news of the day, though Ryan, mindful of the Chief's warning, was careful to say nothing of the important assignment that had been entrusted to him and Grady.

They ate supper in a harmonious silence, that was so different from Ryan's darkness and withdrawn gloom of the past months. It was as though they were back in the early years of their marriage and Ryan felt a great peace steal over him, temporarily easing the horrors of the Munson affair and that of the hideous dreams in which he had been involved.

Afterward, on sudden impulse, the pair went for a long walk through the moonlit streets, where the crisp air quickened the blood and refreshed the senses. As a fitting climax to the evening they shared a bottle of wine at a Viennese restaurant, where a three-piece orchestra played dreamy melodies and which kept open late several nights a week. The proprietor, who spoke English with a heavy accent, knew Ryan well from the years when both he and Ryan were bachelors, and they spent convivial evenings drinking and dining there.

After a discreet interval he joined them at their table and the three spent a nostalgic hour reminiscing about the past, the proprietor sending for one of his best bottles on the house. It was late when they finally left and dark clouds were obscuring the face of the moon as they made their way homeward. Only one slight incident marred the evening. That was when they turned a corner and Ryan, with a sudden start, thought he saw a familiar figure in the far distance. It was just a flickering image beneath a street lamp on the opposite sidewalk. A tall man with a dark cloak and a soft felt hat pulled down low over the eyes. Ryan came to an abrupt halt, with a muffled exclamation. Then he felt the cold steel of his revolver against his chest muscles; he now carried the weapon at all times and it was a tremendous reassurance. Ellie turned a startled face to him and her hand on his arm had a steadying influence.

"What on earth's the matter?"

"Someone's watching us," Ryan said in a low voice. He could not keep the slight tremor from his speech and the girl looked at him anxiously.

"Where?"

"Over there!"

Her eyes followed his and she gave a tinkling laugh that shattered the tension.

"Why, there's nothing there! It was just the shadows of the trees moving on the pavement. And your imagination."

She snuggled into him closely, still smiling. Ryan now saw that he had apparently been mistaken. The dancing shadows of the tree branches had momentarily composed themselves into the semblance of the dark figure that he dreaded. And the rustling of the leaves as they shifted in the breeze could have caused the sound associated with a cloak sweeping the ground. He gave a hollow laugh of relief and the two moved on. But all the way home Ryan could not resist the occasional glance over his shoulder. That Ellie knew this and yet made no comment only increased his uneasiness.

That night he dreamed another strange dream, but this time he felt no fear. He was walking along corridors lined with red plush. Invisible eyes were watching him but they seemed benevolent, urging him inexorably forward. A choir was singing sweetly as though from far away. He had his pistol with him in the dream but he knew there would be no violence or horror in the world into which he was entering. He laid it down on the cushions of a gold and ivory banquette in the corridor and went onward with a contented mind.

He was now aware that he was passing rows of plush seats and then there was a small door. As is the way of dreams he suddenly found himself on the other side of it. Steps covered by a worn carpet — stark contrast to the opulent scenes through which he had just passed — wound downward in a distorted spiral. Two red specks, like those of a smoked glass lantern were in front of him; he was in some sort of cellar, far underground, where a boiler blazed, giving out welcome warmth; soft golden light came from two hanging lanterns. A beautiful girl stood in front of him; she was completely nude and he rushed happily into her arms.

He awoke to find himself clasping the naked body of his wife; his joy was redoubled as they made passionate love, whispering fervent declarations in the blessed darkness of the night. Eventually, he fell into a soothing, dreamless sleep, until the pallid splinters of light, denoting the dawn, struggled feebly through the shutters.

- 12 -

"Now this is imperative! You have your orders! You all know what you have to do!"

The Chief's strained face, tired and tense, beneath the thatch of gray hair, looked grimly round the office, crowded with personnel from the Bureau's highest echelons. A murmur of assent ran through the ranks. Grady caught Ryan's eye and gave him a nod of approval.

The Chief consulted his watch.

"Unfortunately, as always seems to happen, we still have several hours before the plan comes into operation. But we must be in position long before then. I want another thorough search of the building and all entrances and exits must be sealed and guarded two hours before the opening. No one in or out without proper identification. Passes have been issued for this purpose, as you all understand."

The Chief looked interrogatively round the room.

"Has anyone any questions? Now's the time to ask because it will be too late when we get there."

Nobody spoke.

"You all have plans of the building, I take it?"

A general murmur of assent.

"That's good. I think that covers everything, gentlemen. If we carry out the agreed plans all should go smoothly tonight."

Later, Grady and Ryan sat at their desks in the outer office, oblivious of the turmoil about them. They drank mugs of strong coffee, knowing that they had no need to leave the Bureau for another hour. They avoided discussing the assignment in detail; perhaps Grady too, usually so unshakable, was a little overwhelmed at the importance of their task.

"I thought the Chief looked white and drawn," said Ryan, breaking a long silence. "Unusual for him."

"I figured that too," Grady said. "Not surprising, really, considering the load of responsibility he carries."

He shot his colleague a piercing glance.

"Come to think of it, you were remarkably like that some while back, when you were ill, remember?"

Ryan flinched visibly. He felt uncomfortable, remembering the dreadful days and nights that no one else, not even Ellie, was aware of.

"You're right," he admitted. "I was down. But I've put those days behind me now."

Grady lit another of his inevitable cigars and puffed out a cloud of fragrant blue smoke which slowly dispersed in the little eddies of air made by the constant traffic as officers passed to and fro.

"I was afraid the Chief was going to suspend you from active service at one time."

Ryan stared at him for a long moment.

"He consulted you about me?"

Grady gave him an affirmative nod.

"We did discuss it, yes. He knew we were good friends. I was sure you'd pull out of it."

Ryan flushed.

"You told him so?"

Grady looked embarrassed.

"Let's just say we came to an understanding."

"I'm grateful," Ryan said, and meant it. "Like you, the service is my whole life. At least, fifty per cent of it," he hastily corrected himself, seeing the thin smile of his companion's face.

179

"If I were married to Ellie, she would be seventy per cent of my whole life," Grady said.

This was extraordinary for him, Ryan thought.

"I understood you were happily married." Even as he spoke he was conscious of the spitefulness of his remark.

"So I am," Grady countered. "But I'd be willing to make an exception in Ellie's case."

Ryan decided to drop the matter, though he was secretly flattered, as he knew Grady wanted him to be.

The two rode downtown in an unbroken silence, as though the weight of their forthcoming assignment and its responsibilities, lay like a mantle on their shoulders. They were still several hours before time but the Chief had laid great stress on preparation and they were half expecting to see his massive form in front of the building when they arrived. But he was nowhere in evidence though Ryan noted with satisfaction that militia as well as civilian staff were manning all entrances and exits and they were required to show their official passes, even though they were in uniform.

Grady took up his position in the vestibule, at a small kiosk sheltered by potted palms, and Ryan was amused to see that he had brought with him not only a flask of coffee and sandwiches but a fresh pack of cigars with the seals still intact. Grady gave a sly grin as he noticed Ryan's expression.

"The Chief said nothing about home comforts. I look after myself. I take it you brought nothing?"

Ryan laughed shortly.

"True. But I expect I shall be able to find some refreshments before the night is over."

The building was humming with activity as he ascended the main staircase and made his way to his assigned position. Here and there colleagues greeted him with curt nods and once he caught a glimpse of the Chief's burly form as he hurried through a curtained doorway in the distance.

Ryan paused eventually in a long corridor which was dazzling with its red plush and gold decoration. Lines of wall lamps glittered and shimmered in the reflected light of tall mirrors. There was something familiar about the setting though he was unable to place it. However, he had little time for introspection as he suddenly found the Chief at his elbow, nodding with satisfaction.

"Glad to see you're well ahead of schedule, Ryan."

He ran sharp eyes over his subordinate.

"Better let me check your pistol."

Ryan handed it to him and watched while he broke it open and examined the contents of the chambers.

"I see you don't keep a round in the firing position. A wise precaution. I lost a good officer years ago, before your time. The barrel caught in his clothing and he shot himself in the thigh. Bled to death before help could get to him."

He laughed harshly.

"I can see that won't happen to you."

Ryan smiled thinly.

"I try and take care, Chief!"

The big man clapped him on the shoulder.

"That's good."

Then he was swinging down the corridor to confer with two men in civilian clothes who had just debouched from a side passage. Ryan sat down in an ornately carved chair and studied himself in one of the elaborately framed mirrors that hung on the wall on the other side of the corridor. He was glad to see that he looked outwardly calm and in control of himself but inwardly he was seething with excitement. He took the pistol out and checked it again. A militia man in full uniform with rifle and bayonet at the ready stood about halfway down the corridor, but apart from stiff nods of recognition neither of the two seemed inclined to speak.

Ryan thought with faint envy of Grady down in the lobby, where he would be free to smoke and eat his sandwiches in relative comfort. Up here the atmosphere was more formal and the furniture and fittings so sumptuous that it might even seem sacrilegious. He put the pistol down on a carved round table at his elbow and kept a sharp eye on the comings and goings in the corridor. Nothing much seemed to be happening at the moment but one never knew what might ensue on such official occasions. He consulted his watch. There was still almost two hours to go before the party would arrive. Such waiting seemed interminable but was inevitable at ceremonies at this level and of such outstanding importance.

He had a newspaper in his inner jacket pocket but he dare not be caught reading up here, so it had been pointless to bring it. He got up indecisively and took a turn about the corridor, again consulting his watch. Only ten minutes had passed. Then he remembered his pistol on the table and hurried to resume his seat. The time dragged on. People came and went. There were whispered consultations; later, sounds as though an orchestra was tuning up.

Then he noticed in the mirror that the nearest sentry was standing to attention. He stood up, aware that the time was at hand. A military band burst into a heart-stirring anthem. He stood to attention as heavy footsteps denoting a large party, sounded on the central staircase.

- 13 -

Ryan ceased his slow pacing and stared about him. The long corridor with its red plush and lavish fittings stretched before him interminably, due to the reflections of the mirrors on either side. Polite laughter and faint applause came from beyond the curtains to his right hand. The bored sentry at the staircase end of the corridor gave him a sympathetic glance, easing his cramped position with the heavy rifle in the at ease position.

At least, I am able to move about, Ryan thought. He fingered the comforting butt of the revolver, which he had transferred to his outside pocket in case of emergency. He remembered the Chief's words and wondered, not for the first time, whether the upper echelon of the Bureau knew a great deal more of the current situation than they were letting the rank and file know. The probability was that they did, Ryan felt. He ceased his pacing about and turned slowly to regard the end of the corridor. As he did so a slight faintness seemed to overcome him.

His legs felt weak and he sat down on one of the banquettes that lined the corridor here. Something then came back from one of his dreams and he started up, sweat beading his forehead. The outlines of the corridor were beginning to sway and buckle and a delicate mist was filming his eyes. He put up his left-hand to rub them but his arm felt strangely heavy. He must be ill, he thought. What was happening to him? It were as though he was in the grip of one of his weird nightmares.

The noisy laughter and music from the curtained alcove receded and finally ceased. He was directly facing the end of the long passageway now and was aware of two red spots that seemed to be boring into the very core of his being. He commenced to walk forward, feebly at first, and then more firmly. The voice in his dream came back; "He must be fit and well for the great day." Ryan went on like an automaton, his will entirely subservient to some outer force that had him in its power. He paused then, took the revolver from his pocket and laid it down on the nearest banquette. That too was familiar from one of his dreams. He strode on again as though braced to meet some momentous destiny. The soft voices of his dreams were faintly chanting now.

The two red spots had resolved themselves into eyes; an image with which Ryan was hideously familiar. But, curiously, he felt no fear this time. He walked on as though still within the dream, all sounds muted and far away. He passed one or two people in the corridors but on one looked at him, of if they did, saw nothing wrong or peculiar about his demeanour. He was now descending a little used iron spiral staircase, to judge from the dust on the balustrade. Then he was in front of a small, oval, iron-bound door. It opened easily to his touch and he went on, closing it carefully behind him.

There were wide stone steps here and an iron handrail. He negotiated the flights easily, the two red eyes still boring into him. Then he was in a large cellar, with an arched ceiling. It was lit by several oil lanterns hung from beams, and in the right hand corner a vast furnace gave off a reassuring heat. At the far end two familiar images faced him. One, a nude woman, whose face was in shadow. The other the menacing figure in the cloak and broad-brimmed hat. The two red spots receded and seemed to re-focus themselves to form the eyes of the faceless creature beneath the hat brim.

Everything was becoming clear to Ryan now but for the moment he still felt no fear. He advanced toward the still tableau as though this were an everyday occurrence; a normal encounter in the upper world of reality. There was a foul stench emanating from some hidden source that caught Ryan's nostrils, almost making him retch. A thin mist was rising and he noticed that the floor of the cellar was covered with rank foulness through which his shoes made slimy tracks. His head was swimming and he found it difficult to breathe.

The man in the dark cloak moved then and, as in the dreams, Ryan saw that he too was naked. Still Ryan was impelled onward by some unknown force that he was powerless to break. The nude woman moved into the golden glow of the lanterns and Ryan saw, with the inevitability of death, that she was Ellie. She smiled lasciviously, moving closer to the dark man, fondling his naked body beneath the cloak. Ryan understood many things then; the Munson murder; the attempt on the life of the French Prime Minister; the death of Dr. Mandel; his nightmares and the wounds on his throat; the white, drawn face of the Chief and the reasons that had impelled him to give Ryan the most important task this day; it was as though many doors in his mind were opening, one after the other.

The red eyes pierced through to his very brain and he struggled impotently to throw off the horror of what must surely be another dream. The creature in the wide-brimmed hat was up close to him and Ryan could see that the face was composed of rotting tissue with putrescent cracks so black that they seemed to recede to unknown depths. Ryan screamed and screamed without ceasing as he was seized in steel-like claws. The foul thing bent over him and pierced his neck with yellow teeth as Ellie smiled encouragingly. The creature's breath, reeking with the stench of the charnel house was nauseating and then the trio were sinking through the vile detritus of the cellar floor, to unspeakable pits of terror.

- 14 -

Grady was on duty in the foyer and feeling bored and only half-awake when he became aware of a disturbance upstairs. There was a faint cracking sound and then screams and shouts. Others had heard it and startled faces were directed up the staircase. But everyone had strict instructions to stay at their posts and Grady waited to see what was happening. The Army personnel in the lobby too, were well disciplined and remained where they stood, their bodies stiff as they strained to hear what was going on in other parts of the building.

It sounded as though a very large body of people were milling about in utter confusion. Grady reached for his pistol, took off the safety catch and held its muzzle down, ready for any eventuality. Then he heard racing footsteps and walked quickly to the foot of the broad foyer staircase. A man in civilian clothes was rushing down, his face ashen. It was DuCann, one of the very senior officials in the Bureau. He caught Grady by the arm.

"Seal all the entrances and exits!" he said in a hoarse voice. "No one is to leave or enter, no matter who! This applies to police, military and anyone with passes."

Grady, his head spinning in confusion, ran to the main entrance and gave the necessary orders. The lobby was full of hurrying figures now, rushing to transmit the instructions to police and sentries at all doors leading to the street. Grady ran back to DuCann.

"For God's sake, sir, what has happened?"

Wild-eyed and shocked, DuCann could not speak at first. Then he managed to articulate the news that would shortly resonate round the world.

"Mr. Lincoln has been shot! The sentry who should have been guarding him had left his post for a cup of coffee! The police officer on duty was not there and cannot be found!"

The Hunters

by Alexandra Elizabeth Honigsberg

Thoughts race and whirl
    behind eyes that flash,
The silver thread reaches out
    for connection
      as the dance begins
    on a knife's edge
    that sparks
      and cuts the night.

The cry's a song
    that rises on the wind
    in a chorus with

so many others,
Until the voices are one,
Eternal lovers in
the endless bliss
of passage.

A call of joy and grief,
of lonely souls in transit
from here—
to here,
of faces that wear lives
and eyes that speak death
In a game where
trust is the key.

Colors race, red and silver,
as the balance shifts,
paths reform
and the strong give in,
withdraw to a point,
Until there is nothing but
that moment—

And one is left standing.

by Charles Grant

here was chanting, and there was screaming, and a long and constant thunder that never reached the sky; there were orders issued in calm, and orders cried in panic; there was anger, and there was sorrow, and a relentless choking fear.

But most of all, there was the bitter stench of blood.

✠

Severen preferred to ride alone. Taciturn at best, in the company of others he was silent enough that many considered him nothing more than a half-breed mute. He didn't mind. The less he spoke, the less they would find out. And he was good enough that few suspicions came his way.

At least none he couldn't handle.

189

He was, by design and nature, unremarkable. Average in every aspect from height to weight, lean from face to limbs, and the clothes that he wore were as weathered as the skin stretched taut across his cheeks. He was called Gray by those he worked with. That wasn't his name; it came from the horse he rode, as unremarkable as he, and, for the most part, as even in temper.

Most of the time, for weeks on end, there was no trouble at all. He would awaken at first light, dress and eat, saddle his mount, and ride away from fort or village. Unending hills, unending plains, once in a great while the tell-tale plume of dust that signaled riders ahead. He would find the trail, taking his time, and decide if the presence was worth reporting.

Lately, they hadn't been, and that bothered him.

For as much as he knew of the country he lived in, things were changing. Changing fast. Fast enough that he had, years before, decided to do what he could to slow it down. To give the land, and the people, time to adjust.

He smiled then, melancholy and almost bitter, sitting on a flat rock above a dying stream.

Time to adjust.

He cocked an eyebrow. Hell, there was no time — for adjustments or anything else.

The spread of immigrants from east to west was like watching the wind catch the prairie grass in summer — a ripple at one end that didn't stop its undulation until it reached the other, or until the wind died.

And even then…

Even then…

He sighed, picked up a pebble and tossed it idly into the shallow, meandering water some twenty feet below. Behind him, the gray snorted and shook its head, bridle ringing softly in the warm air. It didn't like Severen much, but had learned that carrying him was infinitely better than carrying someone else into battle. Severen knew he was being tolerated and, in some perverse way, that pleased him.

Across the gulch, the plains stretched to a horizon that could have been a thousand miles away. A deceptive vision, the flatness of it, the smooth wind-touched surface; the greens and the browns and the occasional vivid flare of color from a wayward blossom. In truth, the high plains rolled, a vast, slow-motion sea that forever threatened to explode against the mountains the horizon conspired to conceal.

"Damnit," he muttered angrily. This wasn't like him. This mood he found himself in, and had been in for several days, upset him, and it was all he could do to stop himself from screaming.

Something was wrong.

After all the planning, the dreaming, the work, the talk, he couldn't shake the feeling that something had gone wrong. That somewhere along the line he had made a serious miscalculation.

Above and behind him to his right, a low irregular knoll blocked his view of the camp beyond; but not the sound of it.

The gray whickered quietly.

Severen straightened, listening to footfalls come across the top.

"Gray!"

He winced at the bellow, but didn't turn. Instead, he waved vaguely, an invitation to join him.

It was Barnaby Tycke, all buckskins and furs, two gunbelts and a broad knife, fringed deerskin boots, a beard that often held more food than his plate. He was huge in girth and height; Severen was the only man who had ever knocked him off his feet.

Tycke dropped onto the rock beside him, spat into the water, and pulled a length of jerky from a pouch at his side. "You ever think the money's not worth it, Gray?"

Severen laughed. "Definitely not worth it."

The giant stretched out his legs and leaned back on his elbows, chewing thoughtfully. "I don't care for it, Gray." He watched the prairie, watched the sky too sharp and blue to watch for very long. "Two Sons thinks we're gonna get ourselves dead." He shifted. "I think he's gone come morning. Him and Bear."

Severen shook his head. More bad news. The two Crow scouts were important; they saw what others couldn't, sometimes even what he himself couldn't see. If they left, he would have to do the rest all on his own.

That, without a doubt, could very well get him killed.

"I'll talk to them," he promised.

Tycke grunted. "No good, Gray. Two Sons won't listen."

"He'll listen to me."

The giant rolled his eyes. "Oh, really? You his god or something?"

Not quite, Gray thought. Not quite.

Tycke chuckled. "You know, you really are one proud son-of-a-bitch, Gray, it's gonna kill you some day, you're not careful."

Severen bristled but said nothing.

"Anyway, you've lost your chance. He's been up since last sunset, praying and stuff, and he's made up his mind. Soon as he gets some rest, he's gone, Bear with him."

Severen rubbed his thumb over the tips of his fingers. "I don't suppose Reno would—"

Tycke spat again. He didn't have to say a word.

Wrong, Severen thought again. The pieces that should have fallen into place were falling into places they didn't belong. He had to do something, and he had to do it fast. Pride had nothing to do with it; survival did.

With a loud, theatrical groan he pulled his legs up and stood, stretched, took off his battered hat and slapped it lightly against his thigh, raising faint dust from his loose buckskin trousers. Straight black hair faintly laced with silver touched his shoulders. He wore only one gun, tucked into his belt. As he turned toward the gray, he spotted movement in the sky, and he froze.

It coasted without color just beneath the blinding reach of the sun.

Small circles, over and over.

He shaded his eyes with a forearm and waited, but the bird didn't climb or dive.

Small circles, over and over.

"What you looking at?"

He shrugged. *Nothing, just looking.*

"You go blind, staring at the sun like that."

He shrugged again.

Small circles.

Over and over.

His concentration was such that he didn't hear the heavy thud of army-issue boots until a voice snapped at them from the crest: "Hey, you two! We are not on any Sunday picnic, you hear me? Get your asses up here. Now! There's work to be done. Major's orders."

"Bastard," Tycke said, not bothering to soften or hide his contempt as the soldier wheeled about and vanished. He didn't move; he hadn't finished the jerky.

Severen, however, strode immediately off the rock and swung onto the gray, reached down for the reins, and steadied the animal when it protested a little by trying to rear. The struggle was brief; nobody won — the gray didn't buck him off, and Severen didn't saw the bit into the horse's mouth.

As he rode up the easy slope, Tycke yelled something from the rock, but Severen didn't listen. He searched for the bird; it was gone. He checked for another; the sky was empty, except for the sun that broke sweat easily and baked the ground to rock.

Nevertheless, he felt chilled.

"You!"

Blandly, he looked down into the pinched face of a career sergeant hurrying toward him up the campside slope — Cameron Jakes, whose disdain for the army's Indian and breed scouts was notorious. Only orders and a strong sense of pragmatism prevented him from shooting them all.

Beyond, there was dust in the air, constant and constantly moving. It almost hid the encampment like gritty fog. It didn't hide the ceaseless movement of horses and the men who rode them, of wagons being loaded with provisions from other wagons anxious to head back. They had traveled too far too fast, and all of them were weary.

"You!"

Severen didn't move, and the sergeant, scowling and swaying slightly from his exertion, grabbed the gray's reins to steady himself.

"You deaf, mister?"

Severen didn't speak.

The gray turned its head slowly, ready to take a piece of the soldier's rump, but Severen stopped him with a squeeze of one leg.

Red-faced, uniform already dark-stained, and, in places, patched with dusty mud, Jakes pointed west, beyond the dust cloud. "The others have already left, damnit! You think you're on leave or something, you goddamn freak? You get your ass out there, Severen, and get it out there fast. You report back by dark. You understand me? *By dark.* Jesus, man, have you got a tongue?"

Severen only looked at him.

Jakes glared back. "We're moving fast, freak, unless you're blind, too. Just be sure we don't run you down." His laugh was a bark, rough and deep. "To hell with it, get moving."

Severen said, "The colonel—"

"Sorry, freak, but the colonel's got enough on his mind without you bothering him again. Now move your goddamn ass!"

He stepped back and slapped the gray's flank.

The horse reacted quickly, wheeling just in time to swing its tail across the sergeant's face. By the time the man recovered, Severen was already halfway down the slope, angling away from the camp, hearing the man's outraged screams but not listening to the words.

Moving fast. They were moving fast.

He let the gray set the pace, ignoring the troopers who called to him, ignoring the frantic gathering of the colors at the head of each column, ignoring what appeared to be chaos in motion. He had to or the energy that sparked from every corner of the camp would have sparked his temper beyond the point of self-control.

"Freak" was a term most men like Jakes used when they couldn't get a response out of him. They thought he was a breed because of his skin, because of his hair, because of the way he could read the ground and the sky where the rest of them saw only grass and blue. A captain down in Kansas swore Severen's mother had been Comanche. A sergeant in North Platte bet fifty dollars hard coin the father had been Sioux. There had been others; they were all wrong, but he didn't feel the need to correct them, because he had known, when he had seen them, that they were all going to die.

He hadn't done it himself, of course, but he had certainly, and gladly, seen to it that it would happen.

That made him smile, and the smile made the gray falter until he urged the animal on, calming it with a touch and a silent word.

And under the hot sun, he felt the chill again, looked up and saw the bird circling.

The gray snorted.

Severen shuddered and nudged the horse into a slow gallop.

The other scouts had already fanned out across the high plains, seeking more signs of hostiles and their destination than the trail already found. Their orders were always simple, always the same: count the enemy and let us know.

Severen, however, already knew where they would be; what he didn't know, yet, was how many there would be. The army behind him numbered close to six or seven hundred, that number effectively trebled by the weapons they carried. With any kind of luck, it wouldn't be enough.

But still the bird circled, and the chill still walked his spine.

He moved steadily, every few miles allowing himself a drink of water, allowing the gray a drink whenever they crossed a creek or stream. Sunlight became lead on his shoulders. His head began to ache. The plains rose and fell, becoming more rough, more rocky, as rises surged to low hills, eighty to one hundred feet high. The sun peaked and began to slip, and at the same time an uneasy sense of urgency struggled with his common sense.

This was wrong.

This was all wrong.

The bird vanished when he blinked.

The sun glared directly into his eyes.

There was no dusk, no twilight; one minute, the plains were awash in gold, the next they were buried in a black only faintly touched by the gentle stroke of the moon.

Finally he stopped beside a pool of brackish water, urgency now coupling with indecision. He could keep going, ought to keep going, just to be sure that all was as it should be. Or he could go back, just to be sure.

He tethered the gray and stood beside it, searching the moon for an answer.

A few years ago in Kansas it had been simple. He had led the horse soldiers to places where, inevitably, skirmishes had been fought and nothing important had been decided. When casualties finally became intolerable, and frustrations exploded, the soldiers had pulled back, and their leader, the man who led them now, was court-martialed for, of all things, leaving his command so he could visit his wife. At most, the whole affair had been a holding action for the army, and therefore, in some commands, it was considered a minor success; but it also served as a training ground for the commander's enemies. They fought, they died, they learned. They taught others; they spread the word.

Severen did his best to help them.

The moon peaked.

Severen lowered his head and closed his eyes, leaning heavily against the gray.

Where is it, he wondered? Where the hell's the damn mistake?

A few seconds later the horse shifted suddenly, and one hoof stamped the ground. Severen dropped into a crouch, his left hand reaching for his gun, his right braced on the ground. Not fifty feet away a man walked toward him, naked to the waist, in buckskin and soft boots.

"Far enough," he said when the man reached the other side of the pool.

The man started, stopped, and spread his arms to prove he carried no weapons. A bow and a rifle were slung across his back. "You see well," he said in his own language, his voice not quite deep.

"Well enough." Severen recognized the jagged scar that tore across the man's forehead. "What do you want?"

Cuts Deep gestured over his shoulder. "They grow impatient. They don't want to wait."

Severen rose slowly, no sudden moves, no threat. He wasn't afraid, but he didn't replace the gun. "Two days. Maybe three. No more."

"That may be too many."

Anger twisted Severen's voice into a guttural snarl. "It will not be too many," he snapped. The gray shied. Cuts Deep took an uneasy step back. "You stay together and you'll be fine." The snarl deepened, and the gray shook its head anxiously, its eyes rolling to show the white, its ears flat and back. "This will be your last chance, my friend. Patience will serve you. Tell them that. Tell them I said it."

Cuts Deep swallowed and nodded. "I will." He watched the horse for a moment, then stared at the water. "They're afraid of you, Strider, but that may not be enough."

It was Severen's turn to be startled. He knew that Cuts Deep's people called him Silent Strider, because of the way he moved through the night. But they had never called him that to his face. It was neither an insult nor a compliment — it was an expression of certain knowledge.

They knew what he was, although he had never shown them; they knew because they believed in the world beyond the world.

The soldiers had never known; all they believed in was the world.

In spite of Severen's anger, the man said, "Two days," as if it were an order; then he turned and loped away without a backward glance.

196

Severen watched until the Cheyenne disappeared behind a rise, then grabbed a rock and threw it as far as he could, as hard as he could, swearing obscenely, loudly. More rocks, then clots of grass, until he dropped to the ground on all fours, head bowed, sweat dripping from chin and jaw although the night was cool, almost cold.

You really are one proud son-of-a-bitch, it's gonna kill you some day, you're not careful, Gray.

When he looked up again, the world had turned to shades of red, as if his eyes had turned to fire.

A groan, a growl, and he tossed his clothes aside before the wrenching shift had ended. A moment's panting. A moment's listening. Then he launched himself across the ground, running through the red, low and nearly flying. Direction didn't matter, but it didn't take very long to realize his destination.

And when he got there, it was much too soon.

The army, despite the hour, was still on the move.

From the top of a ragged knoll he could see them clearly, night dust rising from hooves and wheels, bridles and spurs muted, weary voices complaining.

No, he thought in disbelief; damnit, no, the man's crazy. If Cuts Deep or any of the others see this—

Dirt sprayed beneath his muzzle, and he wheeled just as a gunshot cracked and echoed across the plain. Shouts and racing horses — a patrol had spotted him. There was no time to do anything else but run. No time to infiltrate. No time to remind the colonel that everything the other scouts had told him was wrong. The commander obviously still believed it, otherwise he wouldn't still be moving.

But what about the others, the infantry that came behind? They were all supposed to arrive together; most of them were supposed to die.

He ran effortlessly through the familiar deep red night, allowing himself one quick grin when he came upon a startled horseman whose mount reared and cried out, spoiling the man's hasty aim.

They may not know him, but they were still afraid of him.

When he couldn't stop a laugh, a distant coyote answered.

And when he reached the gray, it was dead.

It lay beside the pool, its throat slashed, its belly open, its blood black on the grass and in the water.

The saddle was still on its back, a mocking insult.

Severen staggered a few yards away and collapsed. Exhaustion made the shift from red night to black slow and painful; rage at himself made his eyes fill with tears, though not a single tear broke loose; and when he closed his eyes, fists and legs drawn to his chest, he couldn't help but fall asleep.

There were no dreams.

There was darkness and there was light, and he sat up quickly, praying for a nightmare until he saw the gray and its blanket of hungry flies and ants.

He was too weary to let the anger take him again. He knew the dead animal for what it was — a warning. What he had designed was now in motion, and he was neither needed nor wanted anymore. If he tried to take a hand, they would surely try to kill him.

He crawled over to the horse and lay a palm on its head, stroking it between the ears, shaking his head in silent apology. By losing control the night before, by leaving the gray alone, he had broken the compact they had had, and if he could not stop the thunder that would roll across the plains tomorrow, the least he could do was make sure the gray did not die alone.

He dressed and walked away.

The sun climbed.

Every so often he felt faint tremors beneath his feet, and strained to listen to what the dusty wind had to tell him.

It told him nothing, not for several hours.

Then it told him of the thunder.

And it was wrong.

All wrong.

Severen knew he would never get there in time, yet he allowed himself a drink before he broke into a steady trot, following the sounds, feeling the tremors, until he reached the first of several rivers that sliced across the rough terrain. Now he could hear it all, on the wind, and he couldn't believe it.

There was no time left for caution.

He ran.

The black bird circled overhead, mocking him with a cry only he could hear.

And when he could run no more, he walked as rapidly as he could, falling several times, cutting his cheek on a rock, ripping his shirt, paying little attention to anything but the wind, and soon enough, too soon, the awful silence that followed.

One last climb before he could look into the valley formed by rocky knolls and river bluffs.

He sat heavily, not caring that he could be seen, barely permitting himself to think. His legs wanted to cramp; his arms flopped uselessly in his lap. He breathed slowly, deeply, taking in the aftermath as a haze of dust shifted among the clouds of lingering smoke.

The army had come in here blindly, and, incredibly, it seemed as if the colonel had split the column, maybe in half, perhaps in thirds. A major fight down by the river to his left, another down below. And ahead, beyond the center of the three knolls, he spotted what he thought were bodies, but there was no movement. None at all.

He closed his eyes, but not for long.

He had to watch as battered survivors in bloody blue wandered through the depressions and the trees on the river's banks. He watched them take up their dead and cart them away. He watched them shake helpless fists at the cloudless sky. He watched one soldier drop to his knees and weep while another put a bullet in a wounded horse's head.

Tycke was right.

Severen realized it now, and had learned it much too late — he *was* a prideful bastard, an arrogant son-of-a-bitch. Not content with manipulating one man at a time, one incident at a time, in order to shape the world to his liking, he had decided it would be better to turn history around all at once, never allowing himself to understand that dealing with men was not the same as dealing with a man.

And eventually, when the shadows slipped coldly from their places across the shallow water and from between the rocky hills, and the temperature began to drop as if the sun had never been, he pushed himself wearily to his feet and made the awkward descent. A few of the soldiers recognized him and called to him, thinking from his condition that he had been wounded in battle himself. He shook them off with a listless smile, a defeated gesture, until he couldn't do it anymore. After that, he just ignored them as he checked the rows of bodies and the ones that still lay where they had fallen.

As far as he could tell, Barnaby Tycke had missed the fight.

Guards had been posted from the few soldiers who were left, but when he saw the place where the enemy encampment had been, he knew they were unnecessary. The fighting was done.

The enemy had gone.

Once in a while he heard a gunshot.

Once in a while he heard a man cry out in pain.

But only once did he find a body the Sioux and Cheyenne had left behind.

It wasn't the one he wanted.

A few minutes before dark, he made his way up the last uneven slope, veering around boulders that had been no protection at all, stepping over scores of soldiers who had been either mutilated or stripped. No survivors, no wounded; here the destruction had been complete.

Near the crest he paused, smiled grimly, and dropped to his knees, he settled back onto his heels and stared hard until Cuts Deep fluttered open his eyes. There was a hole in the man's side, and half his scalp had been blown apart.

"We won," the man whispered hoarsely, a single drop of blood quivering at the corner of his ruined mouth.

Severen shook his head in disgust. "You didn't wait. You didn't win. And you killed my goddamn horse." A quick look to be sure no one could see him, and he leaned over, smiled and snarled, and gladly tore the man's throat out with one slash of his sharp white teeth.

Then he stood, wiped his chin with both sleeves, and hurried on to the top.

"Damn," he said flatly.

It didn't take him very long.

He found the body he wanted and leaned over it, sniffing at the blood that caked the lieutenant colonel's face, waving a brusque hand to shoo away the flies that swarmed the handsome buckskin jacket. He nearly laughed then, when he saw that the man had cut his hair, the signature yellow it once had been now streaked and matted with red and grime.

"Stupid bastard," he said, waiting for the anger and not surprised when it didn't come. "You didn't wait either, you stupid, prideful son-of-a-bitch."

He blinked once.

He straightened.

He raised his face to the pale moon rising, and he laughed while a bugle sounded.

Then he walked away, alone and silent, through the bitter stench of blood.

Mussolini and the Axeman's Jazz

by Poppy Z. Brite

SARAJEVO, 1914

Stone turrets and crenelated columns loomed on either side of the Archduke's motorcade. The crowd parted before the open carriages, an indistinct blur of faces. Francis Ferdinand swallowed some of the unease that had been plaguing him all day: a bitter bile, a constant burn at the back of his throat.

It was his fourteenth wedding anniversary. Sophie sat beside him, a bouquet of scarlet roses at her bosom. These Serbs and Croats were a friendly crowd; as the heir apparent of Austria-Hungary, Francis Ferdinand stood to give them an equal voice in his empire. Besides, Sophie was a Slav, the daughter of a noble Czech family. Surely his marriage to a northern Slav had earned him the sympathy of these southern ones.

Yet the Archduke could not divest himself of the notion that there was a menacing edge to the throng. The occasional vivid detail — a sobbing baby, a flower tucked behind the ear of a beautiful woman — was lost before his eyes could fully register it. He glanced at Sophie. In the summer heat he could smell her sweat mingling with the *eau de parfum* she had dabbed on this morning.

She met his gaze and smiled faintly. Beneath her veil, her sweet face shone with perspiration. Back in Vienna, Sophie was snubbed by his court because she had been a lady-in-waiting when she met the Archduke, little better than a servant in their eyes. Francis Ferdinand's uncle, the old Emperor Francis Joseph, forbade the marriage. When the couple married anyway, Sophie was ostracized in a hundred ways. Francis Ferdinand knew it was sometimes a painful life for her, but she remained a steadfast wife, an exemplary mother.

For this reason he had brought her on the trip to Sarajevo. It was a routine army inspection for him, but for her it was a chance to be treated with the royal honors she deserved. On this anniversary of their blessed union, Sophie would endure no subtle slights, no calculated cruelties.

The Archduke had never loved another human being. His parents were hazy memories, his uncle a shambling old man whose time had come and gone. Even his three children brought him more distraction than joy. The first time he laid eyes on Sophie, he discerned in her an empathy such as he had never seen before. Her features, her mannerisms, her soft ample body — all bespoke a comfort Francis Ferdinand had never craved but suddenly could not live without.

The four cars approached the Cumuria Bridge. A pall of humidity hung over the water. The Archduke felt his skin steaming inside his heavy uniform, and his uneasiness intensified. He knew how defenseless they must look in the raised carriage, in the Serbian sun, the green feathers on his helmet drooping, Sophie's red roses beginning to wilt.

As they passed over the bridge, he saw an object arc out of the crowd and come hurtling toward him. In an instant his eye marked it as a crude hand bomb.

Francis Ferdinand raised his arm to protect Sophie and felt hot metal graze his flesh.

Gavrilo Princip's pistol left a smell on his palm like greasy coins, metallic and sour. It was a cheap thing from Belgium, as likely to blow his hand off as anything else. Still, it was all Gavrilo had, and he was the only one left to murder the villainous fool whose good intentions would crush Serbia.

He had known the other six would fail him. They were a young and earnest lot, always ready to sing the praises of a Greater Serbia but reluctant to look a man in the face and kill him. They spoke of the sanctity of human life, a short-sighted sentiment in Gavrilo's opinion. Human life was a fleeting thing, an expendable thing. The glory of a nation could endure through the ages. What his comrades failed to fully comprehend was that it must be oiled with human blood.

He raked his dirty hair back from his face and stared along the motorcade route. It looked as if the cars were finally coming. He took a deep breath. As the wet, sooty air entered his lungs, Gavrilo was seized with a racking cough that lasted a full minute. He had no handkerchief, so he cupped his hand over his mouth. When he pulled it away, his fingers were speckled with fresh blood. He and his six comrades were all tubercular, and none of them expected to live past thirty. The fevers, the lassitude, the night sweats, the constant tickling itch deep in the chest — all these made the cyanide capsules they carried in their pockets a source of comfort rather than of dread.

Now the task was left to him. Mohammed and Nedjelko, the first two along the route, were carrying hand bombs. One of them had heaved his bomb — Gavrilo had seen it go flying — but the motorcade had continued toward City Hall with no apparent damage. His comrades between Cumuria Bridge and City Hall — Vasco, Cvijetko, Danilo, Trifko — had done nothing.

The Archduke's carriage moved slowly through the crowd, then braked and came to a standstill less than five feet from Gavrilo. This struck him as nothing short of a miracle, God telling him to murder the villains for the glory of Serbia.

He fired twice. The pistol did not blow his hand off. He saw Countess Sophie sag against her husband, saw blood on the Archduke's neck. The deed was done as well as he could do it. Gavrilo turned the pistol on himself, but before he could fire, it was knocked out of his hand. The crowd surged over him.

Gavrilo got his hand into his pocket, found the cyanide capsule and brought it to his mouth. Hundreds of hands were ripping at him, pummeling him. His teeth cracked the capsule open. The foul taste of bitter almonds flooded his mouth. He retched, swallowed, vomited, convulsed. The crowd would surely pull him to pieces. He felt his guts unmooring, his bones coming loose from their sockets, and still he could not die.

Sophie stood on the steps of City Hall between her husband and Fehim Effendi Curcic, the burgomaster of Sarajevo. Though Sophie and several of her attendants were bleeding from superficial cuts obtained from splinters of the bomb casing, and twelve spectators had been taken to hospital, Curcic obviously had no idea that the motorcade had come close to being blown up. He was surveying the crowd, a pleased look on his fat face. "Our hearts are filled with happiness—" he began.

Francis Ferdinand was white with anger. He grabbed the burgomaster's arm and shouted into his face. "One comes here for a visit and is received with bombs! Mr. Mayor, what do you say?"

Curcic still didn't understand. He smiled blandly at the Archduke and launched into his welcome speech again. The Archduke let him continue this time, looking disgusted. Never once did Curcic mention the bombing attempt.

Sophie gripped her husband's hand. She could see Francis Ferdinand gradually pulling himself together. He was a man of inflexible opinions and sudden rages, painfully thin-skinned, capable of holding a grudge for eternity. He was like a spoiled child, bragging that he had shot five thousand stags, darkly hinting that he had brought down as many political enemies. But Sophie loved him. Not even her children fulfilled her vast need to be needed. This man did.

There was a delay while Francis Ferdinand sent a wire to the Emperor, who would have heard about the bomb. The Army wanted to continue with the day's events, but the Archduke insisted upon first visiting the wounded spectators in the hospital.

He turned to Sophie. "You must not come. The risk is too great; there could be another attack."

Fear clutched at her heart: of dying, of losing him. "No, I must go with you," she told him, and Francis Ferdinand did not argue. When they entered their carriage again, Oskar Potiorek, the military governor, climbed in with them. His presence made Sophie feel a little safer.

The motorcade rolled back through the thronged streets. When they turned a corner, Sophie saw a sign marking Francis Joseph Street. Just as she noticed this, Potiorek sat up straighter and cried, "What's this? We've taken the wrong way!"

The driver braked. The motorcade ground to a halt. Sophie felt something graze the top of her head, a sharp stinging sensation. The Archduke's head snapped to one side. At the same time, Sophie felt something like a white-hot fist punch into her belly.

Through a haze of agony she reached for her husband. He leaned toward her, and a torrent of blood gushed from his mouth. She crumpled into his arms. Attendants swarmed around them, asked Francis Ferdinand if he was suffering. The last thing Sophie heard was her husband replying in a wet whisper, "It is nothing... it is nothing."

They were both dead before the sun had reached its apex in the blazing sky.

NEW ORLEANS, 1918

New Orleans is commonly thought of as a French and Spanish town. "Creole," a word now used to describe rich food of a certain seasoning and humans of a certain shade, first referred to the inevitable mixture of French and Spanish blood that began appearing several years after the city's founding. The buildings of the Vieux Carré were certainly shaped and adorned by the ancestry of their builders: the Spanish courtyards and ironwork, the French cottages with their carved wooden shutters and pastel paint, the wholly European edifice of St. Louis Cathedral.

But, block by sagging block, the Vieux Carré was abandoned by these upwardly mobile people. By the turn of the century it had become a slum. A wave of Sicilian immigrants moved in. Many of them opened groceries, imported and sold the necessities of life. Some were honest businessmen, some were criminals; most made no such clear distinction. The *onorata società* offered them a certain amount of protection from the hoodlums who roamed the French Quarter. Naturally, they required a payment for this service, and if a man found himself in a position to do them a favor — legal or otherwise — he had no choice but to oblige.

The Italians gradually branched out of the Quarter into every part of the city, and New Orleans became as fully an Italian town as a French or Spanish one.

Joseph D'Antonio, formerly Detective of the New Orleans Police

Department, had been drinking on the balcony of his second-story hovel since late this afternoon. Bittersweet red wine, one bottle before the sun went down, another two since. His cells soaked it up like bread.

Two weeks in, this hot and sticky May portended a hellish summer. Even late at night, his balcony was the only place he could catch an occasional breath of air, usually tinged with the fetor of the Basin Canal nearby. Most nights, he had to force himself not to pass out here. These days, few things in his life were worse than waking up with a red wine hangover and the morning sun in his eyes.

D'Antonio was forty-three. The circumstances of his early retirement had been as randomly cruel as the violence that presaged it. A crazed beat cop named Mullen walked into headquarters one afternoon and gunned down Chief Inspector Jimmy Reynolds. In the confusion that followed, an innocent captain also named Mullen was shot dead. Someone had come charging in and asked what happened, and someone else was heard to yell, "Mullen killed Reynolds!"

The yeller was Joe D'Antonio. Unfortunately, the dead Mullen had been widely known to harbor a strong dislike for Italians in general and D'Antonio in particular. No one accused him directly, but everyone wondered. His life became a hell of suspicious looks and nasty innuendo. Six months later, the new chief persuaded him to take early retirement.

D'Antonio leaned on the rickety railing and stared at the empty street. Until last year he had lived on the fringes of Storyville, the red light district. In the confusion of wartime patriotism, somebody had decided Storyville was a bad influence on Navy boys, and all the whorehouses were shut down. Now the buildings were dark and shabby, broken windows covered with boards or gaping like hungry mouths, lacework balconies sagging, opulent fixtures sold away or crumbling to dust.

D'Antonio could live without the whores, though some of them had been good enough gals. But he missed the music that had drifted up from Storyville every night, often drawing him out to some smoky little dive where he could drink and jazz away the hours till dawn. Players like Jelly Roll Morton, King Oliver, and some new kid named Armstrong kept him sane throughout the bad months just after he left the force. He got to know some of the musicians, smoked reefer with them from time to time, warned them when undercover presence indicated a bust might be imminent.

Now they were gone. There were still jazz clubs in the city, but many of the players D'Antonio knew had moved to Chicago when Storyville closed down. They could record in Chicago, make money. And in Chicago they didn't have to sleep, drink, eat, and piss according to signs posted by white men.

Pissing sounded like a fine idea. He stood, steadied himself on the railing, and walked inside. The place had none of this modern indoor plumbing, and the odor of the slop jar filled the two airless rooms. Still, he'd never stooped so low as to piss off the balcony as some of his neighbors did, at least not that he could remember.

D'Antonio unbuttoned his fly and aimed into the jar. Behind him, the shutters on the French doors slammed shut with a report as loud as a double-barreled shotgun in the airless night. His hand jerked. Urine sprayed the dingy wall.

When he'd finished pissing and cursing the freak wind, he wiped the wall with a dirty sock, then went back to the balcony doors. It was too hot in here with the shutters closed, and too dark. D'Antonio pushed them open again.

There was a man standing on the balcony, and the shutters passed right through him.

Francis Ferdinand scowled in annoyance. The first flesh-and-blood creature he'd met since his inglorious exit from this plane, and of course the fellow had to be stinking drunk.

Perhaps his drunkenness would make Francis Ferdinand's job easier. Who could know? When one had to put himself together from whatever stray wisps of ectoplasm he could snatch out of the ether, it became increasingly difficult to fathom the minds of living men and women.

Joseph D'Antonio had a shock of black hair streaked with silver and a pale complexion that had gone florid from the wine. His dark eyes were comically wide, seeming to start from their sockets. "Hell, man, you're a *ghost!* You're a goddamned *ghost*, ain'tcha?"

English had never been one of his better languages, but Francis Ferdinand was able to understand D'Antonio perfectly. Even the drunken slur and the slight accent did not hinder him. He winced at the term. "A *wraith*, sir, if you please."

D'Antonio waved a dismissive hand. The resulting current of air nearly wafted the Archduke off the balcony. "Wraith, ghost, whatever. S'all the same to me. Means I'll be goin' headfirst offa that balcony if I don't get to bed soon. By accident... or on purpose? I dunno..."

Francis Ferdinand realized he would have to speak his piece at once, before the man slipped into maudlin incoherence. "Mr. D'Antonio, I do not come to you entirely by choice. You might say I have been dispatched. I died in the service of my country. I saw my beloved wife die, and pass into the Beyond. Yet I remain trapped in a sort of half-life. To follow her, I must do one more thing, and I must request your help."

Francis Ferdinand paused, but D'Antonio remained silent. His eyes were alert, his aspect somewhat more sober than before.

"I must kill a man," the Archduke said at last.

D'Antonio's face twitched. Then he burst into sudden laughter. "That's a good one! You gotta kill somebody, but you can't, 'cause you're a goddamn ghost!"

"Please, sir, I am a *wraith*! There are *class structures* involved here!"

"Sure. Whatever. Well, sorry, Duke. I handed over my gun when I left the force. Can't help you."

"You addressed me as 'Duke' just now, Mr. D'Antonio."

"Yeah, so? You're the Archduke, ain'tcha? The one who got shot at the beginning of the war?"

Francis Ferdinand was stunned. He had expected to have to explain everything to the man: his own useless assassination; the ensuing bedlam into which Europe had tumbled, country after country; the dubious relevance of these events to others in New Orleans. He was glad to discover that, at least in one respect, he had underestimated D'Antonio.

"Yeah, I know who you are. I might look like an ignorant wop, but I read the papers. Besides, there's a big old bullet hole in your neck."

Startled, the Archduke quickly patched the wound.

"Then, sir, that is one less thing I must explain to you. You have undoubtedly heard that I was murdered by Serbs. This is the first lie. I was murdered by Sicilians."

"But the men they caught—"

"Were Serbs, yes. They were also dupes. The plot was set in motion by your countrymen; specifically, by a man called Cagliostro. Perhaps you've heard of him."

"Some kind of magician?"

"A mage, yes. Also a doctor, a swindler, a forger, and a murderer. He is more than a century old, yet retains the appearance of a man of thirty. A wicked, dangerous man.

"He was born Giuseppe Balsamo in Palermo, 1743. By the time he began his scourge of Europe, he had dubbed himself Cagliostro, an old family name. He traveled the continent selling charms, potions, elixirs of youth. Some of these may have been genuine, as he himself ceased to age at this time.

"He also became a Freemason. Are you familiar with them as well?"

"Not particularly."

"They are a group of powerful mages hell-bent on controlling the world. They erect heathen temples in which they worship themselves and their accomplishments. Cagliostro formed his own 'Egyptian Order' and claimed to be thousands of years old already, reminiscing about his dalliances with Christ and various Pharaohs. It was power he sought, of course, though he claimed to work only for the 'Brotherhood of Man.'

"At the peak of his European success, he became entangled in the famous scandal of Marie Antoinette's diamond necklace. It nearly brought him down. He was locked in the Bastille, then forced to leave Paris in disgrace. He wandered back through the European cities that had once welcomed him, finding scant comfort. It has been rumored that he died in a dungeon in Rome, imprisoned for practices offensive to the Christian church.

"This is not so. His Masonic 'brothers' failed him for a time, but ultimately they removed him from the dungeon, whisked him out from under the noses of the French revolutionary armies who wished to make him a hero, and smuggled him off to Egypt.

"The practices he perfected there are unspeakable.

"Fifty years later, still appearing as a young and vital man, he returned to Italy. He spent the next half-century assembling a new 'Egyptian Order' of the most brilliant men he could find. With a select few, he shared his elixirs.

"Just after the turn of the century, he met a young journalist named Benito Mussolini, who called himself an 'apostle of violence' but had no direction. Cagliostro has guided Mussolini's career since then. In 1915, Mussolini's newspaper helped urge Italy into war."

D'Antonio started violently. "Aw, come on! You're not gonna tell me these Egyptian-Dago-Freemasons started the war."

"Sir, that is exactly what I am going to tell you. They also ordered my wife's death, and my own, and that of my empire."

"Why in hell would they do that?"

"I cannot tell you. They are evil men. My uncle, the Emperor Francis Joseph, discovered all this inadvertently. He was a cowardly old fool who would have been afraid to tell anyone. Nevertheless, they hounded him into virtual retirement, where he died."

"And told you all this?"

"He had no one else to talk to. Nor did I."

"Where's your wife?"

"Sophie was not required to linger here. We were."

"Why?"

"I cannot tell you."

"You keep saying that. Does it mean you don't know, or you aren't *allowed* to tell me?"

Francis Ferdinand paused. After a moment, D'Antonio nodded. "I see how it is. So I'm supposed to dance for you like Mussolini does for Cagliostro?"

The Archduke did not understand the question. He waited to see if D'Antonio would rephrase it, but the man remained silent. Finally Francis Ferdinand said, "Cagliostro still controls Mussolini, and means to shape him into the most vicious ruler Europe has ever known. But Cagliostro is no longer in Italy. He is here in New Orleans."

"Oh-ho! And you want me to kill him for you, is that it?"

"Yes, but I haven't finished. Cagliostro is in New Orleans — *but we don't know who he is.*"

"*We?* Who's *we?*"

"Myself, my uncle."

"No one else?"

"No one else you would care to know about, sir."

D'Antonio sagged in his chair. "Yeah, well, forget it. I'm not killin' anybody. Find some other poor dupe."

"Are you certain, Mr. D'Antonio?"

"Very certain."

"Very well." Francis Ferdinand drifted backward through the balcony railing and vanished in midair.

"Wait!" D'Antonio was halfway out of his chair by the time he realized the wraith was gone. He sank back, his brain seasick in his skull from all the talk of mages and murders, elixirs and dungeons, and the famous scandal of Marie Antoinette's diamond necklace — whatever the hell that was.

"Why me?" he murmured into the hot night. But the night made no reply.

Cagliostro stood behind his counter and waited on the last customer of the day, an old lady buying half a pound of salt cod. When she had gone, he locked the door and had his supper: a small loaf of bread, a thick wedge of *provolone*, a few olives chopped with garlic. He no longer ate the flesh of creatures, though he must sell it to maintain the appearance of a proper Italian grocery.

Above his head hung glossy loops of sausage and salami, rafters of wind-dried ham and *pancetta*, luminous globes of *caciocavallo* cheese. In the glass case were pots of creamy *ricotta*, stuffed artichokes, orbs of *mozzarella* in milk, bowls of shining olives and capers preserved in brine. On the neat wooden shelves were jars of candied fruit, almonds, pine nuts, aniseed, and a rainbow of assorted sweets. There were tall wheels of *parmesan* coated in funereal black wax, cruets of olive oil and vinegar, pickled cucumbers and mushrooms, flat tins containing anchovies, calamari, octopus. Enormous burlap sacks of red beans, fava beans, chickpeas, rice, couscous, and coffee threatened to spill their bounty onto the spotless tile floor. Pastas of every shape, size, and color were arranged in an elaborate display of bins facing the counter.

The aroma of the place was a balm to Cagliostro's ancient soul. He carried the world's weight on his back every day; he had pledged his very life to the furthering of the Brotherhood of Man; still, that did not mean he could shirk small duties. He fed the families of his neighborhood. When they could not pay, he fed them on credit, and when there was no hope of recovering the credit, he fed them for free.

He had caused death, to be sure. He had caused the deaths of the Archduke and his wife for several reasons, most importantly the malignant forces that hung over Europe like black clouds heavy with rain. Such a rain could mean the death of millions, hundreds of millions. The longer it was allowed to stagnate, the more virulent it would grow. It had needed some spark to release it, some event whose full significance was hidden at first, then gradually revealed. The assassination in Sarajevo had been that event, easy enough to arrange by providing the dim-witted Serbian anarchists with encouragement and weapons.

His name was synonymous with elaborate deception, and not undeservedly so. But some of his talents were genuine. In his cards and scrying-bowl Cagliostro could read the future, and the future looked very dark.

He, of course, would change all that.

This war was nearly over. It had drained some of the poison from those low-hanging clouds, allowed Europe to shatter and purge itself. But it had not been purged enough; there would be another great war inside of two decades. In that one, his boy Benito would send thousands of innocent men to their useless deaths. But that was not as bad as what could be.

Though he had never killed a man with his own hands, Cagliostro bitterly felt the loss of the human beings who died as a result of his machinations. They were his brothers and sisters; he mourned each one as he would a lovely temple he had never seen, upon hearing it had been demolished. He could not accept that their sacrifice was a natural thing, but he had come to understand that it was necessary.

Mussolini was more than a puppet; he was a powerful orator and propagandist who would learn to yank his followers in any direction that pleased him. But he was unbalanced, ultimately no better than a fool, ignorant of the Mysteries, incapable of seeing them when a few of the topmost veils were pulled aside. He would make an excellent pawn, and he would die believing he had engineered his own destiny.

The only reason he could be allowed into power was to prevent something far worse.

Cagliostro had seen another European tyrant in his cards and his bowl, a man who made Mussolini look like a painted tin soldier. Mussolini was motivated exclusively by power, and that was bad enough; but this other creature was a bottomless well of hatred. Given the chance, he would saturate all creation with his vitriol. Millions would die like vermin, and their corpses would choke the world. The scrying-water had shown terrifying factories built especially for disposal of the dead, ovens hot enough to reduce bone to ash, black smokestacks belching greasy smoke into a charred orange sky.

Cagliostro did not yet know this tyrant's precise identity, but he believed that the man would come from Austria and rule Germany. Two more good reasons for the Archduke's death: Francis Ferdinand would have made a powerful ally for such a man.

Cagliostro did not think he could altogether stop this tyrant. He had not foreseen it in time; he had been occupied with other matters. It was always thus when a man wished to save the world: he never knew where to look first, let alone where to begin.

Still, he believed he could stop the tyrant short of global domination, and he believed Mussolini was his key. Members of the Order in Italy were grooming him for Prime Minister. The title would unlock every door in Europe. If they could arrange for Mussolini to become the tyrant's ally, perhaps they could also ensure that Mussolini would in some way cause the tyrant's downfall.

Cagliostro finished his simple supper, collected the day's receipts, and turned off the lights. In the half-darkness he felt his way back to the small living quarters behind the store, where he sat up reading obscure volumes and writing long letters in a florid hand until nearly dawn. Over the past century, he had learned to thrive on very little sleep.

D'Antonio was sitting up in bed, back propped against the wooden headboard, bare legs sprawled atop the sweat-rumpled coverlet, bottle nestled between his thighs. The Archduke appeared near the sink. D'Antonio jumped, slopped wine onto the coverlet, cursed. "You gotta make me stain something every time you show up?"

"You need have no fear of me."

"No, you just want me to murder somebody for you. Why should that scare me?"

"It should not, sir. What should scare you is the prospect of a world ruled by Cagliostro and his Order."

"That guy again. Find him yet?"

"We know he came to New Orleans before 1910. We know he is living as an Italian grocer. But he has covered his tracks so successfully that we cannot determine his precise identity. We have a number of candidates."

"That's good." D'Antonio nodded, pretended to look thoughtful. "So you just gonna kill all of 'em, or what?"

"I cannot kill anyone, sir. I cannot even lift a handkerchief. That is why I require your help."

"I thought I told you last time, Duke: My services are unavailable. Now kindly fuck off."

"I feared you would say that. You will not change your mind?"

"Not a chance."

"Very well."

D'Antonio expected the wraith to vanish as it had last time. Instead, Francis Ferdinand seemed to break apart before his eyes. The face dissolved into a blur, the fingers elongated into smoke-swirls; then there was only a man-shaped shimmer of gossamer strands where the Archduke had been.

When D'Antonio breathed in, they all came rushing toward him.

He felt clammy filaments sliding up his nose, into his mouth, into the lubricated crevices of his eye sockets. They filled his lungs, his stomach; he felt exploratory tendrils venturing into his intestines. A profound nausea gripped him. It was like being devoured alive by grave-worms. The wraith's consciousness was saturating his own, blotting him out like ink spilled on a letter.

"*I offered you the chance to act of your own free will,*" Francis Ferdinand said. The voice was a hideous papery whisper inside his skull now. "*Since you declined, I am given no choice but to help you along.*"

☩

Joseph Maggio awoke to the sound of his wife choking on her own blood. Great hot spurts of it bathed his face. A tall figure stood by the bed, instrument of death in his upraised hand. Maggio recognized it as the axe from his own back yard woodpile, gleaming with fresh gore. It fell again with a sound like a cleaver going into a beef neckbone, and his wife was silent.

Maggio struggled to sit up as the killer circled to his side of the bed. He did not recognize the man. For a moment their eyes locked, and Maggio thought, *That man is already dead.*

"Cagliostro?" It was a raspy whisper, possibly German-accented, though the man looked Italian.

Wildly, Maggio shook his head. "No, no sir, my name's Joseph Maggio, I just run a little grocery and I never heard of no Cagli-whoever... oh Jesus-Mary-and-Joseph please don't hit me with that thing—"

216

The blade glittered in a deadly arc. Maggio sprawled halfway off the bed, blinded by a sudden wash of his own blood. The axe fell again and he heard his own skull crunching, felt the blade squeak against bone as the killer wrenched it out. Another searing cut, then another, until a merciful blow severed his jugular and he died in a red haze.

It was found that the killer had gained access to the Maggios' home by chiseling out a panel in the back door. The chisel had belonged to Joseph Maggio, as had the axe, which was found in a pool of blood on the steps. People all over New Orleans searched their yards for axes and chisels, and locked away these potential implements of Hell.

A strange phrase was found chalked on the pavement a block from the Maggios' house: "Mrs. Maggio is going to sit up tonight, just like Mrs. Tony." Its significance has not been discovered to this day.

Maggio's two brothers were arrested on the grounds that the Maggios were Sicilians, and Sicilians were prone to die in family vendettas. They were released by virtue of public drunkenness — they had been out celebrating the younger one's draft notice on the night of the murders, and had staggered home scarcely able to move, let alone lift an axe.

The detective in charge of the case was shot to death by a burglar one week after the murders. The investigation languished. News of the Romanov family's murder by Bolsheviks in Russia eclipsed the Maggio tragedy. The temperature climbed as June wore on.

"I detect Cagliostro's influences still at work on this plane," the Archduke said. *"We must move on to the next candidate."*

Deep inside his own ectoplasm-snared brain, which the wraith kept docile with wine except when he needed to use the body, D'Antonio could only manage a feeble moan of protest.

A clear tropical dawn broke over New Orleans as John Zanca parked his wagon of fresh breads and cakes in front of Luigi Donatello's grocery. He could not tell whether the grocer and his wife were awake yet, so he decided to take their order around to the back door. He gathered up a fragrant armful of baked goods still warm from the oven and carried them down the narrow alley that led to the Donatellos' living quarters.

When he saw the back door with its lower left panel neatly chiseled out, his arms went limp. Cakes and loaves rained on the grass at his feet.

After a moment, Zanca stepped forward — careful not to crush any of the baked goods — and knocked softly on the door. He did not want to do so, but there seemed nothing else to do. When it swung open, he nearly screamed.

Before him stood Luigi Donatello, his face crusted with blood, his hair and mustache matted with it. Zanca could see three big gashes in his skull, white edges of bone, wet gray tissue swelling through the cracks. How could the man still be standing?

"My God," moaned Donatello. "My God."

Behind him, Zanca saw Mrs. Donatello sprawled on the floor. The top of her head was a gory porridge. The slender stem of her neck was nearly cleaved in two.

"My God. My God. My God."

John Zanca closed his eyes and said a silent prayer for the Donatellos' souls and his own.

The newspapers competed with one another for the wildest theory regarding the Axeman, as the killer came to be known. He was a Mafia executioner, and the victims were fugitives from outlaw justice in Sicily. He was a vigilante patriot, and the victims were German spies masquerading as Italian grocers. He was an evil spirit. He was a voodoo priest. He was a woman. He was a policeman.

The Italian families of New Orleans, particularly those in the grocery business, barricaded their doors and fed their dogs raw meat to make them bloodthirsty. These precautions did not stop them from lying awake in the small hours, clutching a rosary or perhaps a revolver, listening for the scrape of the Axeman's chisel.

In high summer, when the city stank of oyster shells and ancient sewers, the killer returned. Two teenage sisters, Mary and Pauline Romano, saw their uncle butchered in his own bed. They could only describe the man as "dark, tall, wearing a dark suit and a black slouch hat."

Italian families with enemies began finding axes and chisels dropped in their yards, more like cruel taunts than actual threats. Some accused their enemies. Some accused other members of their families. Some said the families had brought it upon themselves. Tempers flared in the sodden August heat, and many killings were done with weapons other than axes. Men with shotguns sat guard over their sleeping families, nodding off, jerking awake at the slightest noise. A grocer shot his own dog; another nearly shot his own wife.

The city simmered in its own prejudice and terror, a piquant gumbo.

But the Axeman would not strike again that year.

D'Antonio came awake with a sensation like rising through cool water into sunlight. He tried to move his hands: they moved. He tried to open his eyes: the ceiling appeared, cracked and water-stained. Was it possible? Was the fucking monster really *gone*?

"Duke?" he whispered aloud into the empty room. His lips were dry, wine-parched. "Hey, Duke? You in there?"

To his own ears he sounded plaintive, as if he missed the parasitic murdering creature. But the silence in his head confirmed it. The wraith was gone.

He stared at his hands, remembering everything he had seen them do. How ordinary they looked, how incapable of swinging a sharp blade and destroying a man's brain, a woman's brain. For a long time he sat on the edge of the bed studying the beds of his nails and the creases in his palms, vaguely surprised that they were not caked with blood.

Eventually he looked down at himself and found that he was wearing only a filthy pair of trousers. He stripped them off, sponged himself to a semblance of cleanliness with the stale water in the basin, slicked his hair back and dressed in fresh clothes. He left his apartment without locking the door and set off in a random direction.

D'Antonio wandered hatless in the August sun for an hour or more. When he arrived at the *States* newspaper office, his face was streaming with sweat, red as a boiled crawfish. He introduced himself to the editor as a retired police detective, an expert on both Italians and murderers, and gave the following statement:

"The Axeman is a modern Doctor Jekyll and Mr. Hyde. A criminal of this type may be a respectable, law-abiding citizen when he is his normal self. Compelled by an impulse to kill, he must obey this urge. Like Jack the Ripper, this sadist may go on with his periodic outbreaks until his death. For months, even for years, he may be normal, then go on another rampage. It is a mistake to blame the Mafia. The Mafia never attacks women as this murderer has done."

He left the *States* office with several people staring bemusedly after him, but they printed the interview in its entirety.

After that, he lived his life much as he had been doing before the wraith's first visit. Armistice Day brought throngs of joyous revelers into the streets, as well as a blessed wave of cool weather; it had stayed sweltering through October. The war was over, and surely the wraith would never come back and make him do those things again.

He could not forget the organic vibration that ran up his arms as blade buried itself in bone.

In fact, he dreamed about it almost every night.

Francis Ferdinand returned in the spring of 1919.

He did not muck about with appearances this time, but simply materialized inside D'Antonio's head. D'Antonio collapsed, clawing at his temples.

"He deceived me for a time, but now I know he still walks this earth," said the wraith. *"We will find him."*

D'Antonio lay curled on his side, blinded by tears of agony, wishing for the comforts of the womb or the grave.

Giacomo Lastanza was a powerful man, but he had been no match for the fiend in his bedroom. Now he lay on the floor with his head split as cleanly as a melon, and his wife Rosalia cowered in a corner of the room clutching her two-year-old daughter, Mary. Mary was screaming, clutching at her mother's long black hair. As the Axeman turned away from her husband's body, Rosalia began to scream too.

"Not my baby! Please, Holy Mother of God, not my baby!"

The axe fell. Mary's little face seemed to crack open like an egg. Rosalia was unconscious before her skull felt the blade's first kiss.

D'Antonio lay naked on the floor. The apartment was a wasteland of dirty clothes and empty wine bottles. But his body was relatively sober for once — they'd run out of money — and as a result he was sharp enough to be carrying on an argument with the wraith.

"Why in hell do we have to kill the women? You can't be worried one of *them* is Cagliostro."

"He has consorted with a number of dangerous women. When we find him, his wife will merit killing also."

"And until then, you don't mind killing a few innocent ones?"

"It is necessary."

"What about that little baby?"

"If it had been Cagliostro's daughter, he would have raised her to be as wicked as himself."

D'Antonio got control of one fist and weakly pounded the floor with it.

"You goddamn monster — you're just gonna keep wasting people, and sooner or later I'll get caught and rot in prison. Or fry in the chair. And you'll go on your merry way and find some other poor sap to chase down that shadow of yours."

"The next one must be him! He is the last one on the list!"

"Fuck the list."

A bolt of excruciating pain shot through D'Antonio's head, and he decided to drop the argument.

Cagliostro was reading by candlelight when he heard the chisel scraping at his door. He smiled and turned a page.

The creature crept into his room, saw him in his chair with his head bent over a book. When it was ten feet away, Cagliostro looked up. When it was five feet away, it froze in mid-motion, restrained by the protective circle he had drawn.

By looking into its eyes, he knew everything about Joseph D'Antonio and the Archduke Francis Ferdinand. But the creature upon which he now gazed was neither D'Antonio nor the Archduke; this was a twisted amalgamation of the two, and it could only be called the Axeman.

He smiled at the creature, though its eyes blazed with murderous rage. "Yes, poor Archduke, it is I. And you will not harm me. In fact, I fear I must harm you yet again. If only you had accepted the necessity of your death the first time, you would be Beyond with your beloved Sophie now.

"No, don't think you can desert your stolen body as it lies dying. You'll stay in there, my boy. My magic circle will see to that!" Cagliostro beamed;

he was enjoying this immensely. "Yes, yes, I know about unfortunate ex-Detective D'Antonio trapped in there. But why do you think it was so easy for the Duke to take hold of your body, Mr. D'Antonio, and make it do the terrible things it did? Perhaps because you care not at all for your fellow human beings? 'When they came for the Jews, I did nothing, for I was not a Jew... Ah, forgive me. An obscure reference to a future that may never be. And you will both die to help prevent it."

He reached beneath the cushion of his armchair, removed a silver revolver with elaborate engraving on the butt and barrel, aimed it carefully, and put a ball in the Axeman's tortured brain.

Then he put his book aside, went to his desk, and took up his pen.

The letter was published in the *Times-Picayune* the next day.

```
                              Hell, March 13, 1919
                              Editor of the Times-Picayune
                              New Orleans, La.


    Esteemed Mortal:
    They have never caught me and they never will. They have never
seen me, for I am invisible, even as the ether that surrounds your
earth. I am not a human being, but a spirit and a fell demon from the
hottest hell. I am what you Orleanians and your foolish police call
the Axeman.


    When I see fit, I shall come again and claim other victims. I
alone know whom they shall be. I shall leave no clue except my bloody
axe, besmeared with the blood and brains of he who I have sent below
to keep me company.


    If you wish, you may tell the police to be careful not to rile me.
Of course, I am a reasonable spirit. I take no offense at the way they
have conducted their investigations in the past. In fact, they have
been so utterly stupid as to amuse not only me, but His Satanic Majesty,
Francis Joseph, etc. But tell them to beware. Let them not try to
discover what I am, for it were better that they were never born than
to incur the wrath of the Axeman. I don't think there is any need for
```

such a warning, for I feel sure the police will always dodge me, as they have in the past. They are wise and know how to keep away from all harm.

Undoubtedly, you Orleanians think of me as a most horrible murderer, which I am, but I could be much worse if I wanted to. If I wished, I could pay a visit to your city every night. At will I could slay thousands of your best citizens, for I am in close relationship with the Angel of Death.

Now, to be exact, at 12:15 (earthly time) on next Tuesday night, I am going to pass over New Orleans. In my infinite mercy, I am going to make a little proposition to you people. Here it is:

I am very fond of jazz music, and I swear by all the devils in the nether region that every person shall be spared in whose home a jazz band is in full swing at the time I have just mentioned. If everyone has a jazz band going, well, then, so much the better for you people. One thing is certain and that is that some of those people who do not jazz it on Tuesday night (if there be any) will get the axe.

Well, I am cold and crave the warmth of my native Tartarus, and as it is about time that I leave your earthly home, I will cease my discourse. Hoping that thou wilt publish this, that it may go well with thee, I have been, am, and will be the worst spirit that ever existed either in fact or realm of fancy.

THE AXEMAN

Tuesday was Saint Joseph's Night, always a time of great excitement among Italians in New Orleans. This year it reached a fever pitch. The traditional altars made of a hundred or more kinds of food were built, admired, dismantled, and distributed to the poor; lucky fava beans were handed out by the fistful; the saint was petitioned and praised. Still, St. Joseph's Night of 1919 would remain indelibly fixed in New Orleans memory as "The Axeman's Jazz Night."

Cafés and mansions on St. Charles blazed with the melodies of live jazz bands. Those who could not afford to pay musicians fed pennies into player pianos. A popular composer had written a song called "The Mysterious Axeman's Jazz, or, Don't Scare Me, Papa." Banjo, guitar, and mandolin players gathered on the levees to send jazz music into the sky, so the Axeman would be sure to hear it as he passed over. By midnight, New Orleans was a cacophony of sounds, all of them swinging.

Cagliostro walked the streets for most of the night, marveling (if not actively congratulating himself) at how completely he had brought the city together, and how gay he had made it in the process. No one so much as glanced at him: few people were on the streets, and Cagliostro had a talent for making himself invisible.

He had left the Axeman's corpse locked in the back of the house where it wouldn't spoil the groceries. First, of course, he had bludgeoned the face into unrecognizable mush with the Axeman's own axe. Everything that suggested the murdered man might be someone other than "Mike Pepitone," simple Italian grocer, was in the satchel Cagliostro carried with him.

On the turntable of his phonograph, as a final touch, he had left a recording of "Nearer My God To Thee."

When the jazz finally began to die down, he walked to the docks and signed onto a freighter headed for Egypt. There were any number of wonderful things he hadn't gotten around to learning last time.

ITALY, 1945

Toward the end, Mussolini lived in an elaborate fantasy world constructed by the loyal sycophants who still surrounded him. Whole cities in Italy were sanitized for his inspection, the cheering crowds along his parade routes supplemented by paid extras. When Hitler visited Rome, he too was deceived by the coat of sparkle on the decay, the hand-picked Aryan soldiers, the sheer bravado of *Il Duce*.

He believed he had cost Hitler the war. Germany lost its crucial Russian campaign after stopping to rescue the incompetent Italian army in Albania. Hitler had believed in the power and glory of Italy, and Mussolini had failed him.

Now he had been forced into exile on Lake Garda. He was a failure, his brilliant regime was a failure, and there were no more flunkies to hide these painful truths. He kept voluminous diaries in which he fantasized that his position in history would be comparable to Napoleon or Christ. His mistress Claretta lived nearby in a little villa, his only comfort.

On April 25, Germany caved in to the Allies. The Italian people, the ones he had counted on to save him with their loyalty, turned against him. Mussolini and Claretta fled, making for Switzerland.

A few last fanatical companions attempted to help them escape by subterfuge, but they were arrested by partisans on the north shore of Lake Como, discovered hiding in a German truck, cringing inside German coats and helmets. They were shot against the iron gate of an exquisite villa, and their bodies were taken to Milan and strung up by the heels to demonstrate the evils of Fascism.

All in service of the brotherhood of man.

AUTHOR'S NOTE: Joseph D'Antonio's statement and the Axeman's letter reprinted from the *New Orleans States* and *Times-Picayune*, 1918-19.

The Ouanga

by Fred Olen Ray

riving out to East Bexington was a bitch, for East Bexington lay upon no normal road. The path to the town, which consisted of little more than a hotel pub, rumored to date back 900 years, and about fifteen houses, was a one-lane dirt trail that passed through high grass and missed coming near anything civilized by miles. It was the kind of road on which one car would certainly have to pull into a field to let another car pass, and at night it was worse.

Yet, during his stay in Europe, Howard traveled from Dorchester to East Bexington at least once a week, for that is where Elizabeth Montclair lived. Elizabeth Montclair. In a big manor on the rocky English coast.

He gave her acting lessons; that and a good sound thumping every Thursday afternoon. Thursday being the day Elizabeth's husband, Lord John Montclair, took leave of the Gothic house by the sea for a spot of gin and tonic at the Gentlemen's Club in Dorchester.

The drive was a lonely one, and Howard had always wondered why he had never passed Lord Montclair on the way, but shrugged it off. There was, after all, more than one route to Dorchester, and Montclair had other rich idle friends about the area. They probably met up somewhere nearby, snorted out a pipeful of their favorite cavendish, and drove on together. It was Montclair's ritual. Howard counted on it.

As he pulled up to the manor that particular Thursday, he was a bit taken aback to see the Lord's grotesquely opulent Bentley still positioned like a trophy out front. The sky was clear over the ocean and without even the smell of a rain drop about it. Howard had given Elizabeth acting lessons; he had promised her a bit part in Hollywood. Her ability to give head wouldn't help get them through an impromptu performance, if that's what his Lordship had planned for the afternoon.

He rapped solidly on the door and waited. After a few moments it was opened by Lord John himself — Montclair's servants only being in attendance three odd days a week.

"Howard, my boy," the elder Montclair beamed. "Good to see you. Is it Thursday already?"

"Why, yes it is," he replied and put out his hand in a warm but insincere gesture.

Montclair grasped his hand firmly. "Come in."

Howard followed the raven-haired gentleman into the house he knew so well. The old Lord, being a bit of a self-proclaimed explorer with East Indian interests, had assembled a house of some stature. It looked more like a museum than a home, he had always thought. Exotic animal heads and skins protruded from the walls and weird savage carvings from around the globe rested on every shelf and bookcase.

"Watch the Polar Bear," Montclair said, pointing to a large rug on the floor. "It's getting a bit ratty."

Ratty indeed, he thought. I've screwed Elizabeth on that one more times than I can remember. She liked the softness and it went easy on her knees. "Is Elizabeth ready for her lessons?"

"No, she's not feeling well today. That's why I'm here instead of at the club."

Howard despised Montclair. The Lord had once been a big man, an adventurer and scholar who had traveled the globe, but now he was beginning to wither, his vitality sapped by age. His oversized mustache drooped dramatically about the corners of his mouth, its whiteness in stark contrast with his dyed hair. An old man of wealth and standing with a young wife, as usual.

"Please sit," Montclair said, waving his hand toward an overstuffed chair with a worn antimacassar. Howard smirked, inwardly remembering Elizabeth's nude form crouched wickedly upon it, her face pressed into the fabric, anxious for him to enter her.

"I'd like to see Elizabeth, if that's all right," Howard at last replied faintly.

"Of course. She's in her room — resting. You know where that is?"

"No," he lied.

"Then I'll show you."

Down the long hallway Howard followed Montclair, once almost taking a turn ahead of the Lord out of habit. Finally they came upon the door to Elizabeth's room — her quarters being separate from her husband's.

"Quiet now," Montclair whispered as he edged the door open a crack.

Howard looked inside and saw Elizabeth, as if dead, in deep sleep on her bed. He nodded, satisfied. If only that bed could talk.

Returning to the main hall, Lord Montclair offered him a brandy and the two sat, at a great distance from each other, across a large oriental rug.

Montclair savored his drink, rolling it about in his glass before taking a delicate sip. The vapors arising from the snifter were heady indeed, Howard mused.

It was very old stuff.

After a few silent minutes, he spoke up. "What do you think ails dear Elizabeth?"

Montclair took in a slow breath, held it for a moment, then cleared his throat. "Well, my boy, it's nothing to be worried about. Just a drug I gave her at breakfast this morning."

Howard straightened up. "A drug?"

"Just a bit of root extract that I picked up abroad," he chuckled. "You'd be surprised at what you can purchase on a common street corner in a place like Calcutta."

The Lord a *euthanato*? That's simply not possible. "But why...?" he stammered.

"Why? So that I could talk to you... privately," he hissed, leaning forward out of his seat. "You see, we have much to discuss."

"Such as?" The words slid smoothly across Howard's lips. His stomach began to knot up.

The Lord rolled his brandy about the glass once more, staring into its smoky darkness. "I think you know, Mr. Hughes. I'm talking about your improper liaisons with my beloved wife, Elizabeth."

"I..."

Montclair's hand shot up, halting the protest. "Don't bother, Howard... I've seen the two of you."

Howard sank back into his chair, defeated. "So now what?"

Montclair, smiling, reached deep into his breast pocket. Howard felt a twinge of fear run up his back. Surely this old fool didn't intend to shoot him right here in the living room!

From his pocket Montclair retrieved a doll. A small, ragged, little handmade thing of straw and mud. It had no features and no cloth about it. The old gentleman held it up for Howard to see, twisting it from side to side so as to afford a good look.

"Have you ever seen an ouanga?" Montclair asked slowly. "No, of course not. Well, this is what one looks like."

Howard felt a bit relieved at the absence of a gun, but the old man's crazy smile made him nervous. "What is it? A voodoo trinket you picked up on your travels for a few pounds like you did Elizabeth?"

Montclair blanched. "Speak no more of my wife, you scoundrel!" he burst out. "This ouanga," he said, recovering his composure. "This little figure is you. It cost me a bit, but in the short run, I think you're going to find it most effective. I've used them before, you know. They come from the West Indies."

No, he was not part of a Tradition. Montclair was an amateur. "Sorry, your Lordship, but I don't bite that easily; but I do think I've worn out my welcome here, so..." Howard rose to leave.

"Wait!" Montclair shouted, pushing himself to his feet. "You don't believe in the power of the supernatural? How foolish you young people are today. You don't believe in anything." Lord John turned from Howard and walked over to the stone hearth, soaking in the warmth of its crackling flame. "Dare I but place this ouanga in that fireplace you... you will believe."

Howard stiffened angrily, all his guilt vanishing in the face of this absurd and insulting affront. He strode to Montclair and stared hard into his eyes. The magick was done.

"You will believe," Montclair whispered hypnotically.

"I'll save you the trouble of giving me a hot-foot, old man," Howard sneered and snatched the tiny figurine from Lord John's grasp.

"Throw it in the fire if you are not afraid," Montclair chided. "Do it now and Elizabeth can be yours. I won't stop either of you."

Howard knelt by the crackling flames, feeling the heat flush his cheeks. It was hot. He hesitated. The old fool was crazy, Howard convinced himself — he must be. Either he's crazy or a Technomancer just smart enough to send a man fleeing in fear, never to return to East Bexington.

"Well, we can't live forever, eh Montclair?" he laughed, and threw the Ouanga into the flames.

Nothing happened.

Howard felt his nervousness fly away. Montclair was a bigger idiot than even he had suspected.

Both men watched the mud and straw doll catch and burst instantly in a popping, hissing mass of fire.

Then they both heard the agonized screams coming from the hall. Torturous screams that filled every corner of every room. And the smell. The acrid stench of smoke tangled with that of burning human flesh as it billowed out rapidly from under the bedroom door of Elizabeth Montclair.

As Lord John ran wildly down the hall, Howard Hughes contemplated. Now, he wouldn't need to buy R.K.O. studios. Besides, he had an article due to *Paradigma* about his latest theories in air travel. That would occupy him for a while.

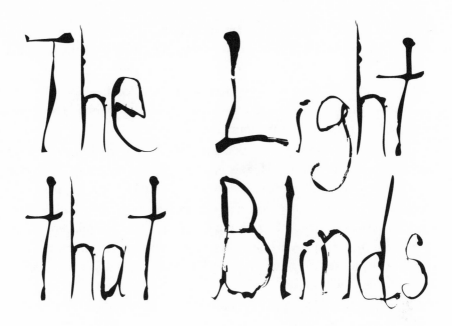

The Light that Blinds

by Brad Linaweaver and Victor Koman

ell the truth, but lead so improbable a life that the truth will never be believed.

—Aleister Crowley

The old man with the white hair shook his head peevishly. "No, no!" he said. "You're getting it all wrong. Let me tell it."

A pleasant summer breeze stirred what was left of the hair on the old man's head, but the wind brought with it the odor of some small animal that had recently died. The second man was older than the first and completely bald. He sat in a wheelchair, inhaling oxygen through a nose tube and wheezing out his words in a thick British accent.

The old man with the white hair hated the way the older man sounded like Winston Churchill. The mere sound of his voice made him nervous and caused perspiration to bead on his clean-shaven upper lip. The deep, rumbling voice could be made out between gasps of breath, saying: "I have all the particulars. We only differ on interpretation. But then, we always did."

"Interpretations?" his companion mocked him, voice breaking. "You claim that *I* lost and *you* won." The angry tone left no doubt that the latter was more annoying to the speaker than the former.

The gaunt, bald Englishman took a deep breath, enjoyed the rush of oxygen to his brain, and said nothing. He was not about to become upset. A good part of his longevity he attributed to knowing when to take it easy. Sometimes he was surprised that his companion had survived as long as he had, given his personality type. But then a certain type of angry, burning soul renews itself. Any practitioner of the Art knew the secret meaning of the burning bush encountered by Moses. You don't tell people how to live unless something more than blood fills your veins with fire.

"Listen," said the bald man, "I rescued the world from the blackest of black sorcerers."

"Well, I escaped," said the other man. "That's not exactly a defeat, is it?"

The bald man had a ready answer: "That all depends on what your opponent is trying to do."

✠

1945 was not a good year for the Third Reich. One balmy afternoon a critic with unimpeachable credentials admitted this fact. "We are losing the war," said Adolf Hitler. He had known since Stalingrad. He wouldn't admit the truth to very many people, but Dr. Paul Joseph Goebbels was an exception. The Führer continued: "I can't even convince Speer that we have a chance."

"If only we could turn him into our Spear of Destiny," replied Goebbels, a thin smile on his thinner lips.

Hitler shrugged. "The man has performed miracles with armaments, but now we need a bigger miracle."

"The V-weapons..." began Goebbels.

"Too few, too late."

"If only the occult nonsense was real," said Goebbels, half to himself.

This offhand comment encouraged Hitler to take a trip down memory lane: "I believed once! The whole thing, the Thule Society, Vril power, Pansophia,

Hoerbiger's "Moon of Ice" theory, all of it. But according to the astrological charts they drew up, we would have enjoyed an unusually warm winter. Instead, we get a Russian winter that would freeze the balls off Napoleon."

Goebbels put in his two marks' worth: "Mein Führer, they misled you. But you've always been able to save our bacon…"

"Anything not kosher," Hitler quipped.

Goebbels cleared his throat, and continued: "You've so often saved the day with political solutions. How can the British and the Americans prefer a Bolshevized Europe to us?"

Hitler was feeling very tired. He shook his head. "My last card, old friend. I wouldn't have been sucked into a two-front war if those bastards in British intelligence hadn't tricked me into thinking they would never accept Stalin devouring Germany."

"We didn't count on the influence of the Jews," said Goebbels sadly.

Hitler put a hand on the shoulder of his old comrade. "Funny, isn't it? We underestimated the Jews! I was too easy on them, and I waited too damned long before giving the SS those verbal orders the brave lads in black wanted so badly to hear. We're not going down alone, and our enemies will have something to remember us by."

"Don't blame yourself," said Goebbels. "I wish black magic were true! I wish we could use the sacrifice of a few Jews to gain you the powers the occultists were always promising would belong to the Führer."

Hitler nodded. A visit from the good doctor always made him feel better. After the propaganda minister left, the leader of the Third Reich couldn't forget the words about sacrifice. Even a thorough-going materialist like Goebbels could at least hope. Hitler had once embraced a faith.

He looked at himself in a mirror, surprised, as always, to witness how the war had aged him — each facial wrinkle was a deep valley telling the story of a campaign won or lost. So what if the occult nuts still insisted that the moon was made of ice? Wernher von Braun was obviously right and they were wrong, if the claim had to be taken literally. But as a metaphor — no, as a secret code — the "moon of ice" could open the door to some kind of victory for National Socialism. He was ready to grasp at anything that could save the heart of Nazism, even if it meant the end of Germany.

Up to now, staying in the middle of the road had always worked for Adolf Hitler. That was how he had sold himself to the German people as the safe alternative to the extreme of Bolshevism on the left and the extreme of unregulated capitalism on the right. It was how he calmed the army by getting rid of the SA leadership. That cautious strategy had given him a third of the world, combined with counting on political solutions when military might proved inadequate. Goebbels was certainly right about that. Now that Hitler had run out of political solutions, and he was running low on fuel, armaments, men and hope... now was the time to try something radical.

He'd heard of a joke that was being told by American GI's: "Since the war is going so badly, Hitler will send out word that he's no longer Mister Nice Guy!" The time had come to make the joke real. The time had come for him to activate an agent whose code name was Tränker.

✙

1945 was not a good year for Aleister Crowley. He felt like shit. "The Lord giveth and the Lord taketh away," he muttered to himself. "So if He can do this with the women in my life, why can't He take away this other kind of pain?"

He was sick in bed (bad enough) at the age of sixty-nine (still worse) in a British boarding house (the pits). All he had in his possession was a lifetime of memories, a single book, and a single goal.

He was known to some as *To Mega Therion*, the Great Beast; and known to others as The Wickedest Man Alive. That's how he'd been introduced to Ernest Hemingway in Paris. He liked Hemingway's reaction. "If that's true," the burly American writer had said, "I'd like to buy you a drink." Crowley accepted.

To think it had come to this. Crowley didn't want to end his life stuck in a little room at the Hastings boarding house called Netherwood, breathing laboriously as his lungs slowly succumbed to the asthma that had plagued him so very long. He'd found a solution to his problem: a solution of heroin to clear his breathing passages!

Condemned as a vile addict, told that his profligate lifestyle would be his undoing, he wondered, between coughs, if a stray German bomb might not get him first. Maybe one of those new-fangled V-rockets would do the trick. Although it hurt like hell, he had to laugh at how many of his detractors he had already outlived.

He thumbed through the tattered, dog-eared copy of *The Book of the Law*. Dictated to him in Egypt by the spirit Aiwass in 1904, it was the foundation of his religion of Thelema and the cornerstone of his magickal society: Ordo Templi Orientis. Filled with obscure symbolism and veiled prophecy, it acted as a Rorschach test for his fellow Thelemites. In his own secret thoughts, though, he much preferred the introductory chapters. They turned out to be more immediately prophetic in light of the events of the past decade. He gazed at the beginning of Chapter Four:

Democracy dodders.

Ferocious Fascism, cackling Communism, equally
frauds, cavort crazily all over the globe.

They are hemming us in.

They are the abortive births of the Child, the New
Aeon of Horus.

Liberty stirs once more in the womb of Time.

He placed the book down on the bed covers and took a long, deep, rattling breath of air. The wheezing took hold once more, constricting his chest and contorting the haggard face beneath the bald skull into a virtual death mask.

"Gwen!" he cried out raspily. "Heroin! Hurry!"

Gwen — a night nurse living at Netherwood whom Crowley had charmed into assisting him — sauntered in after a few minutes, carrying a stainless steel tray. Pointing at him like an evil dagger was an instrument of modern magic: a glass syringe filled with a clear liquid. He wasn't looking at the needle, though, not when there was a woman worthy of his attention.

Gwen's body had been full in her youth, but the war with Germany, and the stress caused by the bombings, had left her, only in her mid-thirties, almost as gaunt as the wan man on the bed. But there was something cute and very much alive in her face that the war had not touched.

"Roll 'er up," she said. Finding a vein in the old man's withered arm, she made a tsking sound and muttered, "Don't see why you don't cure yourself of this, you bein' such a great saucerer an' all."

Laughing weakly, he answered, "The Law of Conservation of Magickal Effort, child. I'm saving up for one last blow against the Hun."

"So what'cha waiting for, luv?"

The diacetylmorphine hit. His brachia dilated almost instantly. He gazed up at her with dark eyes suddenly alive from an internal energy that nearly crackled in the stark room. "Two objects, and a Sign," he answered huskily. Then he slept and dreamed of a world that seemed far more real than the one he inhabited.

Aleister Crowley did not have long to wait. Within one week he recognized the intrusion of a greater universe, involving greater stakes than something as relatively unimportant as the Second World War.

As was his habit, he read the morning *London Times* with a nearly frantic intensity, flipping through the large pages, scanning headlines, noting names. After a quick perusal of the obituaries to raise his spirits, he found the Sign.

An American freelance writer was missing. Of German background, the man had been doing a series about the pseudo-scientific beliefs of the "Moon of Ice" cult for *Astounding Science Fiction* magazine. (Rumor had it that von Braun secured copies of the magazine through Switzerland and loved how the writer made fun of Hoerbiger and his followers.)

The *Times* story suggested that the man had infiltrated one of the Nazi magickal societies and sent word, shortly before his disappearance, that Adolf Hitler had acquired the Spear of Longinus, the weapon that supposedly pierced the side of Jesus Christ as the Savior hung upon the cross at Calvary. The legend was that anyone possessing this spear would be irresistible in battle.

Whether Hitler knew how to use it or not, Crowley was certain that among the sorcerers of the Third Reich there existed one who had the necessary background. Crowley had helped found the German branch of the OTO twenty years before from the German Rosicrucian Movement. In 1935, the Nazis banned all public occult groups. Even his close friend and OTO Grand Treasurer Karl Germer had been arrested by the Gestapo. The German OTO members were victims of Nazism, not collaborators.

Then Crowley read something that chilled him to the core of his being: among a list of religious art treasures looted from the Egyptian Museum in Cairo during the enormously successful African campaign, was a piece noted in the article simply as "Exhibit No. 666, Painting of Horus."

Crowley's mind reeled in horror. *Adolph Hitler and the SS possessed the Stélé of Revealing!*

If Gwen had been in the room at that moment, she would have rushed over with medication. Crowley felt the blood drain from his face. The situation was worse than he could have imagined. *The Book of the Law* had shown him

238

the way to that particular exhibit. To the OTO, the Stélé was the holiest of holy icons. He read further.

The Egyptian treasures had been delivered to Berlin by a man identified only as Tränker.

Crowley reread it. *Tränker!* While the German OTO members were not Nazis, he could not say as much for the head of the group called Pansophia, the man called Frater Recnartus, the man responsible for Crowley's expulsion in 1925: Tränker.

Tränker would know what to do with the Spear and the Stélé.

When Crowley frowned, his whole face seemed to sink into itself. He began quoting aloud from *The Book of the Law*. His concentration was so intense that he didn't notice that Gwen had returned to the room but was standing in a corner, watching, saying nothing.

"Number Four is: Choose ye an island!" he said. "Five is: Fortify it! Six: Dung it about with enginery of war! Seven: I will give you a war-engine. Eight: With it ye shall smite the peoples; and none shall stand before you. Nine: Lurk! Withdraw! Upon them! This is the Law of the Battle of Conquest: thus shall my worship be about my secret house. Ten: Get the Stélé of Revealing itself; set it in thy secret temple...."

He stopped, sighed heavily. Then Gwen dared speak: "Are you all right?"

"Oh," he said, unconcerned over what she might have heard. "Could you bring me a glass of water, dear?"

She did so. Reciting words of power always made his mouth dry. He thought about the meaning of what he had recited. The island dunged about with enginery of war could be the German state. In a world suffused with Magick, it stood as the repository of the darkest sorcery, the birthing ground of the vilest of the black arts.

And now it held two of the mightiest magickal weapons in the world. For those who were prepared, illumination opened the doors to the universe. The light of knowledge grew ever brighter. For those with small, twisted visions, such light was dangerous beyond measure.

The *Times* article openly scoffed at Hitler's ability to do anything with the Spear of Destiny. Crowley smiled. That effete corps of impudent snobs had been wrong before. One of them tried to argue that Hitler had ordered a search for the Ark of the Covenant — a ridiculous charge considering that the Nazis thought the whole story of Moses to be a Jewish lie. They would hardly spend time and money looking for something they didn't believe to exist! In contrast, they did believe in the Holy Grail. It was Himmler's pet obsession.

Hitler had apparently laid hands on his obsession — the Spear of Longinus. Now with the Stélé in his possession as well, the Nazis had a last chance to turn the red tide of war in their favor.

Gwen returned to the room, wearing the I-have-to-interrupt-your-deep-thoughts-expression. "Mr. Crowley, you have a visitor," she said.

He looked up to see a thin man in a black robe with a red descending trigram of fire sewn above his heart chakra. Crowley gazed at an aging magician whose best feature was strong hazel eyes. The thin man touched his head, heart and groin in the traditional greeting, and said, in a voice that made every *l* and *r* sound like a *w*, "Most magnificent Master Therion, I have come to assist you in your most holy mission."

"Mission?" the old man asked, a strange sensation of urgent energy suffusing him. "What mission? Who are you?" He peered closer. "Regardie? Israel Regardie?"

The man in the black robe smiled. He was a slender man, theatrically handsome in a manner reminiscent of the actor Leslie Howard, shot down by Germans nearly two years before.

Crowley brightened upon recognition of his former secretary. "Regardie, you chiropractic quack, what mission are you babbling about?"

"With comments like that about chiropractic procedures, someone might mistake you for H. L. Mencken." The man in the ebony robe withdrew a *Times* clipping from within one of his large sleeves. "I'm going to help you capture the Stélé of Revealing and destroy the Nazis, of course."

✠

The spy's name was Gwen and her face was so beautiful that Hitler felt twenty years younger in her presence. She was one of the Valkyries, female agents who aspired to be a Mata Hari for their Führer. She was proud of her emaciated appearance, convinced that nobody expected a spy to be undernourished.

"This sounds like the sort of thing they worry about in the Thule Society," said Hitler in response to her report.

"I wouldn't know about that," she answered stiffly. "My loyalty is to you, Mein Führer."

"Of course, child," he replied, placing a hand on her shoulder and feeling a slight thrill.

She stiffened her posture even more and her blue eyes stared into his. "Mein Führer, there is nothing amusing about the fact that one of the most dangerous men in the world has decided to take the Stélé from you. Aleister Crowley has no intention of allowing you to make use of the Vril power."

"Do you know where Vril power originates?" Hitler asked.

She had taken the usual academic courses. "They say prehistoric Tibet," she answered.

In the dark, someone laughed. A handsome young man, a perfect stereotype of the Aryan superman with blond hair, long arms, flat stomach, and a mocking grin, stepped forward into the light. He answered Hitler's question: "Vril power was invented by a British writer, Edward Bulwer-Lytton, in a novel called *The Coming Race*. A number of Jewish intellectuals want to immortalize Bulwer-Lytton as an unusually bad writer."

"Is he a bad writer?" asked the author of *Mein Kampf*.

"Of course not," said the young man. "They hate him because he is an approved writer in the Reich."

"Typical," said the Führer, glancing at Gwen who patiently waited for one of the men to address her. The master of Europe continued: "If we had Vril power, we could conquer everything in sight. How do the true believers account for this novel?"

The young man shrugged. "They say that Bulwer-Lytton discovered the power. They see his novel as a kind of bible; and that he received supernatural inspiration. All that matters, Mein Führer, is that the powers are real."

"We will find out," said Adolf Hitler. "May your faith prove the equal of your mettle. Now you may leave, special agent Tränker. I will continue the debriefing of special agent Gwendolyn." He smiled at her. She smiled back. She was a good Nazi.

✠

The Jews stared silently at the massive castle gate. Thirteen of them sat in the back of the troop truck. They were not shackled. They did not have to be. Any spark of resistance, any instinct to flee, had been systematically worked, beaten and starved out of them. They had survived the pogroms, they had survived Kristallnacht, they had survived typhus at Bergen-Belsen. After all they had been through, it was reasonable for them to assume they could survive the next item on the menu.

But as Robert Cohen recognized Castle Burg Werfenstein, perched above the Danube with a Swastika and *fleur-de-lis*, his last hope died. A practitioner of Cabalistic magic, he had been arrested as an anarchist in politics and for being on the wrong side of the occult. This was years before the general round-up of Jews. Cohen knew the significance of the castle. He didn't whisper a word to his comrades, but he silently said a prayer for all of them.

While still a free man, Cohen had known about Himmler's desire to build a Wotanist priesthood, the Armanenschaft. The SS had restored the Knights Templar, the first version of which had been suppressed by the Church in the 1300s. Cohen feared that inside this quaint castle was the Ordo Novi Templi (Order of the New Temple), the traditional meeting place of top National Socialist occultists from all over Europe.

Himmler, as Reichsführer of the SS, was general of the order. If they once caught sight of him in a place holy to the Nazis, they were dead men. Cohen shrugged. They were probably dead no matter what.

The truck passed through the gate, which lowered behind them without a squeak. "Probably greased with Jewish blood," whispered the man next to Cohen, who wished the man had chosen some other image.

The truck stopped. The door opened to reveal not the expected SS uniforms but men in black leather robes. Cohen was the only one to recognize the most dangerous branch of the SS: the Office of Magickal Weaponry, sometimes simply called *die Zauberwaffe*.

The black-robed men ordered them from the truck. In the cold of the evening, dressed only in ragged prison stripes with the yellow and red triangles sewn on their tattered sleeves in mockery of a Magen David, they stumbled out of the back and followed the Zauberwaffen into the depths of the castle proper.

It will be over soon, thought Cohen. He had prepared himself to see Himmler. He wasn't prepared for the sight of Adolf Hitler standing calmly by a black altar, arms crossed, smiling as if he'd been told an amusing story. A woman screamed. Cohen remembered her, a rabbi's wife. She had been prepared for many things, too; all sorts of horrible possibilities that went with the phrase, "Special Handling." This was more than she could bear.

Next to Hitler stood a man whose face was hidden beneath the hood of his robe, his arms outstretched over a manlike form ten feet long. The figure had no face, no fingers, no toes, no features whatsoever. Yet it looked like a thing of real flesh.

To Cohen, the most disturbing aspect of the blank figure was that it breathed. The hideous thing's chest rose and fell rhythmically, yet it had no nose. It had no mouth and Cohen wanted to scream. He noticed an object placed on what passed for the thing's head: a rectangular piece of ancient Egyptian artwork that seemed to shimmer with its own supernal light.

The others — recognizing the image of their nightmares made manifest — shrank in horror. Some fell into prayer, nodding their upper bodies as they recited entreaties to God.

Hitler decided to make their experience complete. He spoke to them in their own language — German. "Go ahead and pray to the devil, Yahweh. We serve the True God. He will hear your prayers, but you won't like how He answers."

As the SS mages took their places on the points of the Swastika inlaid on the chamber floor, red on black, Adolf Hitler, Chancellor of Greater Germany, founder of the Third Reich, and best-selling author (by order) listened with silent pleasure. Frater Recnartus began to utter words in an ancient language, contemporaneous with the runes that he drew in the air about him with the iron spearhead he clutched in his sweating hand.

The runic tracings glowed with a hideous crimson luminosity that hung in the chamber like blood spattered on a wall. The rabbi's wife had stopped screaming. Cohen held her arm tight, and they both moved their lips in silent prayer.

As the incantation rose and runes filled the air about the creature on the slab, pain grew inside her breast as if something grasped her living heart and began to pull. The other prisoners appeared to be enduring the same agony.

Suddenly the voice that filled the room switched to German: "Behold the Jew, whose evil has sapped the youth of our land. Now the Jew can make amends, as fodder. Look, you children of Abraham; look for the first and last time upon the engine of our victory, the unifying symbol of a New Europe. The Star of

David is food for the Holy Swastika. Your devil race will torture mankind no longer. The Übermensch is hungry."

The man on Cohen's left writhed in sudden agony and collapsed to the black and red floor. Something golden shimmered around him; then — as if being sucked down a horrible vortex — the glow swirled into the mound of flesh on the altar.

The thing's form grew more defined, arms and hands reaching out from the stumps and two holes appearing where eyes should be. Another prisoner fell, clutching so hard at his heart that his fingers rent the six-pointed star from his grimy uniform. As he hit the floor, his hand opened. The star shriveled and charred where it lay.

The thing had distinct fingers now, and ears, and eyes, feet, toes, mouth, nose. As the people died, the shape became more and more human. Or superhuman, some might say. Finally there were only two victims left alive.

Robert Cohen and the woman looked at each other. He was moving his lips, silently reciting magic, calling out for an avenger. She was reciting the earliest prayer she had ever learned. There was something almost sexual about standing together on the brink of death, a man and woman bound together by someone else's hate. Their union was real. Not even Hitler could cause them to divorce each other.

She gazed at the monstrosity on the stone table. Fully flesh now, it was ten feet from head to toe. Its body frighteningly humanoid, its head was nonetheless large, as if its skull — covered with soft platinum hair — housed a mighty brain. Eyes still closed, its face possessed the look of an angel in repose.

It was the most horrifying abomination she had ever seen. She stared at the spellborne creature and repeated: "B'shem Adonai, B'shem Adonai, B'shem Adonai..."

The Übermensch opened its steely blue eyes and gazed with curiosity at the woman for a moment. Then it smiled blissfully and raised a mighty arm, at first appearing to salute, but then lowering the arm, hand open, palm out, as if gesturing to the woman. She did not feel her flesh blasted into nothingness; she only felt the incomparable agony of her soul being drawn into the most vile plexus imaginable.

Cohen died last. He stopped praying long enough to speak to Hitler: "You keep finding new ways to lose, you poor bastard."

"Magick is the fire," said Aleister Crowley to Israel Regardie. The two stood in the darkened, six-sided room within Crowley's former mansion called Boleskine, hastily made available by the OTO upon word of his unexpected return. "It gives off its own light to those who can see it," he continued. "Feeble magick gives a dim glow, but the light of a master sorcerer is like a beacon in the night."

"Yes," said Regardie. "That's what I figured."

Crowley was on a roll. "You know, although I've been called the wickedest man alive..."

"You've said that yourself."

"...by people who don't pay attention to life's little details, Regardie, old friend, this slander is directed at me by those who fail to appreciate the great quest to apply the scientific method to the aims of religion."

"Yes."

"By the way, when I've said I was the wickedest man alive, how do you know I wasn't quoting?"

While Regardie pondered the implications of Crowley's question, the great mage performed the Ritual of the Hexagram to cleanse the room of all negative power and imbue it with his own white magick. The ritual proceeded with a scientist's accuracy.

When Crowley finished by crossing his arms over his chest and saying, "L.V.X., Lux, the Light of the Cross," he turned to Regardie and intoned in a vibrant monotone: "The Dark One who has made himself an enemy of Solomon by burning the Seal of his people must face now their ultimate agent of vengeance."

On the catafalque in the center of the Hexagram was an unformed mass of clay. Crowley only wished that he could have imported the clay from Prague, but the home of Rabbi Loew belonged to the Nazis now. Common clay from the holy ground of a London graveyard had to do. So long as the final result didn't talk with a cockney accent, he'd be satisfied. It had taken a bit of trouble getting the clay to Loch Ness for this magickal operation.

The great mage took a break and said, "Before I complete this process, old friend, I have a confession to make." Regardie always perked up at the confessions of Aleister Crowley, who continued with: "I'm glad that nurse isn't with us any longer."

"Where do you think she is?"

"Back in the Fatherland, I imagine, giving a full report to Hitler."

Regardie was stunned. "If you think she was a spy, why didn't you act?"

"I did. I got better."

Regardie was having trouble with this. "How do you know she was a spy?"

"Too thin. No proper English nurse gets that thin. Well, let's get on with it."

☩

The powers of Aleister Crowley left Regardie speechless. As the Master Therion spoke the ancient incantation, the room began to spark with weird lights, swirling, flowing, gushing into the eight-foot-long mass. The thing slowly took form as if a hundred invisible hands were working it into pliancy.

"Yod Hay Vov Hay!" the magus cried. "Yeheshua! Take the holy unspeakable name of God into thine mouth! I — *To Mega Therion* — filled with the unconsumed *amrita* of a hundred times a hundred magickal operations summon forth the agent of retribution!"

At his nod, Israel Regardie placed a slip of parchment on which were penned the forty-two Hebrew letters spelling the secret name of the God of Abraham into the widening maw of the metamorphosing super-being. Finding its clay-slick tongue, he wedged the paper beneath it. Though the mouth should have been cold and firm, Regardie felt a moist heat like breath blow up his sleeve.

Crowley's voice filled the night. "I call upon the Law of Thelema to wrest from the enemy that most sacred of objects, and to do battle with the Dark Ones. 'Drag down their souls to awful torment: laugh at their fear: spit upon them!' I summon forth the Golem of the Jews to rise up and lay waste to *der Führer von dem Volker!*"

The six-sided room shattered and fell away from them. The clay — invested with an unearthly force — took the form of an eight-foot-tall gray giant and rose from its catafalque.

The three — two men and something more than human — stood on a dark hilltop before a stark granite castle above which loomed dark, swirling clouds. Something red and sinister flickered on the bottom of the cloud.

"Where the hell are we?" asked Regardie in utter bafflement.

"Apt choice of words," said Crowley. The Golem said nothing, so Crowley continued: "The spell has taken us to the very center of the storm."

Regardie gasped as the flickering light on the underside of the cloud took definite shape. The castle on the dark mountain stood beneath the malevolent glare of a blood-red Swastika arched across the vault of the sky. It looked as if some impossibly powerful spotlight threw the symbol of the enemy in the face of eternity.

"Remember everything you ever learned about magick," said Crowley. "Your life depends on it."

A few seconds later machine-gun fire turned Israel Regardie into a corpse. Renowned for his practical jokes, Crowley wondered if he should take credit for this one. While he hugged the ground, he allowed the reality of what had transpired to wash over him. He thought Regardie was a pretty good writer and wondered what books the man might have written if he had survived.

Then he thought about guns... and the fact that he'd come without a gun to do battle with Nazi Germany. Of course, he had remembered to bring his Golem. As he watched the clay monster lumber in the direction of the two SS men on patrol, and rip their heads off as easily pulling corks from a bottle of Burgundy wine, Crowley decided that if you were going to fight a war you could do a lot worse than bring a Golem.

He followed the monster down the hill toward the castle, remembering to keep his head low. A guard saw them and opened fire at the Golem. The bullets disappeared in the body and never came out the other side. Magickal clay was a good thing to stay behind. Crowley almost rode his monster piggyback, right up to the castle door.

"Come out and play, Adolf!" he cried out in flawless German. "This is Aleister Crowley, the most evil man alive."

"Says who?" came a voice familiar from too many radio speeches.

"I know what you've been up to," Crowley shouted. "I've come for the Stélé. You can keep the Spear of Longinus if you put it back with the Hapsburg treasures where it belongs."

"You're in no position to dictate terms!"

"Let's get this over with. You should be with your troops in Berlin so you can show them how to get their asses kicked by the Russians."

"I have enough advisors already!"

"Are you coming down to face my Golem or not? If you have any magick, now is the time to put up or shut up."

"Your Golem is a clay pigeon compared to what I've got. Wait right there!"

Then Crowley listened in amazement as Hitler gave orders to his men that they should hold their fire. The idea that Hitler would give up any advantage at this point in the war could only mean that he had used the power of the Stélé and was dying, in a manner of speaking, to try it out.

Crowley was not really surprised when the door of the castle opened, slowly, quietly, to reveal the Nazi idea of the Overman. "So you have a Golem, too," said Crowley as the blond giant came out with Hitler right behind.

"This is not a Golem," said the Führer. "That's Jewish! Behold the Übermensch."

"Whatever," said Crowley.

There was nothing else to say. The monsters did not require orders. They faced each other and that was all that mattered. The human world was a shadowy realm to them under any circumstances. Facing each other, their reality grew stronger — battle would be a consummation for one of them.

They came together with the sound of two freight trains colliding in the night. They did not have human muscles. Nothing bulged on their arms or in their legs. But they stood there, force against force, like two glaciers, each attempting to budge the other. In strength, they were perfectly matched, yin and yang, night and day.

As if by unspoken agreement, they released each other, stood back and stared, impassive face to impassive face. The matter had to be resolved by some other means. The Übermensch raised his massive hands. The Golem did the same as if a mirror image of the other.

Crowley opened his mouth in awe, anticipating the magickal duel that was to come. Glancing over at Hitler, he saw confusion on the dictator's face; but the Führer wasn't worried yet. He'd put all his faith in the Übermensch. At least a dozen Nazis hung back at the open castle door, shadows needing Hitler to give them substance. Crowley reflected how this might be the first time in years that Hitler had faced danger without being surrounded by his men.

A tremendous wind came out of nowhere, its greatest force striking the ground between the monsters. Then the giant Swastika, that was no searchlight pattern, disconnected itself from the cloud above and descended, gently, growing bigger and bigger, until it hung directly over the head of the Übermensch. Now it was the size of the largest flag in the Reich. The Übermensch reached up, touched it and held it, his whole body glowing from the unnatural energy released.

The Golem did nothing but wait, hands still raised as if a child anticipating a thrown ball. The Übermensch struck the Golem with the Swastika and there was a sizzling sound, a burning odor of roasted dead, as clay touched by the magickal symbol grew soft and melted.

"There is hope for the future!" screamed Adolf Hitler. "One war will not spell the end of the dream."

"You never think anything through," said Crowley. "Impatience is your curse."

The Golem defended itself. The Golem went on the attack, and...

✠

"You can stop there," said the old man with the white hair, sweating in the South American sun. The bald man hated the shriveled little man's Austrian accent.

"You never should have shaved off the mustache, Adolf," said the bald man.

"You never should have betrayed Germany, Crowley!" said the man with white hair.

Every now and then Hitler could surprise him. "What are you talking about? I fought you from the start."

"I'm talking about the Great War, the first one, damn you. You were an agent for Germany, and you sold us out to the British Empire."

Crowley laughed. The sensation hurt and he needed more oxygen before answering: "I was a double agent. Besides, I betrayed both the British and the Germans. You could call me a triple agent in that one."

"You've always been a thorn in our side," Hitler went on. "Only recently I found out you were behind our embarrassment with the Swiss..."

"At the start of your little war."

"The German attaché showed the Swiss attaché the smallest spring we had made in our machine shops, a marvel of German efficiency. They returned the spring with little holes they had drilled in it to show how much more advanced they were in miniature work."

"So?"

"My agents tell me you helped the Swiss do this with your magick!"

Crowley laughed again. This time he didn't take a hit of oxygen. "That's paranoid rubbish, Adolf. The Swiss didn't need any help to..."

When Hitler got himself worked up, he wasn't very good at paying attention. He kept on: "You tried to turn me over to the Nuremberg trials!"

Crowley shook his head in amazement. "I never engage in futile behavior, Adolf. I've always agreed with the thesis of Professor Joseph Schulman, when he wrote in *The New Yorker* that the Allies wouldn't have dared try to execute another head of state. They'd never set a precedent to be used against themselves."

Hitler still wasn't listening, an entirely characteristic trait. "You took my Stélé," he said, pouting.

"I won, Adolf."

"You cheated."

"There is no way to cheat when two Golems..." He saw Hitler's withering glare. "Well, when a Golem and an Übermensch duel to the death! You got off easy. When the Übermensch was destroyed, he shrunk down and withered, the hair darkened, and he ended up looking a bit like you! You can't deny that you took advantage of the situation. By the way, was that really Eva Braun in the bunker?"

Now Hitler was listening. "Yes, she found out about the switch and we thought it would be more convincing if she died with me. Ashes to ashes..."

Crowley was feeling stronger as he argued with the man who thought of himself as the Hero of the Second World War. "You have nothing to complain about. Mossad agents have never come close to getting you. You paid off the few who did or had them killed. You are one of the most powerful mages practicing the black arts, a secret master corrupting new generations of neo-Nazis. Yet all you can do is sit here and bitch about the Stélé."

"With the Stélé, there would have been a new Reich by now."

Crowley nodded. "Yes, and that's where I stopped you cold."

"By cheating, by doing one of your cursed practical jokes."

Painful as it was, Crowley leaned forward into the ex-Führer's face. He wanted to make something perfectly clear. "Once and for all, Adolf, I prepared the Golem better than you and your oafs prepared the Übermensch. You wanted the magickal advantages of the Swastika. You should have known better than to take the Tibetan life symbol, and the life symbol of certain American Indian tribes, and reverse it for your foolish death symbolism."

"We were ready for the Star of David. We were ready for the cross. We could have won. We could have been contenders..."

Crowley leaned even closer, and his voice became deeper, more and more like Winston Churchill's as he said: "So all the Golem had to do was take the Swastika and turn it around on your damned Übermensch. You can't face the fact that you were defeated by your own Swastika."

Hitler started trembling. He tried to speak, but only managed to sputter. "Not fair," he muttered. "Using the Swastika that way, rotten thing to do."

Crowley leaned back, completely exhausted, and took another gulp of refreshing oxygen. The sunlight felt good on his bald head. His latest nurse warned him about skin cancer. At his incredibly advanced age, he should worry about such a thing?

Old Hitler staggered to his feet and started to walk off, but something held him back. He was still trying to get some kind of admission out of Crowley.

Crowley figured he was more likely to get an admission out of Hitler. "So, Adolf, are you willing to admit that I'm the wickedest man in the world?"

Hitler shrugged. "Wicked?" he asked. "Who knows from wicked? All I know is that you're the author of *The Book of Lies*."

Crowley could always be impressed by pure gall, in any form. He was being told this by the author of *Mein Kampf*?

"Look, Adolf, we'll leave it at this. I came to South America to retire." He watched the withered, Chaplinesque face mulling over the words. Then Hitler shrugged, and tottered off in the direction of the beach, where girls in bikinis were unlikely to offer stimulating political discourse.

"What's interesting," said Crowley to himself, "is that you've completely forgotten about Israel Regardie. And for everyone who thinks that living well is the best revenge, the only answer is that revenge is the best revenge."

Crowley still had the Stélé. He had learned how its powers could penetrate the veil separating life from death. Hitler was unsure about the personal immortality of his soul. Crowley had no doubts about survival after death; and as was the case with all good practical jokers, Crowley was a very, very, very patient man.

The Skeptic

by Robert Weinberg

ight around *now*," said Captain Hendrickson, with just the proper amount of drama and awe in his voice, "we should be crossing the center point of the infamous Bermuda Triangle."

Mrs. Landers, who gasped at all of the Captain's dramatic flourishes, gasped once more. "The Devil's Triangle! Are we safe?"

Professor Evans, who suspected that Mrs. Landers was much more interested in Captain Hendrickson's marital status than his thoughts on the notorious Triangle, smirked but otherwise said nothing. He wanted to hear the reactions of everyone at their table before making his own views known. It was a habit born of forty years of teaching college. First, let the uninformed reveal their ignorance. Then, cut to the heart of the matter with facts and figures. Though finally retired and on vacation,

Evans could not help but remain true to his own personal standards. Once a skeptic, always a skeptic.

"I saw a movie on da subject once," said Mr. Manconi, a big, red-faced Italian man of indeterminate age. With pasty white skin, tiny pig-like eyes, and heavily starched white shirt, Manconi could have stepped right out of the screen of a hundred Mafia movies. "Da wife," as the heavyset man referred to his spouse, had long since retired, leaving her husband to gulp down glass after glass of red wine. At nearly two a.m., he showed no visible effects of the nearly three full bottles of *vino* he had finished other than a slight slurring of his words.

"Planes, boats, even a submarine, dey all disappeared here without a trace," declared Manconi somberly, his eyes rolling as if he were reciting a ghost story. "None of dem have ever been found."

"I read about those airplanes," contributed Sandy Hayes. "Five of them took off from a base in Florida on a training mission. One minute the pilots were talking to the base on radio, the next *zap*! Nothing. Silent air waves. Planes disappeared. Last anyone ever heard or saw of the men on board."

"Remember the beginning of that *Close Encounters* movie?" asked Jocelyn, his wife, in a muted voice. "That's what started it all, those flying saucers coming and everything. Finding those planes, in exactly the same condition as the day they vanished. Remember that, in the desert? It was so-o-o spooky."

Mrs. Hayes shivered and cuddled up close to her husband. She was a short, attractive redhead, with an abundance of freckles and bright blue eyes. Professor Evans, who fancied himself an expert on guessing people's ages, placed her at twenty-five. She appeared about the same age as her husband, a tall and lanky fellow, with a long, dour face, and already thinning brown hair.

According to Mrs. Landers, who seemed to know everything about everybody, Mr. and Mrs. Hayes were newlyweds taking a cruise for their honeymoon. Not the most spectacular beginning to a marriage, Evans concluded as he stared at the hapless pair. Their features were white as snow, empty of all color, the result of an unending battle with seasickness. They had spent nearly all of their three days on board the luxury ship in their cabin. When they did venture forth, it was only for short periods late at night, long after most of the other passengers had gone to bed. Even then, sitting with the small group of insomniacs who gathered with Captain

Hendrickson on the main deck of the *Tropical Dancer*, they refused to touch any food or drink other than a sip of white wine.

"I've made this trip a dozen times," said Hendrickson, grinning, displaying a mouthful of white teeth. "Gone right across the Triangle, both in the daytime and late and night. Never once had a problem. Though, that's not to say I don't believe." The captain's voice grew low and mysterious. "There's been times I've heard strange noises over the radio. And odd currents run through the water here, that twist your navigation equipment and throw you off course if you're not extremely careful."

"Nonsense." Professor Evans pronounced the word solemnly, breaking it into two distinct syllables for emphasis. It was an old trick he had used in school to gain the attention of his students. "The Bermuda Triangle is a hoax. It is a complete and total fabrication concocted by a few money-grubbing journalists preying on the superstitious fears of the masses. The entire story is an outlandish lie."

"You are an expert on the subject, Professor Evans?" asked the Captain, one gnarled hand rubbing the dark black beard that covered most of his face. "Perhaps you would care to share your knowledge with the rest of us?"

Professor Evans remained silent for a moment, as if contemplating the Captain's request. Slowly, he let his gaze drift across the faces of his companions until he was sure that he had their complete, undivided attention. The professor liked to be the center of attention.

"I have spent my entire life debunking modern myths," he declared, slipping into his best lecture voice. It was a tone capable of freezing a hundred undergraduate students in their chairs, cutting off a dozen conversations in mid-sentence. Filled with professorial authority, it was, in his opinion, the stately sound of reason. "As an instructor of logic, it is both my profession and my hobby."

Nodding to the Captain, he continued. "The whole story began in the late 1950s. The first mention of this so-called Devil's Triangle, this area of the Caribbean Sea bound by Bermuda, Puerto Rico, and Melbourne, Florida, was in an article published in *American Legion Magazine*. The author described half-a-dozen mysterious disappearances in the region during the past fifty years and concluded that some mysterious force was at work destroying ships, hijacking airplanes, and murdering innocent civilians."

Evans paused, gathering in a deep breath. "What was not mentioned anywhere in the piece," he declared, sounding properly offended, "was that all of these alleged supernatural events had perfectly logical, completely rational explanations. Every incident documented had been thoroughly investigated shortly after it had taken place, and the very mundane, very ordinary solution to the vanishing discovered. Since at the time no one had ever head of such a region as the Bermuda Triangle, no attempt was made to link the facts together. The truth was always there, in black and white. The author of the article, the writer of a subsequent best-seller about the region, and various producers of pseudo-documentaries for television and the movies conveniently overlooked them."

"But da submarine?" protested Mr. Manconi. "Da men were snatched right outa da hull."

"What submarine?" retorted Evans, with a snort of derision. "Several young men in an excursion boat reported seeing the underwater vessel while on a fishing trip. Their account, elaborated by gossip, gave birth to the entire story, including the mysterious abduction of the sailors from the submarine compartments. It never existed. Defense Department records showed there was no submarine in these waters at the time described. And later questioning of the students turned up the fact that they had been drinking heavily all day before their sighting. *That* part of their tale never made it into the book."

"What about the naval training flight?" asked Jocelyn Hayes. "Surely, those five planes weren't imaginary."

"Assuredly not," said the Professor. "But they were on a training mission piloted by men who knew little about navigation or flying. They did vanish, *but not over the Bermuda Triangle*. Somehow, the squadron leader became confused and directed the planes out over the Gulf of Mexico. From an airplane, one body of water looks remarkably similar to another. The planes obviously crashed when they ran out of fuel. The wreckage was never found because early investigators were searching off the wrong coast. Only much later, after closely checking the radio log of the trip, did the searchers realize their mistake."

"The ocean tanker in the 1930s?" asked Captain Hendrickson. "An unreported storm?"

"You guessed correctly," said Professor Evans, approvingly. "Another fact completely ignored by the perpetrators of the hoax. Any fact, any evidence that pointed out the basic falsity of their claim, they disregarded. The entire legend of the Bermuda Triangle was nothing more than a case of naked greed triumphing over journalistic ethics. As in all such instances, the supernatural turned out to be nothing more than avarice."

"I take it, professor," said Sandy Hayes, with the slightest smile, "that you are not a believer in the occult?"

"I am a realist," said Professor Evans, chuckling. "I only believe in what I can hear, taste, touch and feel with my own senses. I do not believe in faeries, goblins, witches or demons. They do not exist."

"What about ghosts?" asked Jocelyn Hayes. "I've always been afraid of spooks."

"Figments of the imagination," said Evans. "Nor do I hold with vampires, werewolves, or things that go bump in the night. They are all creations of superstition and ignorance. Sorry, but I am at heart a skeptic. Call me cynical, but at seventy-five years of age, I have yet to be proven wrong."

"How do you explain the *Julie Bell?*" asked Sandy Hayes. Professor Evans thought he detected the slightest edge of mockery in the man's voice, but he couldn't be sure.

"The *Julie Bell?*" answered Evans. He hated being caught by surprise. Or uninformed. "I'm not familiar with that name."

"Fishing boat out of Galveston in 1958," said Evans smoothly. "Crew of seven, all veteran sailors. Calm seas, no storms. There were no reports of trouble. Yet, the boat was found floating off the coast of Bermuda a week later. No one was on board. There were no signs of a struggle. No hint of anything unusual. Except for the captain's log."

"The captain's log?" asked Professor Evans. He hated being strung along. Especially since he had used the exact same method to keep the attention of his students for years. "What do you mean?"

"The book was found open on the captain's desk," said Hayes. "The ship's master had evidently just begun writing his entry for the day. Nothing unusual about the events described. Except that the writing broke off in the middle of a sentence." Hayes's voice sank to a whisper. "Stopped in the middle of a word."

Jocelyn Hayes shivered. "Tell them about the *Pride of Miami*, Sandy."

"Similar circumstances, fifteen years earlier," said Sandy Hayes. His cold tones seemed to chill the night air. "Radio man was in contact with shore, right around midnight. One minute, he's on the air. Next instant, dead silence. Not a word. Channel remained open, but not another sound came through. Boat was found the next morning, devoid of life."

"I never read details of either incident," said Professor Evans. "Neither boat was mentioned in any of the literature about the Devil's Triangle."

"They're the stories the government doesn't allow to appear in books," said Evans. "There's more. Lots more."

"If the feds are keeping this stuff hidden, then how do you know of them, Mr. Hayes?" asked Captain Hendrickson, sounding unconvinced.

"I'm in law enforcement," said Hayes. "It's my business to know the facts. All the facts."

"Well, itsa all pretty interesting," said Mr. Manconi, "but I gotta go to sleep. I'm gettin' sleepy."

The big man glanced down at his watch. "Funny, my watch is busted. Second hand has stopped movin'. Anyone have the right time?"

Captain Hendrickson pulled out his pocket watch. "It's ten after... Wait a minute, my watch has stopped too."

"Ten after two?" asked Professor Evans, checking his timepiece. He frowned. "How can three watches all stop at the same minute?"

"Look at the stars," said Sandy Hayes, rising with unexpected grace to his feet. "They're not twinkling."

"And the waves," said Mrs. Hayes, also on her feet. Her eyes seemed to glow with an unnatural brightness. She no longer appeared so young. Or so helpless. "They're solid as stone. We're frozen in time."

"Impossible," said Professor Evans, nervously. "Time can't suddenly come to a stop. That contradicts every law of science. There must be a rational explanation for this phenomena."

"Perhaps," said Sandy Hayes. He pointed to something moving in the darkness off the port bow. "But explain that."

Staring at the ghostly apparition, Professor Evans was, for one of the few times in his life, speechless.

✠

It was a specter of a ship, moving soundlessly across the unyielding sea. Darker than the night, exuding an aura of incredible age, it painted a vision of wraith-like menace across the horizon. Professor Evans swallowed in a sudden shock of recognition. He knew the dread significance of the rotting hulk, with wood as black as pitch — and sails the color of bright red blood.

"*They who see the Flying Dutchman, never never reach the shore,*" said the Professor, quoting the John Boyle O'Reilly poem he had read as a child.

"Maybe," said Sandy Hayes, glancing over at the Professor. "Maybe not."

"The Flying Dutchman," said Captain Hendrickson, shaking his head, his eyes wide with astonishment. "I always assumed it was a legend. An eternal ship with an immortal skipper, roaming the seas in search of salvation. But finding only damnation."

Hendrickson pushed his chair back from the table. "I'd better go check on my crew. That wreck is heading straight at us. I suspect we are about to receive unwelcome guests."

"Don't waste your time," said Jocelyn Hayes. There was a hard edge to her voice. All traces of the young, flighty newlywed were gone. She was not, Professor Evans sensed, twenty-five years old. There was a certain ageless air to both her and her husband. Ageless and menacing.

"They're frozen solid in time," said Sandy Hayes. His gaze swung around their small group. "As is the case with everyone else on the ship. We are the only ones untouched, and if you move more than a few feet away from this location, you'll be stricken as well. So, stay put and do what we tell you."

"Like hell I will," said the Captain. "This ship is mine and I'll do what I please. Something phony is going on and I mean to find out exactly what." He looked around at the others. "You folks coming with me? Or staying with these," and he paused before he spat out the final word, "*pirates.*"

"I'm wid you, Captain," said Mr. Manconi. A man of limited imagination, he seemed completely unaware of the strangeness of the circumstances. "I gotta go to bed."

Mrs. Landers' gaze darted back and forth between Mr. and Mrs. Hayes and the Captain. She looked like a bird trapped in a cage, not knowing what to do next. Finally, she stepped over to Hendrickson. "Wherever you go, Captain," she said in her most reverential tone, "I'll follow."

Hendrickson stared at Evans. "What about you, Professor? Coming with me to the bridge, or remain with these two frauds?"

The Professor shrugged his shoulders. "I'll remain here," he declared. "I have strong doubts about the Flying Dutchman and this time stoppage. However, being a cynic and a skeptic, I prefer the devil I know to the devil I don't."

"Have it your own way," said Hendrickson. "But if there's trouble, don't blame me."

Turning, he marched away from the table, followed by Mrs. Landers and Mr. Manconi. The trio crossed five yards of the deck before they turned into statues.

"Wise choice, Professor," said Sandy Hayes.

Wood clanged against steel. The ghost ship had made contact with the *Tropical Dancer*. Seconds later, three ropes ending in metal hooks came sailing onto the deck to catch the railing. Professor Evans' eyes bulged in disbelief. The crew of the *Flying Dutchman* was about to board.

"Take my hand," whispered Jocelyn Hayes urgently. "And, no matter what you see or hear, don't move an inch or make a sound. Your life depends on it."

The professor grabbed the woman's outstretched fingers. And gasped in shock. Mrs. Hayes' hand was cold as ice. Her skin was as frigid as that of a long-dead corpse. Staring at her, Evans had a terrible premonition about why the woman's face was so white.

"There's six of them," said Sandy Hayes, his gaze fixed intently on the ropes. Evans dared not ask how Hayes could tell the number of their attackers before they were visible. "Only one of them is really dangerous. He's projecting the timestop. I can't fathom his bloodline. Must be an obscure one. The rest are mere hangers-on."

"Malkavians," said Mrs. Hayes, sneering. Evans had no idea what she meant, though he got the impression she was referring to the religion or nationality of the pirates. "Crazy as loons."

"They probably saw the Wagner opera about the Flying Dutchman a hundred years ago," said her husband, "and decided to make it real. Typical behavior on their part."

Then there was time only for silence. Six gaunt, grisly figures tumbled onto the deck of the *Tropical Dancer*. Horrifying parodies of humanity, they were definitely not human.

The ghostly buccaneers were clad in torn and decayed seaman's uniforms decorated with dozens of gold and silver medallions. Travesties of men, the boarders were composed mostly of bleached white bones held together by strips of dried, leather-like skin. Their eyes glowed crimson, and in their hands they held rusted steel swords. Their teeth, Professor Evans noted in dismay, were long and sharp like fangs.

"Another prize for the Dutchman," said a monstrous figure who was taller and more gaudily clad than the rest. On his head was perched a black captain's hat decorated with a skull and crossbones. His shrill voice possessed all the charm of a squeaking door. Professor Evans gnashed his teeth together in pain, but he remained motionless. "The scourge of the Bermuda Triangle strikes again."

The monster laughed, a dry crackling sound. He waved his sword high over his head. "Pick a dozen healthy specimens," he ordered his crew. "Young ones, filled with life. Take them to the hold of our ship. We'll feast on their blood for months. As always, be certain not to disturb anything else. We want to leave no clues."

The Dutchman's red eyes glared fiercely at his companions. "When I release the timestop, everything has to be like it was before we approached. Make sure of that. No mistakes. The only difference will be that twelve humans have vanished suddenly. One more mystery of the Devil's Triangle for the fools to ponder."

"Time for us to act," whispered Sandy Hayes to his wife. "Before they spread out and make so much of a mess it will be impossible to repair without major adjustments."

"I agree," said Mrs. Hayes. "Hypnotizing the Captain and his friends to forget the timestop won't be hard. But if a bunch of people suddenly find themselves somewhere else on the ship, it would definitely make explaining things difficult. We can't terminate one mystery only to substitute another."

"Cap'n," said one of the pirates, raising his sword and approaching the Professor and his two mysterious companions. "There's some talking going on here. I think we got spies on board."

"Spies?" bellowed the chief of the skeletal crew. "Impossible. The humans all be frozen by the timestop."

"Not true, Dutchman," said Sandy Hayes, stepping forward, a smile on his face. Professor Evans knew without being told that the cloak of invisibility that hid them was no longer in place. "The Amulet of Osiris we wear is capable of dispelling the most powerful of magics. Including yours."

With a casual grace, Hayes reached out and wrenched the sword from the pirate who stood bewildered in front of them. The weapon lashed out like a striking cobra. Metal glistened in the moonlight and the head of the astonished buccaneer tumbled to the deck. An instant later, his clothes followed, as the skeletal body beneath it crumbled into powder.

"Beware," cried the leader of the marauders, "they be executioners!"

For his frightful band, the warning came too late.

Mrs. Hayes, no longer holding hands with Professor Evans, moved so fast that she was almost invisible. In a blur of action, she lanced between two of the pirates, ripped the swords from their hands, and beheaded each of them with a single stroke. Professor Evans gasped in shock. The petite young woman's strength was unbelievable.

Without conscious volition, the Professor stumbled forward, closer to the action. He realized that if he didn't stay nearby one or the other of the mysterious newlyweds, he would suffer the same fate as everyone else on the ship. He had seen too much to risk missing the conclusion of this bizarre confrontation.

The final two Malkavian pirates proved no greater challenge to Mr. and Mrs. Hayes. They dissolved into dust when beheaded. That left only the Dutchman to face the deadly couple. Sandy Hayes had labeled the leader of the band as the only dangerous one among the attackers. The monster proved to be exactly that.

"Halt!" shrieked the Dutchman, stretching out his bony arms, fingers pointed at Sandy and Jocelyn Hayes. "I command you to stop!"

A wave of pure mental force washed over Professor Hayes, filling him with awe and respect. All of the fear, the horror he felt for the monster less than a dozen feet away from him, vanished. Instead, he found his mind overwhelmed with a sense of majestic presence. He knew that he stood in close proximity with a god-like being, the Dutchman. Obeying unspoken commands, the Professor sank to his knees in humility. Close by, he sensed Mr. and Mrs. Hayes doing the same.

"Who be you?" asked the Dutchman, his arms dropping to his sides. "And why be you here?"

"We are Archons," answered Sandy Hayes. "Our master, the Justicar of North America, sent us to find the cause behind the disappearances in the Bermuda Triangle. We've been traveling back and forth through this region on cruises for months, waiting for you to attack. Our mission is simple. We are here to destroy you."

"Destroy me?" said the monster. "Why? Why *now*? I've sailed this region for more than a hundred years. No Justicar ever sought to stop me before. This territory is mine. The Dutchman rules the Devil's Triangle. How dare you question my authority?"

"You've grown sloppy over the decades," said Jocelyn Hayes. Though on their knees before the monster, neither of the newlyweds appeared concerned about their fate. "Years ago, you masked your actions so that they could be explained logically. Skeptics like this one invented solutions for the puzzles you created," and Mrs. Hayes turned her head to Professor Hayes for an instant. And winked.

"But more and more you've taken to conducting raids that cannot be explained even by the most die-hard rationalist," continued Sandy Hayes. "Your actions have stretched credibility to the breaking point. That's why the Justicar sent us on this mission. The Masquerade has been jeopardized."

"As if I care," said the Dutchman, with a sneer. "Your stupid Masquerade means nothing to a true Brujah. I am master of time and space. Playing the role of the Flying Dutchman was originally the Malkavians' idea, but it is one I've grown to enjoy. I plan to continue doing so for hundreds of years to come. You are helpless before my power."

"We are," said Sandy Hayes. "But even your strength and attention has its limits. For example, while you can stop us from attacking, we are still free to tell Professor Evans that now is the instant to obey the command we hypnotically placed in his mind when your ship first approached."

Reacting without thinking, the Professor reached into his pants pocket and pulled out a small pocket lighter, a fact he found quite surprising since he didn't smoke. The Dutchman's jaws were just opening to scream when Evans flicked on the flame and tossed the lighter directly at the creature.

Its clothes, old brittle rags, ignited with a whoosh of white fire. Howling, the Dutchman beat at the flames with his huge arms, but the blaze spread with magical swiftness. In seconds, the skeletal figure was engulfed in waves of crimson. And, with the inferno, the monster's mental bonds disappeared.

"Nicely done," said Jocelyn Hayes, rising to her feet. Though she seemed entirely at ease, Evans noted that her gaze never wavered from the burning figure of the Dutchman. "Your cooperation is greatly appreciated, Professor."

"These ancient ones are much too arrogant," said Sandy Hayes. He was carefully gathering up the empty garments of the other pirates. Their heads had vanished, like their bodies, into dust. Grinning, he tossed the clothing over the side. "The ship is dissolving, too, as the timestop spell wears off. It should be gone right around the same time as the Dutchman. That ties up a major loose end nicely."

"Only leaves us with changing the memories of Captain Hendrickson and his cronies," said Jocelyn Hayes. "Tidy."

"But... but... but," stuttered Professor Evans, feeling very distraught. "The disappearances, the Dutchman, the ghost ship, this Masquerade you mentioned? I don't understand. I don't understand any of it."

Jocelyn Hayes grinned. "The world, my dear professor, is a much darker place than you realize. Suffice it to say that what you believe to be truth is nothing more than a facade. Powerful supernatural beings control the Earth and all mankind. We are known as The Kindred. And the hidden agenda to keep our rule secret is known as The Masquerade."

"You're vampires," said Professor Evans, shuddering as he remembered the fangs of the pirates. "The undead."

"Does it matter?" said Jocelyn. "The real question is what to do with you? Tampering with your memories would be more difficult, considering all that you have seen. And, implanting false thoughts in a skeptic's mind is notoriously unsuccessful."

"We could just kill him," said Sandy Hayes casually. He walked over to the sizzling remains of the Dutchman. "Make it look like a sudden heart attack. Nobody would question that, at his age. Better decide quick. Our pirate friend is nearly ash. We've got to start covering our tracks."

"I think murdering the Professor would be unfair," said Jocelyn. "He did help us torch the Dutchman." She smiled. "I think we should let him live, and allow him to retain all of his memories."

"Huh?" said her husband. "I don't get it."

"Professor Evans is a skeptic," said Jocelyn. Playfully, she reached out and tapped the bewildered professor on the cheek. "He's devoted his entire life to debunking the mysteries of the universe. Stuff like the Bermuda Triangle. If he dares describe what he witnessed tonight, his friends and colleagues would think he's gone insane. Vampires and ghost ships, indeed!

Don't you see? The only way he can maintain his reputation is to remain silent."

Sandy Hayes chuckled. "Instead of exposing a cover-up, he has to become part of one. Poetic justice."

"Exactly," said Jocelyn. "Any comments, Professor?"

For the second time that night, Professor Evans didn't have a thing to say.

Black Casper

by Rex Miller

He could see with his mind's eye. Squinting (in a manner of speaking) through such portals, he envisioned light beams; wide angle views of variegated greens; burning sky; shade, shadow, and blocks of darkness perceived as distant silhouettes.

The sun seared a yellow-white hole in the tangerine-colored sky, and out beyond the horizon the whole world appeared to be on fire.

Inside the fortress-like villa that was his home, and the working field headquarters of Black Casper, the servants toiled silently in preparation for their master's rising. Away from the relentless heat and red dust, behind thick stone walls, it was cool and quiet in the house. The windows were always closed and sealed at noon; iron-shuttered, locked, with long strips of foil taped over every joint. The master's rare ocular disorder would not tolerate direct sunlight.

The servants each busied himself or herself with their particular task, as rice, fish, and tea were prepared, fresh vegetables readied for stir-frying, noodles and nuoc mam awaiting the flame. They were accustomed to working quietly, and only the organic noises — and the occasional whispered comment or instruction — broke the silence. It was a pleasant, if somewhat intense, hour of the day, and a time to concentrate on one's job. Details are everything, the master was fond of saying, and each of the servants knew it to be so.

He always came silently, joining them with a smile or nod, a slender, tall apparition in his dressing gown and sandals. One might be alone and suddenly feel his slim, cool fingers lightly touch the hand in a familiar pat of friendship. A husky, whispered hello, perhaps. He was a gentle and kind man to work for.

Neither voluble nor aloof, it was simply that the master was disinclined to talk upon rising. Typically, he would remain rather taciturn for an hour or two, perform whatever ablutions were necessary, and then do his work. He liked to write during his first hours of rising, and the girl who served him tea generally found him in his small office, cross-legged on the tatami, making thoughtful inked brushstrokes on rice paper. She might get a nod of thanks and a smile, or nothing if he were in deep thought. But if he ignored her, later she might find a beautiful flower in a tiny lacquered bowl, his way of apologizing for an inadvertent rudeness. Small wonder that his servants would kill for the man.

He wrote of the moon, primarily, and of its pull on the earth; on the tides and the effects of such things as magnetic polarity and quantum physics on mortal humans. As he wrote, he did not think so much of astrological charts as he did of fine art; paintings particularly. A Wolfgang Schulz seascape; a still life of great enduring simplicity; a wintry Sewell oil; a sky — captured by Utrillo in lemon-umber oils; a piece he'd never actually seen but remembered from the first edition of the Catalog Luna: these were his mental backdrops.

Against such canvasses he painted word pictures of unusual persistence. ICEX had not yet melted, but he could see beyond its watery grave, beyond the phoenix who would survive it, beyond *its* ashes. These were, however, not the word pictures he created for general publication. He looked into his mind and saw brown water and amber sunset, a hundred ducks — improbable as a cartoon — in a single file, a road of endless ricebaskets drying in the fierce heat, and he wrote of the swollen deltas and the monsoon season that would come, and of the blood that would run from the mouths of the nine dragons and empty into the South China Sea. We have nothing but time and choice, he wrote... and chance.

The smells of the house reached him, and he recalled that April Clifford was coming. He knew they whispered about her; that the servants called her "the master's lady friend" as they prepared the fish for skinning and execution. Camphor, nutmeg, palm oil, saffron, joss sticks, nuoc mam, a dozen more distinct aromas wafted through the house thick as smoke; he had to concentrate and bite down on a momentary jolt of nausea. He never fed before nightfall. He blocked the stench of cooking vegetables and picked up his brush.

Cao Van Vien, commander of the government forces, and Phan Van Phu, commander of Military Region II, were but two of the tens of thousands of Vietnamese who could be numbered among his readers, listeners, and auditors. One of the generals was superstitious, so it appeared, and had misread an omen. He'd proposed a withdrawal without studying his escape route. Another general had listened to bad advice, and his army had been abandoned.

The pullout from Pleiku and Kontum had become such a debacle that the results were quite unimaginable. The planned evacuation via National Highway 14 south to Than An, then east along Route 7B to Phu Bon, had looked efficient on the contour map, but it was raining on 7B, a hard, pelting Asian rain that turned red dust into a quagmire. Down this ribbon marched soldiers, civilians, montagnards, spies, deserters, water buffs, cyclos, bikes, and elephantine Lambretta busses, all rutting out 7B.

First the tanks and tracks rumbled through, scattering troops and civilians alike, then came the elite forces, then the stragglers: thousands of cars, taxis, marching feet, everybody mired in the long ribbon of mud.

On the ground the Army screamed for air support and medevac units — the Air Force told the Army, in so many words, to kiss its royal ass; and the entire Military Aid and Assistance Group sat mired in an unbelievable loblolly. Top echelon brass quarreled, covered its collective haunches, and cast about for plausible scapegoats.

So-and-so blamed what's-his-name, who blamed Tran who blamed Tat who said Phu had misunderstood him, who in turn disclosed that the militia had fled their posts at Ban Me Thuot, whose commander revealed they'd fled to defend their homes against Marvin the ARVN, who were raping and pillaging as they deserted *their* positions. All because of poor advice and a misread omen.

The consequences would be shattering: one general's action would precipitate the eradication of government defenses in the south, the other's would set the stage for the army's total destruction. More importantly, their actions paved the way for the fall.

He took brush in hand and began to write of the consequences of the Ides of March, and of the beginning of the rainy season. The ideogram for monsoon mushroomed like an inky cloud.

✠

The lovely young woman with the very short hair daydreamed out her office window, watching the clock, tapping a pencil on her typewriter keyboard, then on the telephone receiver, then on the desk. A trio of paradiddles. Her mind was on other things. She loved this country… and hated much of it. Loved and hated her work. Loved a man and wondered about him. Hated what she perceived as weakness in herself. Hated the war, loved the action. Felt as if she were being pulled apart, sometimes, by the contradictions in her life. The second hand on her biological clock seemed frozen.

For April Clifford the culture shock of Southeast Asia had been almost too much for her. Beauty and poverty; awesome wonder and brutality; banality and incredible subtlety: This was a universe of morons and geniuses. Paradise and paradox. And to have found love in this ungodly war was the final shattering blow to her central nervous system.

How had she ended so far from home, and in such a frightening world? Footloose and independent, she'd gone straight from Columbia to the Sorbonne. Smart, from a moneyed eastern family, she'd become immersed in the writing life. Music was her focus, and she'd come close to the top, selling pieces to *Rolling Stone*, *Creem*, even stringing for the *New York Times*, before she'd had the shot from *R & R*: the music industry wanted a rocker's perspective of the war. One night she'd torn up her backstage pass to interview one of the major bands of the '70s, and the next day she'd found herself on a 747 bound — ultimately — for Cam Ranh Bay.

The sluggish second hand moved and she pulled herself out of the pit of introspection, picked up the phone, and dialed. She eventually got through to the extension she wanted, and a familiar male voice growled at her.

"2241."

"Don't you ever just say hello like regular folks?"

"Hey, April!" he said, some pleasure in his voice.

"No names, please. This isn't a secure line," she joked. It was her pal Peter Brancato at what was called the Puzzle Palace. "Loose lips sink ships."

"I love the way you say loose lips," he intoned, in a mock sexy baritone. "If only you meant it."

"Listen, Peter. Can I ask you something seriously?"

"Is this for your comic?"

"No. Christ, no! This is for me. I want to ask you about somebody, and I know you can't divulge secrets and all that jazz, but… this is somebody special. Somebody, a friend — OK?

"Yeah?"

"I've heard rumors about him. That he's — you know, one of you guys."

"Gay, you mean?" he asked, innocently.

"No," she laughed, "one of *you* guys… you *bastard*." Peter Brancato was notoriously, in fact infuriatingly, heterosexual. Their friendship was forever threatened by the fact that he wouldn't give up a long-running, if charming, campaign to bed her.

"I don't know what you're talking about, April. So before you say who—"

"— a spook, Peter. I've heard things. I'm involved with this man. I thought we were good enough friends that I could just ask. I don't want to know what he does or who he spies for, but a girl has a right to know something about a guy, right?"

"Sure."

"So you'll tell me?"

"You know better than this, darlin'; you know I can't confirm or deny something like that, even if I knew. You have me very curious now, though. Who are we talking about?"

"If you're not going to tell me, what good will it do if I tell you? Or is this just your prurient curiosity about my personal life?"

"That too, but tell me anyway. I don't know every spook in country, dear, but if it's somebody I think might be on the job I'll say so, provided it doesn't compromise security and provided, of course, I'm just guessing. I can speculate, right?"

"Right. You've heard of Black Casper, I'm sure…" Just as she spoke an operator cut in.

"Pardon?" a woman's voice out of nowhere.

"Working, Operator. Please… *Working!*" They were cut off. She redialed, and there was nothing. The line had gone stone dead. It happened all the time. The fucking Vietnamese telephone system sucked.

She left, and rather than fight with a telephone landline again, got into her battered black Citroen, and joined the parade of traffic out of the city. It was about fifteen klicks to Black Casper's headquarters. Heat mirages shimmered up from the pothole-strewn asphalt; and she drove as fast as the road and traffic would permit.

In the seat beside her was a semi-automatic pistol. It was an ugly, heavy, scary thing that she nearly always loathed, but he made her carry it, and when she was driving out to his place or back to the city, it was a cold and somewhat menacing comfort within grasping distance. April was a terrible shot, and couldn't hit the broad side of a barn with a rifle, much less a pistol, was scared of its noise and recoil, and had no confidence in her ability to use it successfully, but because he'd insisted she'd fallen into the habit of putting it next to her. It was one of the few gifts he'd given her, she realized, not counting flowers, which were among his only passions.

She knew next to nothing about him. He was a complete mystery, a cool and unflappable enigma. CIA, she'd heard whispered around the shop, DIA, Military Intelligence — one of those guys. Tall, slim but iron hard, with rock-steady moves and fast reflexes. Handsome, almost to the point of being pretty, with long slender hands, and the most beautiful feet she'd ever seen on a man. Great feet. She loved to put his toes in her when she was hot, in her mouth, in her butt, inside her — my God, he was such a turn-on.

Dark hair worn way too long, kept tied back in a sort of odd ponytail, very dark eyebrows and that pale skin. The main features were his eyes and mouth. The eyes were white — or close to it — a washed out gray. He'd told her the name of the thing he had several times and she could never remember it. He wasn't an albino, but it was kind of like that thing where sunlight sears the skin, because of the lack of pigmentation, blanco pigmentosa or something, but in his case an eye disorder. Ocularmotor something something.

His mouth was as full-lipped and beautiful as anything Michelangelo might have chiseled. She never tired of kissing him, and he was a *great* kisser. He was — being objective about it — less than spectacular in bed. He was devoted to foreplay, and an ardent practitioner of the most sophisticated cunnilingus, but fellatio and coitus were off limits. She knew that he did not enjoy having his penis touched, and had once tried to broach the subject of impotence only to meet a chilly wall of silence. So she took what there was, enjoying what he could give her, and was becoming accustomed to his idiosyncratic bedroom ways, as the importance of traditional sex faded.

To kiss and cuddle for hours with this gorgeous, giving creature, then to lie back and be virtually *devoured* by a grandmaster of oral eroticism, brought to mini-climax after mini-climax as a world class champion of the art worked his magic… this was hardly a sentence.

She noted that the thought of him had cheered her up, and she felt herself getting excited as soon as the white slab walls of his fortress-like villa came into partial view. She turned off the highway, drove a few hundred meters into roadside jungle, and pulled to a stop in front of Black Casper's.

"Herro, missy," the servant woman said, opening the door for her. "Underwear," it sounded like she said. She followed the woman into the depths of the darkened house. As always, she had to mentally work to keep herself from making some comment — as she had the first few times — about how he kept the place "like a tomb." After all, he couldn't help his physical problem. Once her eyes became accustomed to it, the gloomy rooms weren't so bad. He had a penchant for candles, and there was adequate light to see.

"Hi," he said, turning to take her in his arms. "Safe trip?"

"Mm," she said, through the first kiss. "Uh huh."

"Hungry?" he asked, kissing her answer.

He was naked under his thin dressing gown, and she felt his sinewy muscles as his tongue explored her mouth. She was immediately hot and wet, puddling like the tramp she was — she thought — as she noticed herself shedding clothing and gently being lowered onto a pile of pillows.

After the loving, they dressed and adjourned to the dining area. She ate fish with hot sauce, stir-fry veggies and rice, devouring them hungrily, while she watched him toy with noodles, eating them one at a time, elegantly and carefully. No wonder he was so thin. He never showed any hunger — not when she was around.

She talked with him about events of the preceding weeks, and about her work. He always provided such keen insights; he knew so much about so many subjects.

"You know that guy who does stand-ups for Brazilian News? The guy who always wears the safari jackets with his neck hair showing?" she asked, smiling. "Anyway, this guy somehow bribed his way into the Air America terminal and conned a ride on The Man's chopper yesterday."

"Really?"

"Yeah. So anyway, this guy is on the Air American chopper and he says that they saw all these lines of civilians heading toward—"

He tuned out on her words, his mind far away, as she discussed the problems of the moment, relating her anecdote about a fellow reporter. In a matter of days the last of the dominoes would clatter. He ticked them off one by one: Kontum, Pleiku, Quang Tri, Hue; tumbling dominoes, or mah jong tiles. Whatever.

"— such a total disaster," she said.

"Right," he agreed. He might have been smiling.

✢

The month she'd been named after had been a dark one in the life of April Clifford. On the eighteenth, the evacuations of Americans from Saigon had begun, and it had become — in the words of a senior embassy official who insisted he not be quoted — "the worst Chinese fire drill he'd ever seen."

It was the twenty-second, and a terrible mess had become worse: Saigon was panic city. The U.S. was closing shop, abandoning everything — and everybody — in a mad rush to get clear of the place. Everywhere the streets were filled with crowds of screaming, cursing, shoving Vietnamese angling to somehow hitch a ride out. She had typed the words Hung Dung over and over.

Pham Hung and Van Tien Dung were encamped with a mass of NVA not fifteen klicks down the road from Black Casper's headquarters.

"April!" a voice penetrated her Hung Dung fog. "April! Come on! We're leaving." It was another correspondent.

"Say what?"

"Leaving, let's go — they're ordering all Bao Chi out."

"What are you *talking* about?" Journalists didn't leave, they *covered*, for God's sake.

"All reporters gotta go, kid. That's it. Hey, you knew we were gonna evac, well, it's showtime! Come *on*! We're lining up to make the helo-lift. The Marines are coming in — we're out of here."

"I'm not ready to go — what do —"

"— NVA's just north of the city, April. Let's *go*!" The man turned and sprinted out of the office and up the stairs. There were always chopper noises, but she could hear the *whompwhomp* of rotor blades unusually near. One second she was working, now she was leaving? This was bullshit.

She pulled the page out of her typewriter and for no reason stuck it in a thick manila file of current work in progress. Tried to think what to take and realized it was irrelevant. All she could think about was her man. It was more than she could handle, and for a few seconds her entire body went on overload and she just slumped, suddenly very tired, as the noisy bird thudded down in a storm of noise on the roof above.

There hadn't been enough warning. They couldn't expect you to leave instantly like that... She forced herself to snap out of it and dialed, fingers shaking, trembling on the phone. The line didn't go through at first and she had to fight back the panic beginning to build inside her. She dialed again, carefully. On the first ring he answered, which was even more frightening, as he'd never answered the phone himself.

"Hello?" His voice was maddeningly unruffled.

"Can you hear me all right?" the stupid chopper was deafeningly loud above her.

"Just fine."

"Why are you still there? Didn't you hear that the NVA is just down the road from you? You've got to get out of there."

"I'll be fine, don't worry," he said in that cool, infuriatingly calm tone. "You take care, until I see you again." He wasn't even surprised, and he knew she was leaving.

"How did you know I was going?" It was a stupid question. He always knew.

Her heart was breaking in half. It was awful — this feeling inside. She started crying, blurting it out like a weepy baby before she could stop herself, "It's hell to love somebody who doesn't love you back," but she was crying so much he couldn't understand her.

"What did you say? I couldn't hear you."

"I said —" she forced herself to stop crying, snuffled, and said it again: "It's hell to love someone when they don't love you."

"I've always cared for you — more than you know. Listen, I must take care of some last minute details now. Goodbye, till next time." He hung up, the bastard. She wasn't *ready* to hang up. She was infuriated. She redialed. Got nothing. She couldn't think. Someone called her name. She ignored it, dialed again.

"2241." The voice neither gruff nor laughing, a note of urgency in the man's tone.

"You've got to help me. I've — I can't go without him. He won't leave."

"April?"

"*Yes.*" She started crying again, not caring.

"You've got to get out of there."

"I'm in love and he won't leave and they're going to get him... they..." she broke off, sobbing into the telephone.

"Who are you talking about?"

"Black Casper," she bawled, "that's who." She'd become used to calling him by the company name.

"Who at Black Casper? You don't mean —" He named her lover's real name, a tongue-twister of cs and zs and glottal stops against hard consonants.

"Yes, why won't he go? What is Black Casper?" Again someone shouted to her from the stairs. She could barely hear for turbine noise above.

"Casper was a program. Combined Asian Studies Program for Education and Re-Vietnamization. White Casper was the Studies Group — cover. Black was the covert side. It was a cover unit run by SOG."

"Sog?"

"Yeah. Op 32, they call it. Poisoned horoscopes and stuff. Kid — I gotta go. Forget it — get out while you can." Just as the phone disconnected, hands pulled her from the chair. She tried to resist, but the two who'd come down for her weren't about to let her fall into Charlie's hands. She was in a UH-1 Marine chopper, being strapped down, deafened, her tears drying as they fell, before she could think what to do next, and they were lifting off, and it was too late.

Out at what was left of Casper's headquarters, the first artillery shells were beginning to find their target. But he was safe, far below, in the vault where he would remain dormant until it was permissible to resume his activities. The servants were long gone. He would come back up, and relocate, perhaps in Nicaragua, where the feeding was particularly juicy. He had no enemies, he worked for all sides, simultaneously, a specialist in his trade. The successes of recent months would fuel his fantasies while he waited to reemerge: the twisted omen that caused a member of the general staff to destroy the 23rd RVN Division in its abortive retreat from Kontum and Pleiku; the doctored astrology charts that resulted in Quang Tri's demise, and the annihilation of the First RVN Division; a brilliant stroke in late March, persuading — by meteorological prognostication — the Political Bureau to liberate Saigon before the rainy season; even the interpretation of planetary positions that convinced superstitious officials of the Ministry of the Interior to intercede in the evacuation process where possible... all of that was his work. *His* tumbling dominoes. The fall of Saigon!

Far above him he heard the timers kick in as the self-destruct unit methodically began razing the fortress to rubble. The NVA's incoming "arty" and the planted ordnance combined to send shudders down deep like ten B-52 arc light strikes hitting at once; the tremors reminded him of orgasms from his life before.

He was Ventrue, with endocrine vampirism, not unlike the Malkavians and adreno-genital types, who traded off the ability to become erect, for presentience, and icy invulnerability.

His particular gifts included the ability to convince primitive or superstitious people that the time or the tides bore bad omens. A bad omen misread will take more human lives than any bomb or natural disaster, and massive bloodletting fed his people's life-force.

He would think of these things through the night, and at the exact moment of sunrise he would feel it. The sun in Southeast Asia explodes into the sky as it does in no other place, suddenly, and without warning. But he would be far below, safe and cool, waiting in pitch black.

☩

In sequestered subterranean silence, he fantasizes of mass graves, as invisible demons — guests of honor — hover around the broken shards of his thoughts in search of elusive pleasure, or peace, knowing neither are within their grasp.

Maidens of the Rice Goddess bow to their tasks along the paddy dikes that crosshatch wet, verdant fields; too young for menses, too serious for rock and roll, they work amid the pockmarked fields of cratered, war-torn soil.

The souls of undead ancestors are a solemn, brooding presence, and his eyes open to better see the black.

Getting the Fear

By Philip Nutman

You have to make love with it. You have to know every part of it so that you could pick it up any second and shoot."

— Manson Family member Lynette "Squeaky" Fromme in a scene from the documentary *Manson*, in which she is shown caressing a rifle six years before she attempted to assassinate President Gerald Ford.

> "The best part of it is thae
> when I die I will be reborn
> *in paradice and thei have*
> *killed will become my slaves…*" [sic]

— Excerpt from a coded letter sent by Zodiac to the *San Francisco Examiner-Chronicle* on August 1, 1969, nine days before the Manson family slaughtered Sharon Tate and friends in Los Angeles.

A week following her stepfather's suicide, and three days after she'd laid him to rest, Marcia Gray discovered his diaries in the attic of the old house he'd bequeathed to her on Liberty Street.

That chilly Thursday morning, although it seemed irrational, some inner voice told her she didn't want to go to the gloomy house alone; but Tom Maggid, the old college friend she was staying with, couldn't go with her. He'd left earlier that morning to fly down to L.A. to meet with his Hollywood agent.

As she drove from Tom's Bay Street duplex, nestled on Telegraph Hill, Marcia cursed the persistent headache she'd awakened with. Despite three Tylenol and several glasses of water, she couldn't shake it, and hoped it wasn't going to turn into a full-blown migraine like the others she'd suffered throughout her stay in San Francisco, probably thanks to stress and shock caused by the unexpected turn of events in her life.

As she turned left onto Van Ness Avenue, she noticed dark clouds lowering over the Golden Gate Bridge, as if they were about to devour its towering red peaks. The early morning sky was split between bright sunlight shining from the east over Oakland and the menacing mass of thunderheads advancing in from the Pacific. Another day of bad weather was forecast, and there seemed no end in sight to the pounding Northern California had been victim to for the last week.

"It's the beginning of the end," Tom had joked over dinner the night she had arrived from Chicago.

"Seriously, there are a lot of people out here — and not just fundamentalist Christians — who believe the freak weather and all the other weird shit that's been going on for the last few years are clear signs that the Book of Revelation is about to be opened."

"Interesting," Marcia replied through a mouthful of fettucini alfredo. "But hardly exceptional. This is California. Weird stuff's the norm out here, right?"

"Yeah, but read the papers, there's a definite increase in inexplicable phenomena. And I don't think it's mass hysteria or social delusion. I've researched a lot of it and it's not coming from your typical flake fringe, either. We're talking doctors, lawyers, college professors who swear they've seen this stuff."

Tom was referring to the widespread incidence of angelic visitations and sightings which were being reported on a daily basis in the Golden State. Having written a paper for *The American Sociological Journal* and several articles for national magazines, he'd culled some of the material and turned it into a screenplay called *The Ascension War*, which had sparked considerable interest in Hollywood, hence his sudden departure.

But thoughts of angels and demons weren't at the forefront of her mind right then. She just wanted the headache to go away, but the more its presence bugged her, the stronger its grip seemed to lock upon her throbbing temples. Maybe some soft music would help, she thought, switching on the rental car's radio to an FM station. The cheerful notes of Van Morrison greeted her as she drove toward Market Street, but the music soon faded as the morning news came on.

The lead story concerned President Ford's imminent arrival and meeting with Governor Brown. Within a minute, the newscaster moved to another, even more depressing topic.

"The bodies of two young women in their late teens were discovered at five o'clock this morning by a nearby resident who was jogging through Golden Gate Park. Police are not releasing the names of the victims at this time, nor will they reveal the exact details of the murders, although they have confirmed that both victims' throats were cut and that they had been stabbed repeatedly," the voice droned with mock sincerity.

"The San Francisco Police Department is refusing to confirm any link between these murders and five similar unsolved homicides which occurred earlier this year. Nor will they admit there's any connection to the mysterious coded letters they've been receiving, which, listeners may recall, have been linked to the Zo—"

Marcia snapped off the radio. Disgust and fear churned inside her like oil and water. She knew only too well the pain and terror of physical violation. Eighteen months on from that terrible night, no matter where she went, his specter lurked a step behind her. Suppressing a shudder, she thought about Sallie, alone in the house they shared, wishing she'd called her before leaving Tom's.

Tom Maggid was getting married at Christmas. But Marcia Gray was married to her post-graduate Anthropology studies under Marshall Sahlins at the University of Chicago and, in spirit, to Sallie Hayes, her best friend and lover. Sallie, who had been there for her after the rape. Any romantic, erotic feelings she had toward men were cold in the ground, along with part of her soul, and she was grateful Tom had made no attempt to rekindle the flames of the brief but very passionate affair they had while she was a freshman at Smith College and he was at U Mass. That was another lifetime ago and now it lay in eternal darkness, like the stepfather she never really knew but had buried on Monday. Like her mother, who'd died a little over a year ago, stabbed by an intruder in a Miami hotel while on a vacation Marcia had declined.

As she reached the intersection with 17th Street, she wished her mother was with her to provide insight into the fleeting memory of the man whose will had made her the beneficiary of a substantial sum.

2

Joseph Gallagher had married Alexandra Gray after a six-month, whirlwind romance in 1972. The chance romance had come as almost as much a surprise to her mother as it had to Marcia herself. Then almost as quickly as it had started, the marriage was over, the divorce papers finalized by November of the following year. When asked why, her mother had dismissed the query with a curt "It just didn't work out," the tone of her voice clearly saying, *Don't ask*. So, with her usual rectitude, Marcia never questioned further. She was disappointed for her mother, however, who had been single since Bill Gray had left her and their one-year-old daughter to fend for themselves in Baltimore at the end of 1950. Still, she was less astonished by the news of the break-up than she had been by the wedding itself. As she'd only met her stepfather twice, the union seemed as insubstantial as a desert mirage, especially when she pondered how two people so dissimilar in outlook, interests, and personalities could have wed in the first place.

If the marriage had been a surprise, then the news of her stepfather's suicide and, more important, the fact he had willed the house to Marcia, came as a shock. One she would never understand, she thought, as she stood in front of the immaculately restored Victorian brownstone. Did he really love her mother after all? That and the fact that Joseph Gallagher, a staunch Republican, had lived for the last year on a street lodged close to the heart of San Francisco's primary gay residential area and the *cholos* cruising in their low riders along the hispanic streets of the neighboring Mission district. It was a vibrant, colorful place, but, like her mother, not in tune with his conservative tastes.

She walked up the steps and entered the house, the interior of which, like its neat facade, whispered promises of an era long past. A time of dark, walnut-paneled orderliness and leather-bound decorum shielding family secrets beneath a veneer of respectability, but one which nevertheless was authentic. The coat and hat rack, gold-plated mirror, and the chandelier in the hallway, were the real thing, Dodds, the lawyer, had informed her, and were worth beaucoup bucks. Knowing nothing of antiques or their values, Marcia knew that cataloging the house's contents was going to be an adventure she would enjoy. Much of the antiquated furniture was not listed on Joseph Gallagher's home insurance policy and had been acquired shortly before his death.

Feeling sluggish, with the threatening headache still lingering, Marcia decided to keep today's visit simple — just clear out her stepfather's bedroom. She would drop off his clothes at HomeAid, a local center for the homeless, later that day, and if she felt more energetic, maybe some of the books that filled the fourth bedroom which Joseph Gallagher had used as a library.

She climbed the stairs to the second floor and entered the room where he had blown his brains out with a 9mm Beretta. A dark burgundy stain decorated the wall behind the bed like some crude attempt at a De Kooning, and for the millionth time she wondered why he had killed himself. According to his employees at UniMed, his medical supply company, Gallagher had been his usual self, neither taciturn nor cheerful. Indeed, he was renowned for being a highly focused, hard-working businessman with little time for irrelevant small talk. But he was generally considered a good boss who amply rewarded his workers when sales exceeded expectations. If he had been depressed, no one at his firm had any indication. And as for his health, he'd been in excellent shape for a man in his mid-forties. Even the suicide note, so simple and direct in its intent, shed no light on his motivation: *My time is over. Contact Walter Dodds at Atkins, Bradley, and Dodds concerning the disposal of my estate.*

Marcia turned away from her stepfather's blood epitaph and began busying herself with disposing of his clothing.

3

Two hours later, having placed several sheets of neatly folded linen, pressed shirts, rolled socks and underwear into a number of fresh trash sacks for deposit at HomeAid, the room was empty except for a few items of furniture. While the first floor contained items of value and beauty, the upper levels of the house, especially the bedrooms, were furnished simply, generically, as if reflecting two sides to Joseph Gallagher — the cultured and the spartan. Aside from an old leather billfold containing three hundred and eleven dollars she'd found tucked under a pile of precisely folded handkerchiefs, the man and his house otherwise seemed destined to remain an enigma. Again, she wished her mother were there to tell her more about the man she'd married.

As soon as the unbidden thought formed, she pushed it away. Guilt embraced her momentarily, the inevitable echo of the thought that had haunted her for two years: *Would Mom still be alive if I'd gone to Florida with her? Or would we both be dead?*

The memory of her mother's death revived the same questions concerning Gallagher. *Why* had she married him? *What had gone wrong?* Questions, questions....

Satisfied with her work but bored by its monotony, she decided, despite the lingering threat of migraine, to explore the attic. If the house were a jigsaw puzzle without a definite image to guide her in the assembly of the pieces, perhaps the attic would shed some light on the mystery that was Joseph Gallagher. Attics, the elephants' graveyard of things bought and unused, of non-essential items which became artifacts from decades past, could provide topographical reference points in the mapping of a life.

4

Aside from her first visit to the house with Dodds, Marcia hadn't gone anywhere near the surprisingly clean space beneath the eaves. Like the rest of the house, it was neat. But unlike the other rooms, she noted that the attic was organized according to a more eclectic and erratic scheme, and that it contained items and objects at odds with the otherwise stoic character of the house. Here, in the shadows and dust motes spinning in the pale light that spilled through two narrow casement windows, lay key components of the equation which might add up to the sum of Joseph Gallagher.

No, *eclectic* was too ineffectual a word; the range of junk defied any obvious classification. From hunting trophies to astrological charts, moldering piles of *Guns and Ammo*, *True Detective*, and what looked like the last twenty years' worth of *The Examiner-Chronicle* to framed posters from the movies *The Exorcist* and *Badlands*. When she moved a file box of business records, a pair of handcuffs clattered to the floor; opening an old suitcase freed the aroma of ancient sweat clinging to a selection of lacy women's lingerie. Unzipping a Navy bag, she discovered a hunting rifle and a selection of knives. A packing crate contained a child's train set and a collection of toy cars. In yet another corner of the room, concealed by several boxes of business correspondence dating back to the early '60s, she finally found a trunk containing diaries and bundles of personal correspondence.

As Marcia opened the top journal, a very old, torn piece of typewriter carbon fell out and fluttered to her feet. She stooped to pick it up, and as she read it, her mind froze in confusion. The type was faded and she couldn't make out some of the words very clearly, although the fact that the note had been written in block capitals helped. It read:

SHE WAS YOUNG AND BEAUTIFUL
BUT NOW SHE IS BATTERED AND
DEAD. SHE IS NOT THE FIRST
AND SHE WILL NOT BE THE LAST
I LAY AWAKE NIGHTS THINKING ABOUT MY
NEXT VICTIM. MAYBE SHE WILL BE THE
BEAUTIFUL BLOND THAT BABYSITS NEAR
THE LITTLE STORE AND WALKS DOWN THE
DARK ALLEY EACH EVENING ABOUT SEVEN.
OR MAYBE SHE WILL BE THE SHAPELY BLUE
EYED BRUNETTE THAT SAID NO WHEN I
ASKED HER FOR A DATE IN HIGH SCHOOL.
BUT MAYBE IT WILL NOT BE EITHER. BUT I
SHALL CUT OFF HER FEMALE PARTS AND
DEPOSIT THEM FOR THE WHOLE CITY TO SEE.
SO DON'T MAKE IT EASY FOR ME. KEEP
YOUR SISTERS, DAUGHTERS, AND WIVES OFF
THE STREETS AND ALLEYS.
MISS BATES WAS STUPID. SHE WENT TO
THE SLAUGHTER LIKE A LAMB. SHE DID
NOT PUT UP A STRUGGLE. BUT I DID.
IT WAS A BALL.
I FIRST PULLED THE MIDDLE

And there the sheet of carbon ended, the rest of the note torn off at a diagonal.

What did it mean? Where had it come from? She flipped through the journal, not trying to read the erratic handwriting, but looking to see if the rest of the sheet were hiding elsewhere. Nothing fell out.

The cold, dead weight of the words she had just read pulled her down, and Marcia suddenly felt very tired. As she sat on the steamer trunk, she spied a leaf of paper protruding from one of the other volumes and picked it up. Yes, it was another part of the carbon, the bottom of the sheet, but the tear had not been accidental, for a middle section was missing.

Her mouth turned dry as she read the rest:

AS I CHOKED HER, AND HER LIPS TWITCHED.
SHE LET OUT A SCREAM ONCE AND I KICKED
HER HEAD TO SHUT HER UP. I PLUNGED THE KNIFE
INTO HER AND IT BROKE. THEN I FINISHED THE
JOB BY CUTTING HER THROAT. I AM NOT SICK.
I AM INSANE. BUT THAT WILL NOT STOP
THE GAME. THIS LETTER SHOULD BE PUBLISHED
FOR ALL TO READ IT. IT JUST MIGHT SAVE THAT
GIRL IN THE ALLEY. BUT THAT'S UP TO YOU.
IT WILL BE ON YOUR CONSCIENCE. NOT
MINE. YES, I DID MAKE THAT CALL TO YOU
ALSO. IT WAS JUST A WARNING. BEWARE... I
AM STALKING YOUR GIRLS NOW.

At the bottom of the sheet, in the far right hand corner, someone — the handwriting didn't look like her stepfather's — had scrawled in pencil *Cheri Jo hahahah.*

Marcia frowned. It didn't make sense. Why was this... *thing*... this disgusting note among her stepfather's possessions? She opened one of the journals at random. The entry was dated August 9, 1969, and the neat writing clearly was Joseph's.

The Chronicle had the murders splashed across page one and panic grips the city of Los Angeles so tight you can feel it all the way up here.

"Five Slain In Bel Air" ran the afternoon edition, not naming the victims. But I knew who they were. I didn't have to wait for the later paper.

Charlie was as good as his word. The plan is in place and now it will unravel. The slaughter of Sharon Tate and her friends has triggered a psychic shock wave that will appease and invigorate the Dark Masters. Oh, if only I could tell someone what I know. The newspapers talk of "ritualistic" murders then contradict themselves. If only they knew the truth! But now Jay is gone and our secrets are safe. The game must be played by our rules, the Masters' rules, no one else's.

In six weeks, it will be my time again.

The murder of Sharon Tate? *"Charlie was as good as his word...."*

Manson. Her stepfather knew Manson?

How? It was unbelievable. Joseph Gallagher had been a model, middle-class American citizen: a Navy recruit in the early '60s, a traveling medical supply salesman who eventually started his own business in 1970. She recalled her mother saying something about his involvement with the Freemasons. Maybe this could be some weird attempt at fiction.

She turned to another entry, one dated six weeks after the one she'd just read. The page marked September 28, 1969 did little to quell the confusion gnawing anxiously at her mind.

Afterward, when they have rewarded me, I feel sorrow. Not sorrow born of pity for the victims or of shame for what I have done to them, but a deep, aching sorrow because the hunger is still there, even after my Nephandi masters have given me riches beyond compare. The hunger grows each time I do my work, and now what once would have fed me for months provides nothing more than an appetizer. The longer the torture, the more exquisite the taste as I feed on those who do not know what they are. I feast on their Quintessence, but it is never enough.

Today, I am filled with a deep hunger. Something went wrong last night and both of them are still alive. I only got to taste some of the girl's Avatar even though I stabbed her twenty-four times, and now my masters refuse to grant me my reward. It hurts, and scratches at the inside of my head like an insect trying to burrow its way out.

How did I fail this time? I don't know, I don't

The entry ended abruptly with a small ink stain at the curve of the last character. Marcia turned the page. The next entry was dated September 30, 1969. Again, the handwriting changed, but this time the penmanship conformed to the neat script of the first entry she'd read. It appeared to be her stepfather's work.

The girl, Carolyn Sharp, died this afternoon, but the boy still lives. They haven't announced this in the papers or on the TV yet, but I know because Vaspos, my Magus, visited me while I was asleep and took the pain away. The Others wanted to punish me for my failure, but only my unswerving loyalty and devotion to the cause saved me from months of agony. Vaspos spared me from the hunger by granting me a few crumbs of the promised reward. He told me he has plans for me ,and punishment would only hinder those schemes.

Still, I deserved to suffer, as I always do and always will until I have gathered enough slaves to serve me in the dark paradise. I do not understand what went wrong. The boy, Bryant Hartwell is his name, has Awakened through the trauma of my attack, but his essence is damaged and he will not be a threat. If Vaspos says it is so, then who am I to doubt the word of a Magus?

But I still can't understand why I failed. I should have been able to tell that the boy was the one, not the girl, even though it is always the females who have the power. I keep thinking through that day's events and cannot see where I erred.

It started as it should. The clouds told me to head north, to travel beyond Napa, pointing at Lake Barryessa, directing me to spread the paranoia north, to feed the fear now growing in San Francisco and Vallejo after my activities in December and July. Yet when I arrived up by the lake my instincts failed me and it took several hours to find the victims. That has never happened before and the fact troubles me.

At first I believed the Chosen to be the three young women I found parked outside the A&W, yet something about me spooked them and they drove off before I could read them. Perhaps that was my first mistake, for although I was projecting my big man image, with neat hair, clean-cut and nice-looking, their hasty departure convinced me they knew I was not what I appeared to be, and only a nascent Mage would be able to tell that.

An hour later, I found them sunbathing beside the lake and watched them for twenty minutes. They saw me observing them, and for some reason I was unsettled by their calm response. No panic, no indication of fear. They watched me watching them as if I were no more than a bug walking across their blanket. It wasn't right.

Elsewhere, I found a man and his young son, but the boy had a .22 rifle. They were definitely not the Chosen.

It was shortly after I drove away from them, about a mile west, that I discovered the Hartwell boy's car. It was white, with a black vinyl top, a mid-'50s model. About two hundred yards away, I could see a grove of trees and a marsh. But there was a sparsely covered peninsula reaching out into the lake. Two oak trees stood near the water, and there, laying on a blanket beside the shore, were the boy and the girl.

They were the ones, I knew.

The girl saw me watching them but it didn't matter. I knew they were Chosen. And the presence of a lone cloud hovering over the lake bore witness to the fact, a signpost to sacrifice.

As I approached, I moved into the trees.

The girl was still watching when I reappeared a few moments later, and I could tell she was perturbed by my proximity. The boy, however, continued to lay there as if a tall man weighing over 200 pounds approaching them was no big deal. His attitude suited my actions at the time, but this disassociated nonchalance fooled me.

A small breeze sprung up as I invoked it, sufficient to cast dust into the girl's face. The instant she looked away, I disappeared, circling them.

The neat, almost regimented handwriting suddenly swam across the page in front of her and Marcia rubbed her eyes. The familiar headache was building again, nuzzling the base of her cranium like a faithful pet. She'd been feeling fine before entering the attic, but only now did she notice the claustrophobic suffocation of the stale air, the sense the room was closing in around her.

But she couldn't put the diaries down. It was as if they begged to share their secrets with her. Taking a deep breath, she skipped ahead a few pages and resumed reading.

...then I tied them up with the clothesline.

The boy kept talking, asking me questions. I told him I was getting nervous. I don't know why. Maybe to shut him up, convey I might lose it and shoot him at any time? Or was it to keep the girl quiet? I could taste her fear. But that boy, damn him, he was unsettling me with his constant questions. He should have been afraid. He even asked me if the gun was loaded. I showed him, then turned his head away from me when he started to question again. But the girl...

She knew the gun was primed and her fear increased. It jolted me and I got hard, seeing her lying there, so helpless, so unwilling.

"I'm going to have to stab you," I told them.

That seemed to shut the boy up, but it wasn't why I said it. The girl's aura started to shimmy and dance and I could taste her fear.

Like Charlie used to say, "Getting the fear..."

Damn that boy. Just as the girl started to mewl like a cat, as I drew the knife from its scabbard, he begged me.

"Do me first. I couldn't stand to see her stabbed. I'm a chicken," he kept saying, and I despised his weakness, his cowardice.

Or was it? Perhaps it was some pathetic attempt at being a hero, or a savior. Was he thinking that if I stabbed him I would let the girl go? Or did he know, somehow, I couldn't kill him?

Fool. It only fed her fear.

I stabbed him and cut and stabbed and cut and blood sprayed her face and ran like red rain drops and her fear consumed her essence and it consumed me and then I stabbed her.

In the back, just like I was shown by the Masters, but then she resisted, rolled over and I stabbed her front. Once, the foot-long knife sank to its hilt between her breasts, and then into each breast, her abdomen, and her groin.

Then it was over. My work was done.

I walked off into the enveloping twilight to find a phone and make my call.

Marcia flinched as a cockroach scuttled over her foot, jerking her attention away from the intensity of the words. She slammed down her right foot, crushing the bug, which cracked open with the snap of a dry twig.

Like the bug, she felt the attic, the house, starting to crawl over her, looking for a way in, ready to penetrate her with the intent of the narrator's knife. Like the blade wielded by her attacker, the rapist who had scarred her breasts and belly, threatened to ram it between her legs if she resisted. And for a terrible instant she was back in her dorm room and the incident which had scarred her life more deeply than the faint white marks which decorated her body replayed for the thousandth time.

A rough hand clamped over her mouth, stifling her screams, restricting her breathing, as its mate ran the blade over her breasts, nicking flesh, cold metal on warm skin, the voice whispering in her ear, do what I say cunt and you'll live... and then fingers tore away her panties, entered her, nails scraping her inner self, and—

Marcia gasped. She stood up, almost swooning, gathered the diaries, and headed for the stairs. She wanted to be outside, to feel the sun's furtive fall rays warm her skin. She wanted to smell the scent of the bay, not the blanket of old mothballs and dust which lay thick in the cramped attic.

And so she fled the house on Liberty Street, and in her haste didn't notice the black Chevy following her at a safe distance.

5

An hour later, after she'd returned to Tom's apartment and stood under a hot shower until the tension abated, she went and sat in the living room with a cup of herbal tea and continued reading the diaries. This time, she began at the beginning.

The first entry in the oldest volume was dated June 22, 1964.

I didn't mean to kill her but she laughed at me, humiliated me, just like the girls in school used to every time my back was turned. She spurned me, taunted me when I couldn't get it up, and then she was gone and it was Francis Anderton standing there not a five-buck San Diego hooker and that's when I grabbed her by the throat.

She must have kneed me in the groin but I didn't feel it until later when I thought I'd bled down there. But it was just drying cum among the bruises. I must have shot my wad when I strangled her but I don't remember that either. All I remember was seeing Francis' face, that beautiful taunting face of the girl I loved in high school and who made fun of me in front of the class in science. Francis, who haunted me, came to me in dreams, still taunting years after I left Riverdale and those unthinking, unimaginative dolts at Garton High. All I remember is standing there in the alleyway with the woman dead at my feet, her neck all swollen up and turning purple where I'd crushed the life out of her throat, her skirt hiked up around her waist revealing white, fat thighs bulging over stocking tops.

I was scared. I ran. I don't think anybody saw me. I don't know what to do. Even writing this down doesn't help.

The next entry was dated a week later.

Can't eat, can't sleep. Haven't left the apartment since that night. Every time I hear someone coming up the creaking stairs I want to crawl up into a ball and hide somewhere, expecting a knock at the door and a platoon of cops with nightsticks outside.

Did I leave fingerprints on her throat? Could they trace them through my Navy records?

I must go away, but I don't know where. I can't sleep because every time I close my eyes I see that whore's face and Francis Anderton is with her, and behind them are all those girls from school. And they laugh and point their fingers at me.

The entry was followed by three other lines, but they were scratched out with a thick marker pen and were unreadable. And beneath them, another confession. No date this time, and the handwriting was shaky, like the author suffered from cerebral palsy.

I don't deserve to live for what I've done and I'm being punished for it. The voices keep telling me I'm bad and urge me to do it — that the only way they'll be quiet is if I kill myself.

I want them to go away. I have no choice.

I went to the drugstore on the next block and bought a bottle of aspirin. The woman behind the counter knew I was guilty, knew what I was going to do.

She laughed at me as I walked out the door.

The old guy at the liquor store knew, too, but he understood, and nodded at me when I bought the two bottles of rye.

But now I'm safe. Now I'm home. And in a few hours I won't be able to hear the voices anymore.

The next page was blank, but the one following it was scrawled with penciled symbols. All were variations on a theme, as if the artist were practicing, trying to get it right, and a page over he had. It looked like this:

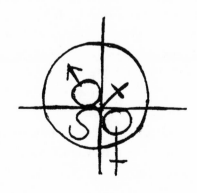

Marcia paused, took a sip of tea, and studied the arcane mark she'd never seen before. Beneath it were several rows of neat, flowing script, the work of a different hand altogether, the penmanship meticulously crafted, and, judging by the indentations in the paper, written with the fine nib of a fountain pen. It read:

The scales have been lifted from my eyes, and for the first time in my life I can see the wondrous, terrible beauty of the world around me. No longer is it mundane, drab, driven by anxiety or bad dreams, or filled with tarnished beauty. Now I have a new life, for I have been reborn into a new world of endless possibilities, of pleasures and treasures undreamed of. But this, the Masters inform me, is only a taste of things to come. For I am the Chosen One and my sacred mission is but a path toward enlightenment leading to the one true Paradise. And there I will have slaves in abundance to serve me.

6

Marcia returned to the house on Liberty Street and found the door was open.

Had she left it unlocked in her rapid departure? Maybe.

Gentle, almost seductive feminine voices drifted down from the second floor.

Slowly, she ascended the stairs, drawn to the sound, the soft whispers of young women conversing, repeating, repeating, as if reciting a nursery rhyme. As she reached the top step, her eyes caught a glimpse of pale movement inside the second bedroom.

The air suddenly turned humid; clung to her like a damp toweling robe, the belt tight across her abdomen. Ripe aromas teased her nose, sickly sweet like Turkish Delight and spoiling jellies. Heavy incense. Marijuana. Musk — a musk so familiar; feminine scent, rich, laced with pheromones. She wheezed with the grace of an asthmatic, moving inexorably toward the ajar bedroom door.

Closer, closer. Not afraid, not feeling anything.

The door swung inward. A naked girl, no more than thirteen, with small, budding breasts, stood beside it, gently waving her forward.

"We've been waiting for you."

Behind the girl, seated, lounging, entwining on the bed were other women. All shapes, all sizes. All naked. Touching, kissing, caressing, a slowly undulating ripple of pliant skin. Hushed moans teased Marcia's ears.

Two women rolled from the bed, providing an unobstructed view of the *menage-a-trois* behind them. A skinny blonde kissed deeply the overweight girl in the middle while an older woman, her face obscured by a curtain of sepia-brown hair, worked something black and phallic between fleshy thighs.

The girl standing beside the door lowered a hand, touching the delicate V between her legs.

"Come in," she said, raising the hand.

Blood stained her finger tips.

Marcia backed away as the girl raised those fingers to her lips and licked.

The woman who wielded the black object looked up, smiling reassuringly in her direction.

Her mother grinned with shameless delight.

No. *No.* This wasn't happening. Her mother was dead—

Chimes rang. And Marcia gasped as she backed toward the stairs, feet tugged out from underneath her, falling backward into the arms of nothing.

As her right arm flailed, knocking the empty mug from the coffee table, Marcia jerked up from the couch, eyes snapping open as the cup landed on the hardwood floor, door chimes tinkling in close proximity.

A nightmare... just a dream... but the images were so vivid, so real, they clung to her like a lover who couldn't say goodbye. Shaking her head, she stood, gathered her robe about her and went to the door.

Looking out through the peephole, she saw a nondescript man in his mid-forties standing on the other side.

"Who is it?"

"Miss Gray? Marcia Gray? This is Dan Leonardo. Walter Dodds sent me. I have some paperwork pertaining to your stepfather's estate."

She hesitated. Dodds hadn't called her. What could be so urgent that he'd send an assistant?

"Just hold on a minute, okay?"

Marcia moved to the bedroom and slipped out of the robe, donning a pair of sweat pants and a T-shirt. Then, as a precaution, she picked up her canister of mace from her purse and slipped it in the pants pocket. A woman alone couldn't be too careful these days. She knew that all too well.

She opened the door with the chain on, and, seeing that the well-dressed man was alone, let him in.

Dan Leonardo smiled politely as he expressed his thanks. Marcia gestured toward the living room.

"What's this about?"

He sat on the couch and produced a large manila envelope from inside his tan raincoat.

"I'm a private investigator, Miss Gray, and Mr. Dodds has hired me to handle a delicate matter concerning the estate of Joseph Gallagher."

"What do you mean, 'delicate?'"

Leonardo fingered his salt-and-pepper mustache, pausing to find the right words.

"It appears... um, maybe you should sit down while we discuss this. It's going to take some time to explain."

She sat and he continued.

"Your stepfather appears to have been involved in some questionable activities, and Mr. Dodds has asked me to investigate on your behalf, and—"

"My behalf? Why? What does this have to do with me? I hardly knew him, and, as Mr. Dodds should have told you, Joseph Gallagher was married to my mother for just under a year."

He held up a hand. "Yeah, I'm aware of that, but what I have to tell you is kind of complicated, okay?"

The threat of the headache suddenly returned, and, nodding slightly as she closed her eyes and massaged her neck, she mumbled for him to go ahead.

"You've heard of Charles Manson?" Leonardo asked.

"Sure."

"Let me throw another name at you: Zodiac."

"What is this, Twenty Questions?" Marcia snorted back, grimacing as a spear of pain pierced her neck. "Of course I've heard of him. San Francisco's mysterious assassin. Didn't he threaten to blow up a school bus?"

"San Francisco's most infamous killer —never apprehended. Zodiac was a masked murderer who primarily hunted couples, at least the few police records confirm that these were his victims. He taunted the authorities by sending letters written in code."

"So?"

What does this have to do with Joseph Gallagher? She wanted to shout it at him, the journals flashing into her mind, but before she could say another word, he added:

"Zodiac wrote the police stating he was killing people — primarily women — to serve as his slaves when he went to paradise."

Tension gripped the back of Marcia's neck.

"But why did you mention Manson?" she asked, feeling her back go cold as she said the last name, recalling the references to 'Charlie' in the strange diaries and the line about gathering "enough slaves to serve me in the dark paradise."

Leonardo paused, blinking. He ran his tongue across his lips, and for an instant, she thought she saw fear in his eyes.

"What I'm about to tell you is going to sound crazy, but stick with me.

"The Zodiac killings started in December, 1968. At least that's what was first thought, but in subsequent letters to the newspapers and police, the killer claimed he'd murdered before. At the time, his chosen method of murder was either by stabbing or shooting, or both. An anonymous tip turned attention to an unsolved slaying in Riverdale, California, that dated back to 1966, and there was concrete proof linking the crimes.

"Zodiac followed his fatal Christmas gift with three more attacks in 1969, in July, September and October. Then, in one of his letters, he stated he was going to change his method of killing — collecting slaves was the term he used — because he was pissed at the police for supposedly telling lies about him. He said he'd make his victims' deaths look like accidents or robberies. He also claimed to have killed seven people by this time — but only five victims had died, and two others had survived. Yet back in August, up in the Alameda Valley area of San Jose, two teenage girls had been brutally stabbed to death...."

Leonardo looked away, leaving his history lesson hanging in the air as he visibly paled.

"What's..."

He held up a hand to silence her.

"Stabbed is too tame a word. Those girls were *butchered*. Their killer stabbed the two of them over three hundred times."

"My God..." Marcia clasped a hand to her mouth.

"It gets worse," he continued. "You wanted me to explain what the Manson connection is...."

Marcia didn't want to know any more; her mind's eye showed her the hacked bodies of two young girls, stabbed, stabbed more times than she could imagine. Involuntarily, she nodded for him to go on.

"Charles Manson had spent most of his life in jail since he was a kid, and for most of the '60s he was in the Bay area. Despite his objections — prison was the best home he'd ever had — he was paroled in early 1967 and immediately gravitated to Haight-Ashbury along with all the other counter-culture flakes. Bikers, dopers, Satanists, cultist—"

"Satanists?"

"Right," he said, taking a cigarette from the pack in his pocket. "Only that's the tip of the iceberg.

"It was there, in the Haight, that Manson started gathering teenage runaways — girls mostly — to be his followers. And where he got involved with the Process Church of the Final Judgment, a cult formed by two former English Scientologists. The Process worshipped Satan, Lucifer, and Jehovah simultaneously, if that makes any sense.

"The fact is, Manson was around the Bay area at the time the Zodiac murders began, and like Manson, Zodiac was heavily into the occult. He only ever killed near water and either on a full moon night or near a new moon, all of which has occult significance. And since the occult community attracted like-minded souls with the gravity of a black hole, the chance that they met is very strong. Anyway, that's the official opinion. I think I have conclusive proof they did meet, but that's not important right now."

Charlie was as good as his word...

Marcia tried to suppress a shudder. If Leonardo noticed, he ignored her response. Considering the almost fanatical, obsessive tone to his voice, he hadn't.

"All right," Marcia interjected, in part out of impatience, though more from revulsion at the subject, "but I still don't—"

Leonardo raised a hand and gave a grim smile. "Please, let me finish.

"Zodiac wrote twenty letters to the San Francisco papers between July, 1969 and July of last year, then — nothing.

"The popular theory is the killer's in jail on some lesser charge, that's why he hasn't written, but there's other evidence suggesting he's still out there and has started killing farther afield." Leonardo paused, toying with the cigarette.

"There have been a series of killings in Seattle, which, after all, isn't so far away. They began in January '74, and the murders there continued until last September. Then the perpetrator, or killers — I believe there's two of them — resumed murdering women in Utah. By the start of this year, the killer shifted his murder spree to Colorado. I have evidence that this man — he's a law student called Theodore Bundy — has been working with someone else, a mentor if you like, who primed him to kill, then turned him loose. That mentor is Zodiac."

"I don't understand the point of all this," she said. "And if you know who's killing these women in Seattle, and Utah, and wherever else, why haven't you gone to the police?"

"I don't have sufficient proof."

Marcia winced as little needles of pain stabbed behind her eyes.

"But this supposed link between Manson and Zodiac—"

"There's more. I haven't told you about the astrological killings or the unsolved occult murders in northern California, which are definitely interlinked with the Manson family, Zodiac, and a Process Church splinter called the Chingons, who practice ritual rape, human sacrifice, and cannibalism."

"That's it! I've had enough!" Marcia snapped, instantly regretting it as pain flared at the back of her head. "This is the great conspiracy theory to end them all! Next, you'll be telling me Lee Harvey Oswald was involved, too."

"He was."

Marcia's temper snapped, and she hurled the mug across the room. It shattered against the wall.

"Oswald unwittingly started it all. But I'm getting ahead of myself."

"What does this have to do with Joseph Gallagher?!" she shouted.

Leonardo lit the cigarette he'd been holding for some time, exhaled and said:

"I have evidence that indicates that your stepfather was the Zodiac killer."

That's insane, Marcia wanted to say. But she'd read enough of the diaries to realize they were the work of a deranged mind, and Leonardo had told her things which connected directly with what she'd read — material that now went beyond coincidence. She took a deep breath, squeezing her eyes tightly shut, urging the increasing throb at the nape of her neck to go away.

"Okay," she said softly. "Okay. It's a great conspiracy theory, and you obviously know a lot of stuff. Why are you involved, and why is Walter Dodds concerned?"

Leonardo moved closer to her and opened the envelope he'd brought with him.

The envelope contained a pile of photographs, some glossy 8x10 black and whites, some color Polaroids, and a selection of yellowed newspaper clippings. As he handed them to her, Marcia saw the photos were all of women.

"This material came from Joseph Gallagher's bank deposit box and was addressed to you. I'm sure you won't recognize any of them, unless you're a crime buff, but this one..." he pulled a press clipping from the file. The headline screamed: TEENS BRUTALLY MURDERED. And beneath it, pictures of the dead girls, one of whom—

"This one was my sister."

Marcia gasped, her mind numbing with incredulity.

One of the girls in the photo — Leonardo's sister — was the girl from her dream.

7

Later, after she fainted and Leonardo revived her, he perused the diaries while she drank the herbal tea he made, nodding to himself as his suspicions were confirmed. Periodically, he read her an extract, explaining its significance, filling her in on details which, before today, she would have dismissed as the delusions of a paranoid schizophrenic. She agreed it might be true — her stepfather could have been an insane killer, based on what she'd read — and after Leonardo told her his story, she began to believe. The day dissolved into a blur of tales, and were it not for the fact that she forced herself to think like an ethnographer, to sift through the data searching for a coherent world view

298

in what appeared to be an elaborate conspiracy, she would have doubted her own sanity.

The sadistic frenzy of Leonardo's younger sister's death had turned his life around. Fueled by a burning desire to see justice done, he dropped out of college and joined a firm of private investigators, and when he wasn't shadowing adulterous husbands or trying to locate teenage runaways, he followed his own leads on the Zodiac case. In doing so, he uncovered startling connections between seemingly unrelated crimes on both coasts and a cast of characters ranging from suicidal neo-Nazi auto workers to Long Island millionaires obsessed with kinky sex, drug dealers and pornographers, to top Hollywood film and music producers — connections which dated back to the mid-'60s, to Charles Manson, the Process Church and its splinter groups, to snuff movies and child pornography.

Marcia again listened patiently, and the more she heard, the more her reality seemed to blur at the edges, quieting the voice of disbelief, drawing her deeper into a web of darkness. As Leonardo continued to talk, she began to feel increasingly disassociated from the world she knew.

"Why do they do it?" she asked, both fascinated and revolted. "Do they actually believe they are serving Satan or is it something else?"

"Most of those involved, the foot soldiers, the servants, are lost souls. Lonely, alienated, dysfunctional. They get lured in through drugs and sex, and then the brainwashing begins. If they resist that, then there's blackmail and the threat of retribution against family members. Fear is the controlling factor. Once you're in their net, death is the only way out. Over a dozen people connected with either these other groups or the Manson family have died under mysterious circumstances during the last six years."

"What about the others, the ones who organize all this?" Marcia suddenly felt very tired, almost slurring her words as she spoke.

"Power, money, the satisfaction that comes from the perverse desire to corrupt and destroy others' lives," he replied. "There are huge sums of money involved from the drugs, the snuff movies, the child smut. But it goes beyond that. I'm convinced some of these people are intent on completely destroying society as we know it. They feed on fear.

"Fear turns them on. It was Manson's big kick. I don't mean in the same way a sexual sadist gets off on his victim's fear. Nothing was straight with Manson. The ghoul's brain is fried like an overdone egg. But one of his mantras in the '60s was 'Getting the Fear.' It was an exquisite physical experience somewhat akin to an LSD trip, from what I understand. But in true Manson-speak, the concept was more than that; the entire substance of expanded consciousness was *fear — fear into infinity. Transcendental fear. Fear was meant to be the key that set you free."*

"I don't understand," Marcia mumbled as consciousness suddenly escaped her.

8

She snapped awake, vaguely aware she'd been dreaming about something but she couldn't remember what. Then Marcia realized she was in a car and it had come to a stop, and that she and Leonardo were outside the house on Liberty Street and she didn't understand why they were there or what had happened and she couldn't remem—

"Get out of the car," the detective said, his tone suddenly as cold as the Chicago wind.

"What?" she said, her voice no more than a whisper.

"Move, you pathetic bitch."

She felt her limbs flex as if controlled by strings, the arms and legs of a marionette, as her brain flashed in panic, *no, no, no…*

Her will fragmented. Confusion and panic were subsumed under numbing waves of automatic compliance as Leonardo took her arm, guiding her up the steps. *Drugged. He drugged me….*

"This is your coming-out party," Leonardo whispered, his voice soft, seductive. "Within twenty-four hours, you'll go down in history."

As they reached the front door, it opened of its own accord, a black mouth ready to swallow her whole. Behind the house, the sun's dying rays retreated, deepening the shadows as it gave San Francisco to the night. Down the hallway, candlelight glowed warmly, but Marcia shivered involuntarily, her breath clouding as the chilling dimness enveloped her like fog.

Like the rape, her mind went into denial. *This… isn't… happen—*

"Oh, yes it is," Leonardo hissed, his voice changing.

He sounded like… like…

The detective guided her to the dining room, and there she saw his promise of a party was a literal truth.

300

Seated at the far end of the mahogany table was her mother, and on each side sat the young women from her dream, and others she recognized from the photos Leonardo had shown her, their flesh a sea of alabaster naked skin rippling like tiny waves in the flickering light cast from the dozens of candles all over the room. Only one woman was clothed, a petite, plain-faced girl wearing a red cotton dress.

What was left of her rational mind screamed silently inside Marcia's aching head. *I don't want to be a victim again.*

Then soft, moist hands touched her right arm, urging her toward the vacant seat facing her mother. She turned to meet the smile of Leonardo's teenage sister, who kissed her cheek before seating her. The girl smelled of rotten mushrooms.

Leonardo walked slowly to the other end of the room and stopped, standing behind Marcia's mother. His hands dropped to her breasts, kneading them like dough.

"It's so good to have you home, Marcy," mother cooed.

Leonardo smiled, and then his face started to run like wax, morphing into the stony visage of Joseph Gallagher.

"I've been waiting for this family gathering for some time," he said, his voice as dry as the rustle of fall leaves. "But the timing wasn't right. And others interfered with my plans. Like your mother here and that crusading fool, Leonardo."

Get out! Run! Get away! she screamed silently, her stomach churning, threatening to rebel. But again all she could do was look and stand still, her body no longer her own.

Marcia stared at him, her mind momentarily woozy from the thick aroma seeping from the black candles. *Can't fight it… nowhere to… go…*

"You have questions," he said, raising his arms. In response, four of the women stood and went to him.

"You deserve answers."

The women undressed him, first removing his blood-encrusted plaid shirt, then his slacks and underwear.

"Leonardo thought he could kill me. He was wrong," Gallagher chuckled as he displayed the gaping bullet wound where his heart should have been. "It's his body you buried.

"And yes, *I* had your mother killed in Miami."

What had once been Alexandra Gray looked up at her former husband, and, smiling, took his erect penis in her mouth.

This is not real! It's the fucking drugs… this is an hallucination…

"No, it isn't," Gallagher laughed. "This is *my* reality."

Then, as he snapped his fingers, Marcia felt nothing, thought nothing. Leonardo's sister guided her to a chair, seated her, then began massaging Marcia's neck and shoulders. With each motion, confusion, fear, and pain eased away.

"She suspected I had secrets, that's why she requested the divorce, didn't you, my darling?"

Gallagher stroked Alexandra's hair, urging her mouth deeper.

"But that's the way I wanted it, because once I met you I knew you were the one. And the plan worked perfectly — better than I dared dream."

The girl's hands moved lower, her fingers lightly tracing circles around Marcia's hardening nipples. A tiny sigh slipped unbidden from her lips and Gallagher smiled.

"You asked if the servants — The Children — believed in the World of Darkness. They do, to different degrees. But only the Egregor, the Council of Thirteen, knows the truth. We are the Chosen, and we serve the Dark Masters. They are the Nephandi, mages who discovered the true path of the Left Hand, and they, too, serve other forces the likes of which you cannot conceive.

"We feed on fear, because fear is the key, unlocking the door of the rational, allowing us to dine on Quintessence, the spiritual essence of all living things."

Marcia felt other hands on her body and realized the women seated closest to her had moved over and were removing her clothing. A steady wetness was building between her thighs, a languorous, pre-orgasmic sensation which was such a relief after the hours of headache.

"The end is coming, and with it a new beginning. We shall rule, and you, dear Marcia, shall serve alongside me.

"I mentioned Oswald earlier. He, poor, deluded fool, helped open the door. When he shot Kennedy, he opened a psychic wound in the national consciousness, and those waves washed away innocence and faith. The door swung wider, and the darkness crept forth across the land, its disciples spreading the word, transporting the fear."

Pleasurable shivers danced over Marcia's body as the women stroked, kissed, and caressed her cold skin.

"Like moths drawn to a flame, they smelled my fear, came to me, and set me free. Their rewards were beyond my wildest dreams, and they kept their promises, because I was chosen. But not everything went according to plan. Drugs are an unreliable tool, and much as they can be used to control and release the fear, they can corrode already weak links in the chain. Manson was one. He served his purpose but is useless now, a hollow joke, and the remainder of the Family have failed us. Except for dear Lynette here."

He beckoned to the girl in the red dress, who got up from the table and went to him, standing beside Gallagher like an obedient daughter.

"Dear Lynette," he said, stroking her face. "Little Squeaky. Charlie's most devoted servant. She's mine now, aren't you?"

The girl smiled.

Gallagher gave a low growl, turned his attention from her and grabbed Alexandra's hair in his hands, moving her head faster.

"Tomorrow morning, in Sacramento, President Ford is scheduled to address the California legislature at the Statehouse. But he'll never make that speech. You, dear Marcia, and Squeaky will shoot him."

As she felt her panties slip to the floor, the girl parted her legs and a tongue probed between Marcia's thighs as orgasm promised to deliver the little death, and she barely heard Gallagher as he droned on, then grunted as he came.

It was all a dream. She was safe in bed with Sallie....

9

The sun shone brightly on the morning of September 5th, rapidly warming the streets of Sacramento, but Marcia Gray felt nothing as Squeaky Fromme drove them toward their destiny. Her body was numb, her thoughts sluggish and no longer her own. The evil that was Joseph Gallagher had drained her will, consumed her soul. All that remained of Marcia Gray was a puppet of flesh and blood, and as such she didn't respond when Squeaky parked the car behind a house on P Street and slapped her.

"I'm the one, not you," she said, reaching for her purse on the back seat. "You're his family, not mine. Charlie chose me. He has the real power, not Gallagher. I'll die for Charlie, I'll kill for him, I'll do whatever is necessary. You don't deserve the glory."

303

Squeaky produced a stiletto from her purse and held it before Marcia's eyes.

"We don't need you. *I don't need you.*"

She thrust the blade deep into Marcia's chest.

In that instant feeling returned, terrible, burning, as the blade penetrated Marcia's heart, freeing her mind and soul from Gallagher's cancer. A tiny sigh escaped her lips.

Squeaky Fromme smiled, admiring her handiwork, then removed a Colt .45 from its hiding place under the driver's seat. Lifting her red dress, she placed the gun in a thigh holster and got out of the car.

"Red is the blood of sacrifice," she said to herself, then began walking the six blocks to the Statehouse.

10

Secret Service agent Larry Burden held open the lobby door of the Senator Hotel for the President, who paused, blinking in the bright sunlight. The Chief Executive was slightly behind schedule, and Burden hoped he wouldn't spend too much time shaking hands with the crowd lining the broad, curving pathway that led to the rear steps of the capitol building. Besides, Burden's nerves were on edge, as they always were when the President was out in the open and vulnerable. It was his job to worry, but this morning he was consumed with anxiety. Despite the glorious weather, something felt wrong.

The President started moving and Burden fell into step alongside the other agents surrounding their charge. Cheers and applause erupted from the friendly crowd as the Chief Executive double-pumped hands, pressing the flesh of loyal voters. Something caught Burden's eye and he turned away from the President.

In that instant, under the shade of a stately magnolia tree, Burden felt his fellow agents tense. All color drained from his face as he saw the president suddenly pull his hand back from a small woman in a red dress.

"Gun!" Burden shouted, leaping at the would-be assassin as he heard a click.

Burden grabbed the girl's gun hand, twisting the large Colt away from the President, and Special Agent Ernie Lutz grasped the Chief Executive from behind as the other agents swarmed around him in a now rapidly moving human shield.

"Everyone get out of the way! Get out of here!" someone shouted.

The agents moved fast as Burden twisted the girl's arm behind her.

"Don't get excited. It didn't go off," the girl said. "It didn't go off. Can you believe that?"

Agent Jim DeMarco took the Colt from Burden as he slapped the cuffs on the girl.

"It's empty," DeMarco said, examining the Colt's chamber. "She didn't pull back the slide, thank Christ."

The girl glowered at DeMarco as he popped the clip and expelled four rounds into his left palm. "Can you fucking believe it? She cocked the hammer but didn't pull the slide."

Burden said a silent prayer.

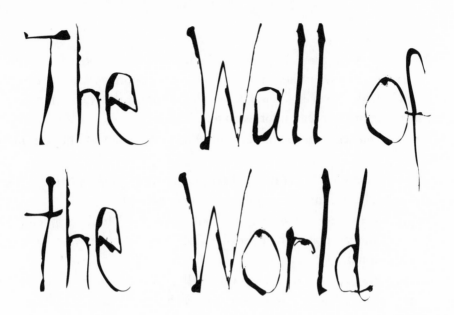

The Wall of the World

by Wendy Webb

The sounds of hammer and chisel sang staccato across the face of the western wall. Those without instruments beat painted cement with swollen, bleeding knuckles and thumbnails that turned deep blue with effort. The Berlin Wall, after twenty-eight years, was coming down.

Words inscribed on the uneven surface in bold strokes of reds, blues and vivid yellow turned first to dust, then salvageable pieces. Pocketed or pressed into the willing hands of those who could say they were here, the tokens of an era would find themselves scattered among the world to rest in bookcases or hide in dark curios under a gathering of new dust.

"More beer, more meat, less Orwell," one segment of the wall read.

"Only those who move feel their chains."

"Get the balance right."

"Monika, I love you."

Monika. It was a name she used this time. A purposeful convenience only. Nothing more. The waif-like, young woman named Monika, scarcely capable of her own shadow, waved a hand across the words on the wall as if to erase their meaning or their reason for existence.

Another message caught her eye, her hand stilled now: "The wall must stay."

The words burned in her mind, then caught in her throat when she tried to say them. The wall must stay, must stay, must stay, must....

But it was over now, and there was only what was left. This sphere, the only facet of human reality she controlled, was coming down. Monika would do what she could.

Closing her eyes, she welcomed the swell of chaotic emotion that ebbed and flowed and grew, as did the crowd, with each passing second. Individually they touched her with past pain and current worry. They became a group with the determination to take a small part of history back to their homes and bury it deep within their hearts. And it was through this collective state that Ascension would finally come. She would do her best not to disappoint them. They had asked, after all, and were more than willing.

It was clear now what she had to do. All was not lost.

The wall must stay, must stay, must stay.

A cheer came up from the press of people at her side.

Monika opened her eyes and watched.

Arms reached down to pull the man in jeans and jacket to the top of the twelve-foot wall. From below, a sea of onlookers encouraged the climb with cheers. A few offered a physical boost that sent him sprawling and writhing on the face of the wall.

Twisting and turning.

The hands reaching. Frantically reaching while his efforts turned to that of a St. Vitus dance with the impact.

An onslaught of bullets from automatically triggered weapons peppered his body and sent him reeling like a puppet at the end of a taut string. His head snapped back, his mouth opened in a scream that was cut short by death. The body slid slowly down the wall, with tracks of red the only reminder that he had tried and failed.

The crowd cheered again and welcomed the man in blue jeans to the top. He saluted like a member of royalty, then danced with intimate friends who only minutes before were strangers.

The waif-like, always young Monika waved a hand across this section of the wall and moved on. There was work to do. The wall was coming down.

A tug on Monika's sleeve attracted her attention. The little girl giggled behind her palm, twirled around to show off her new pale blue jumper, then skipped into the center of a circle of people. There, in the circle, one's arms wrapped around another's waist, the tight group sang patriotic songs and smiled through happy tears that ran in tiny rivulets down their cheeks.

Clamping her arms around her mother's legs, the little girl slid to a sitting position on a square of cracked and chipped pavement.

The asphalt groaned and fissured.

The manhole cover underneath opened.

Raw sewage bubbled up from the cavernous dark, underground system. A rat emerged, blinked in the new light, then scurried off. Noxious gases burned and stung, then dissipated into the dank, night air.

Giggling behind a closed palm, the child accepted the hands that pulled her small body in. And down. It was an escape.

It was a trap.

Hands replaced the manhole cover. Viscous, suffocating pavement shrouded the manhole. And sealed it forever.

Trapped hands came up through the cover, through the asphalt, and begged for release. The sound of lamentation echoed through the narrow underground passageways. Pleas for help traversed below street surfaces and booted feet. Screams of rage for what was right turned frightened, caught, and were finally silenced.

A small hand, one that had tugged at Monika's sleeve, was the last to drown, and slowly disappear, into the drying asphalt.

A palm to cover a quieted giggle.

The giggle turned to a laugh as the circle of singers watched the little girl burst into a song of her own making, then joined in with full voice.

"There is so much color, so much light now," one person said, while stumbling aimlessly through the crowd, then through the open gate.

Another caught the moment and replied: "The eighth wonder of the world."

The crowd responded and whispered or shouted their own mantras of hope and recovery.

"I never believed this would happen. Never."

"They cried for us. They cried."

A blind man, his canine companion close to his side, stopped then breathed deep. "I just wanted to smell the air of free Berlin." He was embraced suddenly, and the hug turned into a rally cry: "Berlin is Berlin again."

"Berlin again. Berlin again," the crowd chanted.

Monika withdrew from this cluster to inhale deep another scent. Beyond the exhilaration, past the short-lived contentment and elusive peace The Traditions would have the people believe was something more. Something hidden deep in every soul that refused to change. Even when a wall came down. Especially when a wall came down.

Because somewhere there was another wall going up.

"Bye, bye Berlin," a painted section said.

And another saying: "Berlin will be WALL-free."

The phrase "I hate this wall" blended like fragile threads of a tapestry into a painted picture of a dove that was composed of two hands joined in an effort at peace. Nearby a large fractured mirror reflected faces of broken promises and shattered dreams.

A rendering of a woman holding a camera to her face while stepping in blood shared wall space with the words: "Too late."

Too late, indeed.

And it was.

History had been unyielding in that regard. The waif-like, omnipresent, timeless Monika had seen it all before. Many, many times. In societies over centuries, across the scope of human existence, it was always the same. The Traditions saw to it that a wall erected by blood kept blood flowing. A barricade to imprison some and forbid others entry had now become an integral component of blood itself. They argued that bringing down a wall raised humanity to greater heights.

And that was the way of this battle for souls. It was why she and The Technocracy were here. That which cannot be controlled must be destroyed. Or confined.

But this time she was too late. Always too late.

The Wall must stay, must stay, must stay.

Monika waved her hand over the message that read, "If you love them, set them free." She paused in her work, then turned to look.

A middle-aged woman walked tentatively toward a frail octogenarian. "Momma? Is it really you?"

The old woman nodded, and opened her arms to her daughter.

The daughter stopped mid-stride. A blur of emotions flickered in her dull green eyes. Her bulky, white coat shimmered in the light.

Sunlight. The glorious light of day, when, for a moment, the shadows disappeared.

A happy celebration.

Her flowing, white wedding gown caught air currents and bounced and swirled as she pirouetted around her beaming groom. The dancing slowed, then stilled, as her bright green eyes filled with a blur of emotions, then dulled. Clutching the bridal bouquet to her chest, she stared with longing at her parents on the other side of the political line. "One day. Together," she mouthed. The tears came then, as they would again.

At the death of her husband, a man her parents never knew.

And again.

At the death of her father, a man her husband never knew.

Still again, at the reunion when she met her mother whom she had so little time to know.

Pulling the bulky, white coat tight, the woman with dull green eyes accepted the arms of a mother she had not touched in twenty-eight years. "It is really you, Momma." Then she cried.

A man in a rumpled, stained suit shuffled past Monika and stood as straight and tall as his arthritic body would allow. A small smile touched his face as he looked at the Wall on the west. His bent, swollen forefinger touched the corner of the painted words and followed them as if he had written them himself: "A white wall is a fool's writing paper." He nodded to himself, and tapped the cover of a well-kept book.

Libraries filled with books.

Words that opened minds and liberated the soul.

His crisp suit rustled as he took his place in front of the classroom to begin the lecture. His clean suit tore when he was taken to prison for speaking against the GDR and for human rights. Deprived of food, water, and human contact, he recited passages from books he had committed to memory.

After his return from prison, his memory began to fail and he wondered whose suits were folded neatly in his drawer. And whose home was this? It seemed familiar, but there were no pictures, no diplomas and awards. And no books. Except one. One that was hidden away for safekeeping.

The man in the rumpled, stained suit held the well-kept book close and smiled. He turned to Monika and spoke. The hint of strength still punctuated the sound. "A library book. I borrowed it." His voice cracked. "Now I can return it." His simple statement made, he nodded to her politely and shuffled into the crowd.

The sounds of hammer and chisel sang staccato across the face of the western wall.

The Wall was coming down. First in a sprinkling of dust, then in salvageable pieces. It was coming down, and in that The Traditions had won and Monika had failed.

But there had been others who had made a difference. She had seen to it. Hadrian's Wall and The Great Wall of China had served their purpose, like the others. As will this one. Eventually. This one held its own special triumph.

The Wall must stay, must stay...

Or should it?

The sound of hammer and chisel...

She closed her eyes, waved her hand across this page of history, this wall, in a final gesture, then turned her attention and talent to the future.

Hammer and chisel. Swollen and bleeding knuckles in a single-minded determination to take a small part of history back to their homes and bury it deep within their hearts.

Yes. They were willing, and she would not disappoint them.

She empowered them to do as their nature directed, and encouraged them to enlightenment. They would pocket the pieces and take them to homes all over the world. Salvageable pieces that would sit in bookcases and gather dust in dark curios.

There they would stay, inert tokens of a fading event. A blip in history repeated.

Until it was time.

A young man from Denver slid a piece into his backpack.

A blond, Italian woman dropped a token into her purse.

A journalist from Japan filled his vest pockets.

All across the Wall small relics of history were gathered by hammer and chisel, and swollen bloody knuckles.

As one wall came down, somewhere, everywhere, in families, communities and nations, there would be other walls going up.

She breathed deep the scent of short-lived contentment and elusive peace, and knew then that the seeds of Ascension, of enlightenment, were being carried.

In time they would germinate and grow.

Okay City One Thousand Times

by Stewart von Allmen

In Bosnia, you must do everything to make what
seemed impossible yesterday possible today...

— Dobrica Cosic, former President of what was
once Yugoslavia, to Radovan Karadzic, leader of
the Bosnian Serbs, at the beginning of the war
in Bosnia

The clean-up progressed slowly, but at least the area was now under our control and we could concentrate on the task at hand. Vaso Miskin Street and the adjoining market area were pulped. Shellfire from the surrounding hills had decimated the busy pedestrian area. The shadows were so thick here, the Shroud so thin, that I mistook for rubble arms and legs and heads as I crawled painfully over the debris. At the same time, I tried to stay clear of the frantic and confused Quick, who earned their nickname as they scrambled to life to escape death in this sudden emergency. Centurion Gusticic, a stern but likable man, stood several feet away and watched carefully for interlopers, his eyes casually flicking over the scrambling people, while I and the five Legionnaires who completed the patrol tried to extricate the dead, the newcomers to our world.

I stood over one victim. A large boulder of concrete, probably a portion of the street disgorged in the vomit of fire induced by the mortar shell, lay across the legs of the woman I tended.

Centurion Gusticic's command was terse, "Hurry, there are others."

It was true. The blast was horrible. The dead were everywhere.

"She might live," I said, but I squatted at her side because I saw immediately that I was wrong — her chest was turning dark, pigmenting her fair skin spot by spot as her heart pumped blood not only out the shrapnel hole in her chest but into her torso as well, where it lubricated her lungs and liver and everything else. I yearned to staunch the blood, to cut her open and compress the artery leaking her life away, and though in life I'd been a surgeon, I could do nothing. Now my work didn't begin until my patient was dead.

I watched her closely, her life a violin string oscillating on key and off. Her eyes flickered open, and for a moment I think she must have seen me. She didn't react differently, though — as one in her situation might in a city not torn apart by war — than she might if she'd found not a ghost by her side but a man from her side of the Shroud. But as I'd discovered little more than a month ago, the Shadowlands of Sarajevo are not darker than the reality of Sarajevo.

I've felt I've always existed between two worlds. Caught between two or more situations or viewpoints. In every facet of my life I personified dichotomy. Certainly as a Bosnian Serb I defied easy classification, caught as I was in a city in a nation that was itself once caught on the crossroads of great empires. The Hapsburgs and the Ottomans made sport of this land for centuries. I was drawn, ultimately drawn apart, by nationalism and patriotism, between my supposed ethnic ancestry and my lifelong devotion to my heartland home of Sarajevo. But there was more. I was a pacifist caught between generations of more serious-minded males: my father the Cetnik Serb and my anti-Serb son. I was an agnostic at the nexus of Catholicism, Orthodoxy, Islam and Judaism. Even in my job as a surgeon, I daily walked that dreadful, teetering axis that is life and death. And now, my life as a doctor offering but a crude glimpse of this damned world, I was suspended in this state between true life among the Quick and ultimate death in the Oblivion.

My name is Dragos Milolsav, and you already know more about me than I could recall for the first many days I wandered these insane streets of the Shadowlands, the land of the dead that almost mirrors the realm of the Quick, or living.

As soon as I realized my ghostly state and tore down layers of denial to acknowledge my appalling situation (imagine a doctor surrounded not by the dying but by the already dead!), I immediately dropped the appellation "doctor." It made no sense in the Shadowlands, and only subjected me to additional scrutiny by those who did not know I was firmly entrenched in the Hierarchy. For some reason everyone assumed I belonged to that despicable class of mercenary vultures called "reapers." The repuation of doctors apparently suffers unfairly even in the land of the dead. Reapers are the zealots of death that hover over the dying in anticipation of that last gasp with a hope that the newly dead, the Enfant, will enter the Shadowlands. The other possibilities are Transcendence — the passing to whatever awaits us, be it heaven or, far more likely, just another miserable hell with new rules for damnation and frustration and isolation — or complete Oblivion, the dark void beyond the Far Shores and beneath the Tempest that is the nothingness of death I expected in life, but which is the absence that I now fear beyond words in this existence.

The Enfant, his or her vision and wits bound into confusion by the plasmic caul which all who arrive wear like an embryonic sac for birth into this new world, is easily tricked by these fiends whose only aim is to gather this new soul for their own profit. Like afterlife bounty hunters, although for reapers "dead or alive" holds no meaning. The souls of the dead have value, for ironically they are all that breathe new life into these lands inhabited by beings — people? — so ancient they are said to be no longer recognized as something once human. Perhaps they were never human. I know so little of this new world…

But I do know that Enfants "rescued" by reapers inevitably end up in chains, as Thralls to more powerful wraiths.

Even in the Shadowlands, and especially in Stygia, the far-flung home of the so-called Deathlords who rule the Hierarchy, there is a need, I suppose, to discover life again and savor its many fragile forms and delicate delights. That city is where the Hierarchy sends the souls we saved, unless the Enfant wishes, like me, to remain and fight as a Legionnaire. The souls saved find solace in a city of death they make beautiful, and the Deathlords and the long-dead souls already inhabiting the city are constantly renewed by those who, if not alive, are at least less dead than they. Admittedly, some reapers gather souls they will send to Stygia for a price, but to exploit in this way for personal gain is clearly a sin, if an agnostic can cast such stones.

But human nature does exist beyond the grave, which is dire news to those who still live and hope for respite from the petty masters who pain them and the idiots who lavish them with indignities. And this is certainly not welcome news for those who have already suffered through hell, such as those in my beleaguered and battered home of Sarajevo, Bosnia.

And that's why I and my fellow Legionnaires are all dedicated to the multi-cultural, multi-religious, by-god-multi-human existence that Sarajevo embodied! All of us are victims of this unprovoked Serbian assault on Bosnia. And all but Mehmed, a Muslim who was killed by a terrorist-led Serbian strike force in the northeastern Bosnia town of Bijeljina where he visited relatives, were killed in Sarajevo itself.

While the world at large may see this war as evidence of the failure of what Bosnia sought to represent, it's really quite the opposite. Indeed, Sarajevo shines like a star of community especially now. For even after almost two months of shelling and sniper attacks that have decimated the population by the death and departures they have caused, there are still Serbs and Croats and Muslims and Jews working and surviving side by side. And they all refuse to leave, as I refused while I still lived, because they believe in what this city represents. So no matter that the world outside the Balkans may turn a dry, blind eye to this "conflict," this war, as they deal with their own small problems, their terrorist threats or sagging economies.

Even if the rest of the world will not move to protect the innocents who live in the city, at least in death Sarajevans can find succor. The Legionnaires of the Hierarchy are at hand to tend them! Unlike the ineffective Blue Helmets of the United Nations Protection Force, we actually intervene, we are actually moved by the tragedy. We are the Blue Helmets of the Shadowlands.

But seeing death on this woman's face before her body itself realized the end was near makes me wonder how we can save the living and replace the impotent UNPROFOR in the Skinlands too. I could not stand for another Vukovar to occur. Vukovar, Croatia fell to the Serbs after a three-month siege at the end of last year, and the people in the city endured days of slaughter in the streets as the Serbs celebrated their victory.

DARK DESTINY: PROPRIETORS OF FATE

It's my Vision that grants me the cruel foresight of a person's death. Just as a truly intact car might appear dented or even demolished from a Shadowlands perspective before the accident that awaits it in the near future, so too can I see death in the faces, on the bodies, of those approaching their time.

A little girl walking the deadly streets seems to have skin pulled back to reveal a skull spider-webbed with fractures.

An old man with an expressionless face and a snaking, rotten core revealed through a somehow transparent torso to be a cancer along the ileum.

A family with withered, crispy skin. All but the oldest daughter who will live because she wasn't with her loved ones when they burned.

Couldn't I follow these doomed souls and protect them from the reapers and salvage their essences for perpetual protection by the Hierarchy? Alas, anywhere but in Sarajevo where the soon to die outnumber not just the dead but seem more prominent too than the living. But at the current rate of death forecast over a period of a couple years — though it's ridiculous to think that even this inattentive, irrational world will suffer the hateful, warmongering fools Milosevic and Karadzic to live even half that long — the dead will outnumber the living and the ghosts of the afterlife will become the guardian angels of the damned. Where else but in Sarajevo would such divine sentinels be ghosts, not angels? Is this the sign of a city torn by ethnic strife? Where even after death we all fight for the other?

"Dragos!" The Centurion's call brought me back.

The woman was dead.

"Yes, sir," I hastily acknowledged, amazing myself that conforming to a hierarchy of command was coming so easily for one always so independent in life. But order was naturally at the heart of the Hierarchy. It allowed all their efforts to run as smoothly as those in Sarajevo, I suppose.

As I watched, the woman seemed to swim across the Shroud. She wavered, drawn perhaps toward Transcendence or possibly to Oblivion, but like so many in this city she was still tied to the life she so recently (and abruptly) departed, so she became a wraith.

Like a diving mask to protect her during that swim through unfathomable depths and unknowable tests on the soul in the Tempest, the woman's caul protected her against the still visible horror of the Vaso Miskin Street massacre. What she saw now would seem only dreams to her later. For an instant I recollected the awful things I dreamt as I wandered in my caul before Legionnaire Gusticic found me. But worse was the disorientation and grief, especially the grief, when the caul was first lifted, so I sighed in relief for the pain Gusticic's order to leave the Enfants cauled would spare this woman for now.

She was gasping and thrashing, but I grabbed her and managed to haul her to Gusticic. There were already two others attached to him by the silken cord he used in such instances. All he'd had at first were manacles, but as the organization of the Hierarchy in the city became better, more appropriate supplies became available.

Though I'd delivered a dozen such Enfants this way, it was still unnerving to leave the woman's side. She was Caucasian, perhaps another ethnic Serb like me caught in the fire of the nationalists who made the claim in my name that I wanted to be free of Bosnia to join them in a greater Serbian state.

The woman was trembling, but there were others suffering more than she, and I turned to face the catastrophic scene again and to look for another ready to flee the hell of Sarajevo into the comforting arms of death.

Looking at the ruptured earth and the mesmerized and stricken people, I tried to imagine the marketplace of Vaso Miskin Street with the perception of a living Sarajevian. Though the Shadowlands I walked mirrored my Sarajevo home, it offered a skewed view. I was distanced from the immediacy of emotion: like the terror and outrage currently engulfed by shock that these mortal witnesses would soon feel. My perspective was becoming more clinical as I sought to do the humane tasks of the Hierarchy and needed to overlook the merely dead to struggle to claim the undying. But I could not forget that the humane task was for these humans, my comrades in life.

So I could imagine the smoke, along with tears, that burned their eyes. The dust that billowed and sought hold in the folds and gaps in their clothing, as well as in their ears, noses and mouths. The heat of the scattered flames, here razing an overturned produce cart, there melting the skin of a middle-aged man whose soul Transcended.

My vantage was grotesque, but grotesquely beautiful. There was a stillness to the Shadowlands. A kind of reverential silence that takes hold in a mosque. And the world is colored grayer. Deader. As if a layer of chalk dust was spread to mute it. Or, as if, I suddenly realized, I saw the world through the purple lens of a kneeling man's robe.

320

My mind wandered again, the urgency of the Centurion's commands fading as I became as incapable of the Sarajevans in the marketplace and allowed the strange beauty of the Shadowlands to mesmerize me. I was a child surrounded by heavenly silence in an Orthodox church and gazed at the bustle of the life through the large stained glass window that dominated one of the walls. I remember craning my neck so I could look at the world through the different colored lenses. Yellow that jaundiced the working faces outside. Red that ripened the cheeks and lent an aura of invincibility to the buildings. Green that gave an unreal clarity to the leaves of the unending rows of trees that once lined the streets. And the purple of the kneeling man's robe. The man was bent in supplication to another. Perhaps presenting a gift. I don't remember. The picture in the window wasn't as important as how it changed my image of the real world outside.

Such a beautiful color purple. I'd drawn more than one demand from my father to sit still as I wriggled to create line of sight with the kneeling man and an object outside. What I eventually saw was a glimpse of Sarajevo from the Shadowlands. The world looked wilted. Greens and reds became browns. As did every vibrant color I could spot. The complexion of the people outside, though, acquired a richness of hue that overcame the general graying and mottling of their skin. They seemed to achieve a depth that ordinary vision couldn't detect. That too was similar to how the Quick seemed from the vantage of the Shadowlands. Even though they might be on the verge of death, they possessed a connection to the world, connections that wraiths such as I also possess, but in a tenuous way that was gripping and raw.

So, through this lens of a kneeling man I witnessed the carnage of the marketplace again. Around the perimeter of the damaged area stood countless Sarajevans mesmerized by the brutal reality of the carnage before them. In the unlikely event this war goes on for long, these same people, the ones not part of the pile of corpses themselves, will react better. Maybe save more lives. Now, only those trained to react can. The implausibility, the seeming impossibility, of bombs dropping on children and in the midst of their city is beyond believability.

It's almost too much for me. But stained glass and death: grotesque beauty. That's my world now.

We worked for another five minutes before the first reaper showed himself. He was a tricky one, but his was a game the Centurion had warned us about. I would never have noticed otherwise. Of course, even so armed I have little conception of all the amazing things the dead can do. This reaper was just showing one of the more common aptitudes. He was skinriding and I noticed him

only because I'd so careful examined the crowd a few moments before. If Centurion Gusticic later disciplined me for being so slow and risking the souls of the Sarajevans, I would have this as my defense.

The man the reaper was skinriding was one in whose face I'd read great horror. I didn't pick him as the kind that would ever harden to such tragedies. So when I saw him assisting the wounded, I paused again. Just long enough to note that the person he was "helping away" wasn't alive at all. Not quite dead either, but almost. I could see through the mirror of the man's blank eyes that his brain had been severely bruised. The concussion of the blast must have been the cause.

If the reaper could move the dying man to a position away from devastation, perhaps behind or in the midst of the crowd where I and other Legionnaires would not see him, then he could steal away with an Enfant's soul as his prize. I could see no sign yet that this dead man might walk again as a wraith, but, as I said, the supernatural capabilities possibly possessed by wraiths, and even my own potential to gain such abilities other than what Centurion Gusticic called my "Vision," was unknown to me. I acted on the assumption that the reaper knew more than I. And I was right.

The reaper started to move more quickly now. Vestigial flickers of life passed through the now dead man. I made certain that at least one of my comrades observed my pursuit before I attempted to negotiate a path on the heels of the reaper. I avoided the Quick as best I could, but even so a few rammed into me and caused some discomfort as I hurried to the corpse's side when the skinriding reaper and his haul fell hard to the ground. Already an Enfant was emerging into the Shadowlands from the corpse.

Because the reaper was skinriding a mortal man and effectively becoming part of the Skinlands himself, he was beyond my reach from the Shadowlands. I could have attempted to cause harm to the mortal he possessed, but my unit and I were here to protect the Sarajevans, so I refused that option. Even so, we were at a stalemate. I was beyond his reach as well. Fortunately, the Enfant was arriving on my side of the Shroud.

The reaper, I believe, was prepared to fight for his charge, but a fellow

Legionnaire, Pasa Sacic, a Bosnian Croat among the first killed by the snipers who fired into every imaginable part of the city from the nearby mountainsides or (as in Pasa's case) from one of the remaining high-rise buildings within the city itself, reached my side to back me up. I don't think Pasa saw the danger, which was proof to me that perhaps I did possess the special vision the Centurion mentioned, but he stood ready to assist me.

"A reaper has possessed this skinlander," I said, indicating the living man by the side of the corpse.

Never had a skinlander stared at me so since I arrived in the Shadowlands. And even though I knew it was really a reaper I'd disenfranchised and not just a man at all, it was horrifying. The man's face was lit with fear and disgust, for on some level he must know that death was touching him, using him, but the burning eyes of the reaper bore through the Shroud into me.

I scolded him, "This soul has been saved, scum." I took the Enfant's hand and prepared to leave, but a haunting whisper rattled into the Shadowlands from the throat of the reaper-possessed skinlander.

"This one was Prince Lazar's, fool!"

I spun to face the reaper. His eyes were glowing a brilliant red and cast a light through the Shroud. I prepared to retort, but I was too late.

The reaper whispered again, "I know your Deathmark now, Legionnaire. Prepare for a new destiny."

But he took no action. Just those brilliant orbs washing my milky figure with bloody light. I turned my back on the prone reaper and guided the Enfant carefully to Centurion Gusticic who immediately took charge of him.

After that our rescue was over. More than a dozen Enfants saved. I knew nothing other than these kinds of numbers, but the Centurion told me an inordinately high percentage of mortal deaths resulted in wraiths in the Sarajevo Shadowlands. So many lives tragically cut short. These people had too many passions for life left unexpressed to pass on.

I surveyed the wreckage of Vaso Miskin Street a final time. At least the Sarajevans could tend their wounded. Their efforts were not thwarted by snipers firing at those who attempted rescues of the wounded or recovery of the dead. Such small happinesses is all that remains for them.

Our clean-up was done, but the Sarajevans were only beginning to count the losses.

Lazar!

I assumed "Lazarus" was the root of the so-called Lazarians, one of the major groups of Renegades that operated in Sarajevo. These Renegades were actually more trouble than the reapers, and I understood that outside Sarajevo they mainly struggled to overthrow the Hierarchy, but I didn't know if they tried to claim Enfants as well. Their time, I thought, was dominated by their conflict with one another, but perhaps their ridiculous battles involved the Skinlands too.

I considered all this as I wandered the empty streets of Sarajevo. It was late and the patrol had disbanded for the evening. Centurion Gusticic didn't sanction wandering alone, but this issue of the Renegades was on my mind and I needed to sort it out to understand this possible new threat. Or at least the personal one. So I deliberated in the way I'd done in my life. I walked the streets of the city, though then the roads had not been littered with fragments of glass, scraps of metal, and chunks of concrete.

And I thought of Lazar. "Prince" Lazar. He was someone else entirely. It made more sense as Lazarus. A band of Renegades established on some premise surrounding the return of Lazarus by the hand of Jesus. Serbian nationalism of a few years ago made it hard to forget that damnable self-proclaimed prince and the Battle of Kosovo where the Serbian noble Prince Lazar died fighting over five hundred years ago.

Actually, it was just over six hundred years ago, and Lazar didn't really die fighting. Serbian poetry and legend has exaggerated the Battle of Kosovo into a great epic of heroism where the flower of Serbian nobility died defending their Balkan lands against the juggernaut onslaught of a nefarious Ottoman army.

I knew this so well because June 28, 1989 was the six-hundredth anniversary of the Battle of Kosovo and it was celebrated with much fanfare and Serbian nationalism near Pristina, Kosovo, at the battlefield of Gazimestan, where the great conflict was waged. This, of course, was a mere three months after the Serbian Assembly in March 1989 passed a resolution that abolished the independent status of Kosovo and made it, along with another province, Vojvodina, the first new components of Greater Serbia. I guess the Serb leader, Slobodan Milosevic, the real architect of the bombardment of Sarajevo and founder of the new destiny of Yugoslavia that has already resulted in over two hundred thousand deaths, needed to possess the battlefield where his Serbian prince was captured and executed before he could personally step foot upon it.

In my mind's eye, though it seemed (and was literally) a lifetime away, I could see the television coverage of the event. Not the official Serbian media, which cast the event as the Second Coming that Milosevic suggested, but the Bosnian coverage that showed Milosevic urging the crowd with puerile rhetoric and threatening the rest of Yugoslavia with violence. I don't remember all the exact words, but he mentioned the struggles facing Serbs and noted the battles were not armed, but that, and this part of I recall because I also remember the chill that ran down my spine, "this cannot be excluded yet."

This disgusting display was all heralded by Prince Lazar. He was dead, yes (though what did that count for any longer in my reckoning!), but the bones of the Prince toured Serbia before the event, and images of Lazar were hoisted and sold in Gazimestan itself. Posters of Lazar sold beside those depicting Christ and, sickeningly, Milosevic too.

Lazar. Killed after his defeat at the hands of the Ottomans. I racked my brains to recall his executioner. Some of the pompous mythology of the event helped. It was the army of Murad I. At the Battle of Kosovo, Murad I captured Serbia for the Ottomans, though he wasn't present to enjoy his victory. He was assassinated before the final clashes by a Serbian posing as a deserter. The Ottoman died in his own tent, where he expected to gain information about the Serbian army from the "deserter." The lack of information, and the loss of the sultan, apparently did nothing to turn the tide of the war.

I thought wryly about that date: June 28th. That was also the day in 1914 when Gavrilo Princip assassinated Archduke Franz Ferdinand, heir to the Hapsburg throne, on Franz Josef Street in Sarajevo to spark the conflicts that eventually engulfed the world as World War I.

All these thoughts stirred my imagination. My dismal surroundings did the same. I couldn't believe what a wasteland Sarajevo was becoming. I'd walked this street with the patrol no more than a few days ago, and already it was transformed. There was more debris. More buildings pounded flat. More holes in the taller, stronger buildings, like the nearby Oslobodenje Building. And something else, I realized with a start: no lights. The electricity was out again. It was an ongoing battle of a different kind for the people of

Elektropriveda, the electricity utility company in the city. They were constantly repairing transformer stations the Serbs attacked, but once that was done a damaged transmission tower elsewhere would already have relieved another area of the city, if not the entire city, of electricity. The power would be back again. Sometime.

The mountainsides now populated by the Serbs were more ominous too. With intervening trees and buildings removed by the shelling, their implacable strength stood revealed, though the details were obscured by darkness.

I wondered if my son were poised out in that darkness somewhere to spring upon those encircling Serbs. It was with him that I last walked this street in life, and it was inevitably of him that I always thought when I walked its narrow way. Now I wondered if I would ever see him on the streets of Sarajevo, but I doubted it would happen. Certainly I would never again see him alive. If he was in Sarajevo, then it would be as a ghost like myself. I doubted that too. If he was fettered to a place, then the memories and passions left unresolved that bound him to this world would surely be in the battlefields of Herzegovina or whatever wasted place he made his last stand against the Serbians.

That was Hierarchy-speak. That much, at least, I had learned of this place. Wraiths, especially those of the Hierarchy, and particularly Centurion Gusticic, spoke of how Enfants, and even older wraiths like Lemures, were fettered to the Skinlands. Apparently that's why people became wraiths at all. In this way our existence here was a sort of Purgatory. I don't know if we could change our fate by our actions in the Shadowlands, if we could alter our inevitable destination, be it Heaven or Hell (or the Oblivion if we failed to reach either), but I know that many tried. Centurion Gusticic, for one, must believe this. Something about him, perhaps things I detected subconsciously with my "Vision," made me think he was not once as kind a man as he was now. I think he sought to change his fate by altering the world into which he was originally born, though from all I've heard and deduced it's more a matter of resolving the entanglements, the fetters, of your prior life than it's changing what you once were. But the belief that you could change persisted. Thankfully, I suppose, or the Shadowlands would be slowly growing as dark and evil as the world of Sarajevo.

My thought shifted back to my poor Kulin. Fatima and I named him with such optimism. We wanted his age to be one recalled centuries hence with the same joy as the time Bosnia was free for over twenty years at the close of

326

the 12th Century under the Ban of the same name. It was time again to forget the racism of men like my father, the Cetnik Serb who'd fought under General Draza Mihailovic, leader of the "other" rebel band during World War II. "Other" to Tito's Communists who came to dominate Yugoslavia's post-war years.

My father, though, was in many ways unlike the general he so admired. Foremost, he was tempted where the general was not by the Serbian nationalist rhetoric of Vasic and Moljevic who I think must have felt that the confusion of the World War was the best time to seize lands for the Serbs, no matter the millions of Turks and Croats and Jews who lived here too. It could have been no worse had Milosevic been my father. I spent part of my rebellious youth seduced by Communism simply because my father despised Tito. Then I discovered that Tito was a mass murderer himself, though the world still allowed him to host the 1984 Winter Olympics. But that was the same world that allowed Sarajevo now, so it should be no wonder.

And for her part, Fatima wished to erase memories of her own father. Perhaps it's because I was not exposed to his hypocrisy day after day, but I cannot fault Ahmed Popovac as I can my father. My father was a close-minded fool who refused even to use hindsight to make his vision clearer. Ahmed was just a weak man. He accepted Tito's harsh laws against the Muslim faithful, like the forcible unveiling of Muslim women in 1950, the very year that my future wife was born. It was only eight years later that Ahmed Popovac gave up his religious faith to integrate (or as Fatima would say, "ingratiate") himself to the Communist rulers of Yugoslavia. Two years after that, in 1960, a mere eleven years after many of his associates and friends in the "Young Muslims" were imprisoned for resisting the Communists annihilation of the Islamic faith, Ahmed Popovac was part of the Yugoslavian diplomatic core in the Middle East.

Ahmed upset Fatima with the degree of his delight of our marriage in 1969. She felt his instant approval of the arrangement was because I was not Muslim, and association with me, a Serb, would win her even more accord in modern Yugoslavia. And Fatima never forgave her father's scolding when she informed them that she had insisted on being listed differently than me in the 1971 census. She was the addition of one to the choice of "Muslim, in the sense of a nation." I suggested that I be listed the same as a show of solidarity, but she insisted that the strength of Bosnia was in it's diversity and variety of ethnic personalities, so I noted myself as Serbian.

Kulin was born in that same year. We listed him as Serbian, because we didn't really care and that's the choice that would cause the least dispute with our fathers. Both, of course, were delighted.

But Kulin's life would not go as pleasantly as either of us hoped, and, I'm certain, so fervently believed it would. He grew up the product of a multi-ethnic society. It was one, of course, that didn't encourage diversity, but options were still there. Something in him, though, sensed the injustice done to Alija Izetbogovic, a former "Young Muslim" and future President of Bosnia, when in 1983 he was prosecuted for pro-Muslim activity.

After that Kulin was wary for signs of political turmoil. He didn't begin to associate with the Muslims even now so much as he disassociated with the Serbs. And this was especially true with the rise of Slobodan Milosevic and his speech in 1989. It wasn't long after that Kulin flew the nest. Fatima's death by cancer in late 1989 — thank God she missed this hell! — certainly precipitated his departure, but his own motives and passions were fully formed as a young man of nineteen, and he joined the Party for Democratic Action, Izetbogovic's SDA, in 1990.

I celebrated beside him on the streets of Sarajevo just a few months ago in March. The day after is when we walked this route. When we stopped here, I realized, at this now burnt out hull of a café, for cevapi, Turkish coffee served in beautiful fildjans, and just a sip of that wonderful brandy, lovovaca. I was hopeful, but he was fearful, and eventually his worries broke me down too. I spoke with Kulin as a father should speak with his children sometimes. We spoke of many things, and I hold those moments in my heart as my last words with my son. I do not have regrets that anything in my life with him, my life for him, was left unexpressed.

Before the end of the month he was gone to defend any number of villages against the assault of Milosevic and Karadzic's Serbs. I only knew he was gone by a brief message on my phone machine.

I wonder if he knew I was dead? That I was killed less than a month later? Or that one week earlier I had buried my father? I smiled wryly on Kulin's behalf when his grandfather was killed by a Serbian shell, like more Serbs die every day at the hands of those who claim to wish to liberate them. I wonder if they'd cared that a WWII Cetnik was put down by them?

And so it was that I wandered the dying streets of the city until dawn. A life does not flash before one only at death, but countless times after death as well. But with the rising light there was also a flash in my mind as the silent ruminations of the night bore fruit. Perhaps it was just my imagination, but the leader of the other major faction of Renegades was a Turk, maybe an Ottoman. Did the dead bear such hatred, such animal animosity, as the living?

I knew so little of this new land of mine. The powers and motivations, and even identities, of the denizens here were unknown to me. How much was there to discover?

✠

A month passed before I learned more. It was a horrible month. The shelling of the once beautiful city was unending. Not a single day passed without more shelling, which made it over two months of constant terror and death for the residents of the Sarajevo.

Unbelievably, the Hierarchy was still the only force within or outside of the Shadowlands that seemed to give a damn. Our Skinland counterparts, the Blue Helmets of UNPROFOR, once cheered and cherished by the Quick of Sarajevo, were now the object of contempt. Just now I've watched a young man hurry to the side of another sniped from the top floors of an abandoned apartment building despite the continuing fire of the Serb assassin. The young man, a civilian, perhaps a baker or chimney sweep, is risking his life while twenty paces away a Blue Helmet stands and watches. When the shooting became heavier he was forced to retreat.

Only after much cajoling, and much time, does the young man convince the Blue Helmet to simply roll his armored car ten paces backwards to provide cover while he continued his rescue efforts. Thirty minutes later the wounded man was dead, and I, left behind at Centurion Gusticic's order, waited to see the fate of the man's soul. He transcended.

He might have made it to a hospital and survived if the Blue Helmet had possessed just a sliver of humanity. Just enough to a bit more quickly bend the non-intervention rules they obey.

It was the first time I was able to pause long enough to actually see it happen. Others I administered had transcended before, but always when I was on patrol. At such times there was not enough time to appreciate this miraculous event. I was too busy racing into the next fire-gutted building or to the side of the next tattered corpse.

It was beautiful. The man seemed not to sink into himself as one does prior to making the journey across the Shroud into the Shadowlands. At the moment of death he appeared to expand. Not physically, of course, and strangely not spiritually either, but mentally. It was the metaphysical parallel to a blind person opening his eyes to see for the first time. It was an awareness, but I could only observe the man himself, not whatever he was encountering or realizing. Then, in a sudden twisting that sent shivers of vertigo through me, the sunlight refracted in circuitous patterns and swallowed the man.

I moved on. I didn't have that much time to spare. I was to meet the patrol at so-called Sniper Alley, formerly Vojvode Putnika, which was the main crosstown boulevard in Sarajevo. It was here that the Serbs had a relatively clear view of Sarajevo citizens on the streets. It was here that people were shot one by one, and very personally because they were specifically targeted, instead of caught in the random destruction of a mortar shell. How a monster could purposely shoot civilian men and women and, yes, children too, and call himself a warrior or even a soldier was beyond my understanding.

The Hierarchy made constant patrols of the area, though, because deaths were inevitable and because the people fell individually instead of in groups, so reapers were expected. The area was also thick with Drones, a kind of mindless Lemure or Enfant that haunted the site of its death or simply wandered without knowledge of its mortal life. I thought this must be because death by the bullet of sniper was a particularly senseless way to die, and one so extinguished must carry a soulful revolt into its afterlife.

I hurried down the northern bank of the Miljacka River. It was not long before I saw that the Oslobodenje Building was in flames. The bastards had finally gotten it. The flames were burning hard in each of the twin ten-story towers, but the landmark that was hailed upon its completion as the most modern building Sarajevo looked like it would yet survive — if only as a skeleton of steel and concrete.

I wondered if Kemal Kurspahic was inside. I hoped the editor in chief and the crew that responded to his call to continue the paper were unharmed. The newspaper, for which the building was named in the Serbo-Croat word for "liberation" because of the paper's origins in 1943 when Tito's militiamen printed it from mobile presses, was still printed every day and the 10,000 available copies always sold out instantly. The words within were disseminated across the whole of the city more quickly than that.

Their voice is one not purely of alarm, but of outrage, which I think was the predominant emotion at least at the time of my death. Of course, that was two months ago. Almost too long for me to still imagine the travails of trying to live. To simply survive! Now I only had to exist. So much easier!

I tried to concentrate on my immediate surroundings, but the burning building dominated my attention. Then I heard sniper fire rattling into the upper reaches of the building — at the floors in flame, I thought. Probably to discourage rescue or firefighting efforts. Surely a patrol was already in the building! I knew the Hierarchy would respond. That calmed me and I watched the street again.

I passed a number of cars abandoned in the streets. The hoods were mostly propped open. The old reaction of attributing this to vandals jumped to mind before I realized that only a few items were being stripped, and one in particular: the car batteries. The power outages were frequent and often long, so people were searching for any means of powering their lights, let alone their stoves and other appliances.

On the other side of the street I soon noted an oddity: a hardware store that was still open. What manner of customers, I wondered, would possibly be in search of material to rebuild their devastated homes? The roof of the store itself was torn by a several feet long gash. But as I passed I saw that there were indeed customers within. People trying desperately to maintain a sense of normality.

As I came within about a quarter-mile of the UNPROFOR headquarters, which was just a scoot away from the still burning Oslobodenje Building, I witnessed a very discouraging transaction. It was the black market in operation. Two men stood ahead of me in an alley recessed from the street. One was nonchalant and seemed oblivious to the war-torn surroundings, while the other flinched with every rattle of gunfire in the distance and almost threw himself to the ground when he heard a shell detonate in the distance. The first didn't seem perturbed at all.

The patient man was clearly in control and enjoying it. His stubble of a beard, wild tattoos, and especially his gleaming and malicious little eyes marked him in my mind as a likely reprobate. The kind of young man who lived on the fringes of society before the war. The kind just waiting for the veneer of civilization that's taken thousands of years to build up to be stripped away so everyone could exist in his realm — a world in which he could be the master.

The nervous, older man was purchasing cigarettes from the "merchant," though he was clearly not enjoying it. He looked the sort of intent, intellectual man who'd once occupied a position in society won with time and effort. Now his position was reversed. I imagined the two as former student and professor. Where once the professor flunked the unruly youth, now he was dependent on him for a quick stroke of nicotine.

I had a wry vision of these men as the two faces of Radovan Karadzic, the leader of the Bosian Serb nationalists. He came to Sarajevo as a young boy from the mountains, rough and looking for chances of promotion into a society to which he did not belong. To enter it he became a professor — I could hardly believe my memories of him as a tenured professor of Psychiatry at the University of Sarajevo. But then he put the old face back on. That of a man driven to be a king, even if it meant that civilization had to be torn down to make it so.

But there was more about this exchange on the streets that staggered me: the price. I could clearly see the bills being exchanged as I drew nearer the two. The professor paid more than one-thousand dinars for a pack of cigarettes! That was fully one-tenth of the average pension of 10,000 dinars a month!

I shook my head in dismay. Perhaps the price would have been less had the man been able to pay in dollars. Our inflation had never been really under control, but this was ridiculous. Each dinar the black marketeer accepted probably lost value every moment.

I could recall a time just a few years ago when that same amount of dinars would have bought well over fifty U.S. dollars of cigarettes. That, I suppose, was a war-time economy. The man didn't look the sort to have a family, so at least that tenth of his possible monthly earnings wasn't necessarily better spent on rations or bread. Still, it struck me as ridiculous.

I resumed my walk, making a large loop around a capsized and shell-shocked street car.

Finally, I passed by the Oslobodenje Building. I saw no evidence of a Hierarchy patrol, but I knew one must be inside. I remained very aware of it burning behind me even as I passed out of its shadow.

Just a short time later I cross the Miljacka and entered a major intersection along Snipers' Alley. Everywhere around me I saw people huddled against walls. Mostly they were pressed against the buildings on the south side of the street, for most of the heavy guns were in the hills south of the city, so this was one means people had of providing a little extra protection. Of course, safety bade them to remain in their homes, but hungry children and a knowledge that their homes were also potential targets of random Serb violence compelled them to the streets. And they needed to cross these intersections.

There a business man clutched his briefcase to his back and sprinted across the street.

There, too, an adolescent boy on some unknown mission backed up to get a running start and darted diagonally across the intersection. It was a longer distance, but it saved two crossings.

From near me a woman toting two loaves of bread said a short and almost silent prayer before hustling the shortest distance across.

And on the south side a young man in jeans and T-shirt shuffled his feet in a repeating pattern for superstitious good luck before dashing into the street.

Watching the Quick like this was like viewing an early black and white movie. They moved in hurried blurs like Charlie Chaplin or Buster Keaton being chased by incompetent policemen. The setting in Sarajevo was a little bit different, though. It was Chaplin mixed with a 1940s war newsreel. Keaton prancing madly about the ruins of gutted and torn buildings. Grotesquely beautiful.

Amid all of this scurrying I was slow to detect the cauled Enfant that walked slowly to the center of the intersection. For one still cauled, this new denizen of the Shadowlands was acting with rare dedication to her task. The Enfant was indeed a woman, and from the deathmarks still plain upon her, and a mouth that was yet wide open and gasping for breath in this airless land, I guessed she'd died by asphyxiation. Perhaps she'd been trapped under rubble when a shell struck nearby.

I watched confused by her. The woman's eyes were wide open and intent, and just visible through the fog of her caul. When she stopped in the middle of the intersection and raise her hands high overhead, I knew she knew where she was. Physically, anyway, if not metaphysically. The psychotic and polychromatic images surely assaulting her since she rose after death had overwhelmed and confused her.

If death wasn't enough, then afterlife would drive you mad. As it almost had me, until Centurion Gusticic had found me.

And this woman, thinking herself still alive and walking Snipers' Alley in Sarajevo, was committing suicide. She was offering herself to the just as mad Serb snipers in the mountains beyond the city. She seemed insane because people she could see and imagine could not see, let alone imagine, her. Insane because images of the past, present and future assaulted her at once. Insane because a patrol had not found her.

Where my patrol was now, I didn't know. Perhaps they were diverted into the Oslobodenje Building. If so, I'm thankful I did not join them, or else I'd never have saved this woman.

But my chance to save her may have slipped my fingers. While I stood in amazement watching her futilely supplicate herself to gunmen that could not kill her, the Shadowland equivalent of a sniper did. A reaper launched himself toward the woman and, before I could shout a warning to him or cry in alarm to the woman, she was shackled at his feet in manacles.

I stared, stupefied. The scene degenerated even further when a number of drones, apparently sensing a commotion, emerged from every conceivable corner of the intersection. They stumbled about ineffectively in a jumbled confusion that was sadly amusing.

I ignored them, though, and challenged my enemy. "Reaper! Unhand her! She is under the protection of the Hierarchy."

The reaper looked up quickly, warily. He was surprised, but did not appear alarmed. He was a stout man and his drawn, Slavic face with its sunken eyes and taut cheeks was mostly covered by a shaggy beard like the kind worn by the Cetniks. I immediately bristled even more.

I shouted, "Now!" as I strode from the corner. My attention was diverted for a moment by three rapid *plinks* of sniper fire as a man ran across the street. The sniper was, thankfully, not very good. An arriving Enfant would dramatically complicate matters.

The reaper leaned over and arranged the manacles wrapped around the woman before straightening again to face me. He stood ready, but didn't appear tensed or especially prepared for action.

He smiled, his beard wrinkling like the rest of his face. "You'll save me a long trip, Legionnaire, if you will take charge of this Thrall here."

I hesitated at this peculiar reply, but did not relieve myself of my momentum and strode firmly to the reaper's side. As I neared, he finally realized that I was ready for action and he tensed himself.

"Just what do you intend, Legionnaire?"

I said firmly, "I intend to rescue this poor Enfant from you. I advise you to release her without struggle to me. Otherwise I will use force. Failing that, I will summon the remainder of my patrol from just down Vojvode Putnika."

The reaper shuffled one foot backward and tightened his grip on the chains. "Is this some new Hierarchy trick?"

His tone was one of incredulity, confusion. I wondered if there was anyway I could take advantage of that, but I was just as confused as he was.

I simply said, "It's no trick, reaper. She is simply not yours to profit from. Her soul is to be safe within the Hierarchy."

It was now amusement that wrinkled his face. With a slight shake of his head, the reaper said, "What in the hell are you talking about? Safe? With the Hierarchy? Are you mad?"

"Mad? Crazy, no. Angry? Yes."

"You must be part of some other Hierarchy, then," he said flatly with a bewildered shake of his head. "Are you part of a Heretic group calling yourself the Hierarchy just to piss off those Deathlords? Like if Karadzic would start a newspaper out of Pale he called Oslobodenje?"

I was so confused by how this Serb was reacting to my demands that I nearly forgot the manacled Enfant at his feet. I considered the possibility that this reaper was in life one of the Serb propagandists responsible for the outrageous lies and deceits of the nationalists. Who else would think of such a scheme as a second Oslobodenje that might claim itself as the true one?

I said firmly, finally, "Release her now that I may transfer her to the charge of my Centurion!"

"You are either stupid or deluded," he spat.

"Damned reaper!" I lunged forward to rip his hands from the chains that bound the woman. Just as my hands swiped cleanly through the air where the Cetnik once was, so too did a sudden feeling like a hot flash wash over me. I ducked without quite knowing why I was in danger. Leaning left to look around my body, I saw the Cetnik, who was suddenly somehow behind me, extended in a kick at where my head had been. I reacted swiftly enough to kick one of my own legs backward to sweep the reaper's other foot from beneath him and send him sprawling to the ground.

I completed a forward somersault to put a couple paces of distance between us. The bound Enfant was now between us and I tugged at the chains momentarily. They were already locked.

"She is my prisoner, Legionnaire! Either pay the Obolus the Hierarchy

335

will give me at Lukavica now, or simply wait. Your damned Hierarchy will have its soul soon enough!"

Regardless of the reaper's threat, I grabbed the chains around the cauled woman and positioned her behind me.

The reaper's face shot crimson, "Very well." He grasped his right arm at the elbow with his left hand. The hand swept down his forearm and reforged the flesh into a long, wickedly pointed sword. "Perhaps now you'll reconsider."

I had heard of such things but never witnessed it. And I wouldn't have believed it without this example. It was an amazing ability. My only weapon was a small relic knife that Centurion Gusticic says I was entitled to after rescuing ten Enfants. Though it seemed petite and ineffective, I drew the dagger and brandished it at the reaper.

"Hold your ground," I warned, "unless you wish to die. It's enough that you would attempt harm to this Enfant, but wait until the remainder of my patrol hears how you slander the work of the Hierarchy!"

He laughed, "You *are* mad! Are you but an Enfant too to be beguiled by such shameful lies? If only Sarajevans in life had been so easy to fool! As easy as the ignorant leaders of the western nations!"

How I hated him! For being a Cetnik Serb. For being a reaper. He was all I'd opposed in two lifetimes. I wanted to sunder his plasmic frame, but something of what he said didn't sound false. Perhaps it was my Vision, but I realized suddenly that this dead man was somehow important to me. Could one see that in others? How convenient, how wonderful!, if those who might shape my destiny always shone with such unmistakable light!

I said, "I will not yield this soul to your possession, but if you have more to tell me, then I will not call my patrol and your existence will be spared."

The reaper stepped back a pace as he languidly dipped and glided the sword that was his arm. He looked at me closely and said conspiratorily, "I suspect you are alone, Legionnaire. First, if you were part of a nearby patrol, then more of them would have arrived by now, or you would have called for them immediately. Secondly, I cannot believe that you are even a member of the Hierarchy if you believe the kinds of lies you've told me. Therefore, it is I... who control this situation." The last he said with a flourish of this edged arm.

He continued when I only glared at him, "Tell me this, Legionnaire: What is it that would happen to this woman if I did release her to your custody?"

I spoke slowly, letting my venom for the man drip with the sound of my words. "As I said, reaper, she would be delivered to my Centurion, who would deliver her with any others we've saved this day from the likes of you and the Renegades or an aimless, confused existence like this one's." I pointed to the woman. She trembled within the links of steel.

"Yes. And what of her fate after that?"

"She would be transferred from this hell-torn city along with all the others saved on this day by patrols across Sarajevo and sent to Stygia to become citizens of the city of the dead."

The reaper shook his head and said, "Wrong."

"Then tell me, reaper. What is her fate when in the hands of the Hierarchy? You mention selling her to the Hierarchy. If so, then perhaps you are less reprehensible than the reapers who well sell her into slavery; but surely whatever fate holds for her with the Hierarchy is no worse than the consignment you would make."

"It's the same, fool!" The reaper's sword slashed the air in frustration. "You've never been to Stygia, have you?"

I shook my head.

"Then perhaps you truly don't understand that you are collecting the souls that become the playthings of the Deathlords and their favored minions. Don't you realize that this woman will be put in the hands of an artificer who will mold her entirely into a relic of some sort, perhaps like that dagger you clench so furiously? Or, if she is weak and worthless, her soul may become a single Obolus?"

This was incredible. "You're lying."

"No, and that's why I reap, Legionnaire. The Deathlords of my life, Milosevic and Karadzic, sent me to my grave. Why, once here, would I fight for their likes again? Or why join the crazy Heretics or the Renegades who are the true cause of the slaughter here, even if it is the Hierarchy that feeds off the carnage."

I couldn't, wouldn't, accept it. "Prove it."

The reaper laughed. "I don't think you have the stomach for the truth."

"I had the strength to face the lies your kind told me in life, Cetnik. I can face the lies you tell now."

He laughed again, not angered at all by the political barbs. "Very well."

He thought for a moment, then relaxed and said, "Take the Enfant to your Centurion. Tonight, after she is turned over, as you say, to the protective custody of the Hierarchy, we will visit her at Lukavica. We will meet again here at midnight. She will not be transported out of the city until later tonight."

"What's the catch? Why release her to me?"

"Simple. When you see that I am right, you will owe a replacement soul."

I said, "And when it is I who am correct?"

"You will already have your prize," he said, motioning at the Enfant who was now entirely on the ground under the weight of the chains.

"True," I admitted. "Very well, I accept. Now release her from these ghastly bonds."

As his right arm melted back into its rightful shape, he presented a pair of keys with his left and calmly unfastened the locks.

I knelt by the woman, trying to assure her that everything was okay. When I stood, I helped her rise beside me. I was relieved with my victory, but the reaper had planted a seed of doubt — one that I might not have heeded had my Vision not shown me that perhaps there was more to be seen.

I said, "Here, at midnight."

"Yes."

With that I wandered away and maneuvered the woman out of the paths of the people still racing to avoid sniper fire.

The reaper shouted one last command to me as I steadied the staggering Enfant. "Remember, Legionnaire, to wear no emblems of your office."

Which meant I must leave my dagger. That's when I knew for certain he was lying, but I would go along with his game.
* * *

I returned at midnight after placing the woman in the charge of Centurion Gusticic and learning that the patrol had indeed been reassigned to watch for casulties in the Oslobondonje Building.

When I saw that the reaper was waiting for me, I realized I didn't know his name. I also realized I didn't want to. "I'm here," I said, announcing the obvious. "Now how do you propose we get to Lukavica? It's miles from here."

"Easy, Legionnaire. We hitch a ride. Let's go to the Holiday Inn."

He started to move, then stopped and turned. "By the way," he asked, "what's your name?"

"Dragos." I made no reciprocal inquiry.

"Serb too, eh?"

"No, Bosnian."

The reaper smiled. "Right."

It didn't take long to walk to the Holiday Inn. The hotel was the last one operating in Sarajevo. It now served as the home to dozens of foreign journalists, among them perhaps the only Westerners to understand the scope of the tragedy here.

Walking across the hotel plaza to enter the building was nerve-wracking. Though it was the early hours of the morning, I knew that snipers were still watching. Waiting for a person lulled to sleep by the hour of night.

Something about one of the snipers here made me recall talking to another surgeon who worked with me when I lived. He made an observation once that absolutely chilled me. He claimed he knew the works of certain snipers when he learned what area the victim was from and could guess the wound before even confronted with the victim. A factory worker from the Bistrik District as shifts changed? Then get some two extra pints of blood because it's a gut shot. Shot in the hotel plaza at the Holiday Inn in the middle of the night? Then prepare to amputate because the bones of the right leg have been shattered by three shots. From Bascarsija in Old Town? Then pack up. She's already dead from a shot clean through the head just above the left ear.

How did he know? And how could he know that last was a woman? I listened incredulously as he described one of the most barbaric things I've ever heard. Some of these snipers apparently fancied themselves artists. So they had to sign their work with signature wounds to the citizens of Sarajevo, like surgeons who stitch wounds in a certain pattern. Not only do they shoot only certain locations, but sometimes only specific targets as well. Not just "only women," but sometimes "only children" too.

But we were invisible to the sniper who aimed for legs, and reached the front doors of the hotel at a leisurely pace that no one living could afford.

The reaper said, "Let's wait to see if someone will open the door. The UNPROFOR vehicles aren't scheduled to pull out for another half hour."

We could step through the doors, but that would hurt. After several moments of silent waiting, and without anyone even lingering near the doors or threatening their use, we had to endure the brief stab of pain that came with breaking the physical laws of the Skinlands.

As we entered the lobby I noted a number of signs that indicated changes to the operation of the hotel because of the siege. The only one I took the time to read notified diners that meals were served in the old conference room because the dining room had a wall of windows facing the hills to the south of the city and people in the room were therefore at risk. It didn't spell out exactly what the danger was: snipers with telescopic sights who could shoot a tine off the fork in a diner's hand if they wished.

Of course, that entire side of the Holiday Inn was nearly obliterated now.

I followed the reaper past the check-in and reservations desks. This area of the hotel seemed just like any I'd ever seen. The clerk on duty seemed perfectly alert, unafraid, and absolutely unaware that she was inside a crumbling building inside the perimeter of a dying city under siege.

I tried to ignore this and followed the reaper to an elevator which led to the underground garage. The reaper tried to exchange words with me twice while we waited, but the clerk was still on my mind. How would this city ever survive if some of the people within it would not even recognize the chaos?

And this clerk surely had wonderful opportunities. When Foreign Ministers and diplomats and UNPROFOR representatives checked in and out, couldn't she at least mutter a word in favor of succor for the 400,000 civilians within the city?

"You are a thoughtful one," the reaper said, finally piercing my haze of concentration.

"I suppose."

"Wondering if I am, after all, correct?"

I said, "That doesn't worry me. You're wrong."

"Then why are you coming?"

"Because it was the price of your releasing the woman to my care."

The reaper shook his head and, for the first time, stroked his beard. "If that's the only reason you're coming, then forget it." He waved his hand.

He continued somberly, "I waive the price. Have the woman with my prayers for you both." He looked at me earnestly and almost repeated, "For both your souls." Then he began to walk away.

At first I was relieved, then I wanted to call after him, to tell him that there was another reason — I needed to know without doubt that I was right. I could no longer simply accept what I'd thought before as fact. Not in light of the truths that surrounded me every moment: ethnic cleansing, genocide, and wholesale destruction. And certainly not in light of what might be truth: a five hundred year battle between the ghosts of a Serbian and an Ottoman warrior and a Hierarchy that was perhaps everything I despised.

But I still didn't call to the reaper.

But nor did I leave after him.

I waited patiently by the elevator. Perhaps there were stairs somewhere. Then I realized that elevators wouldn't be the same as passing through a glass door. While they would seem more complicated for a ghost, they were actually far simpler. All I needed was to embody myself in the Skinlands just enough to exert a little pressure on the buttons.

I concentrated and then pushed the down button. Within moments the elevator *dinged* and one of the doors opened. I noted with some satisfaction that the clerk at least noticed this unexplained arrival and departure of a elevator car. Perhaps she was aware of her surroundings after all.

Soon the doors closed and the elevator hesitated. I embodied myself briefly again and pushed the button marked "Parking." The elevator shuddered and then rumbled down. It opened to reveal a garage full of the largest collection of battered and beaten cars that I have ever seen. Many of them were lettered with graffiti, but all of them sported the wounds of shells and snipers. In a glance I took in a wobbly-tired Russian jeep, some sort of Renault with doors that looked glued on and a battered car of unrecognizable make that had a message written on both the hood and trunk that read "Don't shoot, don't waste your bullet. I am immortel". I didn't spot an intact front windshield anywhere in the garage.

Until I noted the short line of three UNPROFOR armored cars. They were all Panhard scouts. They were all pale white with darkened air vents that lined the sides. Only two-seaters, but I saw just five people lingering near them. Perhaps I'd have a seat to myself instead of hiding among the equipment they carried.

All five of the men were dressed in fatigues and berets. They looked Western European. When one spoke, saying something about the time that I couldn't fully understand, I realized they were French. The French were among the Europeans more dedicated to the Bosnian war, at least if you judge by numbers of "peacekeepers."

It took a moment for me to realize that the passenger side of each car would probably be locked, so I decided to slip in through the driver door instead. The middle Panhard seemed to carry the fewest goods, so I climbed in and pressed myself toward the rear.

The five Frenchmen were soon joined by an officer, and they all immediately dispersed to their vehicles and clambered in. The drive to Lukavica began.

I watched through the slitted windshield as we raced up the ramp of the parking garage, following the Panhard in front, and pursued a course down Snipers' Alley and eventually toward Lukavica. The darkness and my cramped conditions made it almost impossible to see anything during the trip. Fortunately.

I took this moment of relative safety to refresh myself as I prepared to face Lukavica. I'd heard from another Legionnaire who still checked on his Sarajevian family that, only three or four days ago, about 2000 people were deported to the barracks at Lukavica. These were civilian prisoners of war taken directly from their apartments straight to a hell closer to the devil Karadzic.

What the mission of these blue helmeted soldiers at Lukavica was I didn't care. I had my own mission, which I set about immediately after I wrestled out of the passenger door when the Panhard rolled to a stop within the brightly lit grounds around the former barracks, now a concentration camp.

I didn't know where exactly to go. But, after looking around for a moment, I saw what the reaper probably intended to show me. At the far end of the building was a section so dilapidated and rotten that even I felt a chill go down my spine. It was definitely haunted. Certainly an area that no mortal would stray near. Clearly the home of wraiths.

As I neared it, I noted there were two Legionnaires on guard. I wondered what ploy the reaper planned to get past them. Was this even the right place?

I knew it had to be. But could I get in without lying to the guards? I could think of nothing. Nor could I think of a suitable lie since I didn't know what was inside. Was I ready to risk my position in the patrol over a foolish, niggling question? I knew at once I was. If I was wrong, the Hierarchy would prove to be the kind of organization that would forgive me for such a transgression. If, on the other hand, the reaper was right, then my status be damned.

I backed up so I could approach the guards within full sight for a good distance. I immediately drew their attention.

"Good evening," I said as I drew near them.

They remained expressionless, so I pressed, "I need to check inside for a relic of Centurion Gusticic. He lost it here earlier and claims he looked everywhere else. So, he sent me."

They didn't budge, so I rattle on, running my lie into the ground. I wished I had my dagger so I had some proof of my station.

"I'm just a grunt, so I was chosen to come all the way back out here. Just let me have a look, will you, please?"

"Sure," one of them said finally.

"Great," I said before I could think of how foolish it sounded.

Each of the guards drew a key from within their drab gray fatigues and simultaneously unlocked nearly identical padlocks on the bars blocking the doors.

The other said, "Just hurry or we'll lock you in with 'em. They might take you by accident too."

A chill rang my spine dry. Suddenly I didn't want to enter.

"Hurry," the second guard repeated more urgently.

I budged, stumbling forward into the darkness. All I saw at first was that a light source, a fire, burned in the rear of the room. It grew larger and brighter when the doors swung nearly shut behind me.

Then the moans reached my ears. Then the flame of the relic torch illuminated the faces of dozens of Enfants crowded into the room. Most still wore their cauls. My mind leaped in confusion. My plasmic heart beat with alarm. I wondered — no, I hoped — that there was an explanation for it all as I ran the aisles frantically looking for something to prove that this was not what it seemed.

I found the proof. But it was damning, unforgiving. The woman from Snipers' Alley lay crushed between two other women, one an elderly lady killed by a sniper, and the other an adolescent still bearing the marks of the shrapnel fragments that tore her to pieces.

The woman I'd unchained and delivered to Centurion Gusticic as a soul about to be freed was here instead! Chained again. Crowded like a thing, a possession, into this small chamber. Like a veal calf in a dark barn. She still wore her caul and her eyes were large with a fear that sang to me.

I'd spent months fighting not for Blue Helmets of the Shadowlands, who were actually fulfilling a mission of peace, but for the Shadowland Cetniks? Abominable.

I trembled.

A door creaked open. "Hurry."

I almost cried out when that slight opening spilt enough additional light into the room for me to see the babies. They too were chained. One was missing both legs, but all were treated with equal degrees of disgrace and irreverence. Three innocent souls bound for every kind of hell I could imagine.

I tried to think what I might do. The padlocks on these chains were far smaller than the large ones on the door. There was absolutely no chance that the keys the guards possessed would open any of these locks.

I swept a last look at the damned souls. But for my foolish gullibility, here too I would go.

I stumbled out, trembling some more. This time I walked the miles back to the heart of Sarajevo.

╬

After two days of not reporting to my patrol assignment and learning that the Hierarchy, at the behest of Centurion Gusticic who was tracking me down, considered me effectively AWOL, I sat pressed against a crumbling home listening as shells continued to fall upon the city. It was only so much background noise now. Like the children I saw playing in the streets, not even flinching to the distant sounds of exploding shells and sniper fire. It was part of their world now and they'd adapted.

But I hadn't adapted to mine. One particularly nearby explosion roused me.

A picture formed in my mind of the walls the Serb nationalists brought down to end Sarajevan lives. Those same souls that passed into this world afterwards would be twisted by the Hierarchy into objects to make their damn Stygian city even more magnificent. Lives torn down in one world would become an edifice of pain in the next. The new Sarajevan saying was coming true: "We have all lived here together. We will all die here together too."

I knew I needed to decide my next step. I'd discovered that my existence now was much like in life. Again I was caught. Trapped between the stormtrooper Hierarchy and the crazy Renegades.

344

Hours before, as I'd watched a Blue Helmet accept 100 Marks from a Sarajevan for transport out of the city, I'd realized that in death as in life you only mattered if you were one of three things: a traitor, a hero, or a saint.

I wanted to just let the dead battle one another. Their conflicts were grounded in centuries-old disputes I could not fathom anyway. That's what I decided as I staggered home from Lukavica the night before last; but after considering it, I realized how like everyone else that would make me.

The world at large thought the war in Bosnia was just as unfathomable because it was supposedly rooted in centuries of ethnic hatred. But it wasn't. It was the powerplay of a handful of traitorous madmen who created accomplices in the Serbs and now guilted them into completing what had been started.

I also wanted to fight for what I felt was a just cause. I could forge a group of true saviors for the dead of Sarajevo. A new patrol to do the job I thought I'd done with the Hierarchy. Eventually I might halt the transport of Sarajevans souls to Stygia completely. But was that as small-minded as what the Blue Helmets represented? A token response to greater ills?

To be a saint meant to embody the virtues of the hero, only on a much larger plane. Larger, certainly, than anything like surviving a terrorist bombing in the heart of your country, or even something on the scale of Sarajevo, as a horrible a tragedy as that had become. It meant knowing a sense of injustice too large to be sated by heroic action. It also meant knowing that you might be too small to make a difference against something so large. Like I undoubtedly was in the face of the Hierarchy.

But first it meant to care at all.

Then I realized why others before me found it easier to be a hero than a saint. Because the world only responded to heroes. When ennui everywhere is too great for saints, what more could one person do? What less?

The Punchline

by Marc Levinthal and John Mason Skipp

I

S weat and smoke in poseur heaven, on an L.A. night crisp with the last breaths of fall. It is Friday, November 23rd. The year is 1995. Inside the club, it is warm, if not cozy; being on the wrong end of Sunset Boulevard bears little or no stigma tonight. There are stars in the heavens and right here on Earth — right here at Club Lingerie, no less. When a light goes off in the darkness, everybody wants to see.

She should have known that the place would be crawling with vampires.

Sylvie sidles past the doorman, smiles, receives her little rubber stamp. It's only 10:15, the first band's just wrapped up, and already the crowd's nearing critical mass. All *kinds* of fucking vampires here, metaphorically speaking. Ones she knows. Some she even has to call her friends. They're scattered across the dance floor, scattered around the bar, concentrated at the little tables that festoon the balcony above.

347

There's Chester, the guitarist from Trainwreck, down there trolling as usual, with his cheekbone hollows and his leathers painted on. There's Puffy and Skanky, in the balcony dark: a couple of perennial spooky chicks, also out on the boymeat prowl. There are all manner of nameless skulkers and preeners, only some of whom — insofar as she can tell — have souls: groupies, wannabes, hangers-on, psychic leeches latched onto the pulse of the scene.

And then there are the odious A&R vampires: A&R meaning Artists & Repertoire, the guys with the power to sign the bands. To call them vampires, she thinks, is so close to the truth it barely even qualifies as metaphor. Their job is to seduce, to string along, to dangle the baubles of moneypowerfame, until the deal is signed and the teeth go in and every last drop is sucked out of the band.

She recognizes far too many of them. Thinks: *Omigod, it's a feeding frenzy!* Not that she's surprised. She'd known it was going to be this way, but somehow the reality is always a little weirder than one hopes.

You keep thinking that, maybe one day, it might be different.

That goddam rock 'n' roll dream again.

Sylvie looks around, carefully trying to assess whether there is in fact a label that is *not* represented here tonight by one or another bloodsucking creep. There's Hollywood, Interscope, Geffen, Warner, A&M, Capitol, and Sire; you name it, and they are here with bells on... including all those little indies out there scrabbling, now that most of their prime stock had upscaled to the majors.

Big or small, chance in hell or not at all — if there is one band in this town tonight that *everybody* wants a piece of, that band is Everything.

And she is here to bear witness to the slaughter.

Sylvie Press stands above the dance floor, looking down. She is short and smart, twenty-five years old, and she has the kind of eyes that have spent their whole lives looking for a ship that just never came in. She is dressed for near-invisibility, given how goddam cute she is. She is dressed to blend right in.

There had been a time — just a few short years earlier — when she would not have been satisfied with this role; when, in fact, Sylvie Press's main goal in life was to make certain that every eye in the room was focused upon her... and hopefully eyes not even in the room, but half a planet away. Those were the times in which she was the dream and not the dreamer; those were the times in which she had played, and not just written about, the sounds.

But those days are gone, and she kinda likes it, although the dream remains.

And the dream, of course, is the bottom line.

It always comes back down to the dream.

The dream, as it turns out, is what the buzz tonight is all about. This band, from what she hears, is threatening to make people remember why they love this shit in the first place. And that, to her, is a very exciting prospect.

She recalls what she knows about Everything, thinks back on the building of the buzz over the last couple of years. She remembers first hearing a friend of hers — a fellow scenester, name of Tess — going on and on about this show she'd just caught down in San Diego. The way this girl had described it made it sound too good to be true. Tess described tribal grooves so lush, so primitive and true that they dragged her squirming back to her dark jungle roots. ("And I'm from Orange County!" she'd stressed, laughing wildly as she said it.)

She'd gone on to recall dancing more uninhibitedly than she had ever done before. She remembered naked nymphs and satyrs, sprinkling gold dust on oil-slick bodies, gyrating along with and all around her until the whole place took on a pagan abandon that was, she said, "more intense than fucking, and profounder than prayer."

And Tess was not a lightweight. Not even a little. She'd been going to Big Bangs, acid parties, adopted raves and marathon techno-orgies as a way of life, as had so many of her peers. So for her to be this tripped out by one band was no miniscule accomplishment.

Sylvie had indexed the rapturous review, and filed the name in her head.

Good name.

Everything.

Unfortunately, it had been right about that time that her own flame had sputtered and ultimately gone out. Her band, the Triple Hennas, had died the death after a furious two hundred and twenty days of touring every little shithole they could find on God's gray earth. By the end of that, she was so burned out that the next six months were spent in virtual isolation: not seeing bands, not wanting to see bands, not hearing bands, not wanting to hear bands, turning down every opportunity to listen to this or that "new sound" that attempted to gatecrash her ears.

Of course, during that time, the musical revolution referred to as "grunge" had staked its claim, then come and gone. Punk had its night in the sun, as well, and "alternative" had become the new mainstream buzzword: losing cachet with its every success, as trends are wont to do.

It would have been a real good time for her to go out and kick ass, only she no longer had the juice. She was toast; she was burnt; she had kissed so much ass that the flavor was indelibly etched on her tongue; and all she could do was lay in her room and try to remember why she'd been born in the first place. Why, in fact, she was here at all, if the dream was not to be hers.

So slowly, slowly, she began to write about the dream: what she perceived as its purpose, and perhaps even her function in it. First in journals: little scraps that she would scrawl in and out of slumber, little notes that she would make to herself. When she was out and about, she would take along a notebook and pen, to catch the stray thoughts that still spitfired through her brain.

And she realized that if she did this, then possibly she could do with words what her music had failed to do.

Which was to capture the essence of the dream.

And bring it back with her.

Soon she found herself writing for the 'zines — *Ben Is Dead*, *BAM*, the *L.A. Weekly*, then up to *Spin* and *Mondo 2000*. For the first time, she tasted recognition; but more than that, she felt *understood*, the thrill of finally "making it" subordinate to the work of framing the dream and then lighting it up.

So, she thinks, snapping back to here and now, *One mo' time for the cause. And please, God: this time, let them be real.*

Then she takes a deep breath, hits the steps to the dance floor, and descends into the maelstrom.

II

The doorman has the kind of jaded musclehead face you see a lot on L.A. bouncers: seen it, done it, could give a fuck about it, but would be more than happy to snap you in half at the slightest provocation. Probably a TV stuntman or tough-guy extra, when he could land the gig.

Yeah, Carlos imagines him saying, *I'm not REALLY a doorman: I specialize in taking machine gun hits and falling off of buildings.*

The guy flashes Carlos an emotionless glare, sizes him up against the photo I.D. In the picture, Carlos has no hair, but his head is far from naked: a half-dozen rings in either ear, another in the left nostril. And then, of course, the snake tattoo.

Said tattoo remains, open-mouthed and wide-eyed serpentine skullface plainly visible on his right temple under a quarter-inch of fresh black stubble. Behind the collar of his longcoat, the snake's tail descends: down the back of his neck, then coiled in two fat loops around his narrow shoulders.

It was meant to be a mark of some distinction; God knows he suffered enough for it. But he's seen thirty-five people in the last month alone, sporting minor variations on the theme — *arghh!!!* — and so here he is, a casualty of style at the ripe old age of twenty.

The bouncer looks the hairy tat dead in the eye, grunts at Carlos, returns the card. Whew. Carlos puts the fake I.D. back in his wallet, vibrates up the queue. A skinny pale guy rips his ticket in half, invisibly stamps his hand. The blacklight at the entrance to the club reveals the tiny yinyang symbol glowing on the back of his wrist. *Hippie shit*, he realizes, wincing. *Maybe I shoulda brought my parents.*

Then he smiles, as he scopes the young girls in babydoll T-shirts, bright lips, electric hair. The bowl of good reefer he'd smoked in the car unravels its delicate tendrils, clutching his forebrain in a tender undersea embrace.

Lotta freaks tonight, he notes, and not just the regulars, either. It's almost like seeing the Dead in Vegas: lotsa suits, and more neopagans than you could shake a stick at. Near the stage, he spots a couple of people he knows from Cal Arts — Albert, Matty, that fucked up chick from Introduction to Film. He says hello and gets it back, nobody really wanting to have a conversation, too amped up to talk right now.

"Let's party later, all right?" he says, turning back, intent on the stage activity. The DJ is playing some old, slow Bowie song. *I'll make you a deal, like any other candidate.* It seems to fit the mood on stage, as black-clad roadies silently move gear into position and test it.

Buy some drugs and watch a band...

A strange face flickers in his peripheral vision, its smile many-toothed and impossibly wide. When he turns to look, nobody meets this description.

...jump in the river holding hands...

Carlos decides that he has smoked some very powerful weed.

He grins, shakes off the jitter-rush, thinks again about how cool this is going to be. Gwar, Woodpussy, The Boredoms — weird and fucked up as they are, this band is supposed to make 'em all look like Barney the Dinosaur.

Which is good. God knows he can't get enough of weird and fucked up;

351

when you're a struggling young film student, with pretensions to art, you need all the inspirational brain damage you can handle.

Carlos watches the crew for awhile, soaking up the movement, framing shots in his head. Then he fingers the twenty-dollar bill in his pocket and decides it's time for the evening's first overpriced beverage. He inches his way through the room, which is getting more crowded by the minute, finally squeezing up the stairs from the dance floor to the bar.

There is an old cowboy dude incongruously perched on a stool to his left; Carlos checks him twice, just to make sure he's not another hallucination. Pale blue eyes in a strong, gaunt, leathery face rise up to him in passing, then focus on some point over Carlos' shoulder, staring with unnerving intensity.

That's when Carlos turns, and gets his first good look.

At the monster. The rock star.

Drake.

III

She is stupid and tacky and sexy as hell, and what Drake really wants is to fuck her in the brain. All evidence to the contrary, it is a fair bet that she has one. She's just never learned to use it. She is not alone in this. Everywhere he looks — tonight, as ever — the lowing herds of sheep-people graze, splotching the earth with their droppings of untapped potential.

Not that Drake is complaining. He likes sheep just fine; almost as much as he loathes them. Great taste. Less filling.

The morsel of livestock in question is waiting his table tonight at Club Lingerie. She ain't no model/gymnast/kick-boxing stewardess, but her long buxom body is tight; and what she lacks in definitive style of her own, she makes up for with the promise of moist squishy stuff inside.

But her eyes are what truly draw him: great round googly mooneyes that sparkle and flair every time they light upon him. They are the inspiration behind his little brain-fuck scenario: first one socket, then the next, till he spoots cold seed all over her pronounced cranial smoothness.

Of course, tonight he has some bigger fish to fry. But it's an entertaining notion. And who could say? It might yet become an entertaining reality, if the night proves as willing as the waitress in question.

Syd Drake stands, eyeballing himself in one of the three large oval mirrors behind the bar. He looks cool. He likes that about himself. Like a rock 'n' roll

352

hitman, dripping dangerous glamour. His dark facial hair is meticulously sculpted to highlight both his cheekbones and his malevolent allure. His leathers are elegant, neither biker nor plebe; and they are tailored, like the rest of him, to flagrantly attract.

He stretches, feigning caj, and takes a moment to admire the tight abdominal slats above the bulge in his pants. Once again, he is not alone in this. He hears his name on a dozen surreptitious whispers, allows himself to savor the warmth of a hundred furtive gazes. He smiles, locking eyes with roughly thirty reflections, each for what he deems a vastly meaningful microsecond. Just enough to feed.

Then he sits back down.

As he does so, he flashes on the kinds of fables that tend to be told about his kind. They are too stupid for words. It's hard to believe that he ever believed them. Like hating garlic — he loves garlic! — or shriveling in sunlight, or sleeping in dirt.

Or that flat out ridiculous shit about not being able to see yourself in the mirror. If that were truly the case, who would *want* to be a vampire? Why would anyone actually volunteer for such a fate? Drake pictures Michael Jackson, accessorizing from memory, and cackles. No way. Even death would be preferable.

But as he's come to understand, a little disinformation is a wonderful thing. And a lot of it is even better. Better to drown the world in bullshit than give them one glimpse of who you actually are. The less they truly understand, the more they think they do.

And the kick of it is, they'll love you for it, *no matter how much you hate them!*

So, yeah, he concludes. It's fun being famous. Just one of the perks of a life without end. Sex, drugs, creature comforts — they're just the tip of the infinite iceberg. The real buzz here is power, unbridled and pure, unmitigated by moral or mortal restraint. Power to bend wills and shatter souls, dance willy-nilly on the hearts and minds of men, make strong women crawl at your beck and call.

Power. Just because.

If your own creativity suffers for a moment, you simply move in and strip-mine the talent pool. (You always know a true artist. It can't be taught; it's in the blood.) Should the threat of competition rear its ugly little head, you either strafe it in the manger or bend it over, thrust, and make it cry out your name.

And if the whole world should seem to rise up against you — flagging ticket sales, a critical drubbing by the press — you can sit back and laugh, knowing that you will dance on their graves.

Because you live forever.

Because you're on the winning team.

But like old man Renning told him, on the night of his turning, "Nobody plays in the big leagues without an inside connection.

"And son, there's no connection more inside than this...."

IV

Jesus, Erasthmus and Wilbur H. Christ, whispers Slim, the cowboy, to himself.

He is staring at the puffed up leather weasel in the longcoat. It had not been his intention, and he's not liking it a bit. Sixty seconds back, he'd just been minding his own business, quietly drowning his many sorrows.

Next thing you know, he's got the devil in his sights.

Not that Slim hadn't noticed him earlier. He simply hadn't paid a whole lot of attention. Just another prissy bigshot, putting on that he was bad. Kinda boy you'd like to rearrange his nose for him just to pass the time.

But then he'd got an ugly look into those eyes.

And that made all the difference.

He remembers eyes like that from Nam. In fact, the odds are real good that he'll never forget. Not the thousand yard stare of the atrocity burnout, the man who's done and seen so much horror his brain has turned to sloppy joe; Slim remembers that look, too, has seen it on his own face more than once.

No, these are the eyes of a hollow man, a man stripped so clean of all decent human feeling that he's become like some kind of evil machine. Men like that are killers who smile when they do it; you get too close to their ears, and you can hear the roar of the hungry void. Slim remembers one night, on the streets of Da Nang....

Shit. Don't get started thinking about Nam again. Shit.

The last five shots of Jack do a little line-dance, stomping in unison all over the inside of his abdomen. Slim shudders, turns around, slams down the rest of his Bud. He's been sitting at the bar since six o'clock, shortly after knocking off over at the Gower lot; and now he's suddenly thinking that he may have been here too long.

His exposure to Agent Orange made it theoretically possible to sit on his ass in front of the boob tube forever, collecting just enough in bullshit government checks to never quite get by, but he couldn't go for that. He was still plenty strong, despite what the doctors told him. He wasn't about to lay back and wait for the inevitable, wait for the cancer that would not remit, take that final slow ride past pain to death with no one but Gilligan and his own ghosts for company.

No, better the twelve hour days hanging lights on the set, then three or four or five hours with Jack Daniels and a beer chaser. Better not to think about the rats and the trip-wires, the faces blown off and the pieces lost forever. Better not to think about what the defoliant had done to him, done to his marriage (long past over), done to those sweet little girls of his who had died from it, still in the womb.

Better.

He is shaking, and his mind is a monkey. Time to go? That's stupid. What the hell for? Am I scared of that punk? Well, not exactly him, but... aw, hell. He gets the cute little bartender's attention and orders up another round. Maybe you just oughtn't to look at him again, he tells himself, and that seems reasonable enough.

Slim thanks the gal when she brings his meds, tips her well, does the shot, swigs some Bud, and turns to look at the stage. Kids setting up for the rock 'n' roll show. He usually cuts out around nine, nine-thirty, preferring George Jones on the jukebox at his neighborhood bar, but tonight something's sticking his ass to the barstool, some ephemeral bugaboo in his braincase.

He watches them setting up the amplifiers, lights (doing a shitty job of it), projection equipment, computers. Now, this looks kinda interesting, he thinks. Maybe not the usual screaming bullshit, like that last bunch that just got done. Looks like maybe they got something on their minds.

Once, right after Tet, he'd sat around a fire with a couple of kids like that. Hippies. Things ain't changed that much, and more than likely they never will. They were young, those hippies, full of piss and vinegar. Thought they knew it all. Hell, maybe they did know it all. Slim was willing to give them the benefit of the doubt. Took some LSD with them to pass the time.

They'd tried to get him to see something with them. All smiles. "Don't you see it, man?" All that enlightenment crap. Mostly what he saw was a bunch of funny colors, and a handful of pictures that disturbed him no end.

Still, it was clear that they'd been going for something, which, if not exactly good, was at least solidly true. They were searching for some kind of meaning. *In the middle of all that hell. . . .*

He's shaking again, remembering. One of them had blown up the very next day, blown all over seven different directions. Stepped on a mine. Bursting bag of skin. Red spray. So much blood in a human body.

And later, the other one — well, at least half of him got to go home....

Mentally booting himself in the ass — no, stop going back there, you're back in the World, man! Remember what happened the last time. Took you three years to come around, come back out of the jungle. Get out of there NOW. Get out.

Slim raises his beer in a bitter toast. "Hey hey LBJ, how many kids did you kill today?" Next to him, a Latino kid with a snake on his head looks at him like he's crazy.

Not the first time. He gives the boy a big grin. "Cheers," he says, clinks their bottles together. "We used to always say that, way back when."

The kid lightens up. "Right on. That is bobo," he says. Whatever. Slim looks back toward the stage.

"So," says the kid, "I saw you scopin' out big bad Drake."

"Who?"

"That fuckin' dude you were staring at. You don't know him?"

"Nope." Slim's heartbeat revs a little. "And I can't say that I'd care to."

"What an asshole," the kid concurs, clinking his beer with Slim's again. "Total fucking sellout, fucking '80s corporate rock star, back before Nirvana killed the big hair bands, you know? He's like trying to be all 'alternative' now, turning up at these shows, but nobody gives a shit."

"Okay," says Slim. Most of this is going right past him, but he figures it must be bad.

"Not like this next band coming up. You ever seen Everything?" Slim admits that he hasn't. "Dude, you oughta check them out from the floor, man. They're fuckin rad!"

The kid takes his change back from the waitress and says, "Hey! Take care!" then disappears back into the crowd. Slim watches him go, thinks about it for a second.

The question becomes: What have you got to lose? You really want to sit around here, torturing yourself? Or would you rather pick a fight with this Drake character, just to prove that he don't scare you none? Let off a little steam? Maybe get yourself killed?

Just go see the show, you moron. You're already in the door.

Slim shrugs his shoulders. Why the hell not? He picks up his beer and follows Carlos down.

V

Meanwhile....

Kenneth, the guitarist of Everything, pees into the trough on the men's room wall; bright yellow pee, dingy white trough, nasty gray dingy walls below the ugly ceiling, also gray. He takes it all in with an hallucinatory attention to detail, seeing far too much, as usual. There are several squares missing in the acoustical tile ceiling, and he finds himself deep into counting the dots before he forces himself to stop.

There's something about a room like this that always throws him back. He's been in so many of them over the years, over the years and years and years. From the puke-green lower walls to the black tile floor, the dark shitter with its brown graffitoed door, the chipped white tiles lining the bottom of the wall and the gray circular fan above his head, every painted pipe and jagged crack calls to him, speaks to him of other rooms, rooms just like this one, rooms for waiting, waiting for death, always rich with viscid smells.

He weighs the slight heft of his dick in his hand, feels the gush through his urethra, and finds himself thinking, *Wow*. Already nostalgic. *Is this the last time I'm gonna see you or what?* It's always like this at the end of a cycle, the beginning of something new.

It's always like this, but he never gets used to it.

Especially on showdown nights like this...

"Oh, man," says the guy peeing next to him: a transplanted cracker, twenty-something or other, with dark matted dreads and a rich southern drawl. "Everything *rules!* You fuckers are the *shit*, you know it?"

Softly. "Thanks..." Watching his eyes.

357

"I am deeply serious. I caught y'all on Labor Day, at the Nevada Salt Flats? Just before they burnt that wicker man? And when you fuckers cut loose…?" He lets out a whistle, and his irises spark. "I swear I lifted right out of my body."

Kenneth smiles. "But you got back all right."

"Yup. Don't know how, but I made it." They laugh together. "And now I'm ready to do it all over again."

"Well, that's the great thing about infinity," Kenneth assures him. "You will."

By now he's down to the final spritzes. His pal Sandoz taps him on the shoulder, says, "Come on." Kenneth nods, shakes the sprinkles off his single dip.

All at once, the great trough flushes. Sandoz, Kenneth, and the cracker stare. "Holy synchronicity, Batman!" says the cracker. The timing of the universe is a wonderful thing.

Kenneth zips up, smiles and turns. "Take care," he says, heading out of the room. The next guy in line whips agitatedly past him. The line is long. It's that kind of a night.

In the hallway, he finds himself scanning the faces, looking for recognizable signs. More than half of them seem to recognize *him*, but that is not the same. The line to the ladies' is twice as long, but yields the same result.

Where IS everybody? he asks himself. *Where is the Beast, and the tribe of old? Is this really the night?*

Then he rounds the bend.

And stares into the face of his fear.

VI

Renning can't get past the dressing room door, and it is starting to piss him off. Two thousand years old, still at the peak of his power, and some dizzy little purple-haired security bitch is gonna say no to *him*?

"I'm sorry," she tells him. "That's just the way it is. Band doesn't want to see anyone till after the show."

"But if you'll just simply explain who I am…"

"Doesn't matter who you are. Not till after the show."

He thinks about melting her brain on the spot, letting it seep like gray tears from behind her dark eyes. But no. Too many witnesses now. Maybe later. Most likely, in fact.

Renning hangs tough, ancient vampire decked out in the finest Armani shmoozewear. He keeps his longish hair peppered with gray, maintains just enough facial wrinkles to confirm his senior status as Grand Poobah of A&R. He is charming. Wealthy. Authoritative. Powerful. Ultimately, threatening.

He still can't get in the door.

Renning takes a step back, starts waxing ontological. What brought me here? Brought me to this place, this *fin-de-siècle* rock club filled with young, hopeful, hot blood? Renning has no trouble remembering anymore. The power comes so easily now. Whatever you need, Renning. Same bullshit, different century. You need your fix, you will get your fix.

But it's more than just feeding, isn't it, Renny? It's the twisting that you enjoy. It's the ether jar you dig, the actual pushing of the pins through the pretty butterfly's wings.

There's a butterfly inside that Renning just can't wait to see. Her name is Darcie Anything, and he's heard so much about her. Leader of the band — or "the tribe," as they refer to it. Fluent in seven languages and proficient on a dozen instruments. Honor student, college dropout, freelance musical ethnographer. Born into money: right-wing, upper-crust. Now a total bohemian tripped-out pro-sex feminist art witch, all of twenty-four years old. Oh, yes: and beautiful, too.

Renning will *kill* if anyone gets their teeth into her first.

He looks up from his reverie, senses the young man's gaze before he meets it. Appropriate awe and terror there, but something else as well.

"Are you with the band?" he asks on a hunch. The young man nods his head. Another guy steps close beside him, tense. Renning smiles, extends his hand. "I'm Arthur Renning..." he begins.

"I know exactly who you are," the young man says.

VII

Kenneth is staring at the guy, knowing it's High Noon pretty soon. He looks into the eyes that he knows so well, has known and dreaded for so long. He feels a little disappointment at the lack of recognition in — Renning's? — eyes. But that's the way it always goes.

359

To him, we're all the same.

He offers his hand to Renning, introduces himself, says his lines. The drama is behind-the-scenes, a showdown between the actors. The Renning-actor's mask is relaxed, jovial, interested. It cannot hide all the sickness and malevolence behind it. Not from Kenneth. It is all too achingly familiar.

"I'm sorry," he says, at the expected request. "But if you're still interested, after the show…"

Renning chills. "You may regret this," he says.

"Tell me about it," Kenneth agrees.

Thinking, *Man, if you only knew…*.

VIII

Fifteen minutes with the band. I can do something with that, Sylvie thinks. Not the in depth thing I had in mind, but what the fuck? It's just a matter of sussing their vibe, asking all the right questions, and hoping my thesis bears out.

When Sylvie was a little kid, her dad took her to see Sun Ra. Since then, she'd been on the trail of anything remotely like the Arkestra in spirit. She already loved Thrash, Death Metal, Goth, Industrial, but she knew enough to listen to everything. In the process, she discovered Harry Partch, Wagner, Zappa, and a few others who abhorred music in a vacuum — who needed it all together, all at the same time.

Harry Partch called it "corporeal" — using your whole body — singing with dancing in glorious costume while playing on beautifully sculptured instruments, the whole nine yards and then some. It is what she has always craved. More than just music.

Spectacle. Participation.

Communion.

At the edge of the dance floor, by the mouth of the hall, she gets a flash of something glistening in the upward periphery of her vision, something like a vibrating disco ball. When she looks up, there's nothing there but the rafters.

Weird, she thinks, then finishes her slow crawl through the crowd to the back.

Fifteen feet from the dressing room door, she bumps shoulders with a suit. Looks up. It's fucking Renning. He's heading out, doesn't look pleased. Doesn't look healthy, either. Yuck, she thinks.

360

"Excuse me," she says. He sort of scowls at her for a millisecond. Then he's gone.

"Let a smile be your umbrella," she mumbles, and then Lula, her purple-haired bass-playing contact, waves her over.

"Hey!" says Lula, giving her a hug. "Glad you could make it! Come on back! This is Kenneth, our guitarist!"

"Hi!"

"And Sandoz, our light man."

"Good ta meetcha!"

They curtsey, bow, shake hands accordingly. The mood is high, but Kenneth looks deeply wired. Sylvie checks back down the hall, sees Renning glowering after them.

"So… what the fuck did he want?" Sylvie asks. "As if I didn't know."

"He wanted to crash the opening ceremony." Lula hits on her cigarette, exhales. "Nobody gets to do that." She blows a kiss. "Nobody but *you*, baby."

Kenneth shivers. "Don't think we made a very good impression," he sighs.

"Cool," says Sylvie, and they all bust up. "So… are we ready?"

At that, Lula steps aside, a devious twinkle in her eyes.

And Sylvie opens the door into another universe.

IX

It takes her eyes a moment to adjust to the dimness. It is dark in the room, but far from black. Little pools of purple and red and blue swim across the figures that crowd the room: some of them impossibly tall, some of them bizarrely shaped. She steps forward, uncertain, tries to get her bearings; she's been in this room a thousand times, but it's never seemed this *huge*. Lula's fingers rest on her shoulder, the grip reassuring yet surprisingly firm.

"We're here!" Lula yells, cutting easily through the din.

A pocket of yellow light erupts in the far corner of the room. Sylvie blinks at the video camera, the semi-circle of empty seats, and the people standing around them. Several figures turn, as if expecting her. Their eyes catch the light like the eyes of cats.

"'Bout time!" says a tall spindly man in his sixties. He's got a mic in his hand and a white ponytail halfway down to his ass. "They wouldn't let me shoot till you got here." He smiles through gray teeth. "They said you ask good questions."

"Yay!" says Sylvie, stepping full into the light. Then the rest of the band came forward to meet her.

First off is a shavehead with a mean goatee, a wistful smile and purple John Lennon shades. He would be Mojo Cortex, resident electronics whiz. He hugs her, tells her she's brilliant as hell; then he not only quotes from her articles, but from her album as well.

Next up is Loope with his partner, Garoo; they both have sinewy drummer's bodies, naked to the waist, and they are animal to the max. The pheromone count in the room starts to climb; but they're not threatening beasties, just frisky and fun.

Last but not least is Dame Darcie herself, looking every bit as lovely and formidable as her PR would suggest. She has a wild mane of red hair and penetrating gray eyes. She also gives off an intoxicating spirit charge: centered and sexy, transcendent and strong.

"I'm jazzed," she says, and clearly means it. "So let's get down to business, shall we?"

George, the ponytailed gent, hands Sylvie the mic. It seems that they're documenting tonight in its entirety: 16-track audio, 16mm film, broadcast quality video and the fabulous Fisher-Price Pixel 2000. "You're going all out tonight," Sylvie opens, sitting down. "So I gather that this is an important gig for you."

"This is *the* gig," Darcie answers at once. The band has settled into its seats as well; they exchange knowing glances as she proceeds. "If we never play another, there will always be this."

"That implies a lot of pressure."

"Well, let me put it this way. We're gonna try a couple of things tonight that, so far as we know, have never been done. If we pull it off, it should be an extraordinary night. If we don't..."

"It should be an extraordinary night," Mojo cuts in, and there is a burst of laughter.

"So..." She eyes them curiously. "... are you gonna let me in on any of these surprises?"

Darcie leans forward in her seat and says, "How much do you know about shamanism?"

Sylvie shrugs. "A little. I've read my Terence McKenna."

"Good!" Darcie enthuses. Mojo gives her a smiling I *told you so* look. "So you understand the function of the shaman: to bring back an ecstatic healing vision from the other side, for the benefit of the tribe."

"Absolutely."

"Okay. Now, you know that we're a tribal band. What that means is, we're here to assemble the tribe. Out of this fractured, whacked, and anesthetized culture, we've got to somehow pull it all back together. Then give the tribe back its vision, its connection to the Other and Deeper Self."

"And you're doing this through the music?"

"See, the thing is," Mojo cuts in, suddenly earnest, "that we're all actually *made* of music! Okay? *That's* why music's so powerful, and why it's so incredibly important.

"I mean, have you ever noticed how music actually works? How certain grooves just drag you around the room and other ones make you feel like flying? How nobody has to tell you how a song's supposed to make you feel? How certain voices get right down into your soul — no matter *what* they're saying — while other voices can hand you the finest, noblest sentiments in the world, and all you wanna do is get the fuck out of the room?"

Sylvie nods, with mounting fascination.

"You wanna know why? Because on the subatomic level, what we're actually made up of is *energy in waves*, right? We're just this great big boundless universe, vibrating into infinity; and it's just the speed at which you're vibrating that determines whether you're a tabletop or a chairleg, a mosquito or a man."

"And which are you?" inquires Garoo.

"Why, I am... MANSQUITO!" Mojo declares, and everyone applauds.

"*So...*" Darcie concludes, wearily shaking her head at her goofy cohort, "when the music hits us, something radically profound happens. It doesn't just move *through* us. It moves *us*. It literally changes our experience."

"That's also why the Powers That Be have always tried so hard to control it," offers Kenneth.

"Exactly!" says Mojo. "Because they know that it's the secret code. The key to the highway, so to speak."

"And what, if I may ask, is the secret message?"

"*That we are One,*" says Darcie emphatically, and it's as if the air in the room gets suddenly both lighter and thicker at once: fraught with meaning, tinged with danger, tickled by crackling spark and dancing electricity. "The message is that we are all connected: joined at the core, at the center of Being. There is no separation, except when we forget who we really are. The message is that there is no true death beyond the death of the body, which means you can relax, because we never really die.

"But probably the most important message is that *we don't have to be afraid* — that there is nothing to fear *except* that sense of separation, which comes from forgetting who we really are."

There is a moment's pause, like a slapback echo in an empty auditorium. Sylvie takes a deep breath, suddenly aware that she is sweating. Yes, and shaking a little, as well.

"That's why it's so threatening to the Powers That Be," resumes Kenneth. "Because everything they've got is based on fear. And if we're not constantly afraid — afraid for ourselves, afraid of *them* — then we rob them of their power base. And they don't like that at all."

"So…" Sylvie resumes, clearing her throat as she does it, "…without getting too deep into total paranoia: Who is this mysterious 'Them'?"

"Like you don't already know." Lula grins. "Like you didn't slam into one in the hall."

"Okay," says Sylvie, grinning back. "Point taken. So let me ask you this: How do you plan to make this point any better than it's already been made?" She seizes the silence that follows the question: not nastily but tenaciously, as if the answer to it matters. "I mean, you just stated it all very lucidly and clearly; and to be honest, I've heard an awful lot of this before.

"But even if I agree with everything that you've said — and I agree with a lot of it already — how does that change anything? How does that heal anything? Specifically, how does that differ from the fifteen trillion people who've been trying to tell us this shit all along, while the bulk of civilization just keeps doing what it's doing, dragging us closer and closer to the brink while going, 'Yeah, yeah, yeah — but what the fuck do you want *me* to do about it?'"

Mojo smiles. "I *told* you she asks good questions!"

To Sylvie's relief, the rest of them are smiling, too; she'd been afraid that she'd just crossed the line. Darcie, in particular, looks juiced by the question.

Loope, meanwhile, lights a massive joint, hands it off to Lula. The number starts to make the rounds.

"It's one thing," Darcie says, "to have an intellectual conversation. Not that I don't love conversation, but it can only go so far. It's like trying to describe tripping to someone who's never done it. You can say, 'Ooh, pretty lights and pretty colors and shit, and God/Goddess/Whatever is Love,' but that's as far as it goes. And that's not far enough."

The joint has circulated to Darcie now. She takes a deep hit, hands it to Sylvie. Sylvie echoes the gesture.

"The thing about music," Darcie resumes, "is that it totally bypasses regular mind. It logs itself as *direct experience*. It makes you feel before you've had a chance to think about it. And the thing about *experience* — as opposed to theoretical construct — is that it's no longer a matter of faith or trust. It's a *knowledge* that you savor and you hold in your bones.

"It defines, for you, what is real."

Sylvie exhales, then swallows hard.

"So let me ask you," Darcie continues, "have you ever tripped? And do you know what I'm talking about?"

Sylvie says, "Oh, yeah."

"Okay! That's good!" Darcie smiles like the sun, and a cellular warmth seems to flood the room. "So let us tell you — and you may have already heard this before — what we know about the nature of the bardos states."

"The who?" Sylvie passes the dwindling joint off to Kenneth. A ten-foot smiling giant on stilts passes her peripheral vision. *Wow, good pot,* she tells herself, and then settles back into the story.

"When you die," Darcie says, and her eyes are a-gleam, "your spirit explodes out of your body like a rocket. It goes firing off into this astonishing place, this great vaulted chamber that is not physical in nature. It is an arena of pure essence, in which the next stage of the spirit game is set.

"At the summit is the Clear Light of Godhead: the place of Oneness, where all is merged in perfect union. In between us and It are the bardos states, through which we must pass. And back into which we very easily fall."

"Now, the Clear Light," says Mojo, "is like the little bell on top of those sideshow games where you test your strength? You know: take a whack with the hammer; if you make it go *ding*, you get the kewpie doll?" Sylvie laughs; he continues. "And the fact is that, when you die, you've got enough jet propulsion to make it all the way up. All you have to do is let go of your baggage. But therein lies the problem."

"Because most of us want to keep our baggage," Darcie resumes. "We're attached to it; we've allowed it to define us, to the point where we think it *is* us. It's a ridiculous mistake, but a very natural one, judging by how often we all seem to make it.

"That's what the bardos states are for. To strip us of the things that separate us from Godhead: the anger, the hunger, the unfulfilled desire, all the cravings and indulgences and attachments of the flesh."

By this time, a second joint has begun to make the rounds. Sylvie accepts it, feels the world take on a richer texture as the smoke uncoils in her lungs.

"It's almost like going through a series of airlocks, or weird supernatural checkpoints," Mojo says. "At each level, you get met by these guides — some of whom are friendly, some of whom are not so friendly — and then you're exposed to these high-intensity beams which essentially *burn off your karma.* But if you find that you can't handle being stripped down this way…"

"Or if you don't want to, for whatever reason…" Kenneth interjects.

"…there are all these little secret exits that you can duck out of. Little trap doors on every level. The trick is to pick the right set of doors, because that determines where you're going to reincarnate next."

"Now excuse me for cutting in," Sylvie says, a slow grin spreading across her face. "But you guys seem awfully sure about this."

"The Tibetans laid this template out, a very long time ago," Darcie says. "That's what the Tibetan Book of the Dead really is: it's a map of the bardos topography, written as an instructional manual to help guide the dying spirit through the predictable crisis on the other side of the veil. The idea is that if you know where you are going in, you'll be able to decide where you want to go from there. And beyond that, you'll be able to remember the transition."

"The fact is," cuts in Kenneth, "that most people are so freaked out by dying that they just sort of *black out* at the moment of death. Then they wake up in this trippy place full of flashing lights and disembodied entities; and the whole thing is so mind-blastingly phantasmagorical that they panic and, like Mojo said, duck for the nearest exit."

"Then they wake up in their next incarnation, wondering how they wound up with this shitty life that they don't understand," Mojo adds.

"But the bardos states are accessible to us, " Darcie concludes. "Through psychedelics, and through shamanic ritual, it is possible to train yourself — *here, in this life* — so that you can move from incarnation to incarnation with total continuity and remarkable ease. That's why psychedelic research has always faced such massive opposition. That's why Timothy Leary went to jail, over twenty-five years ago. That's why they're still waging a drug war, to this day.

"Because it is really a war on *gnosis:* on direct experience of, and participation in, the Mysteries. It's the same war that keeps our spirituality on the defensive, under the thumb of the Church and the Powers That Be. The psychedelic revolution of the '60s was an attempt to blow the whole thing wide open, to go populist with the details of this deeper reality. That's why it had to be crushed.

"But it changed our way of seeing, from that point forward: Now even network TV flashes us trippy computer graphics, little glimpses of the beyond. Fundamentally, it changed the way we perceive: the way we hear, and the way we think.

"In the process, it has prepared us for the next evolutionary stage in our journey as a species: for freedom from fear and a return to understanding. When we know for a fact that death isn't the end, we are free at last to climb out from under the shadow.

"That is the vision we have brought back for the tribe.

"Have fun at the show, okay?"

Then Darcie stands and, just like that, the interview is over.

"Um… wait!" says Sylvie, startled and stunned. The others rise. The yellow light winks out.

"I'm sorry," Lula says, taking her by the shoulder again, "but it's just about showtime, and we still have some last-minute shit to do. Rituals to perform, ya know? Stuff like that."

"Okay…" Suddenly, they are moving through the shifting dark, the other band members vanished while the strange shapes mill and part. This time, the walk goes by too quickly.

Then Lula opens the door to the world outside: the garish light, the teeming crowds. "Thanks," she says. "When it's done, maybe we can all talk some more."

Sylvie watches the door close behind her.

From the other side, she hears voices.

And drums.

X

Carlos turns when he hears drums erupting from the back of the club. The DJ music fades and the crowd begins to applaud. The lights go off. He hears the entire band coming through to the front, everybody pounding on something. A flash of light. Snapshot of Cowboy Dude standing a few people away from him. No shit, he thinks. Dude actually came down.

The band ascends to the darkened stage, and smoke begins to spread like ether: over the stage, out into the crowd. A low throb rubs and grumbles against his legs, groin, stomach, the bones in his head.

Then it begins: a subsonic thrumming, almost painful, cranium-vibrating, accompanied by quick magnesium flashes on an otherwise darkened stage. In the flashes: portrait of a monkey, mournful gaze turned skyward, hand stuck in a basket.

For a really long time.

XI

Jesus, what are they doing, Sylvie wonders, her body vibrating sympathetically to the low-frequency pulse, teeth jarred halfway out of her jaws. What is this, some kind of Nazi rockstar shit to stir you up? Break you down to your component atoms before you're built up again? She refers back to the interview, deciding that, yes, that's just exactly what's going on.

But is she okay with it? That remains to be seen. There's a strange vibe in the room, greater than expectation but not quite dread. It is an air of *portent,* heady and profound, far thicker than the smokescreen wafting out from the stage.

To her left, a young woman has removed her blouse, sweet breasts revealed beneath a serene gypsy smile. Sylvie'd been told to expect it, but she's still taken by surprise; this is, so far as she knows, a first for ol' Club Lingerie.

The young woman looks like she's about to receive holy communion. And indeed, in that moment, Sylvie comes to understand: this is not a rock show, in any conventional sense.

This is a religious event.

XII

A white noise THWACK! erupts, recedes to a crimson counterpoint fade. Slowly. Again. A low keening chant begins.

The audience starts a slow gentle variant of headbanging. Swaying, slowly moving heads forward and back, resonating with the chant. With the traveling music.

The swaying mass is surrounded by tall wavering shadows: the misshapen overspill of backroom otherworldliness, come to interpenetrate and commingle with the crowd. The balcony also is filled, with far deeper shadows. Still as mannequins. Watching.

There is an almost visible barrier between the watchers and the audience, the congregation. It is a tangible junction between two air masses, one arctic, one tropical. A pressure drop.

A guitar, swimming in echo, twists and stretches a single, sinuous note.

And then Darcie begins to sing.

Every so often, a voice comes along that goes beyond all reasonable human expectations: Yma Sumac, Diamanda Galas, Kongar-Ool Ondar and the Mongolian throat-singers of Tuva. It is not enough to say that Darcie Anything has one of those voices. She is fluent in seven languages, but the sound that flows from her contains none of them and all of them. The sound is beyond language.

The sound is pure language.

It swoops, high, and it is the sound of heaven's flagrant parting. It plummets, then, to the leering devil-rumble of the pit. It sketches the forces of all creation in tones that overflow with passion. Drawing in the forces. Drawing in the crowd.

The shaman, invoking the All.

The shadow-vampires begin to feel the tug of the current, the call of hot mortal blood, amped with the chemical charge of spirit in dawning body ecstasy. Slowly, as if underwater, they begin to push into the junction. On to the floor, into the crowd. The balcony empties.

Suddenly, a flurry of earth-shattering percussion. Bright stage lights reveal bodies, naked skin, tattooed limbs beating on tom toms, car hoods, oil drums, undefinable things. Randomly placed television images scream out life in subliminal flashes: eyeball pyramid money daddy mothersistervirginwhore. Machinebirthfetusgun. Junglemeatsexcitykill.

369

The substance of the world.

XI

This exact second, the electrons dance down the wire, tiny gates shoot yes no back and forth, this dance is flung, and things are occurring. Froth is spewed. Spacetime is diddled. I am here. Mojo is here. I am.

These lights are flipping at near epileptic frequencies and I am pressing down a key and a loop of Fred Astaire is crooning "oh such a hungry yearning" over and over and again. Garoo is beating the universe into being, and I am here again. Again. Now.

The DMT is kicking in. Oh yeah. Sacred mushroom spirit singing. The children sway down below and Kenneth throws down, screaming it. But I know where he is. I stopped going there, I don't know why. It's okay, and I fold in the steel beam echo. The children's pulses rise.

I look at Darcie, naked now, glorious, so beautiful she is giving me a hard-on and laughing at me and gurning with her entire face almost sucked into her mouth, telepathically burning me.

I am hitting the keypad, running a sequence on the six other samplers that activates a helical musical barberpole around the entire room, through speakers all over the place. All around the sides and the back.

And looking back there, seeing something I don't want to be seeing.

Well, what the fuck. Win, fight, go. Let's party, demons. Let's go. Have some fun.

Now I'm starting to fuck with everyone's voices, opening up the Dub. Six sets of custom faders arranged in a circle. I am lighting a stick of incense over it and waving it around. Tweaking the faders. Lula's voice starts blurbering a little then bends fully into basketball dribble echo, folding back on itself. Loope gets it right off and folds into it, rattling a car hood/barrel tattoo.

I twist again, and Loope's and Garoo's chanting becomes resonant insectoid. Something in the twist reminds me that IT IS COMING ON. Like I did last summer.

Which causes me to glance up again at the resident insectoids. Naughty naughty boys and girls. Would you like some too? I think you would. You would like a big piece of us. Okay. Okay. This you shall have. Come on ahead.

The music is mutating into a weird metallic mambo, a bleating and smashing.

And I-I-I like it.

XII

Half of the audience has begun to shed its clothing now, in emulation of the band. Members of the crew wander through the crowd: pouring sacred wine from a bloated skin, smearing naked flesh with a fast-acting combination of KY, DMSO, and DMT.

People begin to writhe against one another, massaging the substance into the collective bloodstream. Visible heat rises from the crowd, drawing the vampires into the mix, slowly eroding their reserve.

Carlos is lost in the rhythm, hypnotized by the insistent chant, resonating with it, blue electric headrushes fountaining up from his spine. He's lost his shirt somewhere; it was too hot to dance in. What the fuck, he thinks, find it later. He and everyone around him are slipping and sliding into one another in a slow sensual mutation-of-mosh, a kind of peaced-out group love-rub. The goo is all over them, lubricating everyone's movements.

I hope there's really acid or X in that shit like everyone says, Carlos muses dreamily, that would be hip. Jeez, maybe I *should* have brought my parents.

Sylvie tries to wipe the stuff off of her arms and face, using the bottom inside of her skirt. This is useless, she realizes. Shit. My clothes are ruined. Maybe I should just take them off, like everybody else is doing.

This is getting fucking wild, she decides. She's trying to get out of harm's way, but to no avail. Sylvie remembers the Fourth of July party she threw a few years back. She had had the same feeling right after every scenester in Hollywood showed up at her house following the big barbecue in Elysian Park and right before same started dancing to P-Funk on her living room table, setting off fireworks in the bathtub, blowing out the stereo speakers, and smashing the front window. It was the exhilaration of knowing that you're part of something, for better or worse, that was about to go completely out of control.

Then she feels the first pre-psychedelic skin-tingles. Sylvie has the sense that before the evening's done, that party will seem like a blue-haired church ladies' luncheon.

XIII

Heat exudes from a sudden torch, held high, borne toward a huge metal trash barrel that has been rolled into the center of the swarm. The crowd steps back as one around it, as the fire comes down.

Renning watches them ignite the barrel and the heat hits him ten feet away, a whoosh of hot, steamy air. A column of flame almost reaches the ceiling, tickling the wooden rafters.

He closes his eyes and falls into another time, another fire....

Always the fire. It always ended this way. The heretics dancing, ecstatic. The soldiers of the Inquisition, surrounding the camp. Then the night, filled with screaming, agony and light.

And power, thought Cardinal Vasquez. More sizzles in the flame than muscle and fat. The exquisite energies of fear and death glow there, the energies that feed me, allow me to continue.

These heretics never would know just how wrong they were, how they challenged not just the Roman Church but the Order of Things.

The three pyres lit the clearing in a yellowed imitation of day. Vasquez drank in the power that pulsed out from their centers. But even as he drank, something came to him: a note of nausea curdling the edges of his rapture. He looked up in time to see a disfigured thing smiling at him from the blaze. As it smiled, its face was darkening, bubbling, crisping. The thing looked at him, chiding. As if the pain were nothing.

"Know yourself, priest," it said. "Hell is between your ears." And it laughed, briefly, until no sound would come from its throat.

Kenneth's head goes back, his hand goes up, and in that instant, he is no longer poised to deliver a detuned power chord. He is in an elegant candle-lit room, caressing a *viola de amor* with a horsehair bow.

The powdered heads that regard the ensemble express the multiple mindstates of their owners: boredom, vacuousness, delight, rapture, contempt, in various combinations.

For a moment, he locks eyes with the Duke, the man who will employ them as court musicians or not, based on this evening's performance. It is obvious that the music does not speak to the Duke, yet it is clear that he is amused. His face betrays his contempt, makes transparent his one true love: power. In that moment of subliminal contact, Kenneth can see that it's more than love. It's need. It's food. This man, this Duke, feeds on the need-energy of others. Their desperation. Their dreams.

He leaves that night without farewells, without respects paid to lords and ladies. He knows what the others want to do, and that they will do it without him. But then, they had not looked into those eyes.

Kenneth remembers the Prussian winter that follows: poverty, malnutrition, a cold that quickly became pneumonia. Death in a freezing, unfurnished room. Then the light, the unburdening. The Punchline.

Kenneth strokes the power chord to life, and looks out across the mosh-pit at the Duke, at Vasquez, at Renning, at whatever he calls himself now, at those eyes staring back.

Renning's reverie ends abruptly as he begins to be jostled by a pulse wave, moving through the growing claustrophobic confines of the dance floor. The disturbance is caused this time by a naked duo, bearing metal buckets filled with something through the crowd.

He watches, amazed, as one naked, bearded pagan faggot stops dead in front of him, grinning widely.

"Hiiiii!!!" the bearded faggot says.

Renning considers that, back in the forties, he wouldn't have hesitated to send this one along to Mengele to use for his experiments, do not pass go, do not collect two hundred *Deutschemarks*. Ah, for the good old days.

The pagan faggot, still grinning from ear to ear, scoops up generous handfuls of whatever he has in his container, and proceeds to smear it down both sides of Renning's face.

"You fucking IDIOT!" Renning howls, but the naked man is gone, making his merry way through the writhing mass. Goo slides down Renning's neck, staining his very expensive Italian suit.

"AAAAAHHHHHH!!!!!!"

"Haw haw haw haw!!!"

Some dreadlocked white trash idiot is pointing at him, laughing his ass off. The same goo is on him, too. "I'll show you funny…" Renning starts to say.

And then the drug on his skin begins to speak instead.

XIV

Slim's got himself caught up in this hippie mess, and figures he might as well enjoy himself. It's getting hot, what with the fire and the sweaty crowd, so he takes off his shirt like everybody else is doing, even the ladies, although he doesn't know if he'd call them that. He ties it around his waist. Soon he's sticky with some kind of mess they've been rubbing on everybody. Behind the alcoholic haze, Slim's starting to feel funny: tingly, kinda hopped up, like the acid trip in Nam.

The pulsing lights start to reach into his head, tickle it a little, then leave. Almost like they were alive or something. Playing with him, trying to tell him something. Like some genius dog on TV. What is it, girl? Ruff! You want me to follow you? Rough rough!

He's all set to follow the Lassie-lights when a cold set of fingers brushes his neck. Then they're gone, but his focus is the crowd now, looking for the cold fingers, looking into a blur of dull smoky light, interspersed with bright glowing and dull greens, snaking in ropy tendrils through a pit of soft bright reds and blues. He can see himself standing on the floor, and another dimension of himself floating on the void.

Through this, Slim realizes that something in the goop has put him in this state, but there is no fear.

Only astonishment.

XV

Kenneth starts a stuttering microtonal birdsong assault at the high end of the neck...

...and then Kenneth inhales smoke from a Lucky Strike with one hand, cradles the horn with the other, fingering the keys. He is standing next to Bird on the stage of a lonely nightclub in Santa Monica. The place is almost empty. It is 1953.

Bird is into his third chorus of "All the Things You Are." He's telling something, some wordless truth, some very funny joke that Kenneth has heard before, has forgotten the punchline to.

He never remembered it that time around; neither had Bird, evidently. They'd both reached for the surrogate: in a bottle, in a syringe.

Then, finally: sprawled on a filthy mattress in a weekly hotel. A needle, holding the dregs of a too-potent speedball, dangling from a vein. As the light and sound fade out behind a frostyfreeze orgasmic numb, it finally comes to him. Oh yeah. That's funny....

Darcie finds her eyes drawn back to Kenneth, watches his attitude, sees where he's traveling behind the notes. Back and back, back and forth, she knows.

She'd traveled far too, through the years and lives and the half-rememberings; through centuries until they'd met again, and recognized each other — dreamily, half-completely — toward the end of an era, the beginning of the seventies.

Of course they hadn't been Kenneth and Darcie then: beautiful-sad hippie children lovers in the flat on the Haight, frozen to the floor behind industrial strength doses of Owsley acid. They'd gone by other names, in other bodies now long departed. They thought they'd recognized each other. But suddenly they knew.

And with knowing came the understanding.

Of what they had to do.

Leary and Alpert's *Psychedelic Experience* gave them the template from which to act: a roadmap to the infinite, for going in. And coming back. This cycle of psychic liberation was coming to its end; but if they acted now, and acted well, they'd be just in time for the next one.

She often wondered who'd found them there, together in that room; and what they imagined had happened, when they did. *More stupid acid casualties. Just say no. Your picture here...*

Kenneth looks up to catch her watching, knows they're both locked into what's going down all over the club. His face is serene, resigned. Darcie suddenly knows without question that the night they'd planned for is finally here. They'd brought the savage garden to them; it blossoms all around them.

And now it's time to open up the gates.

XVI

"Omigod," whispers Sylvie, as the music kicks into the next hyperlevel of overdrive. She is getting spectacular bodyrushes, staggering tangents of thought, but they do not compare to the visual overlay.

Because the place is packed with glowing souls packed into wildly dancing bodies, slick with psychedelic lube and literally *ablaze:* luminous with spirit fire that issues from within, flooding her sight and senses with all the colors of Creation. The effect is somewhere beyond 3-D, stacked in levels of swirling motion; she sees radiant aura over undulating flesh over eye-burning filament core.

And Sylvie is dancing glowing flowing going along with the thundering groove, the primal pulse locked into her and she to it in perfect sync. This is not like mosh-pit mayhem. This is not like L.A. cool. This is not like anything she's ever known.

This is Everything.

Oh my.

If the crowd is glowing, then the band is positively, brain-blastingly *incandescent*; quite apart from the hyperactive light show is their actual spirit charge, pulsating out from the stage in waves like tie-dyed video feedback gone berserk.

In the center, naked writhing wailing Darcie has whipped straight past wet dream to full-blown goddess stature. She is the beacon, the primordial source, the giver and taker of all and more.

Sylvie has never seen anything more beautiful, or more powerful, in her life.

She remembers a slice of Terence McKenna, a description of some jungle ritual he'd once found himself inside; and what he'd said is the closest her rational mind can find to explain what's going on on on fwang fwang oh god ALRIGHT it seems that he was out there in the jungle, right? and all these native guys are there, and she is he is WHOA listening to the music that they play, deep rich ceremonial invocation, shaman piercing the veil between worlds and Terence like Sylvie is there bearing witness to the beauty, the horror, the absolute profundity of what they are creating

and at a certain point, as they reach the peak, the music that they're playing is no longer only music. It is a language s/he can see.

It is the fabric of creation, visually forming out of sound.

And as she thinks this, she feels a terrible glorious *lifting*: a feeling that both the top and the bottom have fallen away, and she is here, right in the center of it, never more fully alive than this, never more aware than in this moment.

She looks up. She does not know why.

And the rafters vanish.

And the ceiling is gone...

XVII

...and the sky peels back, the veil is parted, the space beyond space collides with time: an interdimensional interpenetration, yawning over the dance floor at Club Lingerie like the Grand Canyon upside down.

In that sanity-threatening, too huge expanse, the bardos gleam and beckon: a multi-tiered shopping mall of possible spirit destinations, more staggering to behold than the mothership's interior at the end of Close Encounters. *Smiling lights twinkle and flash, floating in the vastness: the spirit guides that Mojo described, in friendly mode. For the moment, at least.*

While the Clear Light of Godhead shines down upon them, resting above it all like a crown.

XVIII

The perimeter rapidly dissolves; the boundaries between observer and participant are inexorably broken. The wild naked dance is undiminished by the visions; if anything, the Holies are simply more fuel for the fire. The sacred frenzy boils up through the secondary bar level, and those too timid or too cool to be involved — those who'd hung back near the bar or at tables — are swirled into the mayhem.

The psychotropic goo is inescapable; it is all over everything. Everyone, with the exception of the bartenders and waitresses hunkered down under the bar, is tripping HARD.

Carlos, for his part, is humming like a power line. Bouquets of light and color bloom and wither in his skull, and the music becomes sensual, abstract, ceremonial. It's been playing for a hundred or a thousand years.

He opens his eyes and he notices a disco ball, floating in the space where the ceiling used to be. It's vibrating subtly, intelligently. It's actually alive, he sees, speaking to him in telepathic chimings, in words that manifest themselves as image-floods splashing against his head, quick subliminal gestalt transfer from the others in the room. He starts to see different perspectives of the club, mental states superimposed, visuals overlaying his own, shifting by the millisecond. The chiming words begin to modulate, to slow and speed, and the image-states lengthen, then blur together. Gradually they start to reach a kind of equilibrium. Carlos begins to feel, deeply, what's behind the eyes of those around him: some of it smooth and pretty, and a lot of it pointed and deadly.

But the funny thing is that even the deadly, evil, hideous ones have little punctuations of him hiding out in their core, not him exactly but whatever part of him is driving is there driving all the others too: the part he never gets to see because he's too busy wanting and getting and seeing, yammering cause he never shuts up and listens, like he's listening now, like he never wants to hear regular words again, just wants to melt into this mirrorball's metalanguage.

He's seeing a few hundred perspectives at once, sensing millions, billions beyond that, but his fractal POV points updown onto a central ballet, an x-dimensional polyhedron popping up from the background. The mirrorball "holds minds" with him, with this writer woman Sylvie, and with a Pointy-Deadly suit: Ira from A&M, very confused and very hungry.

Their physical bodies draw together through the writhing mass, as if through magnetism; they can see each other through multiple eyes, multiple I-am overload — no secrets now, motives clear — mirrorball wants to deliver this awesome awareness to Sylvie's head, wholesale, needs her to witness. Pointy-Deadly in Hell, overwhelmed by lust-hunger, wanting only to feed, stalking Sylvie, Mr. Death how do you do, all in the Dance, outside Horror or Ecstasy, compelled to converge.

CarlosSylviePointy sees a trail of human bodies, drained of blood, of essence, psyches tapped, remains of Pointy-Deadly's feasts. They see them carted off to some central disposal system, ovens out of Auschwitz (another previous franchise), part of some monstrous conspiracy of silence, never dreamed of but now seen as absolute truth.

In the midst of this psychedelic freefall, Carlos knows that vampires are real, and that they rule the planet. And Sylvie, laughing out loud into the face of Mr. Death, into the absurdity of her figurative take on things turned horribly literal, snatches up Ira's pale blue wrist.

And bites him first, instead.

XIX

"HAW HAW HAW HAW!!!"

"*FUCK YOU!!!*" Renning screams, grabbing the cracker by the throat and squeezing with all his might. There is a pop and a FLASH and a big red squirt, and then the cracker is floating above him. In color.

"You think that's a big fuckin' deal?" the cracker cat-calls, thumbing his rainbow astral nose. *"You think that I'm afraid of that? It's always violence with y'all, you buncha big fuckin' pussies, so scared o' dyin' that you gotta steal OUR lives from US!"*

"SHUT UP!"

"Bite me! Oh, yeah... too late! HAW HAW HAW HAW!!!" He does a cartwheel in the ether.

Suddenly, Renning feels a tug and a tearing from behind. He whirls to see shreds of his Armani in the hands of a grinning glow-eyed teenage girl. "NICE SUIT!" she yells; and before he can strike, she is out of her body and doing backflips with the cracker.

"We're FREE!!!"

"YIPEEE!!!"

"COME BACK HERE, YOU LITTLE BASTARDS!!!"

And that's when Renning notices all the eyes, the watchful eyes upon him. Worse than that, he catches a glint of light from off a camera lens. He is standing there, holding a headless lump of dripping meat with sneakers; and not only are they standing there, staring at him, but THEY'RE GETTING IT ALL ON FILM!

"NO!!!!!" he shrieks, dropping the dripping corpse, shaking his arms as if the blood could leave his hands so easily. They have him now, they have him by rights, they see him now for what he is. All the power he gains from secrecy goes up like piss on a red-hot griddle.

I'll have to kill them all, he realizes.

Starting with that fucking band....

XX

Drake's view of the situation is somewhat different. Drake is high as a fucking kite. He is spinning around the dance floor, his ego expanding in inverse proportions to his diminishing consciousness. The drug has given him what he wants, in a big way. It has given him more of himself.

And what could be better, he considers, wheeling haphazardly, half-moshing, desultorily nipping at swatches of bare flesh, what could be better than MEEEE?

379

Unless of course it was more me.

He regards the spectacle, the band on the stage, magnificent. He hears Darcie's siren cry, the sound of tearing steel and honey-light, and thinks, she is astounding. They are really fantastic. I should be part of that.

I need to be up there performing. I need to show these sheep just how great I really am. And the Others, they need to know just who is next in line, that I am certainly not just another pitiful mosquito like them.

And when they watch me drop my fangs into that beautiful neck, watch me drain her dry, they will know.

And down deep — deeper than he can see, but not quite deep enough that he can't feel it or hear it — an imp is running around his insides, checking out the scenery, knocking on the walls, which respond with a hollow clang. Hollow and empty.

As he makes his way toward the stage.

XXI

Puttyhead descends out of a cartoonland, or a near-enough approximation, and into a late twentieth-century. Into noise and light, into humans swaying and touching, twirling and dying and rising again.

He floats over to the bar, tries to order a martini, shifting into a face like a male mannequin at Sears. The bartender, having done a "duck and cover" under the bar, does not respond. Puttyhead, exasperated, pulls a full, chilled martini glass out of his index finger, makes it extra dry. He turns, then, morphing into a cross between Tiny Dr. Tim and the Lucky Charms leprechaun. He stays that way, serenely pushing through to the middle of the floor, to the center of the sweat-soaked, wriggling crowd. People rub up against him, sticky and slidy against his immaculate white suit: a living membrane which absorbs and dissipates any sort of goo that touches him. He sips his unspilled martini.

Puttyhead is many things to many people. He notices others here tonight that are interdimensionals; a handful of shape-shifters on the stage; and some characters that are simply not quite human, and not very nice. Well, he thinks, how about that.

His green fedora mutates into a black top-hat, his chin lengthens, and fangs press out of the corners of his mouth. His suit clouds to stormy gray, then black. A cape sprouts from his shoulders.

He is Hanna Barbera Lugosi. He is Count Rockula.

Tonight he is one of many ways in.

Or out.

XXII

Kenneth locks eyes with Renning again; this time he's at the front of the stage, and the look in his eyes has changed. He's disheveled and feral. There's torment in his gaze. Desire. Hatred. Hunger. For Kenneth. At Kenneth.

Good, Kenneth thinks, he remembers me now.

The boundaries between the melee on the floor and the action on the stage are blurring. People are on the stage: dancing, caressing...

... and Loope, half-transformed, takes off an attacking vampire's face with one sweep of lupine claw, never missing a beat; while full lupine Garoo takes another vampire's head in the largest set of wolf jaws ever, diddles it playfully with his enormous sandpaper tongue...

... and in the moment it takes for him to sweep his eyes around, Renning is upon him.

"Yesss," the vampire hisses. "I remember..." Reading his thoughts.

We've been at this for a long time, huh? Kenneth thoughtcasts it to Renning, knowing full well that he can grab every word. *Too long for secrets, isn't it?* Pulling his hair back to reveal the flesh of his neck. *Take it. Take what comes with it.*

This is my blood.

MY BLOOD. Renning hear-seeing the words preternaturally vibrating around Kenneth's head. MY my blood BLOOD. And no resistance at all. A cool defiance.

It never stopped him before.

It doesn't stop him now. Renning moves forward with terrible grace, slides razorteeth into the soft slicing skin. The jugular parts like fruit, and he shudders, gulping hot, thick electric blood, drinking light and image, odor, sound, drinking orgasm, even as he loathes himself for it...

... because Renning can see himself clearly now, too: shackled to a chain of rotting carcasses, corpses in infinite regress, slaughterhouse fear fullforce and mounting, enormity of what he has done, what he is

(chittering harpy chorus, dissonant, arrhythmic:

whathehasdone, whathehasdone, whathehasdone...)

and the full knowledge of guilt, physical pummeling awareness of the bottomless misery he has caused, in the service of what Demon? In the terrified preservation of this body, this ego, this id, back and back and back

(detuned bending harpy laughter

and a burning eye,

burning eye like a red-giant sun

in spaceless firmament of mind:

fixed on him, ominous,

silent,

omniscient)

and in this smoking pit of psychic agony, the horror of his desire is death camp silent; his horror, undeniable greedy hunger like a runaway juggernaut, unstoppable.

And the Eye will not judge; it radiates viscous penetrating light-pressure, will only add weight to the stinking corpse chain. As if to say, "This is what you are, Renning. This is what you do...."

Still the music continues to throb: brilliant, ear-punishing. The pounding snapping percussives grind out a counterpoint to the wet pulsing in his mouth, in his throat.

And as he is suffused with life-energy, the disgust, the loathing shifts one-eighty degrees and he sees that This Is Necessary. What he has done. All of it. What he is.

The predator. The prey.

Vibrating with this awareness, mouth locked to flesh, the two bodies rise up toward the lights in the air.

XXIII

Slim comes back out to the realm of the Eye, his Eye, following the snake through the crowd, his friend the snake writhing on his young friend Carlos, following it around, where is this going, and sees it leading up to the stage, up to the fractured lightsound source. It's crowded with bodies and mingling colors, desires, the smell of blood, body fluids, and perfumes, subatomic components of smells.

He can see everything with the Eye. He can see the cancer through his arms, chest, through his skin, reverse shining like a backward x-ray: sucking down black, absence of anything, wild with anti-life, sleeping now, resting comfortably in the wet hinterlands of his bloodvessels, glands, membranes. Yeah. There it is.

But what is THAT?

Slim peers down, deeper, into the microrealms of plasmas and cells, organized self-referring constructs up and down along a web of consciousness, and the construct he's locked to — the Electric Pinpoint Eye — and up past that, subsumed in unknowable meaningless vastness of space, strung along the web of everything, forever.

And he thinks, this ain't so bad. I could just let go.

It would be just fine.

Then back down to here, to the snake and the stage, to the weasel with the evil eye. It's Drake, beyond laughable, wigglin' his hips, ready to sink his teeth into the singer-goddess' neck, grandstanding once again up there in the seductive shimmer-light.

Slim, now in a place outside of fear or courage, thinks simply: Now wouldn't that be a shame.

Then, without hesitation, he jumps up into the light as well....

And Drake is grooving, really grooving, dancing with the nekkid chick, lookit me go! And it feels like all eyes are upon him. Where they belong. On the Chosen One.

Darcie watches him with eyes of fire; if he fucked her in the sockets, it would fry his cock right off. She is smiling as she dances, as if daring him to try.

He strides manfully toward her, takes a grab at the mic.

And then somebody is pinning him from behind.

"I think you're bothering the little lady," the cowboy says, gathering Drake in a bear hug.

"Hey...!!!"

"Why don't you come on with me?"

"NO! LEGGO!" Drake kicks his legs. Like a little kid, scrabbling. He struggles hard, to no avail.

They begin to fly.

Darcie does a little cornball curtsy and blows them a kiss as they rise up, rise up, rise above the madding crowd and leave it all behind. Drake looks at his fans, his miserable subjects, and none of them give a fuck about him now. "DON'T YOU KNOW WHO I AM?" he screams out abjectly.

"YEAH!" Carlos yells, "YOU'RE AN ASSHOLE!"

"AUGHHHHH!!!!!!"

And up into the lights they can see the portals, the subtle variations and gradations, through the entire spectrum of visible out into the infrared and the ultraviolet. The guides floating there don't look friendly to Drake.

But they seem to like the cowboy just fine.

"Hey!" calls a warm ball of spinning light. Slim looks over, takes a gander at the thing. He's really enjoying this flying business. Hell, he thinks. And I could be home, watching goddam TV.

The warm spinning ball is then joined by another. They resolve into a couple of boys that he knows. "Hey!" he says, smiling. "How the hell are y'all?"

"Great!" say the hippie boys. "You see it now?"

"You bet!"

"Nice company you're keeping!" says the hippie on the right.

"Oh, this here?" Giving Drake a squeeze. "He's just bein' a bad lil' buddy, so I figured I'd take him home."

"NO!!!!" screams the vampire. What a wussy.

"Okay! Have fun!" says the other hippie, turning back into a ball. "See you next life!"

"You got it! THANK YOU! And y'all take care!"

"Don't mention it!"

Slim looks up into the Clear Light, grinning. Magnesium brilliance is pouring through the breach. The same brilliance begins to peel him down, exposing him whitelight, a human torch.

They both begin to burn with it, as they rise up toward the pinnacle.

XXIV

Renning, for the first time in a long long time, feels like he is maybe out of his league.

It's been two thousand years since he last saw the bardos states. He did not like them then, and he does not like them now. It's like being stuck inside of a laser light show; and it *hurts*, it *hurts*, every beam slicing into all he's built, all the armor that surrounds him, keeps him being who he is.

This measly musician, this pestiferous spark, clings to him now like an infant to its mother. Only he is the one who is being suckled, suckled by Renning in his bloodhunger state.

He looks up into the Light, teeth still buried in Kenneth's throat, and realizes that he is being beckoned to by a cartoon: a caricature of himself, or at least of his kind, crudely and offensively lampooned. It leers at him, showing its absurd fangs, tips its ridiculous top-hat to him.

"BLUH!" it says to him. "BLUH BLUH *BLUH!!!*" Mocking Bela.

Mocking him.

This pisses him off. The feeding is forgotten, and his hold on Kenneth loosens. The two drift apart. Renning lunges for the apparition, in an attempt to rip it to pulpy shreds: so blind with hate/rage that he fails to see the massive blood-crusted pig-iron cage fall around them.

Too late to escape what the cartoon has ripple-formed itself into.

Now he is caged with something three times his size, a mountain of graygreen mottled stinking flesh, stinking of old chewed meat; something which has hold of a dripping red human carcass, holding it by a stump and slowly, rhythmically beating the headless, limbless body against the bars with a wet smacking thud.

Renning looks into the glowing red eyes, watches the stinking mouth open to reveal two neat rows of long pointed knives, a yellow tongue lolling between them.

The eyes, the mouth close on him, beige spittle rolling down the ancient predator's chin.

Predator, he thinks, in the very last moment before the vile teeth of Puttyhead reach him, tear into him, rend him asunder.

Predator and prey....

XXV

Sylvie watches from the floor as Ira the vampire goes fetal and falls up high into the light. Her mind blown open, she shudders, wiping the clotting blood from her mouth with her sleeve. She sees as if she were there, too, suspended beyond the veil. The mirrorball refracts far more than simple human commonality.

385

It mirrors the pain that the vampires feel.

And their suffering is immense.

THIS IS YOUR PRIDE, says a voice so huge that it dwarfs the music from the stage. And vampire flesh bursts into flames, with the smoldering fat-stench of centuries.

She can see them all, like a row of candles, blazing in the space between Godlight and firmament while the spotlights of deepest reality slice them like beef from the deli, eliciting screams. There is Renning and Drake and Ira, Puffy and Skanky and Chester from Trainwreck. There are all of the fools who gave in to their hatred.

Is God/Goddess cruel?

Does the Pope shit in the woods?

THIS IS YOUR HATE, says the mighty voice, booming; and scars open up on the pale vampire flesh. Poisonous ooze spoots and spatters and sprays while they scream and they scream and the Light rushes in.

AND THIS IS YOUR FEAR, as the hammer comes down: rippling derma and musclemeat, déjà vu dripping.

Sylvie sees the dissolving disease, sees the meatflecks and bloodblossoms sail into Godhead: a great sucking-up, like the vacuum of heaven, taking all of the pestilence into its heart. It is like an embrace. It is awful and wondrous.

So this is Forgiveness, Sylvie thinks.

And you know what?

This shit is *cool*....

XXVI

...but for Renning and Drake and the others aloft, there is still no forgiveness.

There is only the torment.

AND THIS IS YOUR DESIRE, says the voice like an A-bomb, sound like a thermonuclear concussion of the heart. It resonates not from without but from *within*: inside their chests, inside the breasts that burst in ribcage shrapnel and gristle, sluicing and spritzing the ether with heartmuck, the tainted craving for all that they stole, deep and decent desire turned to rape and ugly mayhem.

Just as they had disregarded all the means for all the ends.

"PLEEEEEASE!!!" screams Renning in his pain. "PLEEEEASE!!!" But it is to no avail. The stench of betrayal is the stench of his flesh: long defiled, now burning off toward the Light at his core. Every ugly wish he ever held is burning. Every evil act is kindling for the flame.

And Drake looks back on the lives he's fucked over. The people he played with. The women he's trashed. The fat stack of bodies he's clambered atop of, waving his arms in his hunger for fame.

All of it reeks, and there's nowhere to run now. The cowboy embraces him, whistling all the while.

And if this is the place where it all must come down…

…then fuck it.

Drake releases.

And the pain, at last, is gone.

BUT THIS IS YOUR LOVE, says the voice. And he remembers.

BUT THIS IS YOUR LOVE.

And then the doorway starts to close.

XXVII

Kenneth, weak, drained of blood and energy, falls sideways toward a blinding white whirlpool. Behind him the black killing-cage hangs, broadcasting Renning's flange-warped death-screams, tumbling, shrinking, impossibly receding into some n-dimension. Hell, most likely. Little exit doorway. Oh well. Good luck. Oh well.

And again, he thinks — surrendering, readying himself to fall in — the Punchline. *She said yes, so I shot her.* The beauty is in the telling. *At these prices, I'm not surprised.* So into the story, you forget. You forget. What's on the other side....

So. Into the light. Why not.

Why not?

Suddenly, the cracker appears beside him. Radiant. Smiling. Dead. Dead don't mean shit, and it never has.

It is really good to see him.

"Hey!" says the cracker. "You fuckin' rule! This is the best show *ever!*" He's got a real cute gal beside him.

"Thanks," says Kenneth, fading out. "I'm glad you liked the show."

387

"You're not really gonna *die* now, are ya?" The cracker looks concerned. "That would be a kick in the head. I really wanna hear your next couple albums, soon as I get back."

"I dunno…" Kenneth says. "I can't really say…."

He catches a glimpse of Darcie, about three feet below, to the left. *Coming?* he thinks at her.

Darcie just looks, not thinking, just looking, hair flying around her head, caught in an electrostatic halo. Looking.

Looking very much alive.

As he hesitates, the light falters ever so slightly, but enough to piggyback his doubt.

He drifts a little closer, thinking about junk, his junk, his pain, his fix. About the vampire-life-energy fix. Why? Was he fixing on death energy? Was this continual surrendering to death and rebirth as sick and meaningless in its way as sucking someone else dry in order to continue?

In all these years, struggling to uncover the Light, not once had he ever seen it through: seen what it is to grow old, watched what could happen if he did stick around, to fight for the spirit of the jokester, for the Creative, for the life-igniting spark.

Why?

Exactly, Darcie beams to him, grinning like the Mona Lisa.

The light dulls, diminishes. "See ya later," the cracker says. His girlfriend says, "You guys are great!" Then they are gone completely.

Kenneth begins then, slowly, to fall. Darcie's naked body holds him.

And it is fine. Oh yes, it's fine.

They drift back down together, into the craziness below.

As the sky closes behind them.

And the ritual concludes.

XXVIII

Carlos looks up to see the mirrorball gone, and a perfectly mundane ceiling above. Singed some. He looks around the club and sees the same thing everywhere: people dazed, injured, bloodied. Some down. Some helping each other up.

He is amazed by how many of them are smiling.

He's amazed to be smiling himself.

"Hey," he says to the woman beside him. It is Sylvie. "Hey." He knows her now, really well. "You okay?" he asks, still smiling.

He knows the answer already.

He has seen the Light.

Sylvie stares straight ahead, wipes at her bloodied mouth with her sleeve again. Stunned. Lula comes down toward her from the front of the stage.

The groove at last has ended; it's the end of the show. Lula's still covered with purple fur, but it's rapidly receding, backing up into her skin. "You got a cigarette?" she inquires.

Sylvie nods her head. "Uh huh," she says, feral wildwoman grin attached to deadpan delivery, in answer to both questions.

Because this is the dream. It is all that she'd hoped for.

Now it's time to begin again.

DARK DESTINY II
AGENTS OF FORTUNE, PROPRIETORS OF FATE

EDITOR

EDWARD E. KRAMER
is a writer and the editor of *Grails* (nominated for the World Fantasy Award for Best Anthology of 1992), *Confederacy of the Dead, Phobias, Dark Destiny, Elric: Tales of the White Wolf, Excalibur, Tombs, Dark Love, Forbidden Acts* and other works in progress. Ed's fiction appears in a number of anthologies as well. His first novel, *Killing Time*, is forthcoming from White Wolf. His credits also include over a decade of work as a music critic and photojournalist. A graduate of the Emory University School of Medicine, Ed is a clinical and educational consultant in Atlanta. He is fond of human skulls, exotic snakes, and underground caves.

CONTRIBUTING AUTHORS

POPPY Z. BRITE

is the author of the novels *Lost Souls, Drawing Blood,* and *Exquisite Corpse* (forthcoming), the short story collection *Swamp Foetus,* and the editor of the erotic vampire anthology *Love In Vein..* Her short stories have won critical acclaim and have appeared in *Borderlands, Still Dead, Women of Darkness II,* and David B. Silva's *The Horror Show* magazine. She has been a finalist for both the Bram Stoker and the Lambda literary awards. Poppy lives in New Orleans with four cats and two boyfriends.

NANCY A. COLLINS

is the author of *Paint It Black, Walking Wolf, Wild Blood, In The Blood, Tempter* and *Sunglasses After Dark.* Her collected Sonja Blue Cycle, *Midnight Blue,* was published by White Wolf in early 1995. Nancy is currently working on screenplay adaptations of *Sunglasses After Dark* and the fourth installment in the Sonja Blue Cycle, *A Dozen Black Roses,* plus a romantic dark fantasy called *Angels On Fire.* She currently resides in New York City with her husband, anti-artiste Joe Christ, and their dog Scrapple.

BASIL COPPER'S

long and distinguished writing career spans many genres and more than eighty books. He is perhaps best known for his Mike Faraday mystery novels and the continuing exploits of detective Solar Pons (originated by the late August Derleth). His short stories have been gathered in such collections as *From Evil's Pillow*, *Voices of Doom*, and *Here Be Daemons*. The Mark Twain Society of America appointed him a Knight of Mark Twain for his "contributions to modern fiction."

JAMES S. DORR

is a freelance writer and a semi-professional musician with Die Aufblitzentanzetruppe *(The Flash Dance Band)*. He is a two-time Rhysling Award finalist for his poems "Dagda" *(Grails)* and "A Neo-Canterbury Tale: The Hog Drover's Tale" *(Fantasy Book)*. His chapbook of horror poetry is entitled *Towers of Darkness*.

CHARLES L GRANT

was born in 1942 and has lived most of his life in northwestern New Jersey. He has appeared on numerous radio and television programs both in the U.S. and Great Britain, and has lectured at many schools and colleges on the field of dark fantasy (past and present), editing, writing, and the business of his profession. Charlie is past president of the Horror Writers of America, and served five years as President of the Board of Trustees of HWA. In 1987 he received the British Fantasy Society's Special Award for life achievement. He and his wife, editor and novelist Kathryn Ptacek, live in a haunted Victorian house in Sussex.

ROLAND J. GREEN

is a prolific writer of science fiction, fantasy, action-adventure and historical fiction. He also reviews for the American Library Association and the *Chicago Sun-Times*. He edits non-fiction projects like the "Concordance" to*The Tom Clancy Companion*. He is a graduate of Oberlin College and the University of Chicago, and has been active in the Society for Creative Anachronism.

BRIAN HERBERT

is best known for his science fiction novels, including *Sidney's Comet*, *The Garbage Chronicles*, *Sudanna, Sudanna*, *Man of Two Worlds* (co-written with his father, Frank Herbert), *Prisoners of Arionn*, and *The Race for God*. Brian's forthcoming novel, *Blood on the Sun*, was written in collaboration with his cousin, Marie Landis. Brian and Marie are direct descendants of Rev. John Rogers, the first martyr burned at the stake by Mary Tudor, Queen of England.

ALEXANDRA ELIZABETH HONIGSBERG'S

short fiction has appeared in *Unique* and *Fresh Ink* magazines, as well as the *Angels of Darkness* anthology. This is her first publication as a poet. Professionally, she is a counselor and scholar of comparative religions. Alexandra is also a concert violist/conductor and a song writer. She lives in New York City with her husband and two cats, in the land of the Unicorn Tapestries.

Caitlin R. Kiernan

was born in Dublin, Ireland, the year The Beatles invaded America but has lived most of her life in the Southeastern U.S. She holds degrees in Philosophy and Anthropology, and has worked as a paleontologist, a newspaper columnist, and an exotic dancer. In 1992 she began pursuing fiction writing full-time and has sold stories to a number of magazines and anthologies including *Aberrations*, *Eldritch Tales*, *High Fantastic*, and the forthcoming *The Very Last Book of the Dead*. Her first novel, *The Five of Cups*, will be published in 1996 by Transylvania Press.

Victor Koman

sold his first story to *New Libertarian Notes* in 1976. His novels *The Jehovah Contract* (1985) and *Solomon's Knife* (1989) received Prometheus Awards. Victor's story "Bootstrap Enterprise" in *The Magazine of Fantasy and Science Fiction* was noted as one of the best science fiction stories of 1994. His latest novel is the massive space thriller, *Kings of the High Frontier*. A Hollywood extra in *Star Trek — The Motion Picture*, *Cyberzone*, and *Attack of the 60 Foot Centerfold*, Victor lives in Southern California with his wife and daughter.

MARIE LANDIS

has won numerous literary awards, including the Amelia Award, for her science fiction and dark fantasy stories. Her writing background has been primarily in the news media as a reporter and columnist. She is the co-author of the forthcoming dark fantasy novel, *Blood on the Sun*, a collaboration with her cousin, Brian Herbert.

LISA LEPOVETSKY

has written public service announcements for television and a screenplay for a short horror film. She writes murder mysterie for dinner theatre and teaches writing classes for the University of Pittsburgh at Bradford. Lisa has already written three novels and is presently working on novels four and five. Many of her poems have appeared in publications like *Grue*, *Not One of Us*, *Deathrealms*, and *Dreams And Nightmares*.

MARC LEVINTHAL

is a musician and writer who has lived in Hollywood since 1980. He co-wrote the score for the film *Valley Girl* and the hit single "Three Little Pigs" for Green Jellö. He has played in bands too numerous to mention (or remember). His story "Kids" will be part of the upcoming brain-eating zombie anthology "The Very Last Book of the Dead" edited by John Mason Skipp. Marc recently moved to a new house with his fiancée and four very bad cats.

BRAD LINAWEAVER

is best known for his novel *Moon of Ice* (Tor Books), which won the Prometheus Award in 1989 and was a finalist for the Nebula. His short stories have appeared in over two dozen anthologies including *Dark Destiny* and *Elric: Tales of the White Wolf*. He has worked in radio and film; co-edited *Weird Menace* with Fred Olen Ray and *Free Space* (forthcoming from Tor Books) with Edward E. Kramer; and is collaborating with Dafydd ab Hugh on two *Doom* novels for Pocket Books.

REX MILLER

has been a radio personality, voiceover announcer, and collectibles entrepreneur. He is regarded as one of America's leading authorities on popular culture memorabilia. Rex's novels include *Slob* (nominated for the Bram Stoker Award for Best First Novel), *Iceman*, *Slob*, *Profane Men*, *Slice*, and *Chaingang*. He has also authored over thirty pop-culture publications, including: *Archives*, *Comic Heroes Illustrated*, *Radio Premiums Illustrated*, *Radio Premiums Illustrated*, and *Collectibles Quarterly*.

DOUG MURRAY

began writing at age thirteen for movie-oriented magazines like *Famous Monsters of Filmland*, *The Monster Times*, and *Media Times*. In the mid-eighties, he graduated to comic books as the creator and primary writer on Marvel's *The 'Nam*. Doug has also worked for Comico, DC, and Eternity. His short stories appear in numerous anthologies. His forthcoming novel, *Blood Relations*, will be published by HarperPrism in 1995.

FRIEDA A. MURRAY

is married to Roland Green, and has collaborated with him on the fantasy novel *The Book of Kantela* and several other short pieces. She is a graduate of the University of Chicago, a past member of the Society for Creative Anachronism, and is active in Chicago Women in Publishing. Frieda lives in Chicago with Roland, their daughter Violette, and a black cat named Thursday.

PHILIP NUTMAN

has worn many hats since he first appeared in print at age fifteen. He is a novelist, screenwriter, producer, journalist and BBC TV production assistant. Phil has published over 350 feature articles, fifteen short stories (in, *Book of the Dead The Year's Best, Splatterpunks*, and *Borderlands II*, to mention a few) and one novel, *Wet Work*. A two-time Stoker finalist, he is currently completing two novels and producing *The Last Blood*, an independent action/ horror film.

FRED OLEN RAY

has written, produced and directed over fifty feature films, including *Mob Boss*, *Inner Sanctum*, *Evil Toons*, and *Hollywood Chainsaw Hookers*. He has been featured prominently on such TV programs as *Entertainment Tonight*, *Hard Copy*, *Stephen King's World of Horror*, *CNN's Show Biz Today*. Fred wrote *The New Poverty Row* and *Grind Show*, and edited the horror pulp anthology, *Weird Menace*. He also writes for several national magazines and is himself the subject of numerous magazine articles and interviews.

JOHN MASON SKIPP

has always dreamed of making music, books, and films. Now, at last, he does all three. He is the lead singer for the L.A. band Mumbo's Brain; their first release was the EP, *Excerpts from the Book of Mumbo*. He has directed several videos for the band, including "Sorry" and "Hail Mary (Body of Christ)." His most recent screenplay is called *Black Wing and Pearl*. He has written much hardcore horror fiction — his favorites being *The Cleanup* and *The Bridge* — and he is the editor of *The Very Last Book of the Dead*.

S.P. SOMTOW

(Somtow Papinian Suchariktul) was born in Bangkok and grew up in Europe. His first novel, *Starship & Haiku* , won the Locus Award for best first novel; he won the 1981 John W. Campbell Award as well as the 1986 Daedalus for his novel *The Shattered Horse.* Somtow's other novels include *Vampire Junction, Moon Dance, Forgetting Places,* and *Vampire Junction*'s sequel, *Valentine.* His film projects have included include *The Laughing Dead* and *Ill Met By Moonlight,* a radical departure from *Shakespeare's A Midsummer Night's Dream.*

STEWART VON ALLMEN

got engaged to and then married a crazy but perfect woman, moved into a new house, published two other short stories which appear in White Wolf's *Tales of the White Wolf* and *Dark Destiny,* and wrote a first novel, *Conspicuous Consumption,* to be published by HarperPrism in August 1995. He hopes every year of his life is so harried and fruitful.

WENDY WEBB

is an Atlanta-based writer who has traveled the globe and, as a registered nurse and professional educator, has worked in China and Hungary. An interest in acting landed her roles in movies such as S.P. Somtow's *The Laughing Dead*, as well as work with the Atlanta Radio Theater. Her short stories have appeared in the *Shadows* series of anthologies, *Women of Darkness*, *Confederacy of the Dead*, and *Deathport*. She is the co-editor of the *Phobias* anthologies published by Pocket Books and the forthcoming *Gothic Ghosts* anthology from Tor Books.

ROBERT WEINBERG

is the only two-time World Fantasy Award winner to be chosen as Grand Marshal of a Rodeo Parade. He is the author of six non-fiction books, five novels, and numerous short stories. His latest fantasy novel, *A Logical Magician*, was published last year. He is also the co-author of White Wolf's *Vampire Diary*. As an editor, Bob has compiled nearly one hundred anthologies and collections.

ROBERT ANTON WILSON

has worked as a Futurist, novelist, playwright, poet, lecturer, and stand-up comic. In the area of social philosophy, he wrote such Futuristic projections as *Cosmic Trigger I & II*, *Reality Is What You Can Get Away With*, *Right Where You Are Sitting Now*, *Prometheus Rising*, and *The New Inquisition*. With the late Robert Shea, Bob co-authored the *Illuminatus* trilogy. In 1989, thirteen years after publication, *Illuminatus* became the best selling trade science fiction paperback in the U.S. He also co-authored *Neuropolitique* and *The Game of Life* with Dr. Timothy Leary, starred on a punk rock record in collaboration with the Golden Horde, and is featured in the video *Borders*, shown on many PBS TV stations.